"Maura, let's get married."

"How can we?" she asked Jed. "You're still paying alimony to Denise."

"Well," he said. "We'll just have to find her a husband."

"I don't know," she said, unsure, vaguely afraid.

"Look, we live in a city of eight million people. There has to be someone out there that she'll like. I'm in marketing research and I certainly know the market."

She began to feel slight stirrings of hope. Why not? He was attractive, attentive, in love with her. Willing to go through this.

But how can a man go looking for another man—to marry his wife?

Fawcett Gold Medal Books
by David Rogers:

THE BEDROOM SET Q3528 $1.50

THE GREAT AMERICAN ALIMONY ESCAPE 14132-2 $1.95

THE GREAT AMERICAN ALIMONY ESCAPE

a novel by

David Rogers

FAWCETT GOLD MEDAL • NEW YORK

To that rare combination,
Friend and Agent,
Marcia Amsterdam

THE GREAT AMERICAN ALIMONY ESCAPE

Published by Fawcett Gold Medal Books, a unit of CBS Publications, the Consumer Publishing Division of CBS Inc.

ISBN 0-449-14132-2

Printed in the United States of America

10 9 8 7 6 5 4 3 2 1

Chapter One

"D'ja hear what happened to Mr. Xavier?" the masseur asked, punctuating the question with a right to Jed Lavery's kidney that would never have been allowed by the New York State Boxing Commission. "Terrible," he added, giving Jed a hint.

Jed groaned. "Who's Xavier?" he asked.

"Ah, y'seen him here a hundred times. Big advertisin' man. Tall, good lookin' guy, 'bout forty? Looks sorta like Frank Gifford with a horrible appendix scar."

"I never noticed."

"Ya couldna not noticed a scar like that," Hermie the masseur said, kneading Jed's thigh. He sighed philosophically. "Guess that's what ya get when ya go to your brother-in-law for surgery."

"What kind of scar?" Jed asked, figuring it was wise to seem interested while his body was in Hermie's hands.

"It was kinda a joke like. He sewed him up making it look like Mrs. Xavier's . . . whatchacallit? . . . monogram. T. L. X. Her name's Teresa somethin'. God!" The masseur straightened up, rubbed the small of his own back, and wiped his cauliflower nose on the back of his massive forearm. "The guy's abdomen looks like one of them fancy towels. I allus thought maybe that's why Mr. Xavier divorced his wife."

"Gotta be a better reason," Jed said as Hermie began to work on his calf, thinking, a feeling of stifling, that's a reason. A feeling that life is getting away from you. That if you don't get out now, the rest of your life is all going to be catching the 7:47, dodging United Fund contributions and over-familiar sex twice a week. Although he felt a stab of conscience putting down the sex with Denise even in his own mind, even now, eighteen months after the divorce. Hermie was continuing the tragedy of the monogrammed man but the voice Jed heard was Denise's, echo-chambered with hurt and anger all those months ago.

"Are you in love with somebody else?"

"There is no one else!" Jed's own voice had become angry. Because there was no one else? Or covering the guilt of wishing there was? "I love you, Denise. I guess I . . . I'll always love you."

"And divorce will freeze your perfect passion for eternity?" she had asked bitterly, dropping and shattering a Pyrex dish she was taking from the oven. (Jed had brought up the subject in the awkward ten minutes before dinner.)

"I have always been faithful to you," he had said, ignoring the dribbling mess of chicken, noodles, and mushrooms on the Portuguese-tiled floor, keeping the subject on fidelity because he had always been faithful. "I can't explain," he had continued, and that was true, too. "Jesus! We got married right after graduation. Denise, I . . ." Another bit of truth somewhat more difficult to get out. "I never had any youth."

"You poor thing," she had said, throwing her padded oven gloves into the puddle of food. "Right from college into middle age!"

"I'm not middle-aged!"

"Then why aren't you enjoying the bloom of your

forty-year-old youth?" She had stalked to the door and pointed to the floor. "And clean up that mess before you start making another."

There had been more in the two weeks before he packed up and left. Denise had suggested psychiatry, buying a boat, and, in a moment of evident desperation, smoking pot. For a while she harped on the boys. "Scott's eleven and Keith's only eight."

"I know how old they are."

"They need a father!"

"I'm not dying. I'm just going to live in New York. Dammit, if I can commute to work for ten years, I can commute backwards and see my sons."

By the time they got to the settlement, Denise was feeling mean and Jed couldn't blame her. He gave her everything she asked for: the house, the alimony, the support, the stereo, and even his collection of musical-comedy records. He would start fresh. First he'd buy *Oklahoma* and rebuild from there.

Suddenly, Jed felt a breeze on his behind and realized Hermie had stopped droning. The masseur was standing there, holding the towel. "I said turn over, Mr. Lavery," Hermie said.

"Oh," Jed replied and turned. Hermie redraped the towel and slammed down hard on Jed's stomach. "What happened then?" Jed asked, feeling in his gut that Hermie was offended by his lack of attention.

It had been rough on the boys, Jed reflected, ignoring Hermie's answer. But I did take them away on all their school vacations and I had them to the apartment every other weekend till Maura moved in. But, Jesus, I'll make it up to them . . . I have made it up to them . . . it's not as if . . . and hell, I love the boys, but I'm forty-two and I deserve something for me before it's too late. And God sent me Maura so he must've wanted me to have her, right?

"So here he was, Xavier, nearly forty, an' this terrific chick of twenty-two," Hermie said, beginning on Jed's arm, pressure-rolling the muscle between his straightened fingers. "Her legs was aroun' three miles long an' a nice, big pair. Standin' up at attention . . . nothin' sloppy, y'know what I mean? He met her standin' in line to see a Woody Allen movie."

Of course, that's nothing like my case, Jed told himself. Maura's got the greatest figure I've ever seen but she hates movies and she's not a kid. She's a mature woman of almost twenty-four.

"He was cryin' when he told me about it," Hermie said.

"Crying?"

"Well, we were in the steam room, maybe he was sweatin'. But, I tell ya, jus' talkin' about her, he almost got one on." He dropped Jed's arm and continued, without changing his tone, "Y'oughta tell Franco to give you some exercise for your armpits, Mr. Lavery. They're beginnin' to sag."

"What?" It was a cry of terror.

"Sit up," Hermie instructed, and ran his finger along the line between Jed's arm and chest and pinched a small flap of skin hanging at the apex. "Like there," he said, and added with some concern, "You're too young for that."

Jesus Christ, sagging armpits, Jed thought. Is there no escape?

Hermie walked around behind Jed and began to work the muscles of his upper back and neck. "So this day," he continued his saga, "Xavier forgot somethin' an' he goes home from the office aroun' lunch time an' there she is, in bed with her fencin' instructor."

It couldn't happen to me, Jed thought.

"You're all tensed up, Mr. Lavery. Leggo a little, huh?" Hermie said and twisted Jed's head around as though he was trying to recreate the big effect from *The Exorcist*.

It has nothing to do with me, Jed thought. For one thing, Maura doesn't take fencing. She takes karate.

"So he starts to go for the guy, Mr. Xavier does, and it's a final ironical, ain't it?" Hermie asked rhetorically, building to his climax.

"What?"

"The chick picks up her sword—the sword Xavier gave her for Christmas—and fences him away while the guy puts on his pants and alla time correcting her fencing style."

"How did it end?"

"He lunged and she parried. Got him right in the appendix scar." Hermie grasped Jed in a bear hug and did something Herculean to his sacroiliac, the finale of the massage that usually made Jed feel relaxed and free. But not today. "Well, I can unnerstan' how maybe she felt," Hermie said, Solomon-like. "Like you're shackin' up with a guy an' evvytime he takes off his clothes, you're starin' at his wife's monogram."

Jed rose and folded the towel into itself around his middle, unable to think of any appropriate comment.

"So now she's livin' with the fencin' teacher. I guess she takes the lessons out in trade."

"And what happened to Xavier?"

"He was all strung out," Hermie sighed. "An' that's what's so rotten. He was like a marked man. There was nothin' he could do but go back to his wife."

Jed pushed his feet into the plastic Japanese thongs, thinking about Xavier. He turned and looked at Hermie. "How were his armpits?"

"Oh, jus' fine," Hermie assured him.

Fifth Avenue was empty, quiet, even lonely in the after-work atmosphere of seven o'clock. Leaving the gym, Jed decided to walk, enjoying the warmth of the October evening, a sudden, pre-winter throwback memory of summer before the cold of November overtook the city. The athletic club was roughly midway between his office and apartment, close enough to run in at lunch hour if he had time or walk over on a Saturday from home. He went regularly from the office Tuesdays, the night Maura went to karate class.

Jed had wanted to live in the Village, wanted to recreate the background he had known when he first came to

New York fresh from college, certain it would make him feel twenty-two again. Of course, Denise had been with him the first time, but Jed didn't think the memory of that would bother him. Still, when he saw the rent-swollen, "adorably-Village-y" apartments in the brownstones, the fl. thru, wb fireplace, non-work john hideaways, the charm did not stand up to the memory of the clean, modern, glass-is-better-than-walls, nine-room home he had left behind in Westport. Jed had compromised by taking what was called a Junior Three in a new Village high-rise but was, in effect, a Senior One. After the settlement, it was the best he could afford anyway. It was crowded when the two boys came for the weekends but, oddly, was roomy enough when Maura took up permanent residence.

From the first week in the apartment, women had not been a problem. Sheltered by marriage, he had been unaware of the full force of the winds of freedom the sexual revolution had unleashed. He made the swingier rounds, the Village bars, the P. J. Clark scene, the discos, the Hamptons, amazed at the alacrity with which all types and ages announced their availability, rendering the art of seduction obsolete. At first, he wondered if it had been the same when he was twenty-two, whether this whirlwind would have swirled him up into its vortex had he come alone to the big city back then. Then he ceased to wonder and, like some castaway spirited from a desert island to the senior dorm at Sarah Lawrence, abandoned himself to his elective of the moment. In less time than he would have supposed, his tour of one-night stands began to pall. When he started to think of himself as Mr. Goodbar, he realized he needed some more permanent relationship.

Then he met Maura.

Jed was sharing a beach house in Southampton with three guys whose ad in the *Village Voice* he had answered. They each had their own room and their own shelf in the refrigerator and very little in common. The house rules were as basic and stark as the furnishings. Keep your hands off the other guys' women, towels and diet margarine.

He first saw Maura across a crowded ice-cream shop on Job's Lane. She was accusing the counter girl of serving her a faulty cone. Looking, Jed saw pumpkin ice cream dribble from a hole in the cone bottom onto her yellow jeans and white T-shirt. The word "Chocolate" was imprinted over her magnificent right breast, and "Vanilla" over the left, which was equally awe-inspiring. She was demanding water and a napkin and, as Jed worked his way through the crowd, she was dabbing frantically at the spots. "Can I help?" he had asked. She handed him the ice-cream cone without looking up and continued to deepen both the stain on her breast and his interest.

"I've got a washing machine," he had said.

"With you?" she had asked, looking up skeptically.

"Not far," he had answered and, not wanting to stare at the stain and its firm, round undercarriage, had looked fervently into her eyes, which turned out to be large, brown to the point of black, and quite beautiful, too.

The eyes had stared back into his, then moved slowly to check the face around them. It was a pleasant face, too rough-hewn to be handsome, he admitted to himself, but with dimples unmatured to creases and a generous mouth and teeth that were white and beautifully shaped, albeit prone to cavities. Jed had smiled as charmingly as possible in the crowded shop with people breathing down his neck, yelling "Double-dip mango" and the like.

The girl's eyes roamed over his husky shoulders and the deep chest covered by what Bloomingdale's assured him was this year's knit shirt, down to the trim waist and flat hips and the muscular tennis player's legs under the crisp white shorts.

"Could we walk?" she asked suspiciously.

"I've got my car. Two minutes."

She shrugged, took back the ice-cream cone and, holding it out at an angle as she licked, followed him from the store.

His housemates were nowhere to be seen and the girl seemed neither impressed by the proximity of the house to the ocean nor repulsed by its general tackiness. As he led her into the painted-white, dump-salvaged-rattan living room, he waved rather foolishly at the open kitchen door. "The washing machine's in there," he had said. She nodded and he opened a door leading from the living room. "This is my room."

She nodded again and walked past him into what had been, in a more elegant day, a dining room, now furnished with a chipped garage-sale bureau and a large, necessarily strong, bed. Silently, she dropped the tote bag she carried and pulled off her T-shirt and jeans and threw them to him. With iron control, Jed managed to maintain his cool, pleasant smile, but his voice cracked when he said, "I'll put them on soak," and left the room.

In the kitchen, he threw her clothes into the machine and added some soap. Then, thinking, What the hell? he pulled off his own clothes and threw them in, too. He twisted the dial to "start" and went back to his room.

She was standing where he had left her, more magnificent, if possible, than he remembered. "I figured as long as I was doing a wash, I'd put mine in, too," he said, for something to say. She nodded and Jed closed the door.

"You married?" she had asked.

"No."

"Separated?"

"Divorced," he explained.

"You sure?" she asked. "It's my only rule."

He moved very close to her, sure that in the unlikely event those two magnificent beauties had been technically augmented, the heat from his body would melt them. "I wouldn't want to break your rule," he said.

Thirty minutes later he leaned back against the pillow and sighed, slightly rueful, knowing the rest of his life would be downhill. The girl stirred beside him, shifted her body to its side, and dropped her hand gently on his chest.

"Sure beats the Laundromat," she said.

He turned his head and looked into her big, brown eyes. "I've also got a dryer," he told her.

"Why not?" she agreed.

He rose and, shutting the dining-room door behind him, walked into the kitchen. One of his housemates was standing at the counter, gnawing a salami end, a bottle of Coors in his other hand. He nodded at Jed disinterestedly and watched as Jed took the two shirts, the shorts, and the jeans from the washing machine. "You did a whole wash just for that?" the housemate asked.

"It was worth it," Jed replied and threw the clothes into the dryer, pushed "Permanent Press," and went back into his room.

At the end of the dry cycle, when Jed stumbled to the kitchen and back with the clothes, the housemate was stretched out on the rattan sofa reading a 1967 issue of *Gourmet* magazine that had come with the house. He did not look up. When, dressed again, clean, neat, and terribly relaxed, Jed and the girl came out of the room on their way to dinner, the man dropped his magazine. "It musta been worth it," he said, just before Jed slammed the screen door.

Jed turned off Fifth Avenue, walking around the large old apartment building into the street of brownstones, some still one-family homes impermanently rooted against the encroachments of the two new high-rises. Down the street, opposite his building, he saw the canopy of the restaurant to which he had taken Maura the Wednesday after that weekend. Over brandy in the elegant little open-air backyard dining room, as they swatted at the mosquitoes, he had asked her to come up to his place. "Right across the street," he had persuaded, and added winsomely, "I haven't had it long. I need some suggestions on how to fix it up."

"I have never been in Sloane's in my whole life," Maura told him in a flat tone.

"We could have a brandy," was his next pitch.

"I'm having a brandy," she fielded and, rising, said she

had an early appointment with an author at the office. She was an editor of juvenile fiction at Peter Piper Paperbacks.

The following weekend Jed spent with his kids, but he took Maura to dinner that Monday. He suggested going back to her place, thinking that might be the combination. "No," she had said, "I don't bring people there." It turned out she lived with two airline stewardesses who wanted her out because their numerous guests kept looking like they wanted to move to the wrong section. But she accepted his invitation to Southampton for the weekend. He wondered if she liked him for himself or his beach.

In fact, they never got to the beach at all, and after the weekend, Maura moved into his apartment.

Jed walked past the front of the building, its thin line of decorative hedges securely chained against hedge-nappers. He knew Maura would be home by now, ambling around nude except for the thin gold necklaces she wore in bunches almost constantly. It was an odd fashion trick he found a terrific turn-on. He rushed through the lobby and pushed the automatic-elevator button. It had been four glorious months of returning from his office knowing she'd be there, knowing she enjoyed his body as much as he enjoyed hers, knowing, despite Hermie's crack about his armpits, he was still young.

In the elevator, he thought of the tragic case of the monogrammed Xavier and knew, positively, it could never happen to him.

Unlocking the door, he could see her from the hall, sitting on the closed sofa-bed, a steaming mug in her hand. She was fully dressed, in dark slacks and a long-sleeved T-shirt. A sequined sailboat on the shirt negotiated the tidal waves of her chest, managing to keep its masts unentangled in the gold necklaces. Wondering, since she was dressed, if something were wrong, he said, "Hi," from the foyer.

"Oh, hi," she said, and as he entered the living room, a jean-clad, blond sequoia unfolded itself from the comfortable chair in the corner. "This is Rod," Maura told him, "my karate instructor," as though that explained it all.

It's karate, not fencing, and they are fully dressed across a small room from each other, Jed told himself as he stuck out his hand. Rod grabbed it as though it were a two-by-four he was casually breaking, " 'Lo," he said.

"Don't get up," Jed told him, looking up into his upper branches, knowing he was not being hospitable, just didn't want the dramatic demonstration of the disparity in their sizes. The blond sequoia settled back into the chair.

Jed crossed the room thinking, What is he? Six four? Six five? That's too tall. Awkward. You can't wear clothes well. And with shoulders like that, I bet he can't get anything to fit him. He turned and took another covert glance at Rod. He was right. His shirt fit so badly he couldn't button it above the navel. Jed leaned over Maura and kissed her cheek, saying, "Hiyah, honey, I'm home," feeling absurdly like Desi Arnaz but determined the fact that he lived here be clear to their guest. He sat beside Maura and draped an arm over her shoulders.

"Well," he said as jovially as possible, "how's my little girl doing in school?" Damn! Now I sound like her father, Jed told himself.

"Real good," Rod said. "Real, real good."

They sat for a moment in silence, then Rod drained his mug and grew into a standing position. "Well," he said, with a vague gesture, "I gotta . . . be someplace."

Inarticulate too, Jed thought approvingly and rose as the redwood moved toward the door. The wind that riffled its branches seemed to say, "See you Tuesday," to Maura.

"Nice to meet you," Jed said at the door and could see the blond hair way above him nod just before he closed it.

"He just walked me home from class," Maura said as Jed turned.

"Oh?"

"He said there's a lot of creeps around on the streets."

"That's why you're taking karate."

"I know."

"So what was he gonna do? Wait till you were attacked

and coach you from the curb? What was it? Some kind of in-the-field midterms?"

"He was just being nice, so I asked him up for some rose-hips tea. I figured that was the least—"

"I don't think he's the right teacher for you."

"He's a black belt," Maura began.

"I mean, if you're going to learn karate, you ought to go to a Japanese. I mean, why learn it from some middleman?" Jed was taking off his jacket and hanging it up now, not wanting to look at her, knowing he was being absurd, unable to stop himself. "I mean, a Japanese is . . . is . . ." He made a big deal of pulling off his sweater, trying to think what a Japanese was.

"Is what?"

"Short!" he settled on. "More your own size. They understand your problems. What does he need karate for? Who's gonna attack him? Paul Bunyan?"

"You want something to eat?"

"I had something," he lied. "And besides, I don't like his name. What kind of name is Rod? It's too suggestive."

Maura looked at him, shrugged, and pulled off her shirt and shook out her long, straight, scrupulously clean brown hair.

Now she's trying to make it up to me, Jed thought, get my mind off the subject. He looked at the thin gold chains lying against the heaving off-white velvet of her skin. And it's working, he admitted.

He moved to her, took her in his arms, kissed her, allowed his fingers to trace the thin gold links from the back of her neck down past the mountain to the valley.

"I want a shower," Maura said. "I'm all sweaty from class."

Jed nodded, moved back, watched her shuck off the slacks and drop them neatly on top of the shirt on the floor. After all these months, he was still surprised by her animal-like naturalness, her total lack of self-consciousness. Denise had never walked around nude, although of course the boys were there most of the time they'd been married. Jed had never been able to make the adjustment for himself, but after a few weeks he had been able to roam around in just jockey shorts without thinking about it too much.

He looked at Maura, drinking in the wide, brown eyes, the creamy skin, the slightly pouty, seductive mouth and the magnificent arrangement of bone and muscle and flesh that was her body and knew that she was every schoolboy's fantasy, every old man's post-prostate-operation regret.

"Take your shower," he whispered huskily.

He watched her through the bathroom door, then picked up her clothes, hangered the slacks and left the shirt on her bureau in the dressing room. Then he opened the sofa, got the sheets and pillows, made the bed, stripped and hung his own clothes away, turned off the lights except the lamp beside the bed, and lay down.

Staring at the ceiling, he knew that he was terribly afraid of losing Maura.

He heard the water turned off and in a moment more she slipped out of the bathroom to the bed and lay down beside him. He felt her hand on his chest, the fingers combing gently through the hair, and heard her giggle.

"You were jealous," she said.

"Very," he admitted and turned to grab her, encircling her with his arms, pulling her still-damp body close.

"That's sweet," she said and, before other feelings and emotions flooded through him, he noted his surprise at the sincerity with which she said it.

They lay beside each other in the bed, backs propped against the sofa back. Maura was reading a typewritten manuscript so huge she had lugged it home in two boxes. Jed pretended to watch the eleven o'clock news. She read quickly, her eyes skimming the page in a manner that would have made Evelyn Wood proud. Once, just before he turned the TV on, she had muttered, "Oh my God! The slave screws the mistress of the plantation scene again," and jumped five whole pages. She had recently been promoted from juveniles to romance.

Jed sat, pictures of an African nation whose name he could never place flickering before him, coming to the only decision that seemed viable to him. He rose and crossed the room, pushed the button that darkened Africa in midcrisis. "Maura," he said and turned. She was looking up at him. "Maura . . ." he began again, walked back and sat beside her. "I want to get married."

She looked at him, expressionless, the manuscript heavy in her lap. "You have a girl?" she asked.

"I want to marry you."

"Oh."

He waited till the silence had gone on a beat too long. "Well?"

"Ask me another time," she said.

"I'm asking now."

She didn't answer, looked down into her manuscript, not reading.

"Is it," he asked, "because I'm too old?"

"Oh no!" she said. "Oh, not at all," and automatically reached over to kiss and comfort, spilling the slave, the plantation, and half the Civil War sequence to the floor.

"Then why?" he asked when he was able to move his lips from hers.

"I like things the way they are," Maura said, moving back, gathering the papers, scrunching them together.

"Tell me."

"Let it go," she said.

"I want to know."

She put the papers back in box one, deciding how to phrase it. "It's like . . ." she said and put the lid on the box, the box on the floor. "It's like you're just like my father."

Jed turned and sank back on the pillow. "I am too old," he said.

"Not that. I mean . . . he's living with this girl . . ."

"How old?"

"My age."

"Oh, but your father. I mean, that's ridiculous . . ."

"He's only forty-eight."

"God damn it," he said, hating Maura for the moment. "Where'd he meet her?"

"At graduation," she said reluctantly.

"Whose?"

"Mine. She was my roommate."

"Oh my God!" he said and got up and went into the kitchenette for a glass of water, deciding on Scotch when he got there.

"He wants to marry her," Maura continued to the empty room.

"But?"

"He's been married four times. And he's still paying alimony to all of them except my mother."

"My God," Jed said again, sipping and staring at her from the kitchenette door.

"She's been married three times." Maura kept the record straight.

"You poor kid."

"What's the difference?"

"Well, you can't compare me to him," Jed said and sat in the chair across the room.

" 'Cause you've only got one alimony?" He nodded. "Look, you've got two kids to get through college and if your wife didn't find a guy right away, she never will, so you'll be paying forever."

"Married or not doesn't cost any more. We'd go on just the way we are. But I'd feel better."

"Look, this is swell. Great," she protested too much. "I love it. Can't we just leave it?"

He put the drink down, went back to the bed. "I want to marry you. Doesn't your mother want you to get married?"

"I don't want to get married."

"Does it matter that I love you?" he asked.

"It matters."

"How much more do you need?"

"Jed, how long did it take me to decide to go to bed with you?"

"About two minutes."

"To live with you?"

"A weekend." Then, wondering what her point was, he added, "But I don't think you're promiscuous."

"Neither do I!" she snapped. "I meant, I'm the kind of girl who, when she decides, goes the whole way. And when I get married, I want the whole thing. I want never to read another juvenile or romance novel as long as I live. I want the house, the kids, the cars. This place," she looked around the room, "is fine for what it is but it's not my idea of getting married."

"I'll get it for you . . . all those things . . ."

"I know," she said, and kissed him.

"I mean it," he mumbled around her lips.

"I know," she said, and took his hand, molding it around her breast. "Baby," she whispered, "put it on a back burner. Let's enjoy what we've got."

They enjoyed what they had for a while, but after, Jed did not sleep. He lay quietly beside Maura trying to figure what to do, determined never to lose the girl who slept beside him.

By morning, he was sure he knew how.

Chapter Two

Jed stood, impatient, in the back of the express elevator as it stopped at every floor between sixteen and twenty-five, feeling the righteous satisfaction of a man who has decided on a plan and is on the verge of implementing it. The plaid outer shirt-jacket that he wore over the red flannel shirt over the lightweight navy blue turtleneck that set off his tiki beads dramatically made him stand out in the crowd of suited, vested, tied briefcase carriers around him. He was proud of the difference between himself and the others, all of whom were roughly the same age and income bracket but looked five years older. Seven, he assured himself, and got off at twenty-five.

The sight of his rosewood office door, the words THE LAVERY MARKETING RESEARCH GROUP off-centered in silver on it, sent his spirits up another three points, as usual. He was proud of his office, proud of his firm, proud of the door. The business had grown since he opened it after B B D and O fired him while Denise was pregnant with what turned out to be Scott. The one-room office was now a suite; the staff, once a part-time secretary, was now twelve full-time employees, and Dun and Bradstreet rated him only slightly lower than he rated himself.

He waved good morning to the switchboard girl, typing behind the sliding glass window, and reached the inner door just as she pushed the buzzer. He turned right in the large center room of the office, calling, "Bring your pad, Felicity," to his secretary by way of greeting. He barreled into his corner office, threw his plaid shirt-jacket on the oatmeal sofa that faced the glass-and-chrome table he used as a desk, and dropped onto the black leather executive swivel chair behind it.

"Letters?" Felicity asked from the door. She was in her early twenties but her English accent lent her a certain elegance and maturity. She had come to work for him three months before, when his last secretary left to open a Tiffany-style lamp and homemade bread boutique in the East Village. Felicity had been recommended by Perry Robotham, a VP at McCann-Ericson who used to sit in the advertising car of the 7:47 with Jed in his commuting days. It was only after Jed came to rely on Felicity's intelligence and brisk efficiency that he learned she was living with old Perry.

"No. A list," Jed told the girl as she took her chair, flipped her pad open smartly and, pencil-poised, waited. "Steve Gladstone," he dictated and watched her write. "Lenny Martin . . . Don Phalon . . . Hank Johnson . . ."

"The one at Young and Rubicam or the one at National Biscuit?" Felicity asked.

Jed leaned the chair back, thinking. "Both. I'm not sure about the one at National Biscuit, but put him on."

Felicity wrote, "Hank Johnson X 2."

"Harry Baumgarten," Jed continued, and after a moment's search for one name that had slipped his memory, ". . . and Chris Kellogg." He snapped the chair back and opened a file folder on the glass table. "Type up those names, please, with business address and phone and home address and phone and leave a little space for comment between them, okay, Felicity?" He pulled a computer readout from the file and looked up at the girl.

"Straight away," Felicity said, and Jed turned back to the report, read the heading, and became aware with some surprise that Felicity hadn't moved. He looked up at her again.

"I don't wish to intrude . . ." she said.

"But?"

"But may I venture an opinion?"

"Go ahead."

"None of them will marry her."

The paper slid from Jed's fingers and he had the odd feeling he'd turned white. Wishing there was a mirror in the room so he could check, he stared down at the glass table in front of him but saw only his Gucci loafers. "Marry who?" he asked.

"Your wife."

He sat back in the chair and swiveled it so that he was staring directly into her peaches-and-cream English complexion. In tones of awe, he asked, "How did you know?"

Felicity shrugged. "They're all in their forties, all attractive, all divorced, and all on the list Perry went through last month."

"For his wife?"

Felicity nodded, too delicately sensitive to crush him by saying "Yes" aloud.

Jed swung around to the window, staring toward the half-leafed oasis of Central Park in October to the north. After a moment he said, "I understand Perry's wife . . ." and paused.

"Rhonda," Felicity prompted.

"I understand she's not exactly . . ." He hesitated tactfully.

"She's smashing. If you happen to have an overbite fetish," Felicity corroborated.

Jed turned back, hopes stirring. "Then . . . ?"

For answer, his secretary read back the list with comments. "Steve Gladstone moved in with his secretary last June and says he has finally found himself. Lenny Martin's on Cornelia Street living with an NYU sophomore. Hank Johnson, Y and R, and his wife sold their house in

Teaneck when the kids left home and moved into a Sutton Place condominium. Two months later he moved across the hall to the apartment of a sex therapist with a forty-inch bust who, they say, is frightf'lly good at her job. The wife of Hank Johnson, National Biscuit, left him, taking the furniture, some rather good Impressionist paintings, the bank accounts, the contents of the safe-deposit and both cars. Perry figures she had an accomplice," she explained. "She is now living on Capri with the owner of a trattoria. Hank says he will never marry again. There isn't a woman in the world who's worth it."

Jed heaved an enormous sigh.

"Shall I go on?"

"Let's have it all," Jed mumbled.

Felicity looked down at the list and said, "Harry Baumgarten is living on the West Side with two go-go dancers but will consider taking a roommate. Perry said he looked exhausted. And Chris Kellogg has come out of the closet."

"Chris Kellogg?!"

"He is living in domestic bliss with a construction worker who pumps iron in his spare time and was fifth runner-up in the Mr. New York State contest."

"Hopeless, huh?"

"If I wasn't so besotted with my job and Baskin-Robbins ice cream, I'd go back to London," Felicity said, then added guiltily, "and Perry's frightf'ully sweet," as though she felt disloyal.

Jed stiffened his American backbone. "I have not yet begun to fight," he announced.

"That's what Perry said."

Jed shook his head. "John Paul Jones," he corrected.

"You still want me to type up the list?"

"Never mind," Jed said, and found something bothering him as she started for the door. "Wait a minute," he called. "You skipped Don Phalon."

Felicity stopped at the door. She seemed to be digging something out of her tooth with her tongue. "Perry didn't think of him," she said finally.

Jed had opened his mouth to say, Get him for me now, when suddenly something held him back. Since his mouth was open, he said, "Thank you," and waited till Felicity shut the door. She was a wonderful secretary and he could not question her business loyalty, but . . . still . . .

He dialed Directory Assistance for the number himself, got Phalon's secretary, and gave his name.

"Jed, baby," Phalon said after a slight delay. "I may have something for you the first of the year but I can't talk now. I'm taking off in half an hour."

"Oh?"

"On my honeymoon!"

"Honeymoon?" Jed repeated, cursing himself for not having started a week ago.

"Isn't that terrific?" the voice on the other end crowed.

"It's sort of why I called," Jed said. "I mean, I've been wanting to do that, too."

"Well, go ahead, baby, it's the greatest."

"Can I ask you something personal?" Jed felt uncomfortable but he had to know.

"Give you two minutes," Phalon answered.

"I mean, I figure you're paying your wife alimony and support and . . . Don, how the hell can you afford to get married?"

"Well, I couldn't, Jed baby, till I made the big discovery."

"What?" he pleaded hopefully.

"You just don't pay the alimony and the support and you can afford whatever you want."

"Can't she put you in jail?"

"Let her try. If she can, Sally and I take off for Mexico."

"I couldn't do that," Jed said, mournfully.

"That's what I used to say. We'll have lunch when I get back," Phalon told him and hung up.

Jed stared at the instrument for a moment, then rose and went into the outer office. Felicity was talking earnestly into her phone. As soon as she saw him, she said a quick, guilty goodbye and hung up. He was convinced she was talking to Perry. He walked to her desk and said, "Call Perry back and tell him to forget it. Phalon just got married."

The quick flash of embarrassment in her eyes told him his instincts were right. Their eyes locked for a moment, his expressing righteous anger at her attempted betrayal, hers telling him defiantly what her priorities were. It was Jed who backed off, returning to his office, shocked, dismayed by the proof of her disloyalty, her ruthless descent to any depths to get her man's wife married. He sank into his black leather chair, thinking: My God! It's a jungle out there.

"Excuse me . . ." He looked up. Felicity was standing in the door. "D'you mind?" she asked. "How did Phalon manage?"

"He just decided to skip the alimony."

"Oh."

"I couldn't do that."

"That's what Perry said."

"No, that's what I said," he said firmly, and she shut the door. He turned toward the window, staring out, observing only black, interior clouds. I couldn't, he thought. I've been rotten enough to Denise.

But . . . I . . . Must . . . Do . . . Something!

He swiveled back and dialed another number.

"Dr. Parmalee."

"It's Jed, Og."

"I'm with a patient," Ogden Parmalee answered in the dermatologist's voice he affected on the examining-room extension.

"I have to see you. Can you possibly make it for lunch?"

"Hang on," Og said and dropped the extension, implying, If-your-skin-isn't-falling-off-why-are-you-calling-me? In a second he was back. "I have an *erythema nodosum* at twelve-thirty. Take about a half hour."

"I'll meet you at the Radish. One-fifteen. Oh, and for God's sake, Og," Jed implored, "be sure to wash your hands."

The Radish featured young, fresh-faced wait-persons, both male and female, in red-and-white striped shirts, butcher-block tables, and health food imaginatively distorted to make the customers feel they were eating something both unwholesome and good. Jed hardly knew what he was eating, or cared, but was aware of the ghost of curry in his first bite.

"Og," he said, looking at his friend across the butcher block, "I worry about you."

"Don't," Dr. Ogden Prentiss Parmalee said firmly around a mouthful of papaya salad. As a four-year divorcé, he knew exactly what it meant when his friends said they were worried about him.

"It's not natural," Jed continued, "a man in the prime of life"—forty-seven is close enough to prime, he figured—"living alone, raising children by himself . . ."

"What is it, Buddy Boy? Maura got a cousin?" Og guessed.

"Certainly not. Besides, you're not the kind of man who would be happy with someone young, immature, flighty . . ."

"I like the beads you're wearing," Og commented with a certain venom.

"You need someone more mature, settled, someone who can cope with a home and children."

Dropping his fork, a look of amazement on his face, Og said, "I don't believe what you're suggesting."

"Why not?"

"It would be . . ." Og searched for a word and found "incestuous."

"Nonsense! Nobody's related."

"I couldn't," Og said. "We were all friends. We've lived next door to each other for eight years. I've seen her in her curlers. She will always be your wife to me. It would be like marrying my sister."

"Nobody'd marry your sister," Jed said tactlessly. "Denise is a warm, wonderful woman who just happened to grow in a different direction from me."

"Up." Og specified the direction.

"The kids all get along together," Jed plowed on through his prepared speech, totally unaware they had both skipped over actually verbalizing his proposal. He painted a picture of delightful domesticity, of freedom from Parents Without Partners, and someone to deal with Og's daughter's growing need for a bra. "Even the houses are next door," he concluded. "If you don't want to sell yours, you could build a breezeway."

"After what Lillian put me through," Og interrupted, "I will never marry again. Besides, I still love her. I will always be in love with Lillian."

"Face the facts, she left you."

"She's just trying to find herself."

"That doesn't take four years."

"She's confused. It's the temper of the times," Og sputtered. "All that consciousness raising at the Adult Education Center. It could confuse anyone. Deep down, she loves me. I know."

"Og," Jed pleaded, "you're a man of science, a dermatologist. Don't you see that Lillian was so thoroughly out of love with you that she walked off, taking nothing, not even her children?"

"I'd agree with you if she'd moved to Hawaii or Australia or something," said Og, who had clung to this fact for years. "But she only moved across town to Saugatuck Shores. She sees the kids every day. And if I've ever got a conference, a convention, I can rely on her completely to take them."

"That's not a wife, that's a baby-sitter," Jed countered. "Og, she has built a new life for herself, a home, a successful business."

"Oh, real estate!" Og pooh-poohed. "They all go into real estate. Even Denise."

"Denise went into real estate 'cause she was bored, she needed something to do, and Lillian was opening the office."

"It's ridiculous, Jed. If you want to stay friends, forget it. I'm a one-woman man and Lillian got there first."

Jed saw the anger behind the bifocals and gave up. He had thought the possibility of Og was remote and had only tried because he was determined to leave no bachelor unturned. Besides, Og was his best friend and, despite his squareness and a certain inclination to pompous boredom that might have justified Lillian, he had a firm, old-shoe adjustment to friendship that gave Jed a feeling of dependability.

"Okay," Jed muttered, "I'm sorry. I just wanted the best I could for Denise."

Og smiled, accepting the compliment, the apology, and the end of the conversation. They ate in silence for a moment. Then Jed said, "You have to help me."

"How?"

"Who do you know in Westport that's single?"

"Men?"

"Of course, men."

"Buddy Boy, you're in marketing research. You ought to know. There are no bachelors in the suburbs. Couples move in in their thirties and men move out in their forties. The only singles are women with kids selling each other real estate and antiques."

Jed nodded, then with a sudden impatient gesture pushed the curried whatever away from him. "I've got to get Denise married, Og," he said, his tone so drained and desperate his friend looked at him in concern. "If I don't get out from under the alimony, I can't marry Maura, and I've got to marry Maura."

"I know a doctor," Og said slowly.

"A bachelor?" Jed said hopefully.

"An abortionist."

"Maura isn't pregnant," Jed snapped.

"Oh." For the moment, Og was taken aback.

"I'm afraid I'll lose her."

"Is it age?" Og sounded sympathetic.

Jed sighed and nodded. "Today's her birthday. Twenty-four. That's when a girl starts thinking permanent. On birthdays. Beginning at twenty-four."

"I meant your age," Og explained.

The pretty young wait-person stopped at the table. "Will there be anything else?" she asked.

"Not for you. Probably for me," Og told her and accepted the check.

"There's guys everywhere," Jed said, getting to the root of his problem after the wait-person had cleared. "Maura pulls 'em in like a vacuum cleaner. Without trying. They keep coming out of the woodwork with one hand on their zippers. Y'oughta see her karate instructor. He's maybe twenty-six and built like a brick teahouse."

"Any . . ." Og paused, raised his hand parallel to the table and wiggled it. ". . . hanky panky?"

"Certainly not!" Jed said angrily.

"But you can't be sure?"

"No," he admitted miserably. "That's why I gotta marry her. Then I'd know."

"And you'd move back to Westport, Buddy Boy, and we could commute together again." Sentimentally, Og visualized it all.

"But I gotta find a guy. Don't you know anyone, Og? Another doctor? Even a patient?"

Og thought for a moment. "I've got a rock-concert promoter. He's fifty but he's very jazzy. Denim underwear. Divorced three times. Psoriasis."

"Sounds too flaky for Denise. I need a solid citizen. Good looks, good job, good health. The way I figure it," Jed confided, "he's gotta be better than me or she'll never go for him. Jesus Christ," he said desperately as his eyes searched his friend's face, "Og, how do I find a better man than me?"

"Better man than I," Og corrected his grammar.

"It was nice of you to come all the way in from Syosset," Maura said to her mother, wondering if it was.

"Well, it's your birthday." Her mother made it sound as though she were martyred to the celebration.

They were having lunch at Stouffer's, which Maura basically hated except she found it a nice relief from the good, expensive French restaurants where she usually took authors at Peter Piper's expense. She was thinking that none of the English profs at Mount Holyoke ever told her how fattening being an editor was. The waitress set their drinks on the table.

Her mother picked up the whiskey sour and made the gesture of a toast. "Well, happy birthday, darling, and may this be the year . . ." She hesitated. ". . . when . . . when you finally get it all together." Maura's thank-you smile was as weak and watery as the drink. Her mother set the glass on the table and leaned in on her elbows with a "let's-be-girls-together" attitude and asked, "How's what's-his-name? Everything all right?"

"Wonderful," Maura answered.

Her mother sat back and took a long pull at her drink. Then she smiled at her daughter and said, "Twenty-four! What a wonderful age!" with rehearsed enthusiasm. "When I was twenty-four I was already married."

"Twice," Maura said as the waitress brought the chicken pot pies.

"I never really counted Kenneth," Diana Hunt Malloy Campbell Warren said offhand. "He was really just a fling. We had hot blood and drive-in movies in my day, too. Believe me, I understand," she shot across the table. "It was just, in those days we drew a line before marriage." She poked her fork into the pie, sending up a gravy geyser which splashed across the paper placemat. "Not that we were right," she said hastily, and with her napkin sopped up the spill. "That is, it's nice that women who are . . . nice, can admit to wanting to go to bed with a man now and do it and nobody thinks the less of them. And when it's over, you don't have to go through all that mess with the lawyers and the property, though God knows, Ken had none. You can just shake hands and say 'See you around.' It's really very sensible." She looked at Maura and smiled again. It was, her daughter thought, a really beautiful, charming smile. I bet that's how she landed all three of them. "I absolutely agree," Diana said, and suddenly the smile faded. "Up to a point," she concluded and took a bite of pie.

Maura decided it was better to say nothing and let Diana get it all off her chest. She would anyway, and if Maura kept changing the subject they'd be lunching till cocktail time.

"When I was twenty-four, you were two and I was pregnant with Sean."

"How is he?"

"Fine. The farm is doing very well and only five of the twelve quit before harvest time but he's thinking of going back and doing pre-med." Diana said it quickly, getting it out of the way as though the whole speech was a rubber stamp she applied to oral questions about her son. "All right, Maura"—she switched siblings—"you're twenty-four and you've played the field and I approve of it. I really do," she added when she felt her expression didn't quite hide the truth. "But when you've had three men . . ." She paused, delicately dangling a question mark. Maura ignored it. "Or four?" She tried again with no result. "Or however many"—Diana rushed past the phrase—"you've had 'em all and you simply have to think about having one."

"Must we do this on my birthday?" Maura didn't really give a damn about her birthday but she could see her mother had planned a heavy lecture and she gambled on weaseling out that way.

"It's easy to have a career and marriage both today," Diana continued as Maura lost the gamble. "But no matter what they say, it's still tough for a woman to get anywhere and it's better to have a career with some nice, young"—she underlined the word—"husband who's very good in bed," she put in as an apology, "paying the bills."

"I have plenty of time."

"That's what they all think. But is what's-his-name's wife married?"

"She's forty."

"Are any of your father's wives married?"

"You got married at thirty-three!"

"After two mistakes. Suppose you don't do it right the

first time? Divorces take forever and you've got to give yourself room to operate. It took me till the third time to get it right. And I intend to live the rest of my life with Douglas. He's handsome, sexy, sweet, and carries a lot of life insurance."

Diana took a deep breath and launched her next section with: "You won't always have opportunities . . ." and as she talked on, Maura gently sank beneath the tidal wave of motherly advice. As firmly as she had resolved not to let her mother upset her, Maura had to admit that Diana was getting through. Of course, there were still men everywhere she looked. She could count on at least three propositions a week. (Though the ones from young writers with first novels were suspect and couldn't honestly be counted.) Only yesterday, Rod . . . who was certainly attractive, but equally certainly hyperactive in the field and not as reliable as Jed. She surfaced from the waters of consideration to hear Diana.

". . . look around seriously. And you can't do that while you're living with what's-his-name. It puts people off. Tell me the truth, Maura, has anyone proposed marriage lately?"

"Yes."

"Who?"

Automatically, Maura answered, "What's-his-name," and then corrected it to "Jed."

"But?" Diana asked, assuming some complication.

"He has alimony problems."

"From thirty-five on, they've all got alimony problems or they're gay," her mother told her and plunged into the age section of her lecture.

Maura sank below the surface once more, trying to remember if there had been a proposal aside from Jed's and found there hadn't. I used to get them regularly, she remembered. Why have they stopped? What have I done? She felt a cold flounder of fear swim down her backbone. Upset, she turned her attention back to her mother, whose warnings might be less frightening than her own.

". . . he'd be seventy. My God! He's as old as your father."

"He isn't."

"How is your father?" Diana was suddenly diverted.

"Fine."

"Who's he living with?"

"Nobody," Maura lied blatantly. Then, protecting her father further, "I think he said he was dating a nice widow." Her mother looked disgruntled and Maura felt a little better.

"What if I married Jed?" Maura asked suddenly, unaware that she was going to say it.

Surprisingly, her mother began to cry. Not a heaving, panting production; just tears trickling down enough to begin to dislodge one of her false eyelashes. "I could accept that," she said, "as your first mistake. If you do it quickly. So that by the time you're twenty-seven, twenty-eight, you're a sensibly divorced woman instead of a . . . a used girl."

"Maybe . . ." Maura said tentatively, giving the idea serious consideration.

"But not unless he solves the alimony problem," Diana said intensely. "I've watched it happen. To friends. You don't remember my cousin Grace. The wife has to work and the marriage never does. Resentment. Every week when he writes the check, the wife resents the other wife, the husband resents them both. Not that way, Maura. Believe me, I'm old enough to be your mother and I know."

By the time Maura got back to the office she was not a basket case. But close. She told her boss her headache was beyond Anacin and her boss gave her a manuscript called *Love's Painful Passion* and the afternoon off. She was back at the apartment by three-fifteen. She dropped *Love's Painful Passion* perilously near the wastebasket, threw herself on the sofa, and, for the first time in as long as she could remember, burst into tears.

She was still crying half an hour later when she heard a

key in the lock and looked up to see Jed in the door carrying a Macy's shopping bag.

"Why are you here?" they asked simultaneously.

"I was too depressed to work," Maura said, and started crying again.

Jed moved quickly across the room, bringing his shopping bag, and sat beside her. "What happened?"

"I had lunch with my mother," she panted out.

"Don't cry. It's your birthday," he said, and she cried the harder. He took her in his arms and whispered, "You should've had lunch with your father." She nodded. "Your mother took off on me?" he asked.

"On me," Maura said. "You were just part three, subdivision C." She pulled away from him, wiped her nose, and sat up on the sofa. "What's that?" She pointed to the bag, determined not to continue in this morbid vein.

"I went to Macy's. I bought your birthday present, a steak, a cake, and as long as I was there, I got myself some underwear."

"Were you depressed too?"

Jed nodded. "I had lunch with Og."

"And he took off on me?"

"No."

"So why were you depressed?"

"Same reason you are. Wanna see your birthday present?" Maura nodded and Jed reached into his inner coat pocket and brought out a velvet ring box.

Maura looked at him in some surprise, took the box and opened it. She saw a flash of diamond and quickly snapped it shut. "It looks like an engagement ring," she said.

"Why not?"

"Nobody wears them anymore. Nobody gets engaged anymore. I'm beginning to wonder if people get married anymore."

He grabbed her shoulders, forcing her to look straight at him. "Maura, I'm forty-two. I come from a more enlightened time. Screw 'em all, let's get married."

"How can we?" she asked.

"There's only one obstacle."

"Denise."

"No. Denise's husband. We'll just go find her one."

"I don't know . . ." she said, unsure, vaguely afraid.

"We can do it," he said firmly. "We live in a city of eight million people."

"But four million are women. And they're all looking for husbands."

"We are two intelligent people. One guy. That's all we have to find."

"How do we know she'll like him?"

"I'll find one she likes. For Christ sake, I'm in marketing research and I certainly know the market."

She began to feel slight stirrings of hope. Why not? He was attractive, attentive, in love with her. Willing to go through this. Even if, as her mother said, he was her first mistake, he certainly wouldn't be a big mistake. "Do you think we could?"

"We just need to be logical," Jed said. "If you wanted to meet a guy for yourself . . ." and then regretted putting the idea into her head. "Where would you go?"

She thought a moment and said, "Anywhere."

"That's not specific enough," he told her, although he knew it was true.

"Well"—she thought some more—"I meet them everywhere."

"I'm not talking about your Rods," he said. "We need an attractive guy between forty-five and fifty."

"The publicity girl," Maura said suddenly. "At Peter Piper's? She goes to a place called Close Encounters on First Avenue. She told me. A lotta guys. Some older. Only five percent weirdos."

"We'll go tonight."

"Me too?"

"You're the bait."

"Well," she said doubtfully, "I don't know if that's the way to do it."

"Listen to Poppa," he said and then, mentally slapping

his head, reminded himself to stop using phrases like that. He took the ring box from Maura, opened it, and said, "Well? How about it?"

She smiled and slipped the ring on.

Chapter Three

Close Encounters bore a distinct resemblance to the Black Hole of Calcutta, only the music was louder. Fully four hundred warm bodies were jammed in under the fire department warning that occupancy by more than one hundred and seventy-two was dangerous and unlawful. About a third of them were women.

"See?" Jed said to Maura, only in the darkness he couldn't quite. "Two men to every woman. That means half of them are open to suggestion." As his eyes became accustomed to the smoky, cotton-batting atmosphere from the doorway, Jed decided the action was at the bar. "Follow me," he said and, using his shoulder as a wedge, chipped through the leathered, denimed masses. Managing to get one hand on the Naugahyde lip of the bar, he shouted, "Two Dewars and water" to the barman and turned to Maura. She wasn't there.

Frantically, he searched the human quicksand for some trace of where she had sunk. At last, on his toes, through the galaxy of airborne trays, shifting shoulders, and bobbing heads, he saw her surrounded by three men. Terrific, he thought, she hooked a few already. Starting toward her, he felt a strong hand on his shoulder, and a voice that brooked no argument said, "Five fifty, Mac." He turned and saw the barman half sprawled across the bar.

"Yeah, sure," he said and, digging into what he hoped was his own pocket, pulled out a money clip and put seven bucks on the bar. He picked up the drinks and, elbows out, headed for Maura.

Nearing the girl and the three men, who all seemed to have bought their shearling jackets at a fire sale, he could see they were too young, far too young, for his purposes. "I was at Stowe last winter," Maura was saying to one of them, "but I don't remember meeting you."

"It was Cape Cod. The nude beach," another said. "I remember you. You couldn't forget me. I'm very big—" He paused insinuatingly and finished, "for skinny-dipping."

"You're very small for New York," Jed interrupted and, brushing between them, handed Maura her drink and stood beside her facing the three boys.

"That's cute," said the skinny-dipper. "She came with her father."

"C'mon," Jed said, and, taking Maura's arm, shoved her back toward the bar.

"Look for us in the back room when Daddy folds up," the boy from Stowe said, and Jed decided to pretend he hadn't heard.

Pushing through a few more chattering groups, he paused, casing the bar crowd. "Don't waste your time on the wrong demographics," he said. "Remember we're fishing for a guy in his forties."

"The worm is not responsible for what bites," Maura said with a touch of hostility.

"There," Jed nodded at a turtlenecked, sports-jacketed grey head alone at the bar. "That's a product we could move." And, tightening his grasp on Maura, he pulled her along to an empty space beside the grey-haired man. "Some mob," he said, jostling the man for his attention.

The man turned and looked at Maura. "You think this is

bad?" he asked her, as though it was she who had spoken. "You should see it at Farrah's. I was there before. That's the 'in' place this week."

"My name's Jed. Jed Lavery," he said, trying to get some eyeball contact and failing.

"Hi," the man said, his attention now on Maura's chest. He looked about forty-five and the silver-and-turquoise pendant he wore looked expensive, announcing he had money and thought young. Jed decided he was willing to ignore being ignored.

"And this is Maura Campbell," he said.

"Very glad to meet you," the guy said holding out his hand. "I'm Gary." Maura shook his hand as though she wished it were a Wash 'n' Dry.

"You here alone?" Jed asked.

For the first time he got through. Gary shot a calculating look in his direction. Evidently deciding Jed was acceptable, he said, "I'm here with this terrific chick. Wanda."

"Oh?" Jed answered, wondering, just how serious is he about this Wanda? Did he bring her? Meet her here? "Where is she?" he asked.

"In the can. Had a lot to drink tonight," Gary confided, as though the information was somehow sexy.

Are they a regular couple? Is he interested in a mature relationship or a quick boff? Jed wondered. "Are we intruding?" he asked.

"Hell, no! Wanda's a real, regular guy. Nothing stuck-up, y'know what I mean? And I'm always glad to meet new people." Gary turned his attention to Maura. "I love what it says on your T-shirt," he said and read aloud, " 'Do not fold, spindle or mutilate.' " He chuckled. "Y'know, I spend a lot of my time walking around just reading what it says on people's T-shirts."

Could I trust him with Denise? Jed wondered. Would he respect her? Would he phone when he says he will? Would he see her in the winter? How do you know who to trust? Jesus, Jed suddenly thought, it's tough to be a woman. What a way to go through life. He was glad he had sons.

He dragged himself back to the scene at hand. Gary was ladling out middle-aged charm to Maura, whispering, or, considering the decibel level of the background-music track, more likely shouting into her ear. Jed couldn't hear him, but when Maura laughed, he chuckled too, making himself part of the group. He didn't like it when Gary began fingering the gold chain around Maura's neck. Unless he's a jeweler, he thought, giving a possibility the benefit of every doubt.

A woman behind Jed shoved at him, trying to get past. He turned and saw a tall blond, the V neck of her blouse, which was really more of a U neck, brilliantly constructed to hold her in, but just. It was obviously a clever fashion ploy to divert attention from her face, which, as a tire manufacturer client used to say, had a lot of mileage. Jed shoved against the bar until his belt buckle hurt, allowing her to pass. Gary looked up and cried, "Baby . . . say hello to two friends of mine. Maura and Jud."

"Jed," he said automatically.

Gary leered at Jed and said, "This is the one I was telling you about. Wanda."

"Wendy," she said, and they all nodded.

"Why don't we have another round to celebrate?" Gary suggested and negligently waved a hand at the bar. The barman, who by accident was looking, said, "Yes, sir!" and started to pour. Jed thought he saw a flicker of dismay cross mine host's eyes.

Gallantly pressing on, Gary swung Maura to his other side, putting her next to Wendy and himself next to Jed. "Maura's an editor," he told the blonde, who said something impressed as Jed wondered when Gary had had time to find out. "Wanda reads a lot," Gary told Maura and, looking at his date, "What was the name of that book?"

"The Fire in Cynthia's Crotch," Wendy answered.

"I missed that," Maura said.

"Isn't she dynamite?" Gary asked Jed. "That broad is ready for anything. I mean, anything." He sold heavily, nodding his head sagely.

"Cute," Jed said.

"And yours is neat. Real neat," Gary said. "Known her long?"

"A while."

"Listen, I got a great idea!" Gary said so forcefully Jed almost saw a comic-strip electric light above his grey head. He lowered his voice slightly and pitched his mouth in toward Jed's ear. "Wanda is the greatest ball in the Bloomingdale area," he told him. "You'd dig her like wild. Now, I had it and I figure I owe it to humanity to spread it around a little. You're a great guy, Jud. Besides, Wanda's more your generation. Why don't we switch?"

Jed considered hitting him, then decided in the crowd the man would never fall, would be propped up, solid as a wall, and he'd probably break his hand on Gary's fatuous chin. He saw four people get up from a nearby table as the barman set the drinks down before him. "There's our table, Maura, honey," he called and picked up two of the glasses. "Thanks for the drinks, Barry," he threw over his shoulder as he followed Maura through the crowd, regretting only that he couldn't see the expression on Gary's face.

"What happened?" Maura asked as they settled at the table.

"Creepy bastard," Jed explained and downed about half the drink. He looked at Maura. "This isn't gonna be as easy as I thought," he said. She shook her head and didn't say "I told you so," for which he was grateful. They sat for a moment, a quiet oasis in the desert of make-out chatter; Jed looking for prospects; Maura wondering if he would keep this up long enough to make fighting her way to the ladies' room worthwhile.

"What about that one?" Jed nodded toward a bald man who had been edged far enough away from the bar to be standing, evidently alone, back behind the first row of tables.

"He looks ineffectual," Maura said.

"That's what I like about him," Jed answered. The man could have been thirty-five but looked older because he was bald, or could have been forty-five but looked younger because he had a trim, athletic figure. "At least he's wearing a shirt and tie," Jed said and as the man backed up for a passing waiter, called, "Why don't you join us?" and shoved one of the empty chairs away from the table. The man looked grateful and started toward them, balancing his drink carefully. "If it works, we can give him a toupee for a wedding present," Jed whispered just before the man sat down.

"Thanks," the guy said. "I've got these socks with the elastic, you know? They're digging in." He reached below the table, evidently adjusted his elastics, then sat back in the chair, stretching out his legs enough to say, "Excuse me," when he hit Jed's ankle.

"You come here often?" Jed asked, then thought, Oh my God. I sound like a pick-up.

"Ah . . . ah," the guy sang on a bent note, "once in a while."

"It's tough to meet people," Jed said with what he hoped was deep understanding. "I know," he hastened to reassure the stranger. "Before I met Maura, Jeez it was rough. Oh, this is Maura, I'm Jed."

"Arnold," the guy said, then addressing Maura, "Where did you meet?"

"In an ice-cream place," she said.

Arnold nodded. "Better class of people," he commented. "Place like this, it's a little trampy. How long you know each other?" he asked, but he sounded envious, not calculating like the other guy.

"Four months," Jed said.

"You're lucky," Arnold told him sincerely.

"I'm in marketing research," Jed threw out a line.

"I own a shoe store," was what he reeled in.

Just before he said, "Oh yeah? Where?" Jed thought he heard Maura moan.

"Fifth Avenue. It's called 'The Bootique,' with two O's," Arnold said.

"I bought some boots there," Maura said, reversing her opinion, her eyebrows going up to signal approval to Jed.

" 'Bout a seven-B," Arnold guessed, and as Maura nodded, "We're particular about fit and it's a nice quality, high style line. At a good price. American," he told Jed. "Those imports fall apart when it rains."

"Well, you run a ladies' shoe store, Arnold, you oughta meet a lot of girls."

"I never mix business with women," Arnold said, straight from the shoulder. "Besides," he laughed a little, "I guess I never met the right one." Maura kicked Jed under the table, racking up another point for Arnold. "There's no romance in the shoe business," the merchant was saying. "I guess when the first thing you see is their corns, it turns you off."

"I can understand that," Jed said, trying not to let his hopes rise too high too fast. And what about his age, he thought. I can't say How old are you? If he wanted to borrow twenty bucks, Jed fantasized, I could ask to see his driver's license.

"So I keep going to the mountains, coming to these places, trying to get a toehold," Arnold was saying. "Someday I'm gonna meet the right one. A neat, cute little six-C was a high arch." He smiled sadly, then leaned into Jed. "A guy gets to be my age, he wants to have a kid he can leave his business to."

"Oh you're not that old, Arnold," Jed said, and held his breath.

"Forty-four," Arnold announced proudly.

"If the shoe fits," Maura whispered.

Jed didn't wait to organize his thoughts, just opened his mouth and let it tumble out. "Arnold, don't get me wrong when I say this . . ." A look of suspicion came into the watery blue eyes and Arnold sat back, away from Jed. "We've been looking for just the right guy . . . and I think you may be him." Arnold said nothing. Jed felt Maura's restraining hand on his arm but, seeing the solution to his problem sitting so close in a neatly pressed, navy blue pinstripe, he threw caution to the air conditioning. "We know a girl. Not a girl, a woman. A really sensational woman. Fabulous feet. Not the kind you find in a place like this. I'd like you to meet her, Arnold, because I know you'd love her. It would be so wonderful for all of us."

"All of us?"

"You. Me. Maura. Denise . . ."

Arnold shot up out of his chair. "Are you suggesting an orgy?" he yelled. Then in a momentary silence as the music tapes were switched, he screamed, "You dirty, stinking pervert!" and threw the contents of his glass in Jed's face.

Through the blur of what felt like rum and Coke, Jed could see the whole room staring at him.

"Get away from him, girlie," the maniac shoe vender screeched at Maura. "He's rotten. He'll infect you with his rottenness!" Jed heard several people laughing above the buzz of conversation and stumbled blindly to his feet, dragging Maura to hers. The sound system coughed and a new Afro-Hustle blared out, covering the shoe man's continuing tirade as Jed made for the door. He was aware of passing Gary and hearing the words "lucky escape" issuing from under the grey hair and also aware that he and Maura were getting a pretty good round of applause from the crowd as they made their exit.

There was a couple getting out of a cab right in front of the place and Jed grabbed the door before the man could slam it, shoved Maura in, and gave his address.

As the car shot off, he realized that Maura was shaking beside him, doubling over and rearing back to double over again in helpless, uncontrollable laughter.

When Maura got home from work she found Jed with a newspaper spread before him, making marks with a red pencil. "What are you doing?" she asked.

"I'm looking for a Singles Dance," he said. He had remembered seeing the ads in the Friday edition of the

New York Post from back in his commuting days. "I think they'll have a more refined crowd than the bars."

"Find anything?" she asked.

"I decided to skip the ones that say, 'Over twenty-one.' They'll probably be too young."

"Mmm. I like that one," she said, skimming the page and pointing. "It says, 'Raisin Pumpernickel Sandwiches.' "

"It's in Brooklyn," he dismissed the ad.

"How about, 'Men! One free drink till 9!' "

"I'm not going to the dance to have fun," he reminded her, and she nodded, accepting his logic. He turned back, pointing to another announcement. "How would you feel about, 'Formerly Married, 28 and over. Bagels and Cream Cheese'?"

"It's in Mount Vernon," Maura said judiciously. "At least that's closer to Westport." And, looking further, she said, "There's one with Giveaway Door Prizes."

"Really, Maura . . ."

"I could use a hair dryer," she defended, and dropped her coat and the manila envelope she carried on a chair.

"I'll try this one. It says '28 and over' and it's on East Sixty-fifth Street. And 'jackets required,' so it sounds like it's got a little class." He rose purposefully and went into the dressing room to change.

"How do you want me to dress?"

"You're not going," he said, pulling off his sweater.

"Oh?"

"I mean," he said, feeling guilty, "I think you're a distraction. I think I'll do better alone."

"Whatever you say," she answered and went into the bathroom. When she came out, he was dressed.

"You're not angry?" he asked.

"No," she said, but Jed wasn't sure. "I've got a manuscript to read." She walked to the chair, pulled it from the envelope, and read the title, *"Passion's Painful Love."*

"You read that."

"No, I read *Love's Painful Passion.* That was about an

English girl who became indentured to Jean Lafitte, had an affair with Andrew Jackson, and married the Polish ambassador. This one's about a half-caste Indian girl who stows away on a ship for England. I think she's going to have an affair with Beau Brummel."

"Oh," he said.

"I really would like to get married," Maura said, riffling the pages of the manuscript.

"I don't want you to think I'm keeping you from participating," Jed said. "I mean, there's things you can do, too."

"Like what?" she asked.

"Well, while I'm gone you could call some of your friends. Ask if they've got a brother."

"Okay," she said, putitng her ms. on the table beside the sofa and pulling off her shirt.

Jed got his overcoat from the closet, pulled it on, and looked at her. "I'd really rather stay home."

"Go to the dance, Jed. Maybe you'll meet the man of our dreams."

He said, "Okay," without much conviction, and went to the door. "If they haven't got a brother, maybe you can try fathers," he said, and left.

"I don't want to talk about it." Jed said it from the door before he realized the lights were out and Maura was asleep.

"What?" she mumbled, invisible, a mound of bedclothes outside the square of light that cut the darkness through the opened door.

"I don't want to talk about it." He shut the front door and in the blackness moved the familiar path to the dressing room.

"What?" she said more clearly and, inching up in the sofa-bed, turned on the lamp.

"The dance," he said, hanging up his coat. "It was the worst experience of my life."

Maura shut her eyes against the light, waiting for her pupils to dilate or undilate, she could never remember which. "My poor baby," she said, unable to think of anything else.

"Don't ask about it," he called.

"How many people were there?"

"About a hundred. Eight of them men. There was this kind of hostess. She kept telling me to try the table nibbles."

"What's a table nibble?"

"I don't know. It looked like a chopped-up table spread on Ritz Crackers." She heard a drawer slam. "Maura, I just want to forget the whole thing. Did you have any luck?"

"No." She could not admit she was too embarrassed to call. "Nobody has brothers," she added and, wanting to get him off the subject, she asked, "What were the men like?"

"They looked like a committee to organize a march on the White House for higher Social Security payments." He strode into the living room, barefoot and stripped to the waist. "I was the only one there Denise would have even considered."

"Well, maybe you just picked a bad dance," Maura said trying to be encouraging.

"I will never go to another," he said firmly. "My God, they all kept writing down their phone numbers and giving them to me."

"The women?"

"Even the hostess!" he yelled, pulling several small pieces of paper from his pockets and throwing them to the floor. "One woman even had a Goddamn printed brochure!" He reached into his back pocket and, taking out a folded, glossy-paper flyer, threw it to Maura. He turned on his heel and went into the bathroom.

Idly she opened the brochure. "Nice house," she commented, and, "Is that a Cadillac?"

"I don't want to talk about it," he called, and she heard him brushing his teeth.

"Why did you stay so long?"

He rinsed his mouth and spit out. "I kept thinking maybe the guys came late."

"But what did you do? Did you dance with anyone?"

"You know I can't dance," he snapped from the bathroom door. "I just had some Lysol punch with one of the women. But only to get away from the others."

"Was she nice?"

Jed was pleased to note a minor undertone of jealousy and answered in complete truth, "Very nice. She reminded me of my Aunt Martha. I didn't know if she wanted to marry me or adopt me." He strode back into the bathroom and she heard the motor of the Water Pik.

"You want anything to eat?" she called when the motor stopped.

He came out of the bathroom naked. "I just want to go to bed, Maura." He sounded desperate. He paused to look at her. She was sitting up, the blanket around her waist, a concerned look in her wide brown eyes that seemed to spread over her soft, silky shoulders and down to the glorious, firm, round, worried-looking breasts. "Oh God," he said, awestruck again despite her familiarity, "I have never wanted to go to bed so badly."

He moved across the room quickly, lunged beneath the blanket and grabbed her, pulling her to him, almost in one gesture; feeling the warmth and excitement of her body, kissing her roughly, frantically.

"Hey, take it easy," Maura murmured.

"God, Maura!" he said. "All those people. I have never felt so lonely!"

When Jed went to see the boys that weekend, he was kinder to Denise than he had been in some time. When he brought them home after dinner and two Maalox in the pizza place they liked so well, and even after they had gone to bed, he lingered, discussing more than the usual payment-to-orthodonist subjects they habitually ran down. And, for once, they didn't run each other down. He got home late and Maura was annoyed. He did not sleep well.

The next morning, fuzzy, headachy, and feeling put upon, he blew a meeting with an important client. The VP of the housewares division of a soap company explained the product he wanted Jed's company to test with earsplitting enthusiasm.

"They're like house slippers," the man said, "only they're built on cotton-nylon loops, like miniature mops." He held them up and Jed thought his head would explode. "The customer puts them on, sprinkles her floor wax, and glides around the floor." As the VP put them on he gave his impression of a hard-sell TV announcer. "No more nagging backache!" he yelled. "It's fun to do your floors with Footsie Shiners!" When he began to glide around his wall-to-wall carpet, Jed laughed hysterically and the meeting was over.

"Any messages?" he asked Felicity back at the office.

"Dr. Parmalee wants you to call."

"Get him," he said going into his office.

"How'd the meeting go?" Felicity asked his back.

"I don't want to talk about it," he said and slammed the door. When the phone rang a moment later, he picked it up and barked, "Yes?"

"I'm with a patient!" It was Og.

"You called me," Jed snapped.

"What's the matter?"

"I'm very depressed."

"I'll write you a prescription for Valium later. I've got a *pityriasis rosea* on my table."

"Male or female?"

"Male."

"If you cure him, do you think Denise would like him?"

"For God's sake, Jed, it's an adolescent disease."

"Can't we put a fake beard on the kid? I'm desperate."

"Hold," Og said and whispered a few instructions to his patient. When he came back, he said, "I've only got a moment. He's soaking. But as long as you called . . . There was an ad in the *Wall Street Journal* . . ."

"I don't want a broker. Unless he's a widower. With grown children."

"For one of those adult social clubs. Maybe you could find someone there. I figure if it's the *Wall Street Journal,* the members have to be fiscally sound." Suddenly he screamed, "Don't pick it!" to his patient, then said, "Get today's *Journal.* I'll call you later," and hung up.

Jed went down to the lobby newsstand and found the ad. He read it in the elevator going back up.

"SINGLES! Club How-Do-You-Do? A private club for ladies and gentlemen who want to make new friends. Pleasant, unpressured, homelike surroundings. Under-40 and Over-40 Groups."

At the bottom it said, "For personal interview, call our Mr. Horvath," and a phone number.

Back at his glass-and-chrome table, Jed underlined the number with a felt-tip pen and picked up the phone. As he dialed, Felicity came in with a pile of checks to be signed. Jed slammed down the phone. She put the pile of checks on the table, looking over his shoulder at the newspaper ad.

"Perry tried that," she said in an experienced, I-have-been-there tone.

"Don't say anything negative," Jed snapped.

"I'm afraid—" she began.

"There is nothing to fear but fear itself," he declaimed.

Felicity nodded. "That's what Perry said," she told him as she left the room.

"Franklin D. Roosevelt!" he yelled, but she had already shut the door.

Chapter Four

The address our Mr. Horvath had given Jed proved to be a dance studio on the second and top floor of a Lexington Avenue building in the Forties. Walking up the stairs to the strains of champagne-hour music floating from the door at the top, Jed began to have doubts. He gave his name to an attractive young receptionist who half waltzed down the hall in front of him, opened a door, said "This is Mr. Lavery, Mr. Horvath," and rhumba-ed off, the Muzak having changed beats.

"I don't want dance lessons," Jed said as he went in.

"No, no, of course not," Horvath responded heartily. "We have no connection with the studio. We merely rent space for our completely private, personal, home-style get-togethers. Do sit down."

Jed sat down. Horvath looked good-condition late forties and was attractive in a tweedy way. Both his jacket and his hair were brown flecked with grey, and Jed involuntarily tried to see if his shoes were tweed, too, but they had disappeared behind the desk.

"Now, if you don't mind," Horvath said, "we'll just fill

out your application." As he wrote down Jed's home and business addresses and phones, Jed looked around the little office. There was a desk and the small sofa he was seated on and the usual complement of four walls masked in sheets of plastic paneling that pretended to be knotty pine. They were festooned by eight-by-ten glossies of candid wedding-party shots, doubtless to encourage new How-Do-You-Do Club members.

"Age?" Horvath asked, recalling Jed to the business at hand.

"Thirty-six." He had decided he could get away with that at the mirror in the men's room at the office.

Our Mr. Horvath replaced his pen on the desk with some precision, then clasped his hands in front of him. "Mr. Lavery, it is the aim, the business, and the pleasure of our club to bring together single people of like interests, background, social position, and age"—he only stressed the last word slightly—"in the hopes of their finding new friendships among their peers." His brown eyes, which seemed flecked with grey too, stared into Jed's. "We work very hard to assure a compatibility of interests in our groups."

"Forty-two," Jed admitted.

"Yes." Our Mr. Horvath seemed satisfied now and noted that on Jed's application. Then, softening, either personally or as a matter of business charm, he looked up at Jed again. "There is no stigma attached to maturity, Mr. Lavery. I'm always happy to tell people, I, myself, am fifty-two."

"Are you married?" The question came out before Jed thought about it. He noticed a shadow of irritation flicker across the tweed eyes before Horvath answered.

"The employees of the How-Do-You-Do Club are not permitted to divulge personal information," he said formally.

"Oh."

With a *ready now?* attitude, our Mr. Horvath continued the application form. "Marital status?"

"Single," Jed said.

"Divorced, widowed, or . . ." Horvath hesitated, then made his little joke. ". . . slow getting started?"

"Divorced."

"I see." Horvath made a check mark. "And how long have you been resingled?"

"Eighteen months," Jed answered, wondering why he felt like a roof.

Horvath set his pen down again and leaned forward on the desk, lowering his voice to a pastor-vibrato. "And now you are anxious to establish a new relationship?" he asked. From somewhere down the hall, Jed heard organ music and looked to see whether Horvath's collar had reversed itself.

"Yes. Yes, that's what I want. A new relationship," he assured the now Reverend Horvath.

"A permanent one?"

"If God wills it," Jed said, falling into Horvath's mood.

"Then you won't mind if we call your home number a few times?" Horvath said.

"Of course not. But why?"

Horvath smiled. His teeth were the same brown and grey tweed. "We'll call and ask for Mrs. Lavery," he said.

"But . . ."

Horvath interrupted. "Jed, some men . . ." He leaned back in his chair. "You don't mind if I call you Jed, do you?"

Jed said, "No," wondering if Horvath was going to tell him the Facts of Life.

"Jed, let me be perfectly candid with you. Some men seek to use the Club for immoral purposes, the quick pick-up, the one-night . . ." He hesitated, then chose the word: "flirtation. Jed, we must protect our clients, our friends. We cannot and will not be a pit stop on the way to the nearest motel."

"I see. I understand," Jed said, and wondered what Horvath's first name was. "Let me be honest with you . . . uh . . . Mr. Horvath," he said to his newfound friend. "As I understand it, most of your clients, your friends, are looking for permanent relationships? Marriage?"

"We have high hopes, but, of course, we make no guarantees."

"Yes. Exactly." Jed swallowed, then plowed on. "I came to you because I really felt you could help me. What I'm really looking for is a man. Someone in his forties—"

"What?" Horvath interrupted.

"Forties," Jed repeated. "Well, fifty at the outside—"

"Where the hell do you think you are?" Horvath demanded, rising and ripping the application in two.

"What?" Jed rose too, realizing he hadn't made himself clear. "Wait. You don't understand—"

"Get your ass outa here," the Reverend Horvath thundered. "What's the matter? Have they raided all the gay bars in New York?" He opened the office door.

"That's not what I meant," Jed began, but Horvath outweighed him by twenty pounds and was shoving him now.

"That's the trouble with this goddamn Gay Liberation," Horvath yelled. "So many of you people are out of the closet, you can't tell who's a queen anymore!" He pushed Jed out into the corridor, where several elderly ladies from the dance class that was just over were whispering and staring.

"I'm not!" Jed yelled, half at the ladies, half at Horvath. "You got it wrong!" The dance instructor, a willowy blonde with a moustache, was smiling at him from the dance-studio door. It was the only friendly face in the crowd and it winked at him. "Oh shit!" Jed explained and started down the hall, conscious of their stares at his back and his anxiety to keep his walk as masculine as possible.

He was terribly grateful when a whore approached him near Grand Central Station.

"It's called 'Dining à Deux, Unlimited,' " Maura told him a few nights later.

"Sounds like a gastronomic whorehouse," Jed said

from the depths of his depression. He had, during the week, gone to a lecture in a church basement, an encounter group at a Y, and taken a mystery bus ride.

"I hear it's terrific," Maura said. "One of the senior editors told me it gets a very good crowd. It's so exclusive they don't even advertise."

"Look, it's nice of you to try to help . . ."

"You can't give up now," she said. "Here. Call this number." She handed him a slip of paper.

When he got off the phone, he said, "It's a maybe. Listen, sometimes they call back to make sure you're not married. If you answer, tell 'em you're the maid."

"Yassuh," Maura said.

"Dear, dear, Mr. Lavery," Mrs. Dellaville, his hostess at ten dollars a throw, caroled as she opened the door for him. She was nervously energetic in a hostess gown, huge ropes of pearls, and her late fifties. "Do come in and meet the gang," she insisted in a conscious effort for colloquialism.

It was a large, elegantly threadbare Central Park West apartment thrown open each Friday to the Gang, which this night numbered about ten well-dressed men and twenty-five mostly overdressed women. The ladies ranged in age from about thirty-five to infinity and the men all seemed older than Jed, but he was beginning to doubt he was any judge of that.

Passing the buffet-set table in the foyer, Jed saw the dining room to his left furnished in several small tables, presumably card under the cloths for dining *à quatre* no matter what the club was called. He turned right through an archway and into the living room.

A woman who had not yet resigned herself to her late forties instantly broke from a clump of her contemporaries and bee-lined to him. She had jet-black hair and a dead-white makeup broken only by violet eyelids and a scarlet mouth. She wore what could only be described as a prom dress. "You're new!" she squealed in delight. "Let me introduce you around!" Her arm circled Jed's, tourniquet style, and she said, "I'm Selma Sutter from Great Neck," completing the introductions. "You'll love Mrs. Dellaville's. Isn't she a dream?" she said vivaciously and did about a quarter of an hour of dialogue in a fast-paced three minutes as though anxious to get everything in before she was interrupted. She told him her school background, where she had lived, her premarital occupation and postwidowhood charities, checked for mutual acquaintances, and brought her monologue to a close with an announcement of her goals and life-aspirations much in the manner of a Miss America contestant in the final exciting moments of the Pageant.

"But let me get you some wine," she said after a gasp for breath, as if remembering her manners. "You can meet all of them later." She dismissed the rest of the room with a negligent wave of her unoccupied hand and, keeping her grip firm, led Jed across the living room to a makeshift bar where a high-school boy in an ill-fitting white jacket was pouring wine from a pitcher.

"White or red?" the high-school boy asked.

"Nice to meet you," a woman standing at the bar said before Jed could answer the boy. "I'm Rhonda Robotham. Have some cheese." She shoved a plate of cheese cubes at him.

"Isn't it a small world," Jed mumbled, staring at her overbite.

Perry's ex-wife had no idea what he meant but said, "Yes," to be agreeable. The boy bartender, tired of waiting, handed Jed a glass of white. The group Selma had left descended on him en masse, glaring at Selma, their mouths set in firm, determined lines before they broke into gracious smiles.

Twenty minutes and one glass of Gallo later, Jed, thinking How do I get to the men? said, "Excuse me. I have to go to the john."

"First door on your left." Rhonda Robotham's teeth flashed coquettishly at him as she pointed.

"I'll take you," Selma Sutter topped her.

"Please don't bother," Jed told Selma. "Mummy lets me cross the avenue by myself now," and beat a retreat.

Staring into the bathroom mirror, he told himself You'll have to come out sometime. Then he heard the door rattle and someone knock. Knowing in his heart it was Selma, he opened the door, revealing a tall gentleman in a well-cut black suit with iron-grey hair and a scrap-iron moustache. He stared at the man, sizing him up, trying to visualize Denise beside him, knowing the man was far too much like C. Aubrey Smith. "Sorry," Jed mumbled, "you just won't do," and walked past him back to the foyer.

Mrs. Dellaville was in the archway facing the living room. "Din-din, everybody," she called gaily. "Just sit anywhere you like. In couples," she added, vaguely hopeful.

Peripherally, Jed could see Selma starting toward him. He turned, almost bumping into a woman beside him. "I'm Jed Lavery," he said.

"Gabrielle Marcotte," she answered. "The friends I have left call me Gaby." Jed figured her to be about thirty-seven. She was attractive in an offbeat, not-my-type way. Her face was lively, perky rather than pretty, and she wore an overlay of plumpness that was somehow youthful on a nicely-put-together, petite frame. She looked not as though she had let herself go but as if her baby fat, enjoying itself, had decided to remain through puberty and on.

Selma had paused across the foyer, but Jed decided not to take chances. "Like some food?" he asked Gaby.

"I'd love some," she said, "but I'll settle for what Dellaville serves."

As they joined the line at the buffet, Gaby looked at him. "This is your first time," she said, not quite a question.

"Yes."

She smiled. "You'll hate it."

He laughed. "You're right."

"So do I."

"Why do you come?" he asked, and she just looked at him. Jed felt slightly embarrassed.

"Hello, again," Rhonda Robotham said from behind him in line. Jed smiled at her and turned back to Gaby.

"Are there always so many here?" he asked.

"No. It's one of Dellaville's better crowds."

"I wonder why," Jed said aimlessly.

"Because you're here," Gaby told him.

"You're kidding."

"No. She calls all the ladies when she knows someone new and attractive is coming."

"Good Lord!" he said.

Gaby widened her blue eyes. "That's why I came," she said. "I'd about given up on this club." Jed looked at her in total amazement. Someone put a plate with a chicken crepe and three oily lettuce leaves into his hand.

"Divorced or widowed?" Jed asked. They had gone to the piano bench with their food, the piano serving as a defense from the rest of the crowd.

"My husband, that bastard, ran away with the baby-sitter," Gaby answered pleasantly, and while Jed tried to think of something appropriate to say, she continued. "It's my own fault. Mother told me to use older women." Gaby sighed. "Mother's living with me now."

"And that's why you come to Mrs. Dellaville's," Jed deduced.

Gaby nodded. "Besides, you never know what may happen. Only you do. Really. Nothing will happen." She looked up from her plate and into his eyes. "Will it?" she asked. Embarrassed, Jed looked down at his plate, cut another section of chicken crepe with his fork. He felt like the heel of all time.

"I can't believe you'd have difficulty finding a guy," he said finally.

"Flattery?"

"No."

"I don't go to bed on a first date. Or even a second."

"I didn't mean—"

"I guess you didn't," she said, but Jed couldn't tell

whether she was pleased or sorry. He wanted to explain. She was a nice woman and she deserved it. Except, every time he started to explain what he was doing . . .

"I'm not here looking for someone to marry," he said.

"That's perfectly all right. I understand," she said. "Just don't start talking about the salmon swimming upstream. I'm the type that worries about the roe."

"You don't—"

"You can switch partners when we get to dessert. Dellaville arranges it that way."

"I'm looking for a man to marry my ex-wife," he blurted out, determined she should understand.

"My God, that's considerate," she exclaimed, absolutely stunned.

"No, it isn't," he said wondering why this woman, a perfect stranger, made him feel ashamed.

"Yes it is," she argued. "Even it it's only to get rid of the alimony so you can marry the other girl." Jed was not surprised she had guessed. He was beginning to understand his situation was not unusual. "I mean, for you to go through all this . . ." she said in tones of wonder. "Good God, if Len, that bastard, had done it for me . . . Why, all of us would rather have a man than the money. Don't you understand that?"

"Yes," he said, although he hadn't thought of it before.

Gaby put her plate down on the piano, losing all interest in the food. "What have you done so far?"

He told her everything, even things he couldn't bring himself to tell Maura, like Mr. Horvath. It's easier to tell a stranger, he thought, and didn't resent it when she laughed, realizing it was funny.

When he was through, Gaby said thoughtfully, "So you're living with a twenty-two-year-old C-cup and looking for a husband for your wife."

"Twenty-four," Jed corrected, then asked, "How did you know?"

"Honey . . ." Gaby said, the experience and wisdom of every middle-aged divorcée coloring the word, making explanations unnecessary.

"Any suggestions?" Jed asked.

Yes, she thought. The obvious one. Cut out all of this crap and marry someone suitable. I'm sitting right here. He was attractive, the handsomest man she'd seen since she started out on this circuit. And charming. And kind of funny-naïve with this ridiculous plan of his. Marry me, she thought, and get my mother out of my apartment. He was still waiting for her advice. Regretfully, she replied, "I admire your spirit, but I'm not here to help the competition." He looked decidedly disappointed and she said, "Wait a minute," thinking as hard as she could. We have established some tenuous relationship, I'm a fool if I don't at least try to keep it up. How? On what excuse? Then she thought of Barney. She could almost hear the strains of Tchaikovsky swelling behind her as she realized she could keep this up, at least for an evening, and then, *que sera, sera.* Tchaikovsky blended into Doris Day. "Just how desperate are you?" she asked.

"Very."

"There is a guy," Gaby said. "I met him at Mixed Singles."

"Mixed Singles?"

"Oh, it's another one of these things," Gaby explained as though it were obvious. "Only they do events. Theatre parties, bus trips, nature hikes. Different things. I met this man on a tour of Chinatown. He asked me to marry him on Pell Street."

"Just like that?"

"Well, we had had a Chinese dinner and I showed him how to use the chopsticks. Of course, he's so available, he may be gone by now. That was a month ago. But . . . look, Mixed Singles is having a lecture night. Why don't we go? He may be there."

"Oh, I couldn't take you away from here," Jed protested.

"I was going anyway," Gaby said, "if you turned out to be a frost."

"Sorry about that."

"Yes," she said, as though she were sorry, too, Jed thought.

When they left together, Mrs. Dellaville had little tears of joy in the corners of her eyes and her pearls were heaving.

In the cab, Jed asked Gaby, "If this guy's so terrific, why didn't you take him?"

"I didn't say he was terrific. I said he was available. The guy is a shambles. But," she said hopefully, "he is sort of sweet and I think he's sincere. Call him a diamond in the rough. But I'm not up to the cutting and polishing."

"Look," Jed said as the cab lurched around a corner. "I don't know how to say this. You remind me of Denise, my ex-wife." He hurried on nervously. "I don't mean you look like her. But she's nice. I mean, attractive, smart . . ."

"And middle-aged," Gaby said, thinking maybe the whole project was silly.

Jed sensed an undertone of disapproval. "The point is," he pressed on, "you're as good as Denise. If you didn't want this man . . ."

"Let me put it this way," Gaby said, and sighed. "My ex, Len, that bastard, was a son of a bitch. But he was charming, funny, very good-looking and an absolute smash in bed. Of course, it turned out later he was a smash in half the beds in Riverdale. But I've had the best and I'm not going to trade down." She looked at Jed, her face red in the glow of a traffic light. "My problem is I would never marry the kind of man who would want to marry me."

They rode in silence to their destination. Gaby waited as Jed paid the driver; then he stopped, indecisive, in front of the hotel. "Well?" Gaby asked.

"I don't know."

"We're here. May as well look at him. I know this field, Jed. The competition is out of sight. If you're really desperate, grab what you can and fix it up. It may be easier for a man to reconstruct another man. You'd be more objective. He'd be less suspicious."

"You're right. We're here," Jed said.

As they opened the door to the Mixed Singles conference room, the lecturer, a dauntless-looking woman in a corduroy slack suit and space shoes, was saying, "Any questions on straddles?"

"What is it?" Jed asked. "A sex lecture?"

"Should I sell my IBM?" someone in the audience asked.

"Stock market," Gaby whispered.

"I'm talking about straddles," the lecturer replied.

"Should I straddle my IBM?" the man asked, accommodating the lecturer.

There were only six men in the room and four ladies, though fifty chairs had been set up. Obviously the Mixed Singles membership didn't give a damn about the market.

Jed closed the door, and at the noise, several people turned to look. "He's here," Gaby whispered and nodded toward a man at the back of the group. He nodded back. "Let's sit down. When they serve coffee, we can talk to him," Gaby said.

They sat in the last row of chairs and Jed studied the man. He was distinctly pudgy and the polyester leisure suit he wore did nothing to disguise the fact. The bow tie, a further mistake, was wrong for the leisure suit, if that wasn't a contradiction in terms, and further emphasized his flabby chin and made his face look fatter than it probably was. His moustache, big, black, and droopy, gave him a hangdog look and made his complexion pasty by contrast.

"He's a loser," Jed whispered.

"Winners aren't looking," Gaby answered. "They've found."

"I don't know," Jed muttered doubtfully, then thought, If he looked like Paul Newman I wouldn't like him either.

"It doesn't matter to me. I was only trying to be helpful," Gaby whispered as the lecturer glared at them.

There were a few more off-the-subject questions from the men, and one woman asked advice about insurance, after which the lecturer made a dispirited pitch for customers and coffee and pound cake were served.

"Barney," Gaby said to the prospect, "I'd like you to meet Jed Lavery. Jed, this is Barney . . ." and then she couldn't remember his last name.

"Warburton," Barney said, accustomed to people, women, forgetting.

Jed shook the soft, damp hand Barney offered and was surprised to see the man was an inch or two taller than he was. "Can we talk?" he asked.

"Sure," Barney said, and the three walked away from the rest of the crowd carrying their paper cups and, in Barney's case, two pieces of pound cake.

When they had pulled the gilt chairs around to face each other and were sitting, Jed said, "I understand you want to get married."

Barney looked interested. "Yes."

"Perhaps I can work something out for you," Jed told the man.

Barney looked questioningly at Gaby, then back at Jed. "Who are you? Her brother-in-law? Her agent?" he asked.

"Oh, it's not me," Gaby said.

Barney looked confused.

"Would you mind answering a few questions?" Jed began, wondering how to go about this. Barney shook his head. "Your age?" Jed asked, suddenly remembering our Mr. Horvath.

"Forty-one."

Of course, I lied to Horvath, Jed thought, but this guy doesn't look hip enough to lie. He was vaguely annoyed that Barney was younger than he. "When were you resingled?" he asked.

"Resingled?" The question seemed to throw Barney.

"Divorced," Jed clarified.

"Oh, I've never been married."

"Never?"

"Well, y'see," Barney said, "I lived with my mother," and Jed's heart sank. "She was never really well," Barney continued, "and I . . . well, I couldn't think about marrying. But Mommy . . . I lost her about six months ago . . . and now . . ."

The answer could almost have been funny to Jed, but the man seemed so naïve, so sincere. "What do you do, Barney?"

"Well, I kept the apartment. I've got a lease anyway and I don't like eating out."

"I mean where do you work?"

"Oh. I'm an actuary. For Manhattan Life. The apartment's right around the corner. I took it so I could get home to give Mommy her lunch. It's very . . . convenient," he finished.

Jed admitted he was all for mother love and it was nice the guy could cook, but forty-one and never been married? "Have you any outside interests?"

"Look, why are you asking me all these questions?" Barney had finished his pound cake and was beginning to get restive.

"Trust me, Barney," Jed said. Barney looked to Gaby, who nodded, and then back at Jed. "Any hobbies? Sports? Anything?"

"Well," Barney said doubtfully, "a couple of years ago I took a gourmet-cooking class but Mommy didn't like cream sauces and I sort of lost interest in it. And then there's my coin collection."

"Do you dance? Play tennis? Bridge?"

Barney shook a regretful head.

"How about opera?" Jed tried.

"I don't sing but I don't mind listening," Barney told him. "Look," he said again, "would you mind telling me what you have in mind?"

Jed looked at him a long moment. "Would you excuse us a second?" he asked.

"Sure," Barney said, but he sounded annoyed. "I'll get myself some more pound cake." He went back to the table.

"He's hopelessly square," Jed told Gaby.

"I said he needed work," she replied.

"You keep talking about him as though he was a building," Jed said looking after Barney. "Six more pieces of pound cake and he'll be condemned. And those clothes. I don't think Denise is ready for Mr. Polyester."

"He's the right age," Gaby pointed out. "He's a nice height. And there's a woman talking to him now."

"But he's forty-one and he's always lived with Mommy."

"Okay. He's not an antique and he's not used. It's not so easy to find fresh merchandise in your forties. Put him on a diet. Buy him new clothes. Fix him up."

"I don't know if I could."

"Desperation is the mother of invention," Gaby misquoted.

"He'd have to agree."

"Ask him," she said. "You've been around enough to know what's being offered. Don't hesitate."

"You sound like a carpet salesman," Jed said. The man was coming back to them, the pound cake he was eating dribbling down his polyester front. "Barney," Jed said, "sit down." When he did, Jed rose, trying to find the proper sentence. "I might . . . if this works out . . . I might want you for my wife."

"That isn't even legal," Barney said, his attitude you-can't-fool-me.

"He means his ex-wife," Gaby explained, as Jed seemed unable to speak.

"She's a wonderful woman, Barney," Jed said, sitting again, facing the prospect. "She's lovely looking, warm, sweet, sincere, loving. A wonderful wife and mother. Intelligent, witty, always cheerful. She's the finest woman a man could hope to meet."

"How long has she been resingled?" Barney asked.

"Eighteen months."

"If she's so wonderful, how come she's not married?"

"The divorce was all my fault, Barney," Jed said manfully. "I guess I hurt her, turned her off for a while. What I did was mean and low and stupid and rotten. It would take a good man to bring her out of the wreckage I made.

I want a good man for her, Barney. She deserves the best. I love her enough to make sure she gets it."

"Go back to her," Barney said, touched. "Try to work it out, Jed."

"It's too late. Too much has been said, too much has been done," Jed said tragically, selling the customer the best way he knew how. "Maybe you can help her recapture the spark, Barney. I think she'd like you."

Barney turned to Gaby. "If I'm good enough for her," he asked, "why don't you want to marry me?"

Gaby didn't answer at once, and for a moment Jed thought she was perhaps considering Barney again. He wondered if he had oversold. Finally she said, "It's not you, Barney. I just had something else in mind." Then, to make it sound more convincing, she added, "something shorter," as though she really wanted a street-length dress.

"Are you sure she wants to marry again?" Barney asked Jed. "After what you did, she probably hates men."

"Yes, but you could change all that," Jed answered firmly.

"You think so?"

"I know so," Jed smiled paternally.

Barney thought for a moment. "I'd have to see her."

"Not in your present condition. You'd blow the whole thing."

"What do you mean, my present condition?"

"Well, there are certain requirements Denise has. We'd have to polish you up for her."

"She sounds very damanding," Barney said.

"She isn't demanding anything." Jed wondered if Barney was turning off. "She doesn't even know about this. I just want to be sure when she finally meets you, you'll sweep her off her feet."

"Why?" Barney demanded. "Why are you doing this?"

Oh hell, Jed thought. He's square, but he's not stupid. But if he was stupid, Denise wouldn't give him a second look. "I'll level with you," he said. "I've got to get the alimony off my back. I want to get married."

"To her!" Barney, angry now, pointed at Gaby.

"No," she said, thinking fervently, From your mouth to the license bureau's ear.

"I only met Gaby tonight," Jed said. "I'm engaged to someone else."

Barney looked at Gaby. "What are you getting out of this?"

"Nothing," she told him. "I just wanted to help bring happiness to four miserable people." It sounded phony even to her.

She's a very considerate person, Barney thought, selfless. And she's very attractive. Mommy would have liked her, although, deep down, he knew Mommy wouldn't have liked anybody. I don't know what this Denise is like and why he really dumped her. But I like this one. And before this came up, she didn't even want to talk to me. "All this polishing he wants to do. Will you help?" he asked Gaby.

"Well," she said, looking down at her hands, "it doesn't really concern me." But already she knew it did, terribly.

"I've never seen this man before in my life," Barney said. "I won't do it unless you help." There! See what she says to that.

Oh, I'll help, Gaby thought. Night and day. Anytime Jed wants me. Even when he doesn't. Familiarity breeds marriage as often as contempt. For the first time in months, she was beginning to feel hopeful. "It's really Jed's project," she said, slowly. "I don't know if I should intrude." Then she looked to Jed. "It is a fascinating idea, and if it works for you, who knows? It might work for me."

Work exactly how, Jed wondered, watching a calculating look computering into this strange woman's eyes. I don't want to get him all fixed up and lose him to you. But, on the other hand, she had already said he didn't measure up to Len, that bastard, and there would probably be places where a woman's help would be of value . . . "It might be a good idea," he said, "but I don't know if I can take so much of your time . . ."

Barney watched them staring at each other, wondering if they had forgotten about him.

"What else do I have to do?" Gaby asked. "Anyway, I'm sick of eating Dellaville's chicken crepes."

"One more thing," Barney interrupted, cutting off their satisfied smiles in mid-break. "I'm not changing anything unless I see this Denise first."

"That's impossible," Jed said. "If she sees you like this . . ."

"Mommy always said never buy a pig in a poke," Barney told them, and realizing that sounded rude, added, "Nothing personal," to Jed.

"If she sees him like this," Gaby said, "and we change him, she won't know him anyway."

"Right!" Barney said. "Why don't we all go to lunch together?"

"No," Jed said. "The most important thing is Denise mustn't know I'm bringing you together."

"Why not?" Barney asked.

"Obvious," Gaby answered and turned to Jed. "We'll have to give him devious lessons, too."

"There is one way," Jed said, suddenly seeing it. "Barney can go look at a house."

"I don't want to see a house. I want to see Denise."

"She's in real estate," Jed said. "Pick a fake name and call this number." He found an envelope in his pocket and wrote the office number down for Barney.

"I'm not very good at lying," Barney said.

"What kind of lying?" Jed asked impatiently. "Just tell her you're married . . . being transferred . . . looking for a house for your family." He looked at Gaby. "Would you call that lying?"

Gaby shrugged, noncommitally.

Barney said, "Look, I'm a mathematician. An actuary. I deal in figures. Everything has to be true, correct to the last decimal. I'm no good at making things look like what they aren't."

Jed could see the man was getting upset. "Barney!" he snapped, to shut him up. "You just call that number, but if her partner answers, remember to ask for Mrs. Lavery to show you the house."

"Won't that make her suspicious?"

"She'll be delighted. Figure she's getting a reputation. Do it tomorrow. Saturday's the big day in real estate, you'll get lost in the shuffle."

"Well," Barney sounded doubtful. "Where is it?"

"Westport. Take the Thruway to—"

"I don't drive."

Jed groaned, knowing it was all going to be difficult. "There's a train," he said.

"But what do I say?" Barney sounded almost close to tears.

Very slowly, like the lady on Romper Room used to talk, Jed said, "Your name is . . . Mulligan" he picked out of the air. "You're looking for a house. For you and your family." He slowed down even further when Barney took a pencil from his pocket and began writing the facts down next to the phone number. Oh my God, Jed thought, he plans to rehearse.

"Yes?" Barney said, pencil poised.

Jed looked at Gaby, saw she was about to laugh and hoped she wouldn't. "You live in Ohio," he continued. "You're willing to spend one hundred and fifty thousand top . . ." What I go through for you, Maura, he telepathed back to the apartment. "You need something in a good school area and your wife is particular about the kitchen and your children want . . ."

Chapter Five

"I don't want to hear any more about it, Scott," Denise said. "Either you take Keith or you can't go."

"But he always makes those kissy sounds in the mushy parts," Scott whined.

"Maybe there won't be any mushy parts," his mother said, returning to her bureau to see if she'd left the car registration there when she changed handbags. "It's rated G."

"I liked it better when I was twelve and he was nine and you didn't think I was old enough and you hired a sitter."

"I'll be happy to call a sitter," she said. "The Taylors' little girl sits now. What's her name? The one in your class?" she asked, heavily sarcastic. "You want me to call her?" When he seemed to be considering it with a rather adult gleam in his adolescent eye, Denise changed tactics. "You can go have a pizza before the movie," she said, and gave him a few more dollars.

"Okay." Having gotten a fringe benefit, Scott accepted the contract.

Denise started downstairs to the garage. "Just walk down to the minibus stop and be sure to look both ways when you cross," she threw over her shoulder.

"I know," he answered, pained.

"Where's Keith?"

"Watching *Spiderman*."

"Goodbye Keith," she yelled and, without waiting for an answer, continued to Scott, "and be sure to lock the house. Check all the doors and for God's sake don't lose the key." She didn't actually hear his *I knows*, but assumed them. "And when I get the car out," she said, opening the garage door, "lock it behind me." She turned, finding herself alone in the garage. Sighing heavily, she got into the car and honked the horn till Scott appeared. "Lock the door behind me," she said through the window.

"I know," he agonized, eyes to heaven.

Denise backed out and started up the driveway. At the road, she could see Og in his raking clothes. Evidently attracted by the sound of her horn, he had stopped working and was watching for her. She slowed down.

"Heavy day today?" he called.

"It's Saturday," she answered.

"Love to Lillian," he called, with what he thought was a debonair smile, and Denise drove off thinking, Poor Og. He never gives up.

She drove down Bayberry Lane, turning left into the Easton Road heading for town. The trees that crisscrossed the road above her head were winter-sticklike already and no longer masked the sky, which was battleship grey and threatening. Denise shivered. After Thanksgiving, she thought, the real estate business would trickle off till spring and maybe she could alternate Saturdays with Lillian. She liked the work and it filled the school days, pushing normal household chores into the empty evenings, but Saturdays she would have liked to sleep late, spend some time with the boys. They were good kids, she reflected, even if Scott hassled her about taking care of Keith. And she couldn't really blame him. No, Denise decided, I shouldn't blame him, I should work on enlarging my guilts. But there was Lillian, who'd left her children completely and didn't have any guilts at all. Better if I work on Jed's guilts, she thought. He's the one who left. Or maybe I should have worked harder on finding someone else. Boys need a man around the house, someone to emulate, someone to sleep with Mommy. Damn! she thought, I don't want to think about that.

Determined not to think about it, the memory of Jed flooded her mind. The way he'd asked her to marry him, impulsively, after their second date. ("Why wait? Who you gonna find that's better?") in their junior year at college. Sensible, pragmatic, she had stalled him through their senior year, the dates, the kisses, the holdings and touchings growing progressively wilder, her own instincts harder to deny, but she had held firm. Their wedding night in the Ramada Inn, the crazy honeymoon driving around Cape Cod in her father's borrowed car. His body lying beside hers on the beaches, in the guest-house beds. The shocked old landlady in Truro who had asked them to leave after one night. "Such noises! I don't believe you're married at all!" she had said. "Damn!" Denise mumbled, driving through a stop sign and almost hitting a plumber's truck. The plumber honked insanely but she drove on.

The first Village apartment. His job at B B D and O, and she worked, too, at Ayers, her salary saved. The night she was sure Scott was conceived, Jed got fired. Impulsively, he opened his own office with the money she had saved, but that time he was right, it worked. She was pregnant with Keith when they took a chance and bought the house in Westport, but that worked out, too. And through it all, at the time, now in memory, his body, familiar, understood, an extension of her own flesh and bones, covering hers, fulfilling hers, loving hers. She slammed on the brake, seeing the red light almost subconsciously. Stop thinking! she told herself, and it turned green.

Denise drove on, thinking, the divorce. That was impulsive, too. I held on . . . for weeks . . . thinking he'll get over it. She'd read all the articles on male menopause. In *Woman's Day* and *Family Circle* it all worked out. But not for her. Dammit, she thought. Damn Jed for spoiling what was perfect.

She pulled into the parking lot behind the old house that had been rebuilt so often no one could quite tell what it was or had been. She walked around the new dress shop in the street-level store, seeing the sign, "Final Closing Sale—Everything 50% Off," in the window and thought, I could have told them they wouldn't make it. She opened the street door bearing her name and Lillian's and the words, "New Freedom Real Estate, Inc." and climbed the stairs to the office. New Freedom, she thought. From what? She went into the office.

"Do you know a Mr. Mulligan?" Lillian Parmalee asked from her side of the facing desks, right-angled from the front window.

"Mulligan," Denise said, looking blankly into Lillian's long, thin face. Lillian pulled a pencil from her greying hair and dusted some dandruff from the shoulders of her cardigan. "Mulligan," Denise repeated, taking off her coat. "The tree man is either Mulligan or Shaughnessy. I can never remember."

"Long as it starts with a W," Lillian snorted. "Not the tree man. This one's from Ohio. He called this morning. The phone was ringing when I came in. He wants you to show him a house. He'll be here at eleven-thirty."

"From Ohio?"

"He called from New York. He sounded a little dim-witted."

"I'll show him the Cimini house," Denise said and hung up her coat.

"Nobody's that dim-witted," Lillian observed.

"I wonder why he wanted me."

"Must've been a recommendation. Who do you know in Ohio?"

"Jed once had a tire client in Akron—"

"Whose name was either Cadwallader or Terwilliger,"

Lillian finished for her, washing her hands of the house, Ohio, and Mr. Mulligan.

Denise sat at her desk, idly turning over a few pieces of mail. "Og sends his love," she said.

"Mm," Lillian commented.

"Doesn't it bother you?" Denise said, not having expected to say anything at all.

"What?" Lillian asked.

"Being divorced? Being alone?"

"I wanted it," Lillian told her sensibly.

"But the children?"

"I see them. I love them. I just didn't want to make oatmeal for them every day of my life. Let's face it, Denise"—Lillian leaned an arm on her desk and looked at her partner—"Og's a better mother than I am."

"Oh," Denise said, sounding like she hadn't said what she wanted to at all.

"It's just November blues," Lillian told her. "You're a married type. You should've started going out right away."

"I went out," Denise said defensively. "Three times the first two months. "One was divorced, one was separated, and the third, it turned out, wasn't even thinking of leaving his wife. Two of them jumped on me in the car and the third had rented a motel room before he even picked me up. When you're just divorced they all think you're either desperate for sex or so angry at your ex, you'll do it for revenge."

"Well?"

"I don't want revenge."

"What do you want?"

"I want to be sixty-five so I can stop thinking about it and collect Social Security."

"Take my advice," Lillian said. "Do it with anybody. Three or four anybodies. Doesn't matter who. It just revives your self-respect and then you can decide what you really want. First person that walks in that door. Mr. Mulligan."

"Suppose Og was the first person to walk in the door?"

"Not Og. He'd bore you to death."

"Is that why you left?"

"No. I made a mistake. I'm not the married type. I like being single. You don't have to argue about who gets the Sunday crossword puzzle." Lillian rose and put on her coat. "If I don't see you, it's eight o'clock at Helene's for bridge."

"The only advantage to divorce was I can play bridge with the girls. Except, of course, I lost my tennis partner."

"Win some, lose some," Lillian said at the door.

"Where are you going?"

"I have three gentlemen gym teachers in their twenties and a dog, somewhat younger, who want a rental. I have a feeling there were three under-age girls in the car. They'll be back by now. Do we have any clients who want their homes gutted?"

"Look in the D file, under Death Wish."

It was raining by the time Mr. Mulligan arrived in a grey-green overcoat that Denise thought made him look embalmed. "You must be Mr. Mulligan," Denise said, rising, pumping up her personality as he opened the door.

"Yes!" Barney answered guiltily, wondering why she was smiling, sure she had already seen through his alias. He was terribly nervous, knew that his hands were cold and clammy as he switched his umbrella from the right to the left and shook hers.

"I'm Denise Lavery." Maybe he *is* embalmed, she thought as their hands touched. Then he took off his hat and she moved back, checking surreptitiously to see if he was wearing rubbers. Of course, she thought. Why am I such a good judge of character? "It's such an awful day to see houses," she said apologetically, and decided to show the ones that people said were too dark on sunny days. "The cheeriest house looks gloomy," she announced, setting it up for herself. "Why don't you take off your coat and we'll look through my book?"

"Yes!" The word sped out like a bullet.

Denise sat at her desk and opened her looseleaf "available" book as he laid his coat over the top of the filing cabinet, put his umbrella on top of it and his hat on top of that. "What did you have in mind?" she asked, turning to him.

Barney felt like a fool struggling out of his rubbers, balanced on one foot and her looking at him like that. "A house," he gasped, and the left rubber came off. He dropped it beside the right one and walked to the visitor's chair beside her desk. Sitting, he realized she was between him and what little light there was from the window and he couldn't really tell what she looked like. She had a nice voice though. Cheerful, but soft. Not giggly.

Denise nodded slowly and picked up an index card. "Well, let's just fill this out first," she said, and remembering, she asked, "How did you hear about us, Mr. Mulligan?"

"You were recommended."

"Oh." Denise smiled. "By whom?"

Oh my God, Barney thought, I can't say your husband and Lavery didn't tell me anyone else. "My wife," he answered, figuring that was safe.

"Who is she?"

"Mrs. Mulligan."

"I just thought maybe I knew her," Denise said, her smile frozen firmly in place. She looked down at the index card and wondered, Why do I always get this kind? "Now you are Mr. Mulligan," she said, writing as she spoke. "First name?"

"Stew." It was the first name that came into his head. It sounds ridiculous, he thought. I can't go through with this. I'm unprepared.

Don't make any jokes, Denise told herself. People get very offended and besides, he's heard them all his life. "And you are living now?" Of course he is, she thought, when she heard herself. I mustn't project my opinions, and added, "Where?" to clarify.

"Ohio."

"Where in Ohio?"

"Pittsburgh." Lord, I sound like an idiot. Why did I say

that? "That is," he corrected, "I work in Pittsburgh but we live in a little suburban town that happens to be in Ohio."

"Quite a drive."

"I don't mind," he said hastily.

Denise was thinking it was all unreal as she said, "I need a phone number to reach you in case something comes up."

"Well, I'm in a hotel now in New York," he said remembering just before he gave his number that Lavery had told him under no circumstances to give her any clue to his real identity. "We're moving," he said to make it sound true.

"I know," she nodded. Is there any particular sales approach to the feebleminded, Denise wondered. "It's awfully dark in here," she said, stalling for time, and rose and went to the light switch across the room. Of course, Lillian sold the Donaldson mansion to that woman we thought was too stupid to write her name on a check. "There!" she said, "that's better," as the terrible overhead light revealed the dust around the office.

She's pretty, Barney thought. I like hair like that. Bouncy, curly, brown. And hazel eyes. Or are they a recessive trait? Well, what's the difference, he decided, they're attractive. He was sort of hoping she had a big chest but he didn't want to stare. She was sitting down again. Please, he thought, no more questions. "Could we see a house?" he asked, thinking in a house, an empty house, he'd be safe.

"What were you thinking of spending?"

"One hundred and fifty thousand is my top." He smiled, knowing he got that one right.

No one else is coming in this rain, Denise figured as she nodded to him. Might as well. "How large?" she asked.

He thought a moment and finally said, "Family size."

Denise felt as though she'd stuck her head in a Mixmaster. "How large is your family?" she asked with the brightest smile she could muster.

"Well, there's my wife," Barney said realizing he had

forgotten to look at her legs when she was standing up. Mommy was a better shopper, he told himself sadly, and seeing she was waiting for more, he added, "and my children," remembering Jed told him he had children.

"How many?"

He didn't tell me, Barney thought but dared to ad lib, "Three." Three sounds like a good number, he assured himself.

Well, at least he seems to know that, Denise decided and thought she might make him more comfortable if she talked about his family. "Boys or girls?"

"Boys." That one was easy for Barney, a multiple choice of two.

"Oh," Denise said, sure she was on firmer footing. "I have two boys. Ten and thirteen. How old are yours?"

"Twelve."

"All three?" She sounded startled, and Barney realized it was too late to reverse himself and, hoping that would end the questioning, just nodded.

"Triplets," he heard her say. "How unusual." This is a nightmare, Denise decided, but in the way of nightmares she proceeded unwillingly to her next personality question. "What are their names?"

Barney was totally rattled by now but knew he had to answer at once. What father hesitates over his children's names? "Huey, Dewey, and Louie," he said, automatically.

"Like Donald Duck's nephews?" The hazel eyes widened, the fine arching brows went up.

Oh my God, he thought, that's where they came from. "My wife was related to Walt Disney," he said, and decided he would abandon this whole project if he could figure a way of getting to his coat, his rubbers, and the door.

I better get him out of here, Denise thought. He seems harmless but he could turn homicidal and I'm all alone and even if I pounded on the floor, with a dress sale going on they'd never hear me and if they did, no one would bother, not with mark-downs like that. "Well, let's go look at a four-bedroom house," she said, and ran to the key rack, grabbing the keys to the Cimini house and the one other she vaguely recalled as having four bedrooms.

Well, I got past that, Barney thought, relieved enough to remember to look at her legs, which were very shapely. He got his rubbers and under cover of struggling into them managed to look at her chest, thrown into sharp relief as she pulled on her raincoat. It was more than acceptable.

"We'll take my car," Denise said. If he gets violent and I'm driving, at least I can honk the horn. Stay on main roads, she advised herself.

"Yes," Barney said taking his coat. "I can't drive."

"Then you can't buy a house in Westport," she practically screamed. "You'd starve to death in a week." Maybe he'll just go, she prayed.

I could get out of this now, he thought. But I think I like her. She's nosy but she's pretty. I should check her out further. "My wife drives," he said, "and the boys," making it better.

"They're only twelve!" I shouldn't have said that, Denise thought frantically. Why incite him?

I shouldn't have said that, Barney thought, but I forgot how old they were. "They give them driving training early in Ohio," he tried to pull the chestnut from the fire.

"Oh," she said, evidently believing him. "My car's downstairs."

He was quieter in the car, positively placid sitting beside her, his umbrella clasped between his legs, and Denise began to relax. He's all right, she thought, and with a really good commission, we could take a Christmas vacation. He's probably just tired flying in from Ohio or Pittsburgh or both, and looking for houses can make a man tense. And maybe I'm edgy today. Scott got on my nerves and what Lillian said . . . She tried to remember when her period was due. She turned into the Compo Road heading toward the beach and the Cimini house and began to give him her standard pitch about the town. The schools, the beach club, the summer theater.

She seemed a little hypertense in the office, Barney

thought, but she's better now. He listened more to her voice than her words, liking the tone, the brightness of it. It would be a nice voice to come home to. "Pot roast for dinner tonight, darling," it would say, or "I've made you a Mulligan stew . . ." No! Not that! No Mulligan stew ever! She'd be angry if she remembered, knew what he'd done. She was talking about the house now, the Cimini house, she called it. She was a pretty good saleswoman, obviously smart. The whole idea had sounded crazy when Lavery broached it, but Mrs. Lavery was beginning to seem worth it.

They ran up the walk under his umbrella and Denise tried to point out the shrubbery, which really was nice, and the gracious lawn, which was entirely fallen, unraked, soaked leaves at the moment. The lock stuck and when she finally managed to make it work, one of the door hinges broke, but he didn't seem to notice.

She led Mulligan through the dark, empty rooms, pointing out the advantages, standing in front of the dark, unpainted space from which the refrigerator had been removed while he looked at the kitchen, opening closet doors, admitting it needed paint, aware that he was looking at her more than the raised fireplace and the wet bar in the playroom. He seemed more sensible now, but the staring unnerved her and she decided not to take him down to the basement.

Reject everything till you want to go home, Lavery had told him. Then say you like the last house, ask if they'll come down and say you'll think about it. "No, this isn't for me," Barney said. "My wife would hate the kitchen," and wondered if that was a good reason for rejecting a house.

He's smarter than he looks, Denise thought. It's the worst kitchen in Fairfield County. "Well, I have something else," she said, "but the people haven't moved out yet." She had decided she'd prefer to show houses where there were people around. "Are you in a rush to move?"

"No. But does this house have a refrigerator?"

Denise looked in her book and said, "It's negotiable."

She drove to the Post Road and stopped to phone ahead to the next house.

Barney liked her, he decided. This was the last house he would look at. While she was in the drugstore phoning, he considered asking her to lunch, then decided it might as well be dinner. Why go through this whole rigamarole that Lavery wanted? This is me, Barney Warburton. Add up the figures and decide if you like 'em, Mrs. Lavery. If we had dinner tonight and I asked her to marry me, we could save months of beating around the bush, loneliness, dieting, expense. Except, if I try to date her, she'll ask about my wife, my kids. She'd think I was just another masher. Maybe Lavery's right. I am overweight. And if she likes to dance . . . and if she really would consider me . . . He saw her coming out of the drugstore. It had stopped raining now and her hair was suddenly blown in a gust of wind. But it bounced right back into place naturally, looked just as good as it had, and he liked that. Lavery is right. I do like her. If he was right about that, he may be right about the rest. Barney decided to go back to the original plan.

"Mrs. Robotham said we could come right over," Denise said as she settled back in the car.

"Why is she selling?" Barney asked, hoping to sound like a real buyer. "Is there something the matter with the house?"

"Divorce. It accounts for half the turnover in Connecticut."

"Turnover?" Barney wondered if that was a real estate term or if it were some kind of sexual innuendo.

"House sales. Without divorce half the real estate agents in Westport would starve."

He was pleased her remark had been strictly business. "Is she buying a smaller house?" he asked, to keep the conversation going, to keep hearing her voice, which seemed to have traces of his mother's in it.

"No," Denise answered. "Maybe she's going back to New York to look for another. Husband, not house," she added to keep him from asking. "Lots of them do."

"You didn't," Barney said.

Denise looked at him. "How'd you know I was divorced?"

He looked nervously through the windshield in case a car was coming and happened to catch sight of her hands on the wheel. "You talked about your sons but you aren't wearing a ring," he said, and kept his mouth shut for the rest of the trip.

As he strode quickly through Mrs. Robotham's house, the owner followed him closely and smiled a lot. In the kitchen where her daughters were wolfing down peanut butter and crackers, she asked if he'd like coffee, a sandwich, some of yesterday's spaghetti? "I'll heat it," she coaxed. Mrs. Lavery didn't seem to be included in the invitation.

In the dining room he heard the broker whisper to the owner, "He's married," and her earnest reply, "He can't be. He didn't even ask to see the linen closet."

Back at the front door he told Mrs. Robotham, "I like it. I'll discuss it with my wife and let you know." Even her protruding teeth looked dejected and suddenly Barney realized how easy lying was once you got used to it.

When Mrs. Lavery left him at the train station he remembered to ask, "Will she come down?" although if he had really wanted to buy he'd have paid the full price. The poor woman obviously needed the money for her children's dental work.

By the time Denise got back to the office, Lillian had returned and Og was visiting.

"I got the rental," Lillian said triumphantly as Denise opened the door.

"The schoolteachers liked the house?"

"Not so much the house," Lillian admitted. "It was that little enclosed field in back of it. They thought that was ideal for growing pot."

"Maybe we should look at some of the other houses and rewrite the ads," Denise suggested.

"Been showing someone around?" Og asked her.

She nodded and shook out her raincoat. "He said he liked the Robotham house," she told Lil, "but I don't think he'll buy. Actually, the way Mrs. Robotham behaved, she'd've kept it and let him move in."

"Flirted with him?" Og *tsk-tsk*ed. "A married man?"

"How'd you know he was married?" Denise asked, wondering if the feeling she had was what some people called *déjà vu*.

"A single man wouldn't look at a house that big," Og said, and told himself it didn't matter, Denise hadn't noticed a thing.

"I guess Robotham's desperate," Lillian said. "Her husband's living with someone's secretary."

"How do you know?" Denise hung up her coat.

"I forget who told me," Lillian answered.

"I did," Og reminded her. "He's living with Jed's secretary."

Denise slammed her purse down on the desk, wondering why that made her angry at Jed. At least *he* wasn't living with his secretary.

"Oh yes," Lillian said. "I knew there was some reason I wasn't going to mention it."

"I wouldn't care if Jed were living with someone. Why should I care about his secretary?" Nobody answered, and suddenly Denise realized he must be living with somebody.

"Well, I've got to do my marketing," Og said, and started toward the door. He turned halfway and said, "Oh, Lil, Ellen says she should put something on her hair besides shampoo. What?"

"Creme rinse," Lillian said in a discouraged way.

"Well, if Mrs. Robotham was that impressed, he must've been a terrific guy," Og said to Denise.

"Who?"

"Your client."

"He was a smash," Denise said in a slightly sour tone, and Og drove directly home, closed the kitchen door so the kids wouldn't hear, and phoned Jed.

"She didn't suspect a thing," he said after Jed said, "Hello."

"Who?"

"Denise. And when I asked if she liked him, she said he was a smash."

"Og, for God's sake, what did you do?"

"I just went over to Lil's office and checked up for you, Buddy Boy," Og said in the tone of one who is unappreciated.

"Did you blow his cover?" Jed asked, enraged.

"She didn't suspect a thing. I was very subtle," Og said, justifiably proud.

"I should never have told you. Now, listen, Og. Butt out. If she finds out I'm putting Warburton up to this, she'll never marry him."

"Well, I just thought you'd want to know," Og sulked.

"Besides, she couldn't possibly like him in his condition. Look, Og, forget everything you know about this, and if I start to tell you anything, give me a shot and put me to sleep." Jed hung up and, muttering "Damn fool!" began to dial a number.

"Who's a damn fool?" Maura looked up from a manuscript called *Tender is Your Torture.*

"Og," Jed said. "And me. And . . . Barney?" he asked as the phone was picked up.

"Who's Barney?" Maura asked.

"How did you like her?" Jed asked the phone, motioning Maura to silence.

"I like her. I like her very much." He had thought it out carefully on the train, adding up all Mrs. Lavery's good points, picturing himself with her, introducing her at the Christmas party at the office, sharing a cup of cocoa he would make at bedtime. He had arrived at a trial balance, deciding to go through with it.

"Dynamite!" Jed yelled. "Then we can go to work?"

There was only one thing that bothered Barney. If Mrs. Lavery was as nice as he thought, why would a guy like Lavery walk out on her? "Yes," he said, "if you're sure you won't change your mind. About Mrs. Lavery."

"No way," Jed said, looking over at Maura, naked, ms. in lap, looking at him.

"All right," Barney said.

"I see the boys tomorrow," Jed said, shuffling his mind like a desk calendar. "Meet me for lunch Monday. At my office."

There was one other thing that Barney had decided on the train. Suppose, he had thought, Lavery gets me all fixed up and Mrs. Lavery doesn't like me. Maybe by then Gaby would. He was determined to keep her around. "Should I call Gaby?" he asked.

She might be dangerous, Jed thought again. But you need a woman's touch. Maura? He turned to see her coming from the kitchenette with a yogurt. Today she had draped a couple of her gold chains around her middle. She looked like one of those erotic ads in *The New York Times* magazine section. Fantastic, but not the type to polish a man for Denise. "Okay," he said into the phone. "You call Gaby and tell her to meet us."

"Who's Gaby?" Maura asked.

Barney was so excited he just nodded to the phone, then, realizing, said, "Monday. Twelve-thirty," took the address, and hung up. His stomach was churning and his hands tingling. "Two," he said aloud to the empty apartment. "Two definite prospects." He went into the kitchen, looking for the Fig Newtons, his unvarying reaction to soul-stirring events, whether good or bad. It's worth the effort, he thought. Much more creative, more productive than dragging around to the clubs with their lectures and walking tours and things.

He was on his way back to the phone, eating the second Fig Newton, the box in his hand, when he remembered the diet. He put the box down and the half-eaten cookie on top of it and looked at them longingly, his nervous stomach sending messages to his brain. But we haven't even decided on what kind of diet, he rationalized and, popping the rest of the Fig Newton into his mouth, picked up the box and carried it to the phone, thinking, I'll start Monday. He was eating the third as he dialed Gaby.

"Hello?" she said.

"It's Barney Warburton," he said, windshield-wipering his teeth with his tongue.

Gaby sighed with relief. She had been thinking it was all too wild, too crazy, too much a hot inspiration of the moment that freezes out when cooler heads prevail. "Did you like Mrs. Lavery?" she asked.

"She's terrific. Really terrific," and then, remembering, "almost as nice as you."

"Oh, come on, now, Barney," Gaby said, thinking, He is rather sweet. What a pity he's such a lump. But Lavery? . . . She smiled, recalling the husky body, the offbeat kooky way of thinking that she found intriguing, the wide, generous mouth, and the beautiful teeth. She'd always had a weakness for teeth—perhaps, she thought, because my father was a dentist.

"We're meeting for lunch on Monday to get organized. Will you come?"

"Well, if you really want me," she said, determined to be an integral part of the plan. Jed Lavery may have a bird in hand, she thought, but twenty-four-year-old C-cups have a way of flying off, leaving the older unmarrieds to look for two new ones in the nearest bush. Which was exactly where Gaby intended to be nesting. Meanwhile, she would be able to fix up the lump so Mrs. Lavery would be out of the way, and keep Mr. Lavery under surveillance till the iron was hot.

"I do," Barney said.

What a lovely phrase, she thought, and said, "Give me the address." She wrote it down, hung up, and called the beauty parlor for an early appointment Monday.

The taste of the yogurt was still in her mouth; the scent of his Aramis, which she occasionally splashed on after a shower, was on her breasts; the gold chain, which he had not allowed her time to remove, chafed between them, catching and snagging his hair, oddly arousing him further, if that was possible; pulling him to new heights of exertion, and, he felt, to new depths within her. He heard her moan but drove on exhilarated but controlled, his body a wildly ecstatic locomotive chugging through Paradise; his mind a computer of joy in the knowledge that it had solved the problem, won the squirming prize under his body for now, for always. Two months, he thought, ten weeks at the outside, and I'll have her forever. Nothing can come between us . . . unless the government declares her body a national treasure and puts it in the Smithsonian. My God, he thought, I'm humping the Statue of Liberty, and, in time to the music of *The Stars and Stripes Forever* that suddenly exploded in his brain, he brought the explosion to his body and hers, and to the cheers of the crowd, or at least a satisfied little yelp from Maura, he settled quietly on the upholstery of her body.

"Wow, that must've been some phone call," she said.

"I didn't want to tell you till I was sure it would work out."

"You found her a guy!" Maura guessed.

"And he likes her."

"Does she like him?"

"She hasn't met him yet."

"Then how does he know he likes her?"

He told her the whole story and Maura only interrupted once to say, "Get off. You're heavy." When he finished, she looked at him in awe and said, "You really think you can do it? Change him like that?"

Jed nodded. "Yes. And knowing Denise as I do, Barney will be absolutely made to measure for her."

"You're sure you can't find her a ready-to-wear?" Maura asked.

"I been out there, honey, and there's nothing but remainders, irregulars, and odd lots. This is the only way."

"And what about this woman? This Gaby?" she asked. "Why do you need her?"

"It needs the woman's touch. I may not think of everything."

Maura thought that over. "Why can't I do that?" she asked.

"Honey," he said, "the demographics are wrong. We're prepping him for a market you wouldn't understand."

"What does Gaby look like?" she asked flatly.

"Short . . . lumpy . . . grey," he ad-libbed. "Your average little brown wren."

It didn't quite add up, to Maura. "So why is she doing it?"

"She was excited by the concept." This at least was true. "She figures if it works for me, she'll try it for herself."

That sounded true, Maura thought. It *is* an interesting concept. Her mind flipped a page, dismissing Gaby for the moment. "Do you really think it'll work?"

"Absolutely."

Maura rose and went into the bathroom. Jed heard the water splashing into the tub and Maura reappeared, evidently thinking hard. She went into the kitchenette and came back with the message pad and pencil and sat on the comfortable chair. "Tell me again how and where you looked for him," she said.

"You going to make notes?"

She nodded and said slowly, "It's a book, Jed. It's a terrific idea for a book." The pace of her speech increasing with her excitement, she said, "It's the original *How to. How to*'s sell like crazy. *How to Make a Million in Real Estate. How to Make Love to Your Lover. How to Grow African Violets,* and this is bigger than all that. *How to Marry Off Your Wife.*" She threw the title at him and quickly wrote it down.

"I don't want you to do that," he said, feeling vaguely uneasy.

"It'll sell in the millions. How many men do you know that can't get married because of alimony payments?"

"How many men do I know?" he asked.

"And that's just New York!" Maura pursued. "Think about Cleveland. St. Louis. Denver. My God!" Her brown eyes went even wider as she saw it all before her. "Think how it'll sell in Beverly Hills!"

"But . . ."

"Jed! We'll make so much money that even if the experiment fails, we can still afford to get married."

"If the experiment fails, you won't have a book."

"Well, it won't fail," Maura said savagely. "Not when I'm onto something like this. Why it's almost supplemental reading to *The Joy of Sex,* and you know how that sold! Jed"—she stood in her fervor, a naked Joan of Arc with a gold-chain bellyband—"you make this work and I'll make you the new Messiah!"

"I don't want my name used."

"I won't use your name. I could get sued."

"Then how can I be the new Messiah?"

"Since when do you have a religious hang-up?"

"I don't know," he said and, rising, he found his robe and pulled it on, went into the bathroom and turned off the water. When he came out, he said, "It's like commercializing on Denise's problem."

"We won't mention Denise. We'll just show men how to take a clod, any clod, and fix him up for marriage. Or women can do it, too. *How to Create Your Ideal Husband.*"

"They've been doing that since Eve," he said. "Your bath is ready."

Maura talked right over him. "And the clods can do it for themselves and the clods' mothers who want to get their sons married off. And my God!" she soared dizzyingly on, "we can do a companion piece on women. *Fix Up Your Wife So You Can Dump Her.* Change your sister-in-law and get her out of the guest room! The possibilities are infinite!"

Jed had never seen her so excited.

"No," he said, the whole idea seeming somehow an invasion of privacy. "For one thing, I don't want you involved in this."

"I'm not involved! I won't go near anyone! All you have to do is come home and tell me what happens every day. I'll just write it down. I'll start on the initial search while you're with the boys tomorrow. Now,"—she flipped open her notebook and made notes as she talked—"you're meeting Monday. I know this boy who's a fantastic photographer, so I'll send him over to the office to get a few pictures of . . . what's his name? Barney!"

"No pictures!" Jed screamed. "You'll frighten him off."

"Just a couple befores and a couple afters," she said, "and maybe a few durings."

"He won't want his name used."

"I'm not using his name, just his picture."

He stood in front of her and yelled down, "No photographs!"

She rose and put her arms around his neck. "Baby, don't you see what it means? If I can pull this off, I'll never have to read another *Love's Longing Lust* again. No more milliners who become the king's mistress, no more pirates who screw the queen!" She put her hand inside his robe, massaged his nipples and smoothed her way down his body. Her mouth nuzzled into his neck as his robe fell open. She moved her hands and pushed the robe off his shoulders, pulling his body into hers. "Just think, Jed, no more of that crappy sex," she whispered. "Oh God!" she said, as the feeling began to overcome them both. "Let's do it in the bathtub!"

Chapter Six

Miffed. Felicity was decidedly miffed. Her boss had arrived before she had, evidently mucked about in her file (and for what? she would have liked to know), and buried himself in his office with the door closed. Her three investigative trips to the door had been repulsed. At about ten, he had buzzed her on the intercom and said, "I'll need the conference room at twelve-thirty."

"There's nothing on your schedule?" she said, not bothering to look at it, leaving a hooked question mark between them, but he did not bite.

"I know it's not on the schedule," he said, mockingly pronouncing it as she had, without the C, and making it an accusation of prying. "This is a private meeting."

"Will you want lunch?" she asked in the hurt-angry tones of a woman whose husband said he was reserving their bedroom for a meeting to which she was not invited.

"I'll take care of it," Jed said and switched off.

At noon, when the crone with the aluminum tea-cart tinkled her bell in the outer hall, Felicity went out and bought a sandwich, determined not to leave her post while she was uninformed. "There's some jiggery-pokery afoot," she told Irene, the receptionist, slipping back into her native tongue under tension.

"Oh yeah?" Irene commented with total lack of comprehension and went back to typing the third draft of a motivational research questionnaire.

At twelve-fifteen Jed came out of his office carrying his attaché case. He did not speak to Felicity, but she watched him cross the room and give what were evidently make-busy instructions to Irene until he saw something, or someone, through the receptionist's window and rushed out to the lobby. In a moment, he was back with a fat, moustached man in a grey-green overcoat. Jed hustled the man quickly into the conference room.

Felicity switched off her typewriter, went to the door of the conference room, and rapped. Her boss opened it about a quarter of an inch. "I thought you might want me to hang the gentleman's coat?"

"Never mind," he said and shut the door.

Felicity stalked to Irene's desk, "Who was that?" she asked as casually as she could.

"I dunno. He ordered three lunches," Irene said, and they both looked through the window as the rosewood door opened. A woman in her late thirties they'd never seen before walked toward the window, smiling. His wife! Felicity thought. Has to be. And that fat man's a solicitor—attorney, she quickly translated for herself—and it's something to do with the divorce. Except, of course, they're divorced already. So it's . . . could Jed have found someone for his wife?

"Mr. Lavery," the woman said. She was short and a little plump, but smart looking.

Felicity smiled back. "He's in a meeting."

"With Mr. Warburton?" the woman asked, and Felicity sort of nodded, thinking, Warburton. Who is Warburton? "I'm supposed to join them."

"May I tell him your name?" Felicity asked to be sure.

"Mrs. Marcotte."

Wrong! thought Felicity and, angling for whatever she might get, "Mrs. Marcotte from where?"

Mrs. Marcotte looked as though she didn't understand the question and finally answered, "Riverdale."

"One moment," Felicity smiled, and walked back to the conference room. Well, he's not introducing the man to his wife . . . but it's something to do with it, I'll wager. Now, if he could find a prospect that quickly, and he's not all that bright, is that bugger Perry faking? She rapped on the door rather more sharply than she had intended. Jed barely opened it at all. "A Mrs. Marcotte from Riverdale is here," she said.

"Show her in." He closed the door again.

When Felicity returned with Mrs. Marcotte he was obliged to open the door, and Felicity slipped in behind the guest and walked directly to the man who was still standing, holding his coat, scarf and hat. "Can I take that for you, Mr. . . ."

"Mulligan," Jed introduced them hastily. So that was who Mr. Warburton was, Mr. Mulligan, Felicity thought, and took his coat and the woman's, too. Jed said, "You may go to lunch."

"I brought it from home today. When yours comes, shall I slip it under the door?" Felicity's acid tone accused him of a lack of trust.

Thinking, if a secretary behaves like this, imagine how hard it must be to have an affair when you're married, Jed said, "Thank you, Felicity," and closed the door, determined she should know as little as possible. After all, Perry was looking for someone, too, and Jed had been in marketing research too long to let the competition know what he was doing. If it works, he thought, walking to the head of the table, Perry can buy Maura's book and do it for himself.

"Please sit down," he said and opened his attaché case. Then he gave them his standard meeting opening line. "The Lavery Marketing Research Group has been doing precisely this sort of work for fourteen years."

"I thought you were going to help me get married," Barney interrupted.

"Exactly," Jed said, "and as I see it, this is a marketing research problem."

Gaby made a strange noise, somewhere between a laugh and a cough, and Jed looked at her. "Excuse me. I sneezed," she said.

"Marketing research," Jed plowed on, "is any planned organized effort to gather facts and knowledge to help in winning our fair share of the market." Dramatically, he pulled Denise's picture from his attaché case and pinned it to the corkboard behind him. "That is our market!"

"Oh, she's lovely," Gaby said, meaning it.

"And a very nice personality, too," Barney assured her. "She took me to see this house—"

"Please." Jed called them to order. "Normally we would run some motivational research in the market area but I think that can be dispensed with. In this case, I know what motivates Denise." He looked around the table but no one argued and he knew he had the meeting well in hand. "Now, we know our consumer"—he gestured to the picture—"and we have our product"—he looked at Barney. He paused and asked rhetorically: "Do we need a marketing theme?"

"How about 'O Promise me'?" Gaby suggested.

"I'm serious," Jed said.

"Can't we take a less formal approach?" Gaby began.

"Bear with me, Gaby. This will serve to clarify right at the top and make our work simpler in the end." But he decided to skip the theme he had borrowed from the '76 Dodge campaign. "Now, the two most important factors in getting a product moving," Jed continued, "are packaging and performance." He moved to the blackboard catty-cornered to the end of the corkboard wall and wrote the words in chalk. "Shall we begin there?"

"Anywhere," Gaby said. Barney looked like he was losing interest.

"Do we have a package that will reach out and grab the consumer?"

"Not till I know her better." Barney sounded shocked.

"Would you stand up, Barney?" Jed asked, and added "over there, where we can see you," as Barney lumbered to his feet.

Barney moved to the opposite end of the room and Jed, taking his '76 Dodge questionnnaire as a guide, moved down behind Gaby's chair and they looked at him. "Design?" Jed asked, looking at the questionnaire.

"Basically, quite good," Gaby said, and Barney smiled. "He must be at least six-two and the shoulders . . . broad . . . with a nice forward thrust. It's just . . ." She sighed with the effort, either of thinking or tact. "The lines aren't quite sleek enough."

"Twenty pounds have to go," Jed suggested.

"Thirty," Gaby decided. "That means diet and exercise."

"Now wait a minute," Barney said, annoyed.

"It would improve performance," Gaby encouraged him.

"Make you more competitive, too," Jed said.

"Of course, would that affect his engineering?" Gaby asked. Jed thought he caught the hint of a giggle again.

"My engineering is just fine," Barney said firmly. "I have an annual tune-up!" he threw defiantly at Jed. "Even an EKG for my motor."

"We're only trying to help," Jed said with exaggerated patience, but, realizing Barney's temper was growing short, he pressed on. "Let's get to styling," he said.

"Barney, darling, I'm sorry," Gaby said, "but it's definitely inferior."

"Not modern enough," Jed agreed.

"And no dash," Gaby added.

"I don't like a lot of chrome," the product announced. "In my business they want something sturdy and dignified."

'But not something that's only driven by a little old lady on Sundays," Gaby said, caught up in the spirit.

"Everything's too square." Jed made a check mark on

his sheet. "You're going to need a complete new wardrobe."

"That's expensive," Barney said.

"After we trim the design, nothing's going to fit anyway," Jed reminded him.

"But . . ."

"Look," Jed said, in the tone he used for clients who were about to give their wife's opinion, "if you want the customer to take you off the shelf you need a new package." Seeing that Barney had no more to say, he asked, "Anything else?"

"The hair," Gaby said. "It must be the only crew cut left east of Kansas."

"Don't have your hair cut," Jed said. "When it grows in I'll have my guy style it."

"I don't know if I'd go that far," Gaby said, and Jed glared at her. "And the moustache. I hate it," she continued. Then, deferring to the expert, she looked at Jed. "What are the percentages on moustaches in our market?" As she said it, Irene opened the door, without knocking, Jed noted, and Felicity brought in the lunches.

"I like this moustache!" Barney exploded. Felicity was staring at Denise's picture pinned on the corkboard. "I just grew it. I think it makes me look swingier."

"Thank you, girls," Jed said. "Don't bother unwrapping."

"How do you like his moustache?" Gaby asked Felicity.

"Love it," she said. "It makes Mr. Mulligan, or is it Mr. Warburton . . ." She hesitated, just a luft-pause that gave Jed the chance to answer "Mulligan" and Gaby to say "Warburton," before Felicity raced on: "It makes him look most distinguished." She got out of the room before her boss could fire her.

"Why am I Mulligan today? I thought that was just for Saturday?"

"I'm just experimenting to see which has more consumer identification," Jed exploded. "Forget it. And the moustache goes!"

"Don't I have anything to say?" Barney fingered the moustache as though judging its value and how far he would go in its defense.

"We agreed that I'm in charge," Jed reminded him.

"Can we eat now?" Barney demanded angrily, and sat down.

"Of course," Jed said. He gave them each one of the foil-wrapped plates, pointing out, "It's the Radish's diet special. Better get used to them."

"If we're putting him on a diet," Gaby said practically, "shouldn't he see a doctor first? For a thirty-pound weight loss . . ."

Barney pulled the silver paper from the plastic plate and groaned.

"You're right," Jed agreed. "I've got a friend who's a doctor." He picked up the conference room phone, dialed a 9 and then Og's number.

"Dr. Parmalee."

"Og? I'm with Mr. Warburton and Mrs. Marcotte. We would like you to see him this afternoon."

"Mr. Warburton? Is that Mr. Mulligan?" Og asked in a slightly snide way.

"Yes."

"Oh well," the doctor said, "I don't know anything about that."

"Og . . ." Jed's voice held a certain irritation.

"You told me to drug you if you said anything to me about that whole project."

"I didn't mean that, Og. I was upset. Look, it's very important that you see him," Jed coaxed.

Alarmed, Og asked, "Good Lord, Jed, you didn't pick up someone with a skin disease?"

"We want a general checkup." There were times when Og's obtuseness got through to Jed.

"I don't do that. And I'm booked until five—" Og began.

"Five would be fine," Jed said, eyebrows up to Barney, who nodded agreement.

"I can't stay late. I've got to get home and pick up Steven at his rehearsal. The high school is doing *Antigone*."

Trying to control his irritation, Jed asked, "Can't Lil get him?"

"She doesn't like to do that," Og said, adding, "He's playing Creon," in a literary non sequitur.

"Please, Og. For Pete's sake, you could tell her you've got an emergency."

"Well . . ." Og drew it out. "I suppose I could." His desire to get a look at the prospect overcame Og's annoyance with Jed's behavior Saturday. "I could tell Lil I've got a *pyoderma gangrenosa*."

"What's that?"

"She won't know either," Og sighed. "She was never interested in my work. Five o'clock," he said and hung up.

Jed took a forkful of the diet special and said, "Five o'clock," around it, swallowed, and stood up again, moving back to the blackboard. "Let's get on to performance."

"Just what do you mean by that?" Barney asked. "Remember, there's a lady present." Gaby nodded her appreciation.

"I mean," Jed said, "there are certain requirements I know Denise will have in a husband." As the chalk squeaked, irritating them all a little more, he wrote the words, "Tennis, dancing, bridge." "Can you?" he asked Barney.

"No. Can you?" Barney asked sounding hostile.

"Only tennis," Jed admitted.

"So why do I have to do all of them?" Barney demanded.

"Denise is used to the best. I have to find some way to make you look better than me."

Barney glared at him. "You could never work in insurance," he said.

"I think you said something about driving," Gaby said in a small voice.

"Oh God, yes!" Jed added that to the list.

"Who's going to pay for all this?" Barney demanded.

No one answered.

The door opened and Felicity entered, announcing, "Mr. Zabriski."

"This is all going to be very expensive." Barney worried his own bone.

"Who?" Jed asked Felicity as she stepped aside, allowing a strikingly handsome young man in a leather jacket and jeans through the door. He was already uncapping the camera that hung around his neck.

Oh my God, Maura's photographer, Jed remembered, having hoped the girl would forget.

"You didn't tell me so much was going to be involved," Barney accused Jed. "Did he?" he asked Gaby, who shook her head. Jed saw Felicity reading the blackboard.

"Felicity," he began, and Mr. Zabriski, looking from Jed to Barney as his hand fumbled in the leather bag over his shoulder for a flashcube, asked, "Which one?"

"Driving lessons might be of some value." Barney said it as though he didn't believe it. "But tennis? Dancing?" He picked up his plastic fork and stabbed at a forgotten lettuce leaf.

"That one," Jed said to the photographer. "Felicity, you may go."

"New clothes, and for heaven's sake, a hair stylist!" Barney groused around the lettuce leaf, half out of his mouth. Mr. Zabriski flashed and snapped. "No pictures!" Barney said, with the angry dignity of a major motion-picture star being booked for a felony.

"I think she wants him standing," the photographer told Jed, "but make it snappy, huh? I'm booked at Bonwit's at one-thirty."

"Barney, would you just stand over by the wall?" Jed asked, deciding it was wiser not to argue with Maura.

"Why?"

"You'd be doing me a favor." Barney rose reluctantly and moved to the wall. Jed turned his attention to his secretary and barked, "Felicity, what are you doing here?"

"I just thought Mr. Zabriski might like some coffee," she said with saintly forbearance.

Jed said, "No," while Zabriski said, "Terrific," and Felicity sped off.

Focusing, the photographer instructed Barney, "A little to the left, huh? Gimme the stomach."

Barney, automatically doing as he was told, turned left and demanded to know, "Why is he doing this?"

"We . . . that is I," Jed phumphered, "just wanted a few 'before' pictures." Incredibly, Felicity was back with the coffee.

"Who's going to pay for him?" Barney pointed at Zabriski just as he snapped.

"Oh, no charge," Zabriski smiled a very engaging smile at Jed, showing teeth as perfect as Jed's were but much younger. "I'm doing this for Maura."

Jed felt himself go pale. "Just leave the coffee, Felicity."

"Cream or sugar?" she asked brightly.

"Both," Zabriski said, but Felicity lingered long enough to hear him ask Jed, "You Maura's boss or something?" and Jed's tight-lipped "Something" in return. Felicity registered a broad smile that came over Mrs. Marcotte's face.

"Yeah," the photographer said, "I figured you were too young to be her father." Felicity went for the cream and sugar. Again Zabriski focused on his subject. "Head down, huh, that way I get the double chin." Barney put his head down and the flash went off.

"That hurts my eyes," Barney said.

"Where did you . . . uh . . . meet Maura?" Jed asked, against his better judgment. Gaby looked at the young man, awaiting his answer almost as eagerly as Jed.

"At the American Booksellers' Association convention," he said, squinting through his finder. "I was doing a layout on famous authors. And then she posed for me."

"Pretending to be Harold Robbins?" Jed asked in a dangerous tone.

"No. At the studio," Zabriski explained and, the

memory diverting him from Barney, he turned to Jed. "What a body on her! That's why the pictures are free. I figured I owed her one."

For what? For what? the words screamed inside Jed's mind.

Felicity, incredibly in the room again, asked brightly, "One lump or two?"

"Two," the photographer said, not thinking, still remembering. With a wistful expression he vocalized his thoughts. "That Maura's got an ass that's outa sight."

"I certainly hope so," Jed muttered.

Turning for his coffee and seeing Gaby, Zabriski said, "Excuse me," apologizing for the frankness of his memory.

"It's perfectly all right," Gaby practically sang, seeing Jed's face, knowing her instincts in the matter of Maura were correct.

"Go to your desk, Felicity." Jed sounded murderous.

"I'll just tidy up the dishes." The World's Best Secretary moved regally around the table.

"And if you think I'm going to pay for bridge lessons . . ." Barney inserted, feeling the attention that he deserved had somehow gotten away from him.

"I play bridge," Gaby said, a new plan burgeoning in the warmth of the room. "I can teach you that. That'll save something." She directed the last to Jed.

Sipping the coffee, the photographer, anxious to repay the hospitality, asked, "Would you like a group picture?"

"No," Jed snarled.

"Finished?" Felicity indicated Jed's half-filled plate.

"Yes," he answered, the knife in his voice cutting her Christmas bonus in half.

Zabriski said, "Lemme get one safety of the guy and then I gotta split. It's getting late."

Later than I thought, Jed realized, and, seeing the need to bring the whole of Operation Denise to a speedy conclusion, said, "I'll pay for everything, Barney, except the clothes."

"Nice meetin' ya," Zabriski said. "Ya need me again,

here's my card." He gave Jed the card and a bone-crushing handshake and was gone.

"What a nice young man," Gaby said.

"Sexy," Felicity agreed, smiled at her boss and, taking the photographer's soiled cup, departed, the picture of efficiency.

The half of the diet salad Jed had eaten was swimming squidlike in his stomach, its cabbage tentacles grabbing at his vitals. Suddenly weak, he sank into a conference chair and gave them Og's address.

"I'll be there at five," Barney said happily, freed of the financial burden of his conversion.

"I'm counting on you, Barney," Jed said more fervently than he expected to.

"Count on us both," Gaby said, and reached across the table to pat his hand with a devastating smile.

"He's dressing," Og said to Jed and Gaby as he came into the waiting room.

"How is he?" Jed asked.

"He's perfectly fine," Og said in the reassuring tones with which doctors suggested a "but" was coming. "Heart, lungs, blood pressure . . . tiptop. Except . . ." He sighed regretfully.

"Except what?"

"Well"—Og looked at them both—"he looks like a chronic *epidermato phytosis.*"

"What the hell is that?"

Og adopted a pedagogical manner. "It's caused by *thrichphytum rubrum,* I think . . ."

"Does it rule him out?" Jed snapped, demanding basics.

"Considering how much Denise likes tennis—"

"Tennis! What the hell has he got? Tennis elbow?"

"Athlete's foot."

"Athlete's foot! For Chris' sake, Og, how could you scare me like that? Give him some foot powder. The guy's perfect."

"Don't snap at me," Og said self-righteously. "I thought you wanted a complete physical."

"I did. And you could've just said apart from a minor irritation below the ankles, the guy is terrific."

"He's thirty pounds overweight," Og justified himself.

"For that, I don't need a doctor," Jed snarled.

"What about a diet?" Gaby asked as Barney came into the room.

"I'll give him one," Og answered, looking at the patient. "Nothing complicated. Just the usual give-up-everything-that's-good."

"Even cheesecake?" Barney sounded doubtful.

"You're an actuary," Gaby persuaded. "You know thinner is better."

It's going to be difficult, Jed thought and shut his eyes. Immediately, a picture of the toothy-engaging smile of the photographer flashed on the inner lids and he opened them quickly. "When you know a good woman's love, Barney," he said, sounding as much like Grandpa Walton as possible, "you forget about cheesecake."

Barney nodded, a little down in the mouth.

"Maybe you better give us a copy of the diet," Gaby suggested. "I don't see Barney as a tower of will power."

"I'll get one," Og said and went back to his office.

"Get your coat," Jed told Barney.

"Where are we going?"

"To my gym," Jed said and followed Og into his office.

From the closet where he was changing out of his whites, Og said, "The diet sheets are on the desk."

Jed picked them up, asked to use the phone, and started dialing his own number before Og nodded.

"Hello?"

"It's only me. I'll be late for dinner," he said.

"No problem. How did it go?" Maura asked.

"Terrific. I'm taking him to the gym now."

"Get his measurements. For the before."

"Okay," he said wanting to ask about Zabriski, knowing he shouldn't. With a mighty mental effort, he came up with a dodge. "Oh Maura," he asked, "when was the American Booksellers' Convention?"

"I don't know . . . May. Or June, I think."

Jed was flooded with half-relief. Whatever he was now, at least she had met him before she knew me.

"Why?" Her question caught him unprepared.

He came up with "I may do a market analysis for Waldenbooks," which seemed to satisfy her.

When he said goodbye, Og was at his side. "I'm sorry I frightened you before," he said nodding toward the waiting room. "He'll do. He's a little flabby but you can fix him if anyone can, Jed. And when his feet clear up, I know Denise'll go for him."

"You really think so, Og?"

"Yes." Og slipped into his jacket. "You don't see many guys hung like that. Wow!"

They stopped at Barney's apartment on the way. Jed sat on the heavy old sofa and looked at the living room crowded with overstuffed chairs and highly polished tables, themselves crowded with statues, dishes, vases. The walls were overburdened with mirrors, sconces, and department-store oil paintings depicting woodland scenes, and the windows were shrouded in maroon brocade drapes. Dark, Jed thought, dark and depressing, obviously reflecting Mommy's personality. This guy should get out of here, quick, no matter what.

Barney came out of his room bringing, as instructed, his bathing suit, a T-shirt and towel. "I don't have sneakers," he said and held up a pair of bedroom slippers. "Will these do?"

"For tonight," Jed said. "Get some sneakers tomorrow."

Barney dumped the things into an old flight bag and followed Jed obediently to the gym. It was not what he expected. To begin with, there was not the remembered old-sweat-sox smell from his college days. Something sort of powder-perfumey drifted through the lobby over the wall-to-wall carpeting, around the crystal chandelier, and bounced off the powder-blue walls. A high-busted girl sitting at a reception desk called, "Hi, Mr. Lavery," and Jed introduced Barney, said he would be joining. "It's a fun place, Mr. Warburton," she told him with professional cheeriness. Jed asked if Franco was around and the girl summoned him over an intercom.

Franco bounced out of a door to the rear, a short, dark Italian with a broken nose and a physique that was muscular but not ridiculous. He wore a T-shirt and white pants. He welcomed Jed like an old friend, was happy to meet Barney, and spirited him off to a little room. Barney was grateful that Jed followed them.

"Okay, Mr. Warburton," Franco said, sitting at a small desk, "first we gotta getcha weight down okay and firm you up, then we build up your chest okay and your arms and legs. We put you on a monthly program, establish goals, and make sure you make them okay."

"Okay," Barney said in Pavlovian response.

"You gonna feel great okay we get done with you, Mr. Warburton. We build up your stanima okay and we give you a total health remigen. Okay."

Jed, accustomed to Franco's consonant inversions, put in: "We gotta get his weight down fast, Franco. There's a time problem."

Franco nodded. "We get his health speficication first okay." He pulled a printed form from a stack on the desk, asked Barney's age, then went through a list of physical impairments, heart trouble, asthma, varicose veins and so on, all of which Barney denied having. He only hesitated over the question, "Hemorrhoids?" knowing he had them but feeling it too personal to admit in front of Jed. How do I know, he thought, maybe that would disqualify me, he thought, and, besides, I won't be exercising that part of my anatomy.

"Okay Mr. Warburton, you done any exercise the last six months?"

"No."

"Could you say when maybe you did exercise last?"

"In college," Barney mumbled, vaguely ashamed, adding truthfully, "It was mandatory."

"Manatdory in college," Franco repeated. "Okay you go change. I meetcha on the exercise floor."

Jed took Barney into the locker room and found two empty lockers. He threw his coat into one and said, "Let's get dressed." Barney, still in his overcoat, took off his shoes and socks. "Take off your coat," Jed said, "it's hot as hell in here."

"I'm okay," Barney said.

Jed stripped and tried not to watch as Barney removed his trousers, hung them, then buttoned his overcoat and turned away from Jed facing the wall. After a series of contortions that would have made an escape artist's mother proud, Barney dropped his shorts.

Jed noticed another man down the line of lockers staring. "Barney, for Chris' sake," he whispered, "there's only guys in here." He hoped he was only wising Barney up as a friend, that it was not residual curiosity or envy brought on by Og's comment about the man's equipment. Denise deserves the best, he told himself firmly, and, shit! I don't care! Let her have a bonus. "Barney!" he snapped because the man hadn't answered him.

"I'm very shy about my person," Barney whispered and took his bathing suit from his flight bag and turned away again. Having got the shorts on without exposing more than his knees, Barney removed his coat, jacket, shirt, and undershirt and put on the fresh T-shirt.

He was a mountain of solid flab loosely draped over respectable shoulders. Jed wondered if what Barney had in his pants could possibly make up for what hung over them. When he brought Barney on to the exercise floor, he thought Franco looked sort of daunted.

"How much time we got okay, Mr. Lavery?"

"Some kind of shape in a month," Jed said as though it was possible.

"Madonna mia," Franco mumbled and crossed himself.

Franco took Barney's measurements and weighed him, deeply embarrassing to Barney, not only because Jed was there recording them on his chart, but because of the other men, maybe ten, working out on the floor. Three of them were obviously into body-building, their massive, bull-like bodies sweating, biceps expanding, thighs rippling as they pumped away, lifting and releasing huge weights in infernal machines. A couple of the others had bodies like Jed's, human but good. Barney decided to concentrate on two elderly gentlemen with sagging chests and flabby stomachs to get him through.

Franco put him on a stationary bicycle, said, "Two minutes okay," and from then on the next twenty minutes were a gasping, painful melange from which Barney could only surface enough to catch occasional words.

"Legs over this bar, feet under that bar. Lift. Ten times. Roll over . . . hamstrings . . ." He heard, "We divide your body up into separate parts okay," and screamed a, "NO!" deep inside but without the breath to say it aloud. "Center grip . . . pull down . . . bring up to the pecs . . ."

"Pecs?" Barney was able to gasp.

"Pectorals okay . . . lie down! . . . pull up . . . ten times . . . good for the lats . . ." accompanied by a vague underarm gesture. "Okay . . ." Standing on a disc that slid from side to side. "Wide grip . . . shoulders straight . . . twisters . . . trim your waist up okay . . ." Handed a small pair of weights he could barely hold. "Elbows in . . . lift . . . breathe out coming up, breathe in going down . . ." Off the beat, unable to breathe either way. "Don't let it touch . . . keep the weight on you . . . build your pecs . . . lats . . . tris . . ."

Oh God, Barney thought, I went to the friendship clubs for romance.

At last the exercise was over and Franco was giving him further instructions. "Steam room . . . three minutes . . . you can tell okay by lights flicker every two minutes . . . sauna . . . dry heat . . . three minutes . . . you want the sun room? Shut your eyes . . . bell rings every two . . . shower . . . take a swim . . . the whirlpool

. . . 110 degrees . . . no more than five minutes . . . hair dryer if you want okay."

Jed pulled him through it all, handing him towels, soap, reminding him what was next, timing things as Barney tottered from steam to sauna to shower, his pores opening and closing in frantic confusion. At last he stood at the edge of a large boiling bathtub and Jed said, "Three minutes," and pulled him into the heat, the bubbles, forced him to sit on some invisible underwater bench, the water pushing and pulling and pounding at him. After three minutes he looked at Jed. "I think I'm soft-boiled," he managed to say, and Jed took him out, allowed him to lie down on a deck chair by the pool for a minute.

"Want to swim?"

He shook his head weakly and Jed said, "Let's get dressed." They went back to the locker room. Barney took his towel, his underwear, and his pants and went into a little stall that had a pull-across door. Once inside, he realized he was in what Franco had called the sun room and turned away from the blinding glare of the light, dried himself quickly, and put on his shorts and trousers. The bell rang signaling two minutes . . . from when? Barney wondered . . . and he jumped out, zipping up, afraid he had overdone the sun.

Jed left him in the street in front of the gym, giving him the address of a dance studio and saying, "Seven o'clock tomorrow."

"Tomorrow?" he strangled out, feeling the pull of what should have been the muscles in his stomach, his legs, his back. "How will I be able to dance tomorrow?"

"Seven o'clock," Jed said sternly, then softening, "You're doing great, Barney," and walked off down the street.

Barney was rarely extravagant but he hailed a cab.

Bone-tired, Jed opened the apartment door. Even the sight of Maura, stretched out on the sofa wearing just a Corot bib, did nothing to revive him.

"Jed," she said, sounding worried, "how can you ever

transform this glunk?" She held up an eight-by-ten glossy of Barney, moustache, pallor, and stomach, in Jed's conference room.

"How'd you get that picture?"

"Stan dropped them by. Wasn't that sweet of him?"

"Very," Jed said to her, and then, silently, to God, *Help me!!*

Chapter Seven

The girl was young, maybe Maura's age, and very pretty. She was dressed with a flair that suggested to Jed she was probably an actress who hadn't worked the twenty weeks required for unemployment insurance and was teaching dance in order to eat. She had given a twinkle-footed, twirling skirt, girlish-laughter Ginger Rogers performance as she shoved him and Barney around the floor for their "dance analysis" and an impression of Rosalind Russell career-girl efficiency as she marked their charts. Now, seated in the corner of the studio, she was Greer Garson, devoted teacher, as she gave them the results.

Gaby sat between the two men, her dance ability unanalyzed. "I'd need a male instructor," the girl had June Allyson-winsomed at her.

"That's all right," Gaby had said. "I can dance. I just thought I could help."

"That's the spirit!" the girl had answered.

Actually, Jed had planned to send Barney to the dance school alone, but the subject, pleading shyness, had insisted Gaby go along. Fearing too close a friendship might ensue as they hustled around the floor, Jed enrolled himself too, as unwilling as he ever was to dance.

"On a scale of ten," the girl was saying to Jed, "I gave you two for grace." She smiled encouragingly. "Three for rhythm, one for variety." She hurried past that to the good news: "But you got a seven for confidence and that's the most important thing, isn't it?"

"Skip the rest," Jed said and nodded toward Barney. "Go on to him. He's the important one."

"All our pupils are important," she told him loyally but switched her analysis sheets and attention to Barney. "Well, of course, Mr. Warburton," she smiled radiantly (Audrey Hepburn) at Barney, who looked dejected, "you did admit you had never, never danced before." And then, as though she could hardly believe it, "Not even at the high school prom?"

"I didn't go," Barney said, and to explain further he mumbled, "I had dandruff."

"Well, it's better this way," she said with Katharine Hepburn's ringing sincerity. "You don't have all those terrible things to unlearn!" She looked at Jed, who evidently had them. He nodded and the girl looked down at Barney's analysis sheet. It seemed to discourage even the Katharine Hepburn facet of her personality and she looked up again. "Listen," she said, forthright as Mary Tyler Moore, "it's wonderful that you want to learn to dance . . . and you can. You both can. I know it. However, I think you should think in terms of a life membership." She smiled brightly, confidently, and launched into the many benefits; the number of lessons, the weekly dance parties, the "swell people" they would meet.

"No," Jed said bluntly when she paused for breath.

Effortlessly, she switched into a pitch for the three-month full course of instruction with no loss of enthusiasm.

"We don't have ninety days," Jed interrupted. "He has to learn to dance now."

"Well . . . ten lessons . . ." she said as though it was

hopeless but she'd give her all. Jed wondered what her commission on the ninety-day number was.

"We'll see how far we get and we can extend from there," he told her, hoping to bring the sunshine back into her smile.

"Okay," she said, unenthused, "let's start with the box step."

"Him first," Jed said, and the girl rose and turned on the music.

Jed and Gaby stood watching Barney take the girl in his arms awkwardly. "Now, this is your basic step," she said. "Once you have this, everything else is merely an adjustment to it."

"Mm," Barney said.

"Now," the girl said, pulling him along with her. "Step . . . side . . . together. Back . . . side . . . together." Barney tripped. "That's it," the girl said, flying in the face of the evidence. "You'll have it in no time. Step . . . side . . . together."

Unable to watch any longer, Jed turned to Gaby. "I can do this," he said.

"Well?" she asked, waiting. He held up his arms and she slipped between them, taking his left hand with her right, feeling his arm around her, the hand spread wide on her back. Not much, she thought, but something. A warm body next to mine, a body I find very exciting. Involuntarily, her back moved, almost rippled beneath his hand and they began to dance. She looked up at him and smiled. "It's been a long time," she said.

"Yeah. Me too."

From across the room, Gaby heard, "Step . . . side . . . together . . . feel the music . . . in time . . ." and Gaby felt the music as she felt the strong back of the man in her arms.

"You're easy to dance with," Jed said and then he stepped on her foot.

"All right . . . you're getting it," the instructor said and, leaving Barney's grasp, "Keep going." Robotlike, he continued to step, side, together by himself as the girl walked to Jed and Gaby. "Switch time," she said brightly, and Gaby moved to Barney. Awkwardly, he put his arms around her, trying not to lose the step. She adjusted hers to his; lurch . . . fumble . . . recover . . . lurch . . . fumble . . . recover, Gaby counted, achieving Barney's rhythm.

"I can't do this," he whispered, perspiration streaming into his worried eyes.

"Of course you can," she told him. "Just relax." Suddenly Gaby thumped him on the back and, startled, his rigidly held shoulders fell. "That's it," she said. "Now take smaller steps till you get the idea. You won't fall out of rhythm as easily, and if you do, your partner may not notice."

"I can't," he said again, but he took smaller steps and Gaby was able to shove him slightly, push him into time with the music.

"That's better," she said, and seeing him watching himself in the mirror behind them, she danced with a little more style, keeping her steps small and her rhythm obvious but making them look better, trying to feed him confidence.

When they switched again, Jed was more clumsy, a rigid lump shoving Gaby around, and she could see that Barney had tightened up again, the authority figure of the girl making them tense. "Easy . . . take it easy . . ." she said, more to Barney than her partner, but it reacted on Jed, too.

"I don't know anything fancy," he said. "I only got one for variety."

"You're fine," Gaby answered. "Just be a little more definite," and twirled herself away from him in a little break. When he pulled her back in, losing the beat of the music, he held her somewhat tighter. She got him back on the beat, her body warming again in his embrace. "Just fine," she said again, and, suddenly daring, he swirled her around and pulled her into a dip, letting her body rest against his, letting her feel the deep, strong chest she knew was lurking under the jacket, the sweater, the beads.

"Dipping is out, Mr. Lavery," the girl's voice came at them from across the studio.

Shut your Goddamn mouth, Gaby thought, as Jed righted her and stumbled on off the beat again.

Jed made a mental note that dipping was out, wondering when it went. It used to be the most fun back at college dances, he thought, the quick, legal feel. And Gaby had something to feel. And she was easier to dance with than Denise. Denise lasted one chorus of something slow and said her shoes hurt or her Living Bra was pinching, but he always felt it was his dancing that bored her to death. He had never danced with Maura, he realized, and decided that was one of the ways he kept her.

At the end of the lesson, Barney did not look much better. As they arranged a time for the next lesson, the actress-instructress told Jed privately, "Maybe you're right. Ten lessons will be enough." She sounded discouraged and had no personality Jed could immediately recognize. Maybe that's *her,* he thought.

Barney passed the written test easily. He just took the little pamphlet home, memorized the laws, the rules, the road signs, and sailed through with a perfect score. When he handed in his paper, the clerk looked at him as though he was awfully old for this kind of thing. "Never had a license?" he asked.

"Never."

"Phhh," the clerk commented.

Barney was rewarded with a learner's permit, called the nearest driving school in the Yellow Pages and booked lessons. Arriving at the driving school, he found a small store with a desk and a filthy ashtray, two folding chairs, and an insurance company's calendar. A bored, white-haired little man in a ratty cardigan told him to wait. In a few minutes, a bored, pudgy young man in a ratty toggle coat entered.

"This here's nine o'clock," the little man said.

"Yeah," the pudgy boy answered and motioned to Barney to come with him. They went out to the curb where the car was parked. Automatically, Barney started for the seat beside the driver's. "No, no, no! Wrong!" the pudgy man said, managing to make a sentence without s's sound sibilant. "You can't learn to drive there!"

Obediently, Barney walked around the car and sat behind the wheel. The young man sat beside him. "That's the ignition," he said and pointed. "Headlights, windshield wiper, heater." His finger roamed around in front of Barney, informing him of nothing except that the pudgy young man bit his nails. The instructor shifted his foot across the lump in the middle of the floor and pumped first one pedal, then another. "Accelerator, brake," he said and pulled the leg back. "The key," he said and produced one on a chain and handed it to Barney. It was the first intelligible word, the first recognizable object Barney had seen. "Okay." He nodded to Barney.

"Okay," Barney said.

"So start." The young man seemed annoyed.

"I don't know how."

"Just figure it out. I'll correct you."

Barney looked at the key and stared in front of him. There was a lock. He put the key in the lock.

"No, no, no! Wrong!" The young man said petulantly.

"I know how to put a key in a lock," Barney said.

"You didn't fasten your seat belt." His tone was such that Barney wondered if he was a kindergarten teacher who had been dismissed for perversion. He sighed and, fishing around on the seat, found the belt and connected it. "I know how," he told the young man sarcastically. "I've been on planes."

"So, go awready," his companion replied.

Barney twisted the key in the lock and there was a roar from the front of the car.

"Fine," the unfrocked kindergarten teacher awarded him.

"What now?" Barney asked.

"Put it in gear! Put! It! In! Gear!" The young man seemed to be short-tempered.

"You're supposed to teach me," Barney snapped.

"You can't be taught to drive. It's like swimming. You jump in and I correct you."

"I don't know how to put it in gear. Whatever that is."

With a sigh of ruptured patience, the young man slapped the gear shift. Barney lifted his hand but before he touched it, the boy was saying, "No, no, no! Wrong!" again.

"What's wrong?"

"You didn't put your foot on the brake."

"You didn't tell me to!"

"I'm correcting you!" the young man screamed, wild-eyed. "That foot. That pedal." He pointed. "No. That pedal!" Barney shifted his foot. "If you don't put on the brake when you put the car in gear, you could just explode out of your parking place and kill God knows who!" The boy addressed Barney as though his actions were a personal affront. They sat and glared at each other. "So, go awready."

Barney shoved his foot down on the brake as hard as he could and moved the gearshift to drive. The car sort of burped.

"So, go!"

"So, how?" Barney asked.

"Ease up on the brake . . . gently! Gently!" As Barney began to unlock his knee joint, the boy was already screaming, "No, no, no! Wrong!" Barney turned to him. "You didn't look."

"At what?"

"Anything. In front. Behind. Anywhere. *And*"—he made this a big point—"you didn't signal."

"What signal?"

"There's only one," the instructor said quietly, snidely, and pointed to something else in front of Barney. Barney pushed on the thing and a green light began to flicker somewhere in front of him. He was sweating profusely.

"Was that right?" he asked.

"Perfection," the young man smiled at him. "Now, go."

"Where?"

"Anywhere! I don't care where! Anywhere!"

Gently, ever so slowly, Barney pulled his foot off the brake. The car, to his surprise, began to roll. "It's moving!" Barney yelled and, from some primordial, inbred knowledge, slammed his foot back onto the brake. The car stopped abruptly, swinging them both forward with a whine of springs. "No, no, no! Wrong!" the young man shrieked.

He had only driven a foot in his life, but already Barney knew he had picked the wrong driving school. Again, he lifted his foot from the brake and vowed as soon as the first five lessons he had already paid for were over, he would switch to another school.

"No, no, no. Wrong!" the young man said in a tired tone. "This is the parking lane. Get out into the traffic. Pull the wheel to the left . . ." But as Barney complied, he screamed, "Brake!" and Barney slammed his foot back on the brake.

"No, no, no. Wrong?" Barney asked.

"Wait till the bus passes," said the young man, who had gone quite white.

"Two men? Why invite two men to dinner?" Mrs. Danton asked. "You can't get a man that way, Gaby. They'll frighten each other off . . . cancel each other out. It's what they call overkill." They were clearing the table, moving the dishes from the dining el into the small rectangular kitchen hacked out of the living room.

"We need four for bridge," Gaby explained, patiently, to her mother.

"I know you need four for bridge!" her mother snapped. "Don't patronize me. I'm a life master at duplicate." She slammed some dishes down on the counter and scraped chicken bones into the garbage bag. "Two men," she said in annoyance. "It's nine months since Mr. Leonard Marcotte walked out and you haven't even found one in all that time. Nine months! Do you realize how long that is?"

"Time enough to have a baby," Gaby sighed, and rinsed a dish and put it in the dishwasher.

"That's one thing you don't need," her mother said. "Two is plenty. If it weren't for babies and baby-sitters—"

"But you'll teach them?" Gaby interrupted, hoping to get her mother off the track and failing.

"I could have sat with them," Mrs. Danton was saying. "Why didn't you call me?" She paused under the beaded portiere that led to the dining el and turned to look at her daughter. "I know the whole divorce thing was a shock to your system, Gabrielle, and sometimes women around your age get very strange ideas, but . . . you're not thinking of . . ." She didn't quite know how to phrase it. "Thinking of doing something with both of these men?"

"No."

"Are you interested in both of them?" Mrs. Danton wanted it perfectly clear in her own mind.

"No."

"One of them?"

"Yes."

"Is he interested in you?"

"Not yet."

"Oh." Mrs. Danton collected the coffee cups and the children's milk glasses and returned to the kitchen. "Well, if you're only interested in one of them, why can't I just teach him to play bridge?"

Gaby had hoped to avoid a complete explanation, but saw there was no way. "He doesn't have to learn bridge. His ex-wife likes bridge and he's training him for her."

"The other one?" Try as she might, Mrs. Danton was having trouble grasping the concept.

"Yes."

"Then why can't I just teach the other one to play bridge?"

"Because you need four."

"I know that!" She put the cups in the dishwasher.

"But why should you care if this strange man's ex-wife plays bridge? Is she a life master?"

"Because he can't get married until his wife gets married." Gaby put the soap in the little trap and snapped it shut irritably, knowing the next question already.

"And he wants to get married?"

"Yes."

"To you?"

"No."

"To somebody else?"

"That's what he thinks!" Gaby slammed the door of the dishwasher so hard they could hear the dishes rattle.

"But you're going to change his mind?" her mother pressed on.

"Right!"

The expression in her mother's eyes was the one that Gaby recognized from long ago. It was the one that preceded getting out the thermometer and the Vicks and the vaporizer. "Have you been having hot flashes?" her mother asked.

"No," Gaby practically shrieked, turned on the dishwasher and went into the living room. Her mother followed her. "Look," Gaby said, "It's nine months. I haven't seen an unmarried man I'd hire to wash the windows. This one, I like. He's living with a twenty-four-year-old but he'll never marry her."

"He's living with her," Mrs. Danton pointed out.

"And Len, that bastard, is living with the baby-sitter. But they haven't got married! They never do! It's a matter of time. Eventually, this girl will walk out on this man and I'll be there! And meanwhile, I'll have helped him get his wife married to the other one so there'll be nothing to stop us. That's why I want them both to learn bridge. Will you do it?"

"Of course," her mother said as though she'd agreed an hour before. "I told you when you first brought Mr. Leonard Marcotte home and he said he couldn't play and wouldn't learn that he was not the man for you. And look what happened!"

Gaby dumped herself on the sofa and asked, "Is Saturday all right?"

"What will we do with the children?"

"They'll be spending the night with their father."

"Oh yes," Mrs. Danton smiled. "They like that. They enjoy seeing the baby-sitter."

" 'Ey Mr. Lavery, good news! Okay Mr. Warburton just broke five on the sit-ups!"

"I thought you'd be out," her mother said when Maura answered the phone.

"Then why did you call?"

"I haven't heard from you since your birthday."

"I've been busy."

"With what's-his-name?"

"Well, yes," Maura said, "but more than that."

"Oh?"

It was only a monosyllable but Maura could hear in it as many questions as there were on a loan application. "I'm writing a book," she told Diana almost fiercely, denying with the information that she was doing anything about her marital status.

Diana decided that showed some action in some direction and told her daughter, "That's wonderful. What about?"

"It's a long story . . ." Maura began.

"Yes, but those sell well now. Look at that Australian thing," Diana said.

"That's not what I mean," Maura replied, and since the call was on her mother's bill and Jed was out giving Barney his tennis lesson anyway, she continued, "It's about how to find a husband for your ex-wife."

There was a long pause and then Diana guessed, "Science fiction?"

Maura explained Jed's project, realizing halfway through that she was opening herself to another barrage of questions.

"You mean you're engaged to what's-his-name?"

"Well, sort of."

"Maura," her mother said, "when I was your age and I got engaged, I called my mother. Every time."

"Well . . . yeah . . ." Maura apologized.

"When are you getting married?"

"We have to wait till Denise gets married."

"When is that?"

"I don't know."

"Well, who is this man? Does what's-her-name like him?"

With a sinking feeling Maura admitted, "She hasn't met him yet. Exactly."

This "Oh" told Maura Diana thought the whole thing was ridiculous and quite probably a stall on what's-his-name's part and Maura was really right back where she was when they last discussed it.

"Jed gave me a ring," she said defensively.

"Nice." Diana's voice denied the opinion.

"He's supposed to be a very sweet guy. His name's Barney."

"But you haven't seen him?"

"Not yet. They just sort of have to fix him up before he meets Jed's wife."

"They?" Her mother's reading of the word spotlighted all of the doubts and suspicions that had already run across the stage of Maura's mind and more.

"Jed's got this woman helping him," she said as though it were usual in these cases.

"Have you met her?"

"She's a delightful old lady. Looks sort of like the wicked witch in *The Wizard of Oz,*" Maura lied outright.

"Well, if that's the way you want to live your life," her mother washed her hands of it verbally and, without a breath between thoughts, continued, "I think you should come out for Thanksgiving."

Maura began her excuses at once but Diana talked right over them: "What's-his-name'll be with his kids anyway." And, hearing Jed's key in the lock, Maura accepted just to get her mother off the phone.

Jed looked exhausted. She kissed him and he ran his hand absent-mindedly along her bare fanny. But it wasn't erotic. More like patting a spaniel.

"How was the lesson?" she asked.

"Oh much better," he pasted false enthusiasm over the depression in his eyes, "this time he got the ball over the net three times."

"I think you really got this thing licked, Buddy Boy," Og told Jed as they settled down at a table at the Radish for lunch.

"Oh?" Jed asked, but seemed despondent.

Og opened the menu. "I saw Barney yesterday and I really think it's all going to work out."

"Og, premature optimism is one of your major faults," Jed told his friend.

"No. Really. I guarantee. One more week and you'll never know he ever had athlete's foot." Og turned to the wait-person. "I'll have the rhubarb parfait," he said.

"We'll play the first hand open, so I can explain," Mrs. Danton said and dealt out the cards.

"Would anyone like more coffee?" Gaby asked, standing, one hand on her chair.

"I don't like conversation at the bridge table." Mrs. Danton snapped. The two men shook their heads "No," and Gaby sat opposite Barney. Jed picked up his cards. "I said open," Mrs. Danton told them, her eyes flashing, and hastily he dumped them back on the table. "Arrange them in suits," she said with admirable forbearance. "You know the names of the suits?" she asked Jed, struck by what could have been the ultimate horror.

"I played poker in college," he said.

Mrs. Danton nodded. "In bidding the ace is four—" she began.

"Four what?" Jed asked.

"Four points."

"Which ace?"

"Any ace," Mrs. Danton said and took a deep breath.

"The king counts three. Any king," she interrupted herself to specify in his direction. "The queen is two, the jack one, unless they are unprotected, in which case you deduct one. Any questions?"

Nobody dared.

"A void counts three," Mrs. Danton continued, feeling a martyr to Gaby's matrimonial prospects, "a single two and a doubleton one." She looked around the table. "Count," she challenged them.

"Thirteen," Barney said at once.

Mrs. Danton scanned Barney's cards and said, "Very good," and looked at Jed.

"What does unprotected mean?" he asked.

Gaby decided to stop thinking for the rest of the evening. Asking the two men to dinner, with the excuse of bridge, had been a calculated risk. Balanced against showing herself off to Jed as a gracious hostess, an excellent cook, a charming homemaker, was the certain knowledge that her mother, difficult at best, became a monster at the bridge table.

"Bid!" the monster was nudging her.

"One diamond."

Jed said, "Four hearts."

"Four hearts?" Mrs. Danton soprano-ed. "You don't have four hearts!"

"Right there. The king, the nine, the seven, and the three."

Gaby drifted back to the memory of her own bridge lessons at twelve. She had learned to play and play well as a defense against those horrible evenings when Mother lacked a fourth. Others remembered acne as the worst of adolescence. Gaby remembered bridge.

Barney had bid a spade and when asked why explained with precision, winning a smile from Caligula. They went round twice more and Barney won the bid at three spades. Mother announced they would not play it out but would bid another hand.

Dinner had gone well, Gaby thought. Of course, because of Barney's diet, she had been forced to serve fruit for dessert . . . "Pass," she said with the quarter of her mind that was on the cards . . . and she had not been able to show off her baking, but it was good and dietetic. She had missed Jed's bid but the informative reply from her mother was a screech.

"You don't have an opening bid!"

"Twelve points," Jed answered. "I counted three times. You said that was mandatory."

"Fourteen is mandatory. Twelve you have to have a six-card suit!" She turned to Barney. "He passes."

Barney said, "One heart," smugly.

"Good," Mrs. Danton cooed.

Jed muttered, "He's got the worst backhand I ever saw on a grown man," but, seeing Barney's hurt expression, regretted it.

"One spade," Mrs. Danton said.

Gaby said, "Pass."

Jed said, "Pass."

Mrs. Danton singsonged at him, "On a count of twelve you must respond."

"Doodah! Doodah!" he yelled back.

"Bid!" she screamed.

"Two no trump," he bellowed, wondering what it meant.

I'll make it up to you, Gaby told Jed silently across the trenches. I'll burn all the cards in the house and we'll make love beside the fire. Her eyes focused on his wide, sensual mouth, bidding it to press against her own and pass along down her neck, trumping her breasts, willing him to bring their vulnerable bodies together in a grand slam.

Tactfully, through the evening, Gaby played as badly as she could, hoping her mother would be assuaged by winning big. But Barney proved brilliant and by the time he had won three consecutive rubbers, even the one with Jed as partner, Mrs. Danton's face was as divided as a portrait by Picasso, half frustrated rage at losing, half tutorial pride in a student who had "Come Through."

It was clear that Barney's precise, actuarial mind made

him a natural at bridge and that Jed was more than hopeless.

When the two men had left after a night in which Gaby first feared that her mother might destroy her chances with Jed, then hoped that Jed might destroy her mother, Mrs. Danton said, "I invited him to Thanksgiving dinner."

"When?"

"On Thanksgiving," her mother snapped.

"When did you ask him?" Gaby stared into the refrigerator trying to fit in the dinner leftovers.

"When you were talking to the other one. He said it was the first Thanksgiving he'd be alone and I felt sorry for him. Besides, I thought we could ask Aunt Harriet and have a really good game after dinner."

"You asked Barney?" Gaby shut the refrigerator in her dismay, allowing the remains of the roast to knock over a bottle of salad dressing.

"The other one's hopeless. If Barney's wife really wants a bridge player, you'll never make it with that one."

"It's not Barney's wife. It's Jed's wife. He's the one I'm helping. He's the one I like!"

"That one!" Her mother's voice soared to the stratosphere. "Gaby," she said and threw the empty wine bottle into the garbage can, "will you never learn? He's . . . he's . . ." She searched her mind for some way to express it, get through to her daughter. "He's got less card sense than Mr. Leonard Marcotte." Having delivered this final condemnation, she rattled through the beaded portiere and went to bed, spitefully leaving Gaby to cope with the mess in the kitchen.

She had it all cleaned up, was wiping the counter with a dishrag when the phone rang. Startled, it was after midnight, thinking it might be Len, that bastard, with news of a dreadful accident to the children, she grabbed the instrument and said, "Hello?"

"I just wanted to thank you," she heard Jed's voice. "It was really a terrific meal."

"Oh." The tension slid from her voice. "Well, I

couldn't really let myself go. Barney's diet and all," she answered.

"No, terrific," Jed said sincerely. "I mean roast beef and baked potatoes . . ."

"Without sour cream," Gaby pointed out.

". . . and that beet Jell-O kind of thing . . ."

"It's a salad. Non-caloric."

". . . it was sensational," he concluded. Suddenly, there in the phone booth, the evening's tastes remembered in his mouth, it seemed the months of yogurt with Maura, the plain broiled fish, the cabbage salad he was unable to tell her gave him gas for fear of sounding too old, seemed a payment or a penance for the delight of watching the girl assemble the ghastly meals, topless, bottomless, and acquiescent.

"I'd have made a soufflé," Gaby said.

"You make soufflés?" he asked, impressed, remembering the runny, soggy mess that Denise had tried once. Obviously, Gaby was a better cook than Denise who, herself, was not chopped liver.

"Chocolate, lemon," Gaby told him, "but they're so fattening. I was afraid . . ."

"Barney said you asked him to Thanksgiving dinner."

What was that tone? Gaby wondered. All at once, she realized this was the point of the call, but what did it signify? What was it she heard in his voice?

"I'm sorry. Mother . . ." she began and then realized she had heard jealousy. Definite jealousy. She changed her sentence almost unnoticeably in mid-breath. "Mother was so awful about the bridge."

"Doesn't matter," he said. "If she ever played with your husband, I can see why he left. Certainly not over the food."

Hmm, she thought, maybe it's not so bad Mother asked Barney. Jed sounds a little wistful. "I would have asked you," she said, carefully, "Thanksgiving, but I thought I'd use it to polish up his game. We're having my Aunt Harriet, too."

"Oh, it's okay," he said. "I have my kids that day."

"Maybe you can come up one night when Mother's at a tournament and we'll just eat soufflés all night long," she said, deciding to pursue what seemed to be her advantage, having other, unspoken ideas for an evening with Jed.

"Swell," he said, and the phone clicked, the recorded operator beginning her dismal warning of interruption.

"What's your number? I'll call you back," she said, wondering why he was calling from a pay phone.

"Never mind," he yelled over the operator. "I'll call you tomorrow. Thanks, again."

He hug up and she realized he couldn't phone from home. The twenty-four-year-old C-cup would be there . . . but not for long, she told herself . . . He sounded jealous. He called from outside; maybe C-cup is jealous. She took the *Gourmet* cookbook from the shelf and carried it to bed with her, opening to soufflés for a little light bedtime reading.

Maura had decided the entire day would be the pits anyway and she might as well dig them as deep as possible. Plunging headlong into her holiday masochism, she mashed onto the Long Island Rail Road, joining the screaming masses of couples in their thirties dragging small, wailing children to Grandma's, or, conversely, city-trapped grandmas, highly made-up and carrying gifts to grandchildren whose parents had fled to the suburbs. For entertainment, she had brought the least likely manuscript in her office pile and devoted the trip to Syosset to *To Kiss a Pilgrim,* a story of sexual intrigue aboard the *Mayflower*.

Doug Jr., her stepfather's son by his first marriage, picked her up at the station, signaling that she had Doug Third, a sticky-fingered, screechy three and his mother, Annette, who brought a new meaning to the word nitwit, to look forward to. As they drew up in front of her mother's house, Doug Jr. added to the delights of the day. Slamming the car door, he said, "I think you'll really like Will. He was my best friend in junior high."

The short walk up the flagstones was long enough to build a consuming rage in Maura. When her mother opened the door with a delighted cry of "Darling!" and embraced her, Maura whispered into her ear, "How dare you?" with enough passion to clue Diana in at once.

"He's in publishing," she whispered back and drew her daughter into the living room.

Maura kissed her stepfather, waved to Annette, patted the top of Doug Third's head with just the tips of her fingers, and was introduced to Will Trolander.

"Doug's told me a lot about you," he said.

"I have to go to the john," she answered graciously and went upstairs, furious, but admitting to herself he was attractive, with bright red hair and the terribly clean skin of someone who swims a lot. But obviously hopelessly square. Who wears a shirt and tie to a family Thanksgiving?

Diana followed her into the bathroom. "You're writing a book," she reminded Maura. "He's in publishing."

"So am I," she snarled, washing her hands.

"He's in hard-cover," Diana bragged or defended. "A senior editor at Defrees, Wayland and . . . and those other people. Just moved back from San Francisco and doesn't know a . . ." She hesitated. ". . . a writer in the East."

"Hmphh," Maura commented as she viciously wrinkled one of her mother's best guest towels.

"I would have invited him even if he was a girl," Diana testified, and Maura turned to the mirror, pulling a comb through her long, dark hair. "Listen, I know you're not interested in another man even if he is adorable, lonely, and has bedroom eyes."

"Bedroom eyes?" Maura turned to look at her mother. "No one says 'bedroom eyes' anymore, Mother. You're dating yourself." She knew that would hurt. She tucked her severe, cowl-necked sweater which had nothing written on it (already a concession to her mother) more firmly into her slacks, checked the mirror to be sure it outlined her breasts more distinctly, and went downstairs.

Diana didn't have the gall to bring it up herself, but after the turkey was carved, Will said, "Doug says you're writing a book."

"Isn't everyone?" Maura asked. Diana looked pained.

"What's it about?"

When Maura hesitated, Diana began, "It's the most wonderful idea . . ." so Maura told him herself.

"That is good," Will said. "How'd you think of it?"

Maura answered carefully. "I know someone who's doing it."

"What's his name?" Will asked, and Diana said, "Yes."

Maura had no intention of letting this creep take her home, but the family made it so obvious, having Doug Jr. drop them both at the station for the same train. It was crowded, there were no seats, and obviously she could not continue reading about how the Pilgrim Fathers achieved that status standing up, and could find no excuse not to stand with Will. At least he had the good grace to discuss nothing but the publishing field and establish a few mutual acquaintances.

At Penn Station he offered to take her home.

"Never mind," she said. "I'll just grab a cab to Tenth Street."

"I live on Ninth," he said, in happy, fake surprise, and the next thing she knew they were both in a cab. He was polite, but she decided she hated him. He wore a hat, scarf, and gloves. Coming from California, he probably had thin blood.

When the cab reached the house on Tenth Street, he paid the driver, dropping the money into the little rolling slot as he sat in the curbside seat, effectively trapping Maura till he was ready to get out.

As she slid across the seat and angled herself out of the cab, Maura was thinking, Okay, here it comes. Can't I come up for a drink? Just a nightcap? You don't have a roommate, do you? She was on her feet in front of him, staring into the bedroom eyes, waiting for it, planning something nasty in reply.

"I figured I'd walk from here. It's only two blocks," Will said. Maura just nodded, waiting.

"Basically, I like to walk," he said. "People walk a lot in San Francisco. That's why I like it better than L.A."

It certainly takes him a helluva lot of time to get to the point, Maura thought.

"About your book . . ." he said,

Can I come up and look at your rough draft? Maura finished for him mentally.

"Do you have an outline?" he asked.

"No," she said. "I'm just writing it down as it happens."

"I'd like to see it," Will said.

Uh huh.

"How much have you got?" he continued.

"Not much."

"When you get some more, will you call me? I think it's the kind of thing my firm might be interested in."

"Maybe," Maura allowed.

"Or I'll call you?" he said. "Would that be all right?"

Jesus, she thought, I've had affairs that took less time than this guy asking for my phone number. "Sure," she said, on the off chance that he was legit. Maybe it was more than an off chance. Anybody this slow-moving had to be legit. "Call me at the office. I'm not home much."

"I'll do that," he said and smiled.

There was something in the bedroom eyes, but not much, Maura decided. He tipped his hat, and when's the last time you saw someone do that? she asked herself. "It was nice meeting you," he said and walked off.

Okay if you don't want to kiss me, she thought, but you could at least shake hands!

Given the circumstances, Jed felt queasy about seeing Denise. After all, he was spending most of his time, to the detriment of his business, constructing a golem to be her mate. His fiancée, which he found a more comforting term than roommate, was writing a book about his experiment, which he felt should more properly have been conducted in an ancient castle in a dark wood with lightning crackling around the tower than in the full light of *How To* publication. And Denise, the object of the full concentration of Gaby, Barney, and Maura, as well as himself, was totally unaware of what they were planning for her. So he asked Og to drive the boys down for the football-game-and-restaurant Thanksgiving dinner he had planned. He met them at the stadium in New Jersey.

The boys enjoyed the game, but Jed's mind wandered away at the kickoff to thoughts of the Thanksgiving dinner in Riverdale. What truly was Gaby's purpose in all this? he wondered. And Barney's? I have broken the eggs, he thought, but is the soufflé to rise to the wrong woman? And, watching the boys, red-cheeked in the cold, screaming with excitement at the game, What if the plan works? Will Barney be taking them to a game next Thanksgiving? In all the honing and shaping and polishing of Barney, he had considered only Denise's requirements, forgetting that Barney, if elected to the post of husband, would also be serving as surrogate father. Of course, I'll see them just as much, just the same. But day to day, he'll be there fixing bicycles, wrapping Ace bandages, loaning the car when they're old enough for dates. Was Barney up to that? Was Jed up to allowing that? Well, of course, he reasoned, I have already abdicated much of fatherhood . . . and I won't let go of any more. Impulsively, he hugged Keith, who sat beside him.

Og, not a football fan, read *New York* magazine during the fourth quarter and ordered a double Scotch, saying he was frozen, as soon as they sat at the table in the Jersey roadhouse restaurant.

"How come you're not with your kids today, Mr. Parmalee?" Keith asked over the soup.

"Dr. Parmalee," Jed corrected.

"Whatever," Og said.

"It took you eight years, you deserve the Doctor," Jed told him.

"They're with their mother today," Og told Keith. "I

have them the rest of the time, they get holidays with their mother."

"Sort of upside down," Scott observed. "You're having Thanksgiving dinner with us and Mom is having it with Mrs. Parmalee and your kids. It's, y'know, crazy. We could at least have had it all together."

"Even if Ellen's a girl." Keith allowed Og's daughter a left-handed welcome to the group.

"Could we do it for Christmas, Dad?" Scott asked. "I mean just the four of us. At our house?" Then, realizing he might be being rude, he turned to Og. "Then maybe you could bring your family over later, y'know?"

Jed said, "I'd like that, Scott. If it's okay with your mother," and hated himself for wondering in quick succession what he could possibly tell Maura, what condition Barney would be in by Christmas, what Gaby would be doing.

After dinner he walked the boys back to Og's car, kissing Keith, who still permitted it, and indulging in a roughhouse bear hug that Scott would interpret as wrestling and Jed could consider an embrace.

Jed drove home in the depths of depression, accusing himself of selfishness and general shit-heeledness as far as the George Washington Bridge. On the bridge, he tried self-justification, his own needs and happiness, his constant visits with and concern for the boys. I make a better father if I'm happy, he told himself sadly; and down the Henry Hudson Parkway and through the cluttered Manhattan streets to the garage, convinced himself of his current happiness by envisioning Maura, the thin gold necklaces twinkling over the lush breasts as she puttered over her manuscript, writing away at the proof of his perfidy to Denise. He concentrated on the breasts, the feel of her skin, the soft round perfection of the handhold her rump made in the act of love.

By the time he got out of the car in the garage in University Place, he could hardly wait to get home. He strode briskly down Eleventh Street to Fifth Avenue, turned south for a block and, rounding the corner into Tenth, saw her standing with a man in the light-spill from the lobby in front of the building.

Her mother's! She said she was going to her mother's! The words stabbed into his bowels like hot steel or warm prune juice, causing them to boil and bubble. He slowed his pace, watching them. They were talking, obviously unable to pull themselves apart, unwilling to say goodbye, uncaring who might be watching. When Jed was halfway down the block, the man tipped his hat . . . surely a signal: watch out, he's coming. Something like that. Nobody tips his hat anymore. Nobody wears a hat anymore. Unless it's a disguise . . . Having given the signal, the man turned and walked away from Maura toward Jed. No kiss. Not even a handshake. HE HAD NOT EVEN TOUCHED HER! Obviously, sated by unimaginable sexual Olympics, they no longer had the strength to touch. Or dared not, Jed thought, could not risk a further flaring of the torch that might enflame them so that they would leap behind the chained-down hedge and couple there as unmindful of the passersby as the average Greenwich Village passerby would have been unmindful of them.

The man was twenty steps away from Jed, advancing quickly. The hat shadowed his face and Jed could get no reading of his appearance except youth. Young. Un-old. The body, swathed in winter clothing, disclosed nothing, but left to Jed's imagination muscles, trim waist, tight, unsagging armpits. Mutely, he let the searing curse, Oh balls! explode inside him and quickly thought, those, too! adding them to the enemy's weapons.

He hurried on into the lobby, saw the little electric eight above the elevator door light up, knew that Maura in her postcoital ecstasy was stepping into the hall, pulling the key to their . . . to his apartment from her purse. The little lights descended and the elevator opened. He rushed in, pushing "eight" and "close" with separate fingers at the same time. Going up, he thought: Calm, cool. Don't say anything. Don't let her know you saw. He forced himself to walk slowly out of the elevator and down the claustrophobically narrow hall, telling himself a jealous scene would only weaken his position. Putting the key in the lock, he decided to concentrate on being glad to see her, being charming, warm, lovable. He opened the door and saw her standing between the hall and the living room, caught in the act of throwing her coat toward a chair. "I saw him!" Jed yelled. "Who was he?"

"Who?" she asked.

"You were supposed to be having dinner at your mother's!"

"Oh him," she said and pulled her cowl-necked sweater over her head. Waiting till she could see again, peeling the sleeves from her arms, she continued, "He was my stepbrother's best friend in junior high." A likely story. "Mother asked him 'cause he's in publishing. She thought he might be interested in the book."

Could he believe her? Jed wondered. Maura disentangled her arms, threw the sweater in some general direction and gently scratched her nipple. "I've got to go back to bras," she said. "That sweater itches."

If it was a ploy to distract him, it was working. Pulling himself back to the matter at hand, he asked, "Why did he bring you home?"

"They left us at the train together," she said, and moved to him, opening his coat, his jacket, pulling up his sweater and running her hands up his chest. She kissed him, her hands beneath the sweater going around his back and down, digging beneath his belt and the elastic of his shorts to cup his buttocks. "Jesus, Jed, be nice to me. I spent the day with my family!"

"Honest?" he asked, wanting to believe.

"Honest," she whispered. Her hands, snuggling in the warmth of his shorts, confined at the wrists, inched their way forward around his hips to meet in front for a constricted frolic. He leaned down to let his mouth cover her nipple and she moaned. How could he have suspected a thing like that of a nice girl like Maura, he wondered, while he was still capable of thinking.

Somewhere between where they stood and the sofa-bed, he managed to undress completely, he was not sure how, perhaps Maura helped him from the inside out.

As they sank into the wrinkled sheets and bliss, "How could you think I'd cheat on you?" she whispered, "with a man who tips his hat?"

Chapter Eight

Franco strapped Barney into the machine and showed him how to push down on the bar that would move the pulley and lift the Buick. "Four hunnerd times okay? A grand slam vulnerable!" Barney strained at the bar and a shower of playing cards hit him, their suit symbols not clubs or spades but hot buttered rolls and he heard Mrs. Danton's voice screaming, "You can't respond to a demand bid with hemorrhoids!"

He was dancing with Gaby in the whirlpool bath. She was naked. Barney wore his overcoat. "No, no, no! Wrong!" the dance instructress cried in the voice of the driving teacher and he removed his coat, bundled it around Gaby and, crimson with embarrassment, covered himself as best he could with his hands. Franco rose from the bubbling water and said, "Okay three for rhythm."

Barney ran from the whirlpool, past the swimming pool as Dr. Parmalee jumped from a deck chair, pointing at him, yelling, "Athlete's foot!" Everyone in the gym stared at him, then checked their own feet. Three muscular body-builders leaped as one from the leg press and lifted

Barney high in the air, rushing him through the lobby to leave him standing, naked, in the snowy street.

A cab pulled up and Jed got out, bringing Mrs. Lavery, who wore a wedding gown. "No," she said looking at Barney, "I wanted something with three refrigerators and no bathroom." She got back into the cab and drove off. Jed held his tennis racket like a weapon and screamed, "Get it up! Over the net!" and Barney realized with horror he was having an erection.

The snowy street evaporated, replaced by his secretary's office. Elderly Miss Friedman, with her hair in her usual bun, wearing her cameo brooch, was staring at his erection. "I admire your stanima," she said.

He fled into his office. Mrs. Danton was seated on his desk holding a whip. "If they don't want you, I'll take you," she said hoarsely. "You can be my life master." She threw the whip to him. Barney looked down to see that he was huge, muscular, pecs, lats, biceps, thighs, calves. He advanced on Mrs. Danton and with one steel-like hand picked up his desk with her on it and moved to the window, opening it with his other hand. He threw the desk up for the serve and his mother's voice cried, "No, no, no. Wrong!" and Barney woke up.

He lay quietly, breathing hard, wondering which part of his body would ache the most when he finally moved. He pushed his body up with his right arm, feeling the ache from the tennis lesson, deciding it was the definite winner. Rising, he changed his mind. It was his stomach muscles from the sit-up torture bench. On the way to the shower he gave some consideration to the claim of his hamstrings from the leg press and his lats from whatever that thing was called and finally gave up, unable to arbitrate between the sections of his body. He made the shower very hot.

Drying himself, he looked in the mirror on the bathroom door. He had, he realized, never been so conscious of his body in his life. Of course, it reminded him of itself with every aching move he made, doubtless angry at the unaccustomed extra work he was making it do while at the same time cutting down its rations. He dropped the hand with the towel to his side and looked more closely. He was obviously losing weight. Not that it was much of an improvement. His body looked as dumb and flabby as it ever had, but now, two weeks from Christmas, there were sixteen pounds less of it to embarrass him. He lifted the towel and saw some flicker, something maybe lumplike in his upper arm. A growth? he wondered. Should I see Dr. Parmalee? Not much of a doctor, but he's free. He turned from the mirror, studying his arm directly. My God, he thought, it couldn't . . . it couldn't be a muscle?

He ate the half grapefruit and the cup of black instant that had become his breakfast as slowly as he could and then dressed, the notch in his belt two over now, the pants bunching up in a funny way around his waist. For the first time, he noticed the collar of his shirt was tight and wished Mommy was there to move the button. His hair was beginning to dribble over his collar. His jacket billowed like a windless sail even when he'd put his wallet, his pad, his pen and the other things in the pockets. Gaining and loosing, he thought. I look worse and nothing fits. Well, he decided, I'll probably be able to pay for the new clothes with what I'm saving on food. He no longer ate lunch out, brought a paper bag from home with two apples and a container of cottage cheese in it. He hated restaurants now, especially when they put the little basket of rolls and the dish of butter on the table. Before all this started, he realized, I used to dream about cheesecake and becoming vice-president of the company. Now I dream about hot buttered rolls and erections. Is this an improvement?

He took the paper-bag lunch and left the apartment, zombied through the walk to the office. I was foolish to try this, he thought. It's hopeless. I'll never be able . . . I should have just waited for my pension and moved somewhere . . . Samoa, Tahiti . . . both of which sounded nice, removed . . . lived out the rest of my life . . . he made a quick actuarial estimate of how long it was likely to be . . . alone.

He moved unseeing from the elevator to hall to Miss Friedman's office, took off his coat in front of her closet. She came out of his office and when he saw her he blushed, ashamed of his dream. He had hired her because she had the comfortable look of an aunt, and now . . .

"Good morning, Mr. Warburton," Miss Friedman said and watched him hang his coat. She knew it was foolish for her to worry about him, but he seemed . . . she couldn't define it exactly, but almost like a nephew. And here it was, only six months since his mother left him and he was wasting away, his clothes hanging on his almost emaciated frame and a swelling in the neck. Visions of dread diseases hovered over her typewriter. With an effort of will, she smiled, knowing how important it was to be cheerful and said, "I put the mail on your desk," brightly, making it mean, I'm here, I know, I care. He bent to retrieve his fallen scarf and put a hand on his buttock groaning in agony and said, "Good morning," and vanished into his office, shutting the door. What kind of dread disease strikes in that place? she wondered as she sat at her desk.

She heard a cry from inside his office and suddenly the door burst open and he stood there waving an envelope. "Dear God," Miss Friedman murmured involuntarily. They've told him he's only got six months.

"My driver's license!" he cried, rushing to her desk. "I got my driver's license!"

"What?" She didn't understand. Perhaps he wasn't sick, just crazy.

"I got my driver's license," he cried in obvious delight. "The first time I took the test, I got the license."

"Oh that's wonderful." Miss Friedman understood, was relieved. Then suddenly the auntly fear returned. "But you're not going to drive in your condition, are you?"

There were ten shopping days to Christmas and Maura, who never shopped, had finished one hundred pages of her book, *How to Marry Off Your Wife for Fun and Profit*. She lay propped up in the open sofa-bed, rereading what she had, trying for an objective, professional evaluation. She finished Chapter Five, "Re-Doing Your Frankenstein," decided the word was tactless and changed it to "Candidate." Satisfied with what she had read, she clipped the pages together again and put the manuscript on the night table. She had gone as far as the book and real life went for the moment.

Maura settled down in the bed, stretching her arms, her legs; swastika-ing herself on the empty mattress, feeling neglected. Jed was at the gym again. With Barney. Or possibly . . . again the thought assembled in her mind: With Gaby? Why has he never let me meet her? I can understand him not wanting me to meet Denise. But Gaby? Jesus! She thought, resentfully, here I am not only living with a guy but engaged to him, and I've got so much free time I've written half a book.

She rolled over, punching the pillow into a semblance of a torso, and curled around it. Jed had explained this desperate, time-consuming, headlong plunge into Barney's rehabilitation; the need to get Barney into shape quickly before he became discouraged and endangered the whole project. He had begged Maura to "hang in there," see him over this hump that would lead to their eternal happiness. "Considering you're out every night," she had told him, "you could delete the word 'hump.' "

Squirming in the memory, suddenly Maura sat bolt upright. Enough! she thought. Reviewing in her mind what she had read, she decided Jed had gone far enough. Barney had lost almost twenty pounds, he had a driver's license, he evidently played a helluva game of bridge and could apparently pass muster in the fox-trot and the hustle. So what if he didn't know his backhand from his lob? And the cha-cha was an unnecessary luxury for Denise. She would have to make some compromises, too.

Barney and Jed had done enough. She would tell Jed tonight when he came home. She felt the time had come.

And enough! She enlarged the sufficiencies. I have

enough to show the book. God knows, I've bought books far less written than this one. I could get an advance. Maybe enough to buy the wedding dress. The whole trousseau! Oddly, as their conversation centered almost entirely on a marriage for Denise, Maura had found herself regressing to more traditional concepts than she would ever have dreamed possible. She wanted Jed and she wanted the rest of the ball of wax. The showers, the church wedding, the honeymoon. Despite the fact that it would please her mother, she was determined to have them all! She decided that in the morning she would call that tip-your-hat creep and make an appointment to bring her manuscript to him. Then she wondered why she had to wait till morning, and justifying herself with the thought that perhaps Peter Piper Paperbacks would resent a call like that from the office, dialed Directory Assistance and asked for a new listing for William Trolander ("I can't spell it. How many new listings can there be with that cockamamie name?") on Ninth Street.

He answered on the third ring. "Hey, how are you?" he asked when she told him who it was.

"I'm fine," she said, businesslike. "I wondered if you were still interested in my book."

"Yes, sure. You bet."

"Well, then, I'll send it over to you tomorrow. At your office."

"Fine. Or I got a better idea," he said. "Why don't you meet me for lunch?"

Lunch? she thought. An author's lunch? From the other side of the table? "Why?" she asked.

"We can talk about it."

"You haven't read it."

"Well . . ." he said, "I like to get a feel of the writer I'm dealing with."

I never said that to a writer, she thought. But then, I never wanted to feel one of them. And why the hell not? If I smile and bat my lashes, maybe the advance goes up. "Okay," she said.

"One o'clock? The Italian Pavilion?"

"I'll be there," she said, and hung up.

She considered the possibilities for a few minutes, then picked up a manuscript she had brought home. With half her mind, she followed the romantic absurdities of *The Lust of a Nightingale* (Florence follows a Cockney stud to the Crimea) as the other half decided if she had a chance of selling her book, she'd have to get it finished, which meant, even more, that Jed had to finish his part of the job.

When he opened the door she looked up from a scene of orgasm on a primitive operating table and said, without preamble. "Jed, this crap has got to come to a screeching halt," and proceeded to tell him exactly why.

Jed had come to an uneasy truce with Felicity. He did not want to add breaking in a new secretary to all his other problems, but he was convinced she listened to his phone calls and had once accused her of opening his mail.

"But that's my job," she said with some justification and, embarrassed, he gave her three hours off to go to the dentist.

Determined not to phone Gaby from the apartment under Maura's watchful ear, he got to the office early, anxious to beat Felicity in so he could concentrate on his conversation without worrying whether the extension had been lifted.

"I think it's time," he told Gaby, who said, "Wait a second," dropped the phone, and gave the children their paper-bag lunches and told them not to dawdle on the way to school.

"What?" she asked, returning to the phone.

"I decided last night." Though it had been Maura who decided, arguing that Christmas was the perfect time for Denise to meet Barney. "Everyone's depressed around the holidays," she had claimed. "Her defenses will be down. Ask any psychiatrist."

"Decided what?" Gaby asked.

"He's ready. At least enough to let them meet. He can continue at the gym, the tennis."

"But he's got another ten pounds to lose," Gaby said, thinking, Barney may be ready but I've got more work on you.

"So we'll get his new clothes on the tight side. What the hell? The worst comes to the worst, he can have them altered."

"I think it's too soon. I don't know if he's ready emotionally."

Jed gave her all of Maura's arguments including Christmas, which Gaby agreed was strong. The only thing he didn't tell her was Maura's plan that he should tell Denise he was getting married as the final softening blow before the introduction.

"Still," Gaby said after she had reluctantly agreed, "I think we should try him out once first. Give him a dry run. We've got too much riding on this to move too fast."

"Dry run? With whom?" Jed asked, his old suspicions of Gaby surfacing. She had never told him anything about that Thanksgiving dinner except that Barney had set Aunt Harriet four tricks on a little slam, redoubled and vulnerable.

"Why don't we take him to Dellaville's?" Gaby suggested. "See how the women there react to him, how he behaves with them."

"No," Jed said. "Denise isn't as desperate as Dellaville's gang," and then remembering where he'd met Gaby, he slapped his head, punishing himself for his tactlessness.

"Got a better suggestion?" she asked, a slightly sour tone in the question.

"No," he said and, by way of apology, "it's a very good idea. Would you call her and say we'll be three on Friday?"

"What about his clothes?"

"We'll get him some tonight."

"Tonight?"

"It's Christmas, all the stores are open. I'll get him a haircut and a shave tomorrow morning."

"It's exciting, isn't it, Jed?" she said, breathless now

that the decision was made. "It's like a Broadway opening."

"Dellaville's is just a summer-stock tryout. But it'll give us a chance to change his costumes and fix his second-act curtain." Struck by a thought, he added, "I wish we could have him propose to someone. He could back out later."

"After all the work we've done on him, Jed, don't turn him into a heartless little tease."

"I guess you're right," Jed said regretfully.

"Will you tell him?"

"We'll both tell him tonight. Look, you call him, tell him to meet us in Bloomingdale's men's department at six. I'd call myself," Jed said, lowering his voice, "but I'm afraid my secretary suspects something."

They told him right in the middle of Better Sportswear, an anxious salesman hovering on either side of the little group.

Barney turned white. He retreated three short steps to a small bench and sat down. "It's too soon," he said, the bottom falling out of what was left of his stomach. "I'm not ready yet."

"Before Christmas is the best time psychologically," Jed told him.

"But after Christmas"—Barney looked around at all the suits and overcoats—"there'd be clothing sales."

"We'll only buy enough to get you started," Gaby told him encouragingly. "We can finish your trousseau in January."

Barney nodded a weak agreement.

They bought him a vested suit in a conservative dark grey pinstripe material but with a high-fashion design and construction. Then they selected a navy blue Cardin blazer and light grey slacks.

"I can't breathe," he said, modeling them.

"They'll be perfectly fine when you lose the other ten pounds," the salesman assured him, entering into the spirit of the occasion. "If not, bring them back and we'll alter them. After the Christmas rush," he specified.

"I can't wear them to the office," Barney complained.

"Wear your old things to the office," Gaby suggested.

They bought him a classy-looking storm coat and when he insisted that if he didn't wear a hat he always caught cold, they compromised on a cap they hoped looked sort of rakish.

They got some shirts and ties and finally Gaby herself bought him a white turtleneck sweater. "A graduation present," she said.

Jed took Barney to his hair stylist the next day.

Jean-Pierre viewed Barney with alarm. "What 'as 'appened to 'is 'ead?" he asked. "It resembles a crew cut that 'as grown out."

"That's what it is," Jed admitted. "Do the best you can."

"But is zere enough?" Jean-Pierre asked the barber god as he riffled Barney's hair with his fingers.

"There always was," Barney answered tartly, resenting their talking over his head as if he were a poodle.

"Fake it," Jed instructed Jean-Pierre, "but cover the ears."

The stylist pulled a lever and the barber chair catapulted Barney backwards, heels over head, his neck resting uncomfortably on the rim of the sink. Hot water gushed into his hair. He had never had it washed by anyone except Mommy and even she had stopped when he objected strenuously at seventeen, and he resented it.

In a minute, Jean-Pierre righted him and toweled off his dripping head, then attacked it with a razor. "It's still wet," Barney said, and when Jean-Pierre ignored him, "You'll give me pneumonia!"

"It weel be vairy fresh, vairy moderne," Jean-Pierre assured him negligently, put down the razor and picked up a blower and a brush.

"I don't want a blow dry!" Barney said, by now definitely angry, feeling somehow an affront to his masculinity.

"I do it all the time. I have my own at home," Jed said.

Barney glared at him.

When he was finished with the dryer, Jean-Pierre stepped back to review his work. "Not bad," he said. "Not bad at all. I can do better when eet grows out a little more," he told Jed.

"Fantastic," Jed told him over Barney's head.

Barney stared into the mirror and howled, "Don't you understand it won't do? I'm in insurance!" He raised his hand to rumple the creation and Jean-Pierre, with a cry of, "No!" struck his arm away, grabbed a spray can and swished enough lacquer over Barney to keep his hair in place until Easter.

Jed put a hand on Barney's shoulder and looked at him in the mirror. "Trust me," he said, sincerely, then turned to Jean-Pierre and instructed him, "Get rid of the moustache."

"No!" Barney yelled and leaped from the chair, turning to stare at them defiantly, a lion with a lacquered mane defending his person. "It's mine and I like it!"

"I am a 'air stylist, Mr. Lavery," Jean-Pierre reminded Jed grandly. "If you want a shave, go to a barber shop."

Without the reinforcement of Gaby, Jed was unable to fight.

Petulant, Barney would not speak to Jed as they rode down in the elevator. In the lobby of the building, Jed said, "Gaby and I will pick you up at seven tomorrow."

"Why?"

"To go to Dellaville's."

"I'll meet you there," Barney said angrily.

Jed paused, wondering just how difficult Barney was going to get. "We thought we'd just check out your clothes. Give you some last-minute tips, you know?"

Letting out his rage and with the odd feeling he was talking to his mother again, Barney yelled, "I can dress myself. Even the buttons!" and three passing secretaries laughed. Without another word, Barney walked off into the wind caroming off the Madison Avenue buildings, hoping it would blow his hair back into a crew cut.

When he got back to his office, Miss Friedman stared, horror-stricken, as he hung up his old coat, and her eyes followed his coiffure all the way into his office. A moment after he sat at his desk, she came in and closed the door behind her. "Mr. Warburton," she said emotionally, "I hate it! You look like one of those go-go dancers!"

They sat, Gaby and Jed, on the piano bench, their left hands holding crepe-loaded plates, their right hands, forks; not eating, not moving, staring over the piano at Barney.

He had arrived half an hour late but beautifully dressed. He wore the proper shirt and tie with the pin-striped, vested suit and the storm coat and the cap. He had seemed tense, high-strung, like a baritone breaking in a new role at a provincial Italian opera house; one where the audience was known to throw things. When the cap came off, Jed was relieved to see Jean-Pierre's work was still intact. Gaby, apprised of yesterday's scene, said, "I love your hair," hoping to give Barney confidence.

"It feels like concrete," Barney said with something of yesterday's fire. "I'd have washed it to get it back to human but I was afraid to go right out with a wet head."

As Gaby and Jed watched, damp-palmed with first-night nerves, Barney had gone into the living room alone. To solo.

Mrs. Dellaville's gang, which seemed, by and large, the same as before, took to him like Halloween kids to Tootsie Rolls. After a shaky start with a faded, aggressive blonde, Barney recovered, took the measure of Selma Sutter, the Great Neck Prom Queen, and not only charmed her, but got rid of her in an incredible three minutes.

From then on, it was not quite so much a question of his circulating through the ladies, but of standing, living room center, while they eddied and whirled around him. As Gaby and Jed watched, he seemed to grow in confidence and charm. Now, in the midst of dinner, he held forth to three matronly types on their life expectancy from the actuarial standpoint. Another two listened, leaning on the curve of the piano, waiting for a break to move in on the New One. As Jed watched, one of them turned to the other and said approvingly, "A man like that, he'd carry a lot of insurance."

"That's plenty," Jed whispered to Gaby. "We better get him out before he gets interested in someone."

"It's a triumph," Gaby said. "A triumph. You've done wonders with him, Jed."

"We've done wonders," he corrected, looking at her, meaning it. As one, they put their plates down on the piano and he squeezed her hand.

They rose and made their way to the contender. "Barney," Jed said to attract his attention. "We've got that other party we're supposed to make."

Barney turned. They had made no agreed signal to get out, not knowing one would be necessary. Barney didn't turn a concrete hair of his head. "Oh yes," he replied and, turning back to smile at the ladies, he said, "I'm sorry. I hope we'll be able to talk about this another time."

Gaby was sure she heard one of the ladies moan ecstatically under her breath, and another said bluntly, "Can I call you?" and, realizing that was too much, added hastily, "about a policy?"

"I don't sell," Barney said with just the proper shade of put-down in his voice, smiled again and said, "Let's get our coats," to Gaby and Jed.

"How was I?" he whispered at the coat rack in Dellaville's back hall.

"Sensational," Jed told him.

"Couldn't have been better," Gaby said. "I just know it's going to work."

Jed, excited, clapped his pupil on the shoulder. Struggling into their coats, they went back into the foyer where Mrs. Dellaville was greeting a late-arriving woman. As they neared the door, the woman turned and, recognizing Jed, said, "Hello, there! You were here a month ago!"

"This is dear Mrs. Robotham," Mrs. Dellaville reminded Jed. "She's been with us ever so long," she explained, as though she was ready to remainder Mrs. Robotham. Mrs. Robotham did not look too pleased.

"Oh yes," Jed said and remembered meeting Perry's wife the other time. "Nice seeing you again. I'm sorry," he said to both of them, indicating his companions, "but we have to go."

Rhonda, ignoring Gaby, looked immediately at the other man. Her ever-open lips widened further around her teeth and she squealed in some delight, "Mr. Mulligan! What ever are you doing here?"

For a moment, Barney considered denying ever having been Mr. Mulligan. Gaby was confused and Jed was wondering how . . . when Rhonda Robotham plunged on. "Did you ever find a house?"

"No," Barney gasped, having hesitated too long.

My God, Jed thought, understanding Denise had showed Barney her house.

Mrs. Dellaville, looking confused, turned to Gaby. "But you said his name was Warburton."

Rapidly, Rhonda Robotham remembered. "And Mrs. Lavery said you were married!"

Mrs. Dellaville, her confusion turning to a suspicion that her lovely club was being used for some probably immoral purpose, gasped. Jed could only hope Mrs. Robotham didn't remember his name was Lavery.

With singular presence of mind, Barney strangled out the word "Widowed."

"In the last month?" Rhonda Robotham's voice was a creamy textured medley that expressed shock, sympathy, and the certain conviction that here was a prospect, whatever his name was.

"He can't bear to talk about it," Gaby said and, grabbing Barney's arm, threw a "You understand" over her shoulder and pushed Barney through the open front door.

"Who is he?" Rhonda asked Jed.

"I'll see you next Friday," he answered and fled.

"Good night, Mr. Lavery," Mrs. Dellaville called after him as she closed the door.

"Lavery?" Rhonda Robotham repeated.

"Is she likely to mention it to Denise?" Gaby asked. The three of them were seated, despondent, over coffee cups in a little luncheonette around the corner.

"No," Jed said with a determination he didn't feel. "They're not friends. At least, they weren't. I knew Perry from the train but even I didn't know his wife. I guess Denise was just showing her house."

"Still," Gaby mused, "she could show that house again."

Barney hailed the waitress and ordered cheesecake.

"There's no reason to suppose Robotham would even think of telling Denise," Jed said. "She may never show that house again. It may be sold. We have no choice but to go on as planned."

"And if Denise likes you"—Gaby looked on the brighter side—"after all, Barney, you were a smash tonight. Those women would have eaten you up."

"Yes!" Jed backed her up.

Gaby continued, "Maybe it will all be settled quickly. And if Denise finds out later, it simply won't matter."

"Does that woman know who you are?" Barney asked Jed.

"No," Jed lied, Mrs. Dellaville's goodbye ringing in his ears. "There's nothing to connect me to Denise." Then, seeing a way to put the setback to some use, "But she recognized you, Barney, and I think the only reason was the moustache."

"Yes," Gaby caught on immediately. "The moustache will have to go."

Barney shook his head. "The whole plan was nutty," he said.

"Christmas is Monday," Jed barreled on. "Call Denise at the office Tuesday morning and try to make a date to see a house that afternoon. If it goes well, you can look till dinnertime and ask her to dinner."

"But don't let her show you that woman's house!" Gaby cautioned.

"Just knock her over like you bowled over Dellaville's

gang tonight. You can do it, Barney!" Jed tried to remember the technique of his high-school football coach at the half. "You're everything she wants. Tell her you're a bachelor . . ."

"No," Gaby said, "a widower! At his age, he mustn't look as though no one ever wanted him."

"Right," Jed agreed. "And don't mention your mother."

"Mothers are very square," Gaby put in.

"You're a widower but you're thinking of marrying again. You want a house big enough to bring a wife to. And if she asks if you have anyone in mind, say no."

"Say yes," Gaby ordered. "Say you're thinking about a couple."

"Right," Jed agreed again, impressed by the woman's devious thinking. "That way you're obviously open to marriage, you have a few women on a string so you're desirable, but there are enough to make it clear you haven't committed yourself!"

"Exactly!" Gaby cried.

They looked at the man, clearly struggling with his doubts. The waitress set the cheesecake in front of him and as she added it to the bill already lying on the table, he stared at it longingly. The waitress put the bill down again and left. Barney, sighing, picked up the cheesecake and set it in front of Jed.

"I'll take off the moustache tomorrow," he said.

Jed played Ping-Pong with the boys after dinner while Denise was straightening up the kitchen. He was surprised that Scott could beat him now, that he really had to play hard to keep Keith from winning.

The boys had called him, told him Denise had agreed to them all having Christmas together and, of course, he had gone. For a while he wondered if he should bring her something and, if so, what was an appropriate gift for an ex-wife. He had settled on an antique garnet ring he had found in the jewelry section on Forty-seventh Street, knowing she loved old jewelry, figuring garnets were inexpensive enough to make it look like a thoughtful hostess gift rather than anything more serious. The boys loved the presents he had brought for them, the dinner was in the traditional Christmas vein but one of Denise's finest efforts. The atmosphere was pleasant, almost familial, as though some unwritten contract to make the day a happy one for the kids had been concluded between them.

Denise, to Jed's surprise, gave him a thin gold neck chain. She had always hated the idea of men wearing jewelry.

She came into the playroom during his second game with Scott and said it was time for Keith to go to bed. "Will you come up and talk to me?" the boy asked Jed, reviving his father-memory of the way it used to be.

"Sure," he said. "Get undressed while I finish this game with Scott."

He sat on Keith's bed, an arm around the boy, and they talked for half an hour of school and Keith's friends, of a movie he had seen and "Charlie's Angels," which the boy thought was keen. At last the boy got to "remember whens," but all of them were from the long ago, the time before the divorce.

"You better go to sleep," his father said, at last.

"I know," the boy said and when Jed kissed him and rose, Keith grabbed his arm, holding him at the bedside. "I wish . . ." he began, and could not continue,

"In a way, I wish it too, Keith, but it isn't in the cards. We'll do the best we can," he whispered and bending over, kissed the boy again.

As Jed closed Keith's door, he heard Scott call him from his room and went in. For a moment he was surprised that Scott, with his two-year majority, was in bed. Then Jed realized the boy wanted what his brother had had.

They talked too, of other things, including, for the first time, girls. It made Jed feel older. "I liked this," Scott said when Jed told him it was time for him to go. "You'll do this again?"

"As often as I can," his father said.

"Mom liked having you here," the boy said, more subtle than his brother.

"I'm sorry, Scott," Jed said, meaning not the day but all the days before, all the days to come.

"I know," his son answered and Jed went downstairs.

Denise had added a log to the pre-dinner embers in the living-room fireplace and it was blazing up as Jed walked in. She looked up from her book. "I guess it's time for me to go," he said.

"Have a brandy," she suggested, and when he hesitated, "It's a shame to waste the fire."

He nodded and she rose. "I'll get it," he said.

"You're a guest," she answered, a lemony twist in her voice, and left the room. Jed wandered to the window, looking out at the remains of week-old snow on the ground. The trees, their branches stark and leafless, revealed Og's house next door, the living-room window lit. I wonder if Lil brought the kids home yet, he thought, and where was Gaby having Christmas dinner? And Barney? Maura was with her father, his roommate was with her mother, her mother's husband with his children and so on to infinity, Jed thought.

"Here," Denise said. She was at his shoulder, he had not heard her come back into the room. He took the glass. Her eyes moved to the window.

"Peaceful, isn't it?" she said about the view.

"That's why we liked the house," he answered.

"I remember." She looked at him and raised her glass. He clinked his against it and they drank. Denise went back to the sofa and sat down. Jed chose the armchair by the fire.

"Thank you for the necklace," he said.

"I thought you should have something . . . the boys . . ." she added vaguely, then, "I love the ring." She held her hand at arm's length and stared at it.

"It looked like you."

"Antique and slightly tarnished?" Denise guessed.

"Old-fashioned and reliable. With an incandescent sparkle way down deep." She shrugged and smiled and sipped some brandy. "You're looking very well." Jed really thought she was. Her hair was styled in a new way, her makeup perfect. She wore gold earrings and a long beige dress.

"I look fine for a woman of my age," she said flatly.

"No more than five years older than when I first saw you."

"Flattery," she said.

"No."

"Then nonsense. I've got a mirror, Jed. I'm forty-one and I look it. In good condition, but forty-one and I don't mind. It's logical to be forty-one the year after you've been forty. I'm not Ginger Rogers and I don't have to try for twenty-four."

He was sorry she chose that particular age because it made it impossible for him not to compare. "How is it going?" he asked to stop his mind pursuing what he did not wish pursued.

"What?"

"Everything. The job. The boys. Life."

"It's all right," she said. "Not easy but all right."

"Do you need more money?"

"No," she said at once. "You were very generous." He waved the comment away and she said, "Always. And Lillian and I do pretty well. It takes care of the extras."

He drained his glass and rose. "I've really got to go," he said, but he hadn't looked at his watch.

She stood and walked to him before the fire. "I'm really happy you were here today, Jed," she said.

"I appreciate your asking me."

They stared at each other for a moment, the light from the fire flickering across her face. "Kiss me good night?" she asked.

Jed moved his arms around her lightly, prepared for something short and simple, but when his lips touched hers, when he felt her body press against his, felt her return his kiss with unexpected intensity, he tightened his grasp, pulling her to him, pressing his mouth against hers.

He held it for as long as it took to remember other nights and other kisses, then he released her.

"The boys must be asleep," she said and reaching up, pulled off her earrings. It was a gesture he remembered very well, an invitation he had never once refused in twenty years.

He wanted her, he realized, with a desire of the now, hopelessly entwined with passions of before, memories of her hands upon his body, his lips upon her breast, a thousand or six thousand nights of wonder and excitement and finally, familiar, warm comfort.

Then he remembered. "It would be wrong," he said.

"It never was," she answered. "Those papers that we signed changed nothing."

"I'm getting married."

She looked as though he had slapped her. After a moment's searching of his eyes, she backed away a step. "I'll get your coat," she said and walked into the foyer.

He followed her and when she turned, the coat in her hands, he spoke as best he could. "I wouldn't want to . . . under false pretenses. I planned to tell you . . . But . . . I wouldn't want to hurt you." She nodded and walked to the door, opened it.

"Thank you for coming," she said, as hostesslike as she could manage. "It was wonderful for the boys."

"And for me," he told her, sincerely, in the doorway.

"Who is it?" she asked. "That girl you've been living with?"

"How did you know?"

She smiled. "You haven't had the boys to your apartment since August. I hope you'll be happy. I'm sure she's young and beautiful." When he opened his mouth, she shook her head to stop him saying what she was sure he had in mind. "I'd hate her," she explained and shut the door.

Chapter Nine

"He's getting married." Denise slammed her purse down on the desk and Lillian looked up from the ad she was writing.

"Who?"

"Jed."

"Og never said."

"Then he doesn't know. He always tells you everything."

Lillian pushed her chair back and sighed. "When we were first married, I thought that was good. But after a while . . . have you any idea how boring it is to be told everything?"

Denise pulled off her coat without answering and went to hang it on the coat rack.

"Who?" Lillian asked.

"Who what?"

"Who's he marrying?"

"That girl in his apartment."

"Og mentioned her."

"Has he seen her?"

"No."

Denise sat down and stared across the double desks at her friend. "Oh, shit!" she said.

"That's right," Lillian said comfortingly. "Cry. Get it all out."

Denise said, "Double shit!"

"There are other foul words," Lillian suggested. "Use them."

Denise used them, then sat silent for a while. "Now what?" she asked at last.

"Now," Lillian told her firmly, "you know what you should have known eighteen months ago. It's over. Completely over. Now tell yourself the hell with him, and do something with the rest of your life!"

"The hell with him," Denise said, but without much conviction.

"What are you going to do?" Lillian asked.

"I don't know, what are you going to do?"

"Finish writing next week's ad and then go look at a house on Crooked Mile." Lillian picked up her pencil and worked on the ad. Denise sat faced in Lillian's direction, not seeing her partner. When Lillian dropped her pencil, Denise came to.

"Oh shit," she said again.

"So?"

"I'm getting married."

"May I be the first to congratulate you," Lillian said. "To whom?"

"Don't be so damn grammatical," Denise said irrelevantly. "I'll marry somebody. There's always somebody around."

And then the phone rang.

Denise picked it up and said, "New Freedom Real Estate, Mrs.—" and corrected herself: "Miss Lavery speaking."

"This is Barney Warburton," a man's voice said. "I'm looking for a house." Instantly, Barney realized she had, in her first sentence demoted (promoted?) herself from

Mrs. to Miss. He took it as an encouraging sign. She was saying, "Where did you get our name, Mr. Warburton?"

"Out of the phone book," Barney answered without even thinking about it. Over the long weekend he had reviewed the evening at Dellaville's, scrutinized his body in the bathroom mirror, gone to the gym without even being told to, washed his hair and with the gym's blow-dryer had managed to get it looking almost the way Jean-Pierre had it, and celebrated Christmas Day by shaving his moustache. He knew that nothing could stop him now, not even an unexpected question.

"Were you looking for a family home, Mr. Warburton?"

"No. I'm alone." Lillian, who was watching Denise, saw her smile. "I want something small," the voice continued, "but not crowded."

"I'm sure I can do something for you, Mr. Warburton," Denise said, her voice suddenly lower, suddenly projecting more than professional charm.

"Could I come up this afternoon?" he asked.

"Let me check my book," she said, and put her hand over the phone. "God is on my side," she told her partner. "It's a bachelor."

"Go home and put on your red knit," Lillian advised.

Denise took her hand off the phone. "I think I can be free at three o'clock, Mr. Warburton."

Lillian had planned to be there when he arrived to offer moral support, to check him out and, if she liked him, she admitted to Denise, "to push you."

"I don't need pushing. I'm determined."

"Even so," Lillian had said. Then the boiler burst in a rental house and she had to dash off to fix the blame on the tenant at once, so Denise was alone when Warburton came in.

"Hi." She rose and smiled, went to shake his hand. "You must be Mr. Warburton." Cute, she thought, no, even better than that, elevating him at once from cute to suitable.

"Miss Lavery," Barney said, remembering her title correction, shaking her hand, smelling her perfume. She was staring at him. She recognizes me, he thought at once. It's less than two months. Nobody changes that fast. And Rhonda Robotham . . . even though I did take off the moustache . . .

"Let me take your coat," Denise said and helped him out of his storm coat, checking the Bloomingdale's label as she hung it on the coat rack. She turned back to him. Tall. Taller than Jed. Nice figure. Maybe a little heavy, but still . . . He wore a navy blue blazer over a white turtleneck shirt. But no jewelry. No necklace, thank God. He'd lose two points for a necklace. His hair was over his ears in a cut that said fashionable but not faggy.

She keeps staring, Barney thought. I'm sure she knows. His palms began to sweat. She walked back to her desk, inviting him to sit down. She looked even better than the first time, her clingy red dress showing off her figure. She opened her book.

"You said a small house? You'll be living there alone?" Denise said it as though she was refreshing her memory.

"For the moment."

"What does that mean?"

She sounded disappointed, almost resentful. Why? Still, she hadn't said she recognized him. "I may get married," he told her. "I want a place that's big enough if I do."

Oh you may get married, may you? Denise thought. Another aging divorcé shacking up with someone young enough to be his daughter! How dare you call a respectable real estate agent and suggest you're unattached so I go home and change when you know you've got some broad . . . "Wouldn't it be wiser for you to look at the house with your fiancée?" she asked and snapped her "available" book shut.

What is she angry about, Barney wondered. How have I offended her? "I don't have a fiancée." He smiled, hoping to restore their pleasant relationship.

"Oh." Denise backed down. She reopened her book,

thinking, getting married? No fiancée? Goddamn indecisive. She looked at him, reevaluating.

I sound like a fool, Barney thought and, remembering Gaby's advice, said, "What I mean is, there are a couple of girls . . ."

He's got eight or ten on a string. I'm a fool! And why am I bothering? For the commission, she answered herself. "Then you probably want something with a very large bedroom!" she snapped.

"I don't know. I'm looking to see what's available."

"There must be a lot," Denise said. "You're a very attractive man."

I am? he thought, wondering at the change of subject. Of course I am, he decided. Look at all the work I've put in.

"What's your price?" she asked.

"What?" He couldn't believe she wanted to buy him. She had told him he was attractive and he knew there were men who . . . still, he couldn't believe it. Not of her.

"How much do you want to spend on the house?"

"Oh," he sighed, relieved. And she had said he was attractive. "Nothing more than ninety," he said. "Less if possible."

Well, she thought, business is business and there will be other men. She managed to smile and say, "I'm sure we can find something." She rose and got the keys for a couple of houses the usual twenty thousand more than he wanted to pay.

Barney rose too, bucked up by the fact she was smiling.

"We'll take my car," she said.

Driving to the Old Hill section, Denise did her standard routine on the town, leaving out schools as he was obviously a sex-mad swinger, assuming she was being as client-charming as usual. Barney, who had heard the routine before, could detect the mechanical performance and knew that, for whatever reason, she was still annoyed at him.

"It's old," Barney said in the foyer of the house.

"One of the oldest in the area. 1750," Denise told him

proudly. "Of course, I can't substantiate it, but they say George Washington watered his horse here."

"Oh." Barney looked around as though there might still be splash marks.

"And it's so beautifully preserved," Denise said. "Just look at those old floorboards."

Barney looked. "They seem strong enough to walk on," he agreed.

"Oak pegs," Denise said curtly and moved him on into the living room. They roamed slowly through the house, the agent pointing out corner cupboards, the old warming oven in the fireplace, the tiny keeping room.

"What's it for? "Barney asked.

"Keeping," she answered, and, discouraged, "I have a feeling you might like something newer."

"Could I see it?" he asked.

Looking at him, she decided, he's a monument to indecision.

Looking at her, he thought, why doesn't she like me?

I'll show him the dog, she thought. If he's really interested in buying, it'll soften him up.

Back in the car, she said, "Now, this one's a terrific starter house. It's in walking distance of the town and only a quarter-acre so there isn't all that outside work. And a steal at ninety-five thou."

"Fine," Barney said and, unable to think of anything else, allowed himself to be driven through dark, muddy streets, over a bridge spanning gray, bilgelike water past a small shopping area with a gas station. Denise pulled into a driveway beside a small, pink-painted ranch house past the gas station. The front door opened directly into the living room. "Now this one's only ten years old," she said.

"I'm not very smart about looking at houses," Barney admitted. "I never have before." It wasn't exactly a lie. Mulligan had looked. Warburton was an apartment-dweller.

"I suppose your wife always did it for you?" Denise asked.

"My wife?"

"Aren't you divorced?"

Widowed, Gaby's word, sprang to his lips but before it fell from them he remembered Denise's reaction to the Gaby-coached announcement of several girls. Phooey, he thought. Suppose it works. Suppose I could marry her, I'd have to pretend to a first wife for the rest of my life, make up a name for her, a personality. Mary Jane always loved chocolate pudding and like that. Pretend to be sad on the anniversary of her death. The thought depressed him. I'm Barney Warburton, he decided, I'm all polished up and if you don't like me this way, then what's the use. "I've never been married," he said.

"Never?"

"Never."

Feeling as though a sunbeam had burst through the living-room window that overlooked the pile of old tires behind the gas station, Denise thought, he isn't used. How sweet. How unusual at my age to find one you can break in.

She was staring at him again, not, he thought, as though she recognized him but as though she were reshuffling her mental file on him in the light of this new information. I guess I added it up wrong, he thought, and, if you don't like that, you'll hate this. "I lived with my mother. She . . . she wasn't well . . . and . . . and, well, I lived with her. Took care of her." She was still staring, no change of expression.

Unbelievable, Denise thought, emotion translating the backfire of a pickup truck in the street into the sentimental poignance of a violin. A man like that . . . in this time and place.

"She . . . she passed away in the spring," he said because no one was saying anything.

"I'm sorry," Denise said.

He shrugged, indicating it was not her fault but he appreciated the way she felt about it. "I want to get out of that apartment," he said. "I want to change my life."

"Get a house, get married," she explained for herself.

"Yes," he answered vehemently. "Sounds dumb, I guess."

"No." I wonder how many girls there are? If there are several, he can't be serious about one, Denise decided and smiled broadly. "Forget this house," she said. "It's tacky, over-priced, and insulated with Kleenex."

They went back to the car, both of them radiant, though Denise had a minor qualm that if anyone ever heard what she had just said, she'd be drummed out of the Realtor's Association.

"I've got one that's an absolute jewel. It's in Weston but you don't care about that, do you?"

"No," he said, "I don't care," caring a lot that she wanted to show him another.

The car sped through picturesque country roads, the old snow, neatly banked at the sides, reflecting an orange glow from the sun, sliding over the countryside from an oblique, coquettish angle between the clouds and the horizon. The pine trees swayed gently in the wind, their needles rustling.

She turned off the road between two concrete pillars and went up a long driveway. "This one's got four acres and wait till you see the view!" she said and, turning a corner, brought the house into sight. It sat at the top of a small rise, an explosion of glass held together by slats of redwood. The sun beamed red across the wide living room and into the hall, causing Barney to shield his eyes as they entered.

"Isn't it gorgeous?" Denise asked, smiling, her face spotlit by the sun.

"Yes," Barney said, looking at her, ignoring the house, and she noticed it.

He looked at the house a long time. First because he truly liked it, the sleek, modern openness, the expansive view, the bathrooms so much more modern than the one in his apartment. He could fantasize living in this house with the woman who was showing it to him. Second, the sun was going down and when it finally did, he could ask her to dinner.

"I'd like to think about this one," he told her, "but I would like to see some others."

"Well," Denise said, "of course. But it's gotten too dark to look at any more today."

"So it has," he said looking to the window, as though surprised the sun had gone away. Then, turning back, he said, "Why don't you have dinner with me?" and realized his blend had been rather abrupt.

"Yes," she said immediately, without thinking, having spent the last half hour wondering how she could put a binder on their relationship.

I've done it, Barney thought. I've made myself into an attractive, desirable man. She didn't even stop to think before she answered. Could I have gone all the way up to lady-killer?

My God, I can't look that forward. Denise thought and trying to recover a little, she asked, "When?"

Or maybe not; Barney's palms dampened a little. Maybe she misunderstood. Now she'll do the I'm busy tonight and tomorrow and so on. "Now," he said, tensely.

Okay, I coyed around enough, Denise decided. At my age, at his age, I can't afford to waste time. "Fine," she said.

They went back to the office first so that she could drop her book and the keys and freshen her perfume and lipstick. They were almost out of the door when she remembered her sons.

"Oh," she said, "I ought to call home."

He smiled, impressed with what a good mother she was. "Tell the boys you won't be home to dinner," he said. Then his smile faded as he realized it was Mulligan who knew she had boys.

How intuitive he is, she thought. And, of course, if he doesn't like kids it's better to know now. "I'm divorced," she explained.

"I figured," he answered, relieved she hadn't noticed his mistake. "How old are they?"

She considered lowering their ages then decided that

would be ridiculous if anything came of this. "Ten and thirteen."

"I bet they're wonderful kids," he said.

Relief gushed up from her ankles to her smile. "Sensational," she answered, and then had to maintain a cheery, one-sided conversation against Scott's whining when she told him he had to defrost something and feed Keith.

Barney insisted on taking his car. "I can drive," he told her as though it was an accomplishment and she wondered about it for a minute. Behind the wheel of the rented Buick, he said, "Where to? I want the best place around here."

"It's too expensive," she said and realized she sounded like a wife, not a date. A date, she thought, I haven't been a date in twenty years. How did I act then? How do they act now? It must be different, what with inflation and all.

He had meanwhile been telling her expense was no object, a little difficult for him to get out, but still, he figured, that ought to impress her.

She figured what the hell? and directed him to Stonehenge, a French restaurant whose menu was covered in cream sauce and whose decor was confusingly early American.

They decided separately to forget about their diets.

He asked about her kids.

She asked about his mother.

He told her about his job.

She told him about her real estate business.

Through the dinner, there was never a pause, an awkward hole in the conversation. He told her about his decision to restructure his life. Without mentioning the coaching team, he said, "I decided to do all the things I always wanted to do and never had time for. I go to a gym. I learned to dance. I'm playing tennis and bridge."

God, she was thinking, although she was not religious, you really did create him just for me.

"I feel terrific," he was saying. "Now I want to live in the country and . . ." He stopped short, not wanting to go too far, then realized he had already admitted he wanted to get married. But still, he couldn't quite say it. "Find someone," he finished. She didn't say anything.

It's too perfect, she was thinking, I can't let myself hope too much.

"I know I've improved my life expectancy," he said, hoping that made him sound like a better risk.

"And you're thinking about . . ." What had she meant to say? Me? Or a girl? I can't say that, Denise decided and said, "a house," instead.

"Yes," he answered, staring at her, moving his hand across the table. She knew he was going to take her hand but the waiter came and put the bill between their outstretched fingers.

He drove her home, wondering if he should kiss her.

She sat beside him wondering what to do if he should make a pass. She felt sixteen again.

He felt sixteen for the first time.

He walked her to the door and Scott opened it, obviating the problem for both of them.

"I defrosted a pizza and it burned," Scott said, "so we ate corn flakes."

"This is Mr. Warburton."

"Hi," Scott said. "Could you make us a sandwich?" He left abruptly.

So much for whether they like each other, Denise thought.

"He's a fine boy," Barney said. "Can I see you tomorrow?"

You're not supposed to look anxious, Denise remembered. "Well . . ." she said doubtfully, "I've got . . ."

"More houses to show me," he prompted.

"Four o'clock," she said, unable to think of a house, wanting the appointment to be near dinner time.

"I'll be there," he said and drove away. Then she remembered her car was at the office.

"Hello?"

"Jed, it's Barney."

"How did it go?"

"It was absolutely wonderful. The best evening I ever had in my life."

"She liked you?"

"Don't sound so surprised," Maura called from the other side of the room. "That's what you wanted."

"She liked you! That's terrific!" Jed said, reversing himself at once, pouring on all the enthusiasm he gave a client with a hopeless product he'd been asked to re-research. "She didn't know you?"

"Not as Mulligan, but . . ." The square voice smoothed into a dreamy elliptical sound. "It was as though she did know me . . . as though we'd always known each other."

"Oh."

"I took her to Stonehenge."

"For dinner?" Jed was trying to remember whether they rented rooms there, too.

"Canard à l'orange," Barney told him. "Expensive."

"Well, I'm proud of you, Barney. Now, I think we should meet for lunch tomorrow with Gaby and figure your next move."

"That's okay. I already made my next move. We're having dinner tomorrow."

"Two days in a row?"

"She likes me." Barney made it sound like that was the proof.

"But I already booked the tennis court," Jed heard himself say, knowing it was irrelevant, vaguely annoyed that Barney had moved on his own, maybe bypassed tennis altogether.

"I'll make it up."

"I still think we should meet tomorrow . . ."

"I don't need to, Jed." Barney sounded enthusiastic. "I mean it couldn't have been greater. We talked and talked . . ."

"Barney, face it. You're still very inexperienced."

"I'm doing all right." Barney began to sound annoyed at being doubted.

"You've never been there, Barney. Listen to a guy who's screwed half of—" Realizing Maura was listening, he changed directions. "I got Denise to marry me. I know the way. Do what I tell you."

"No!"

"Barney, if it wasn't for me—" He was shouting now, and Barney shouted back.

"I'm a grown man. I've been voting since Eisenhower. I won't be treated like a child!" and Jed heard the click of the phone being hung up.

He was still holding the phone when he turned to Maura and said, "He's very headstrong."

It was dark in the room and Maura was just at the point of falling asleep when she heard Jed say in tones of wonder, "It's funny. There's a girl was married eighteen years to me . . . and she actually likes him!"

By the time they reached the second house it was almost dark. Denise switched on a lamp in the living room. "It's furnished," Barney said, surprised.

"The owner's in Florida. She's a little old lady."

"Who only uses the house on Sundays," he said and she laughed.

"Let me show you the terrace before the sun goes down," she said and led him through French doors at the end of the room. It was a large deck, cantilevered over a slope that led down to a small stream. There was some ice but the water that remained unfrozen plopped and gurgled comfortably. Although there were no leaves on the trees, there was not another house to be seen.

"It's so peaceful," Barney said. "When you come from apartments, you don't even think there is a place like this."

Denise looked at him, turning from the sun, the red-orange rimming her dark hair. "In the summer . . ." she began.

"It must be," he answered, understanding what she meant. They stared at each other for a long moment, perhaps hearing the rippling and bubbling of the stream, each afraid to make the first move. She led him back inside and they went quickly through the rooms. Coming back into the living room, she switched off the lamp and sat on a sofa faced into the cold fireplace. "With a fire going, this room is so cozy," she said.

He sat beside her and put his arm on the sofa back. He was sure that he must have done it correctly when she moved her body closer, brought her face up to his. He kissed her. Awkward. Overcoats. His cap. But still, his hands on her back, her lips on his.

"We really should be going," she said.

"Can we have dinner?"

"Yes."

In the car, his, he said, "Don't you have to call the boys?"

She said, "No. I told them when they left for school."

When he left her, remembering this time to leave her at the office, he said, "Tomorrow?" and she nodded. He said, "Six o'clock," and she nodded again. They didn't mention houses. "And Friday?" he said, "and Saturday and New Year's Eve?"

"We'll talk about it tomorrow," Denise said.

When Barney got home, he decided not to call Jed.

Jed stared at the phone on the chrome-and-glass table. He had hardly slept for two nights. Wednesday he had insisted on waiting up for Barney's call, not turning out the light till one. "Call him," Maura had urged, and he refused. "If he's so damn smart, let him do it himself!" He had stared at this same office phone most of Thursday, accomplishing practically no work, and moped through Thursday night till Maura had said, "If you don't call him, I will!" It was twelve-thirty when he dialed Barney's number, and there was no answer. Maura had turned out the light but Jed had thrashed and tumbled in the sofa bed (singly, Maura went right to sleep) till three-thirty or four.

Either he screwed the plan or he screwed Denise, Jed

decided again. And then he was ashamed to call me. Why? There's no reason to be ashamed to tell me he slept with my ex-wife. Or is there?

He picked up the phone and dialed Gaby's number.

"Did you hear from Barney?" he asked when she picked it up.

"He said it went like a house afire," she replied.

"When?"

"Tuesday. He sounded like a schoolboy in—"

"Well, what happened Wednesday?"

"I don't know."

"He blew it. I'm sure he blew it. Otherwise, he'd have called." For a moment, he thought he heard a click that indicated Felicity was listening, but concentrated on Barney, afraid he was being paranoid about Felicity. He went on: "I told him Tuesday night we should have a meeting. Call Gaby, I said, we'll figure the next move. But he was so damn pigheaded . . ."

"It's his romance, Jed. We've done all we can do."

". . . just in common decency . . . after all this work . . ." I am not paranoid, he thought. "Felicity, get off the phone," he yelled and, as Gaby said "What?" Felicity buzzed him on the other line. "Hold a minute, Gaby," he said and punched the button. "You were listening!" he screamed.

"I didn't know that wire was engaged," Felicity said, clipped-English grand, and, before he could comment, "Mr. Warburton is on six-one."

"I'll be right there," he said and switched back to Gaby. "He's on the other line. I'll call you right back." He pushed the button again and said, "Barney? Why the hell haven't you called me?"

"I've been busy," the voice came back. "Can you meet me for lunch?"

"Oh, you screwed it up, did you? Didn't want to take my advice, knew just what to do and now it's too late—"

"Everything's fine. I just ran out of clothes."

"What do you mean?"

"I've worn the blazer twice and the pinstripe once and

I don't want to repeat tonight and tomorrow. And I certainly need something dressier for New Year's Eve."

"You've seen her every night?" Jed became aware that Felicity was standing in the doorway and he waved her out.

"She's just great, Jed." The actuary's voice was covered in honey. "We've looked at houses and had dinner—"

"Alone? Dinner? You should have played bridge. We told you. Lead from strength."

"I'm doing fine. My way." Barney sounded a little truculent.

Felicity had closed the door and come further into the room. Jed put his hand over the mouth piece. "Get out!" he hissed. "You can't run this show yourself, Barney. You need a man who's—" He stumbled over the phrase that came to mind and changed it to "—your own age. And wiser. You're going too fast. You'll frighten her off!"

"I'm not holding a gun in her back. She wants to see me every night. And I need an overcoat. I can't wear that dumb storm coat all the time."

Defiantly, Felicity sat down on the oatmeal sofa.

"This is my operation, Barney," he screamed. "If you see her every night, whatever you have for her will wear off. Keep her guessing. Insecurity is the foundation of romance!"

"All right, if you don't want to meet me, I'll go myself," Barney said, then asked hesitantly, "Bloomingdale's?"

"Cancel tonight, Barney. Let me handle this. And wait on the clothes. For God's sake, it's Christmas week. Next Tuesday every suit and coat in New York'll be on sale!"

"Damn the expense. I'm in love!"

"Barney!!"

"I'll call you," he said and hung up.

Jed smashed the phone into its cradle and looked at his secretary. "What the hell are you doing?" he demanded. "I told you to get out!"

"I can't help it," she gasped, "I'm desperate!" and burst into tears.

"Felicity . . . for God's sake . . ." Jed was always ill-equipped to deal with crying women. "I've got troubles of my own." And as she sobbed, "Felicity . . . the whole point of English secretaries is they're unemotional."

"Please, please," she begged, "I must know what you're doing." Around a massive gulp aimed at self-control and missing, she gargled, "Or I'll lose him," and wept again.

Wearily, Jed sat down beside the girl and patted her hand unconvincingly. "Explain, Felicity," he sighed.

"Perry's wife," she managed to gasp out.

"Yes?"

"She happened to mention—" She paused a moment trying to control her breathing. "She happened to mention that Mrs. Lavery had shown her house to a Mr. Mulligan who was married." Caught up in her story, Felicity's breathing became easier and she rushed on. "Then a month or so later she met him at some singles club, but he was widowed and his name was Mr. Warburton."

"Why did she tell Perry?"

"Perhaps because he was with you at the singles club!" She vocalized an exclamation point accusingly at him.

"Well, why does that make you desperate?"

"That doesn't." She waved the exposition away with an impatient gesture. "In point of fact, I know Mulligan /Warburton was here! In our conference room with some other woman."

"Felicity, none of this concerns you."

"It does! Perry concerns me!" She began to cry again.

"What's he got to do with it?"

"Mrs. Lavery!" she managed to get out between sobs.

"What's she got to do with it?"

"You found her someone! You found her Mulligan /Warburton. And Perry can't find anybody for that beastly woman with the overbite. I don't know,"—she waved her hand vaguely—"maybe it has to be a man with an underslung jaw so they'll fit like a jigsaw puzzle," and she wept again.

"Felicity," he said, this time patting her shoulder with the same ineptitude.

"It's been ages," she said, "and Perry's frightf'lly fed up . . . and . . . and . . . and . . ." She seemed to be coming to the climax of her story. "And he's seeing another woman. An older woman. A rich older woman. A rich older woman of thirty. He's thinking of marrying her, I know it! Because she could pay Rhonda's alimony!"

"I can't give you a raise," Jed said automatically.

"I don't want that. I want to know where you found Mulligan-Warburton." Her voice rising to a dizzy crescendo, she exploded, "If you've got an ounce of human decency, you'll tell me!" and, doubling over on the oatmeal sofa, face in lap, she abandoned herself to her tears.

Jed patted his sobbing secretary's back, the only body plane available to him, thinking, if Rhonda told Perry, she might tell Denise. Oh my God! What do I do now? Get rid of Felicity for openers, the voice of reason answered. He pulled her up to a sitting position. "Felicity, I have worked long and hard on this project and I'm sorry, but I can't reveal my sources."

"I'll tell Mrs. Lavery," she blackmailed.

And she would, he thought. The girl is obviously bananas. "Okay," he said, "if it works, I'll tell you, I'll tell Perry the whole thing."

"You will?" There was a ray of hope in her despair.

"On the day they get married. But if you breathe a word to Denise, you'll blow it and not only will I fire you, I'll hound you out of the country!"

"As long as you swear you'll tell, you'll help us."

"I will, I will," he said, already preoccupied with other worries. "Now wash your face and go type something."

He watched her from the door of his office until she turned the corner toward the ladies' room. Then he shut the door and, dashing to his chrome-and-glass table, dialed Gaby.

"What happened?" she asked.

"Disaster! Rhonda Robotham told!"

"Denise?"

"No."
"Then who?"
"My secretary. She knows everything."
"Well, who cares about her?"
"She's threatening to tell Denise."
"Oh well," Gaby minimized the threat. "Just push her into her typewriter and X her out."
"Very funny."
"Does Barney know all this?"
"He doesn't know anything. All he knows is he's in love."
"Well, what more can you ask?"
"He's doing it all wrong. Seeing her every night. She'll get suspicious. My God, Gaby, he even wants to buy more clothes. At regular prices!"
"If she wants to see him every night, Jed, it sounds like it's going just the way we wanted."
"He's out of control, Gaby. He'll probably propose before I even write the speech for him."
"Jed," she said gently, "the boy has graduated. Just keep your secretary quiet and let nature take its course."

When Jed hung up, Gaby made herself a cup of tea and reviewed the bidding. Round one, Barney and Denise seemed to be going splendidly. Of course, round two, the girl Jed was living with hadn't moved out yet, but once Denise was married and Jed was vulnerable . . . that was the nervous moment. Maura could accept the contract. But, more likely, the girl would renege and drop out of the game completely, leaving Jed open for a new and permanent partner. And Gaby was ready to make her bid. Deciding that perhaps Barney needed a little encouragement, she called him at the office.
"Jed says it's going well," she said.
"I've never been so happy," he practically sang. "Can you meet me for lunch? I need some more clothes."
"It's Christmas holiday. The children are home."
"Bring 'em along. They'll be good practice for Denise's kids."

"Bloomingdale's at twelve-thirty," she said and hung up.

It was a huge party, to which Denise would not have gone without an escort. When Barney asked her out for New Year's Eve, she decided it was time to see him against the background of her friends and that a large party was ideal. A failure would be less noticeable in a crowd and a success would not necessarily mean a commitment to Barney.

He slid smoothly and imperceptibly into the group. Not too great with the ad agency people, but okay with the oil company executives and a positive smash with the local lawyers and doctors and real estate people. He wore a burgundy velvet jacket and dark slacks she hadn't seen before that seemed to hit the nail of overstated suburban elegance right on the head.

They circulated through the evening, not spending too much time in any one place. When there were single women in a group, Denise instinctively moved them on, recalling only later it was the way she used to act at parties with Jed. That must mean something, she thought.

At first, seeing the mob, Barney had felt uncomfortable, but within minutes he realized this kind of gathering was easier than a small dinner. He was not obliged to become seriously involved and conversation could be convivial, shallow, easy. He liked several of the people and was impressed with the way the others behaved to Denise. She was obviously popular, respected, and being with her, he was accepted readily. He knew he was doing well when a strange woman hand-fed him a cheese puff and asked him if he was new in town when he went to get Denise a refill at the bar.

They were in a cluster of real estate agents in the center of the living room around eleven-thirty, when, over Denise's head, in a group of late arrivals in the hall, he saw Rhonda Robotham. He was very proud that he didn't panic.

He took Denise's arm and whispered, "C'mon," and led

her from the crowd, through the dining room, and into the kitchen.

"What are you doing?" Denise asked.

"Wait here," he said. Checking from the door that led from the kitchen to the entry hall, he saw that it was Rhonda-less. He moved forward carefully and peeked into the den where the coat rack had been set up. Finding it empty, he ran for their coats and, clutching them, ran back again. He was facing the kitchen door when someone tapped him on the shoulder and a voice that could only have been that of the woman with the overbite said, "Who are you tonight? Mulligan or Warburton?"

He didn't turn. He breathed deeply and said, "Luigi's catering service, ma'am. My quiche is burning!" and pushed into the kitchen. He grabbed Denise's arm and pulled her through the outside kitchen door, snatching up a bottle of champagne, with great presence of mind, on the way.

"We can't leave," Denise said, vapor billowing with the words in the cold. "It's almost midnight."

Inspired, he said, "That's why I want to leave. I want to be with you . . . just you . . . at the stroke of midnight."

She smiled, charmed, and said, "Just let me tell Helene good night," and took a step toward the door.

"No!" he said intensely. "This moment is mine!" It sounded a little melodramatic but it worked.

They sat, silent, in the car as he drove, not knowing where, over the dark roads, brilliant stars scattered through the moonless sky. I did that like a real grown-up, he was thinking. There was danger, I acted. I was caught, I lied. I am ready to take my place with other men of the world.

He switched on the radio and waited for a time check. When the announcer said, "Five minutes to midnight," he pulled over to the side, stopped the car and turned out the lights. He fumbled on the seat beside him and found the bottle.

"What's that?" Denise asked.

"Champagne," he answered, ripping the foil from the cork, trying to pull it out in the restricted space behind the wheel.

"There's a little wire," Denise reminded him.

"Oh yes," he said as though he'd opened a bottle of champagne before. He turned on the interior light, unwound the wire and opened the car window, pointing the cork out as he shoved it off with his thumbs. It made an exhilarating pop but didn't bubble over. He turned back to Denise and offered her the bottle.

"You think of everything," she said.

"I forgot glasses," he admitted, and they both drank.

The radio announcer began a countdown to midnight. At seven, Barney put the bottle on the floor of the car, jamming it up against the side with his leg, feeling clever, daring, romantic, even swashbuckling. Exactly as the man said "Midnight," he kissed Denise.

It was twelve oh two according to the announcer when he drew away, breathing deeply, and switched off the radio.

"It's a New Year," he said, and Denise nodded. "Let's make it a new life, too. Will you marry me?"

Chapter Ten

Though it was after two in the morning, Denise washed and creamed her face carefully. After all, it was possible that it would be seen without makeup again, possible that a man would be sharing her bathroom, her bedroom, her bed.

"Will you marry me?"

It was only the third time she'd heard those words, and she could not remember the name of the first boy who had gasped them to her, more in unavailing back-seat persuasion than in earnest.

When Barney said it, she had felt joy, delight, smug I've-still-got-it satisfaction, and a moment of triumphant conclusion. Followed by instant fears. Of him . . . what did she really know? Of herself . . . what did she really feel? The boys. The sweeping changes it would mean. And Jed. Jed found his way into her thoughts as well.

"Let me think," was what she told Barney, but he insisted on an answer. "Too soon," she had said. "We've seen each other every night . . . but it's only a week . . . I have to think . . ." And finally, she said that she must have a week without him, told him to keep away till Saturday and not to phone. "On Saturday," she said. "I'll tell you Saturday."

I'll sleep on it, she told herself in the bathroom mirror and, switching off the lights, got into bed, but her mind did not switch off as automatically as the lights.

A week, just a week since Jed said he was getting married. And just a week since I told Lillian that I'd get married, too. And just a week since I met Barney. Good Lord, think of all that's happened in a week and Keith still hasn't put his Christmas presents away. Barney's sweet and kind . . . or so he seems . . . but anyone can manage that for such a short time. No, she decided, he really is. I'm sure enough of my own judgment. And it is what I want.

Isn't it?

I'm tired of having too much room in bed and dealing with the man at the garage and trying to understand what the Lawn Doctor is prescribing and having no one to talk to when the boys go to sleep. And the boys need a live-in father. They're getting to their teens and they'll be harder to handle. They'll be going out with girls and someone has to tell them . . .

But is Barney the one to tell them things like that? He hasn't pressed me . . . not for sex. Does that mean he's considerate and kind and moral? Or a homosexual who wants a cover?

And the boys? They would be bound to resent him.

How can anyone resent a man who's so open and anxious to please?

Well, they could. They're kids. What do they know? What do they know about being a woman alone in a world made up of couples? Especially in the suburbs. And they'll grow up and go away and I won't even have Scott to sit with Keith any more.

That's ridiculous.

What do I want?

A good night's sleep.

What else?

What else occupied her till she heard the TV go on in Keith's room and crawled out of bed to give him breakfast.

She somnambulated around in slacks and an old sweater, picking things up, dusting an occasional table, writing half of the first-of-the-month checks. At two, she was making brownies, always good for concentration, when she heard a car in the driveway. Barney? she wondered, half hoping, half fearing. He couldn't . . . I told him not for a week . . . unless he decided to force the issue. She stood, the spoon half in, half out of the mixing bowl, and heard the doorbell.

"I'll get it," Keith howled from somewhere.

"Wait!" she cried, dropping the spoon, running frantically for the stairs, her bedroom, her comb, her lipstick. But it was Lillian standing in the door.

"It's my day with the kids," she said, "so I thought I'd stop on the way. How was the party?"

With a look at Keith, Denise said, "Come into the kitchen."

"That good, huh?" Lillian said, following her.

Denise shut the door. "It was Helene's regulation New Year's Eve. Champagne, cheese puffs, a baked ham, *la toute* Westport braying like asses, and Barney asked me to marry him."

"Helene always over-glazes her hams," Lillian said and dropped her purse on the counter. "That's wonderful, Denise," she said sincerely.

"Mmm," Denise said and went back to the bowl of batter, picked up the spoon, looked at the brown gook and said, "It's supposed to be three hundred strokes but I lost count."

"Would I be prying if I asked what you answered?"

"I told him I'd tell him Saturday," she said and began counting arbitrarily at one-seventy-five. Lillian watched her. When she reached three hundred, she dropped the spoon and said, "I'm going to marry him." Lillian whooped in joy, a real Indian, Custer's-last-stand-in-a bad-movie rolling cry of delighted exultation that brought both the boys tumbling into the kitchen.

"What happened?" Scott asked.

"Nothing," Denise said.

The boys looked at Lillian. "She told me I could lick the bowl," she explained.

"Get out," their mother told them affectionately.

"When did you decide?" Lillian asked when they were gone.

"On stroke two-sixty-three," Denise answered, which was quite true. "But I won't tell him for a week."

"Why not?"

"I don't want to look anxious. I want to break it to the boys. I want to give myself some time to change my mind."

"Don't you dare change your mind," Lillian said. "I like him." And she spent the next five minutes selling so hard, it was as if she had a bank ready to write a mortgage on the man.

"Don't worry," Denise said as she saw Lillian out. "He's the most marvelous man in the world. I'm absolutely certain. I think."

Lillian got into her car and drove the thirty feet from Denise's driveway to Og's thinking, we don't walk enough in the suburbs.

Og hurried her into his kitchen, closing the door, before she even saw the children, telling her he had to talk to her, offering her coffee and Danish. Seeing he was determined and guessing what he wanted to talk about, she agreed to fifteen minutes and coffee.

Pouring the coffee, Og reviewed what he had decided to say. He had spent a lonely New Year's Eve waiting to be called to chauffeur the children back from the parties they had gone to; a night that screamed for a reassessment of his life. The recent focusing on love and marriage, Denise and Barney, Jed and Maura, had brought the dermatologist's desires and frustrations to the surface like a pernicious rash. Steeling himself, he fluttered and fussed with paper napkins and the sugar bowl and creamer as though Lillian were not accustomed to pouring milk directly from the carton in this same kitchen. Finally, with the familiar tone of exasperation he knew and loved, Lillian said, "What is it, Og?" and he sat down and answered, "Four years."

Anxious to see the children and hating the brand of coffee he used, she decided to double-jump the conversation. "I don't want to come back to you," she said.

"You haven't found anyone else!"

"I don't want anyone else."

"Exactly!" he cried triumphantly. "Because you still love me."

"I'm fond of you, Og," she admitted, "from the distance. I suppose I must have loved you when I married you but that's so long ago, I don't remember." He was beginning to pout and she felt slightly guilty. "I had no intention of messing up your life," she said. "I just discovered I'm not a married person. I'm sure we're all much happier this way . . ." And, seeing him open his mouth, she added, "including the children. Can I take them bowling now?"

"I'm a hot-blooded man, Lillian," he said, hesitating for a second, possibly allowing her a moment to laugh, she thought, but she restrained herself. "I won't wait forever. It's easy for a man to find someone new, Lillian, someone young." He thought a little dig like that might get a rise out of her but she did not react. "Like Jed," he pointed out.

"Have you met Jed's girl?" For a moment Lillian looked interested.

"No."

Trust Og, she thought, to tell you everything except what you want to know. She rose, bored with the rerun of the conversation. "Forget me," she said melodramatically. "I'm no good, Og. Marry a high-school girl that you can train into the wife you want." She dropped back to a natural tone and said, "If I don't get to the bowling alley by four, I'll miss my dinner reservation."

"You'll grow old, Lillian, and you'll be alone."

"That's exactly the way I've planned it."

"You're being flippant, but I know how difficult it is for a woman in her forties to find a man."

"How would you know?"

"Never mind, I know," he said wisely.

"If I wanted a man, Og, I could get one like that. Don't think there haven't been opportunities."

"You're having affairs!" he accused.

"None of your business."

"Who?" he demanded.

"The point is not age," she told him. "If you look like you want to get married, there is always someone there to marry."

"For a man," he interrupted. "But for a woman, it takes planning and work and sweat and toil. It's the roughest thing I've been through since medical school."

She was angry now and wanted to finish what she was saying and go. "One week ago, Jed said he was getting married and I told Denise to get married, too. And she found a man she thinks is the most marvelous man in the world and last night he proposed at Helene Dinsmore's party and she's going to marry him. And all in a week. And she doesn't look any younger than I do. Screw you!" she said and started for the kitchen door.

Furious, he yelled, "Maybe Denise did it, but nobody's going to set that up for you, Buddy Girl. You walked out on me. I don't have any alimony problem at all!" Og was satisfied to see that stopped her, one hand on the kitchen door.

Lillian turned. "What are you talking about?" And his earlier statement percolated through, full-bodied and aromatic. "What's the roughest thing you've been through since medical school?"

He regretted having said it at once. Trust Lillian, he thought, she only gets interested when I say something I shouldn't. He had to get her off the subject, say anything, quickly. "She's going to marry Barney?" was what he picked.

Lillian moved slowly back to the table. "How did you know his name was Barney?"

Og picked up the coffee cups and took them to the sink. "Jed told me," he said cautiously.

"Jed knows nothing about him. She only met him last week."

Rinsing the cups, Og said, "She must've told him or how could he have told me?"

"How indeed? She hasn't talked to him since Christmas."

A cup dropped from Og's shaking fingers and shattered. Thinking attack is the only defense, he turned. "Do you mean to say she would marry a man without even telling the father of her children?"

"She just decided half an hour ago," Lillian said. "She won't even tell Barney till Saturday. Unless . . ." She implied a threat.

"Unless what?"

"Unless I tell her Jed is behind this whole thing."

"Tommyrot! How could he be? He doesn't even know about it. You said Denise hasn't talked to him since Christmas."

Lillian zeroed in and placed a shot right through the hole in his defense. "Then how do you know?" she asked.

Oh God, he thought, and seeing no other way, decided to throw himself on Lillian's finer instincts, if she had any. "It was the most beautiful, selfless act I've ever heard of in twenty-five years in medicine."

"What was?"

"You won't tell?" he pleaded, guilts welling up in direct ratio to his blood pressure, the vision of Jed's red-faced anger hanging in the air before him.

"Tell me exactly what I'm not supposed to tell," she said from her position of power, "or I'll call Denise right now and tell her."

"But if I tell, will you tell?"

"I'll decide when you've told," she said and sat down, as if the houselights were dimming and the curtain about to rise.

She got it all. No matter how Og tried to elide, skip over, gloss around, Lillian's pragmatic real estate agent's mind poked in every corner, scratched the weatherstripping of his story, looked for termites in the foundation and paced the boundaries of Jed's action.

"It's incredible," Lillian said at last.

He knew he would have to do something, say something that would keep her quiet. Passionately, he cried out, "Jed only wants her happiness!"

Flatly she replied, "He only wants out of the alimony."

All right, he thought, I'm in the operating room and the patient's heart has stopped beating, as indeed it seemed his had, it's time for a desperate measure. "If you tell," he almost sobbed, "you'll destroy Denise's happiness and Barney's and Jed's as surely as you have destroyed mine and the children's. Lillian, can't you feel the atmosphere of romance? It's all around us. Only you can make everything come out right. Lillian, allow your true feelings to come out. Keep your mouth shut and marry me!"

"Marry you!" she screamed as she rose. "I escaped once! You were always a blithering bore, Og, and in four years you've worked yourself up to a hopeless idiot. If I wanted to marry again, I'd marry anyone else in the world. Nixon!" she shrieked as the most unlikely candidate who came to mind, and stormed out of the kitchen.

I've still got it for her, Og thought. I can still make her gasp for breath when she talks to me, make the blood come rushing to her face, release the passions she keeps so firmly locked deep down inside. But I proved it and now the hell with her! It's over, Lillian, he told the kitchen door. You can't talk to me like that. If Jed can do it, so can I. There's plenty of girls . . . young girls. They come trooping into my office with their mothers' advice, "Marry a doctor," ringing in their ears. Patients! What's her name? Every other Thursday at nine-thirty. Twenty-two, thirty-eight bust, legs that won't quit. As soon as I clear up her acne, I'll make my move. That's my New Year's resolution, he vowed.

He went back to the kitchen sink, picking up the pieces

of the cup, watching through the window as Lillian drove his children away, cutting his finger. She won't tell, he decided, nobody could be that cruel. Not even Lillian, who, much as he loved her, he admitted had a vicious streak. And Jed, he thought, after all the time and money he's put in, he deserves to know what Lillian told me. But not, he decided, his hand on the phone, what I told Lillian.

They were still in bed when the phone rang. They had gone to a New Year's Eve party given by a friend of Maura's, so Jed, the only guest over thirty, had insisted on staying till five A.M. They woke at noon, had some yogurt, Maura changed her necklace, and they had returned to bed to catch up on some work.

Maura was writing a report on *Of Rape Remember'd* (Regency convent girl, deflowered by duke, struggles upward to become Wellington's mistress and arranges her ravisher's death by horse-trampling at Waterloo. Unbelievable trash. Recommend first printing of two hundred and fifty thousand copies).

Jed was working on a questionnaire for an oatmeal survey and was stuck trying to think of a euphemism for "lumps" when he grabbed the phone and said, "Hello."

"Jed, something's happened I think you should know," Og said.

Jed sat bolt upright, the lumps melting away and a cold sweat breaking out on his forehead. "Og? What happened?" he asked. Maura, sensing a major breakthrough, dropped her pad and pencil.

"Barney," Og said, knowing for once he had his friend's full attention and deciding to capitalize on it.

"What happened to Barney?" Jed asked tensely and Maura, frightened, reached over to touch his stomach, to let him know she was there, behind him.

"Last night," Og said.

"What happened last night?" Jed asked and, as Maura nervously began to knead his abdomen, threw an abrupt, "Stop that!" at her.

"Stop what?" Og asked.

"Nothing. What happened last night?"

"Barney proposed."

"Barney proposed." Jed filled Maura in and, hope rising, she moved her hand down his stomach, kneading, scratching, rubbing in her growing anticipation. "How do you know?" Jed asked the phone.

"Lillian."

"How does he know?" Maura whispered and, unable to hold his hand, let her fingers slip further down, holding him elsewhere, finding their own solid base in a world of insecurities.

"Lillian told him," Jed said, aware of two rising excitements and not, for the moment, wanting to be bothered by the second. "What did she answer?" he asked Og.

"Well, it seems they had a date for New Year's Eve. Went to Helene Dinsmore's party . . . half the town goes . . ." It was the best story Og had ever had to tell and he was not going to fudge the suspense in any way.

Maura had both hands on Jed now and he was amazed that his body could go off in that direction while his mind stayed glued behind. "Please," he said to Maura, and Og, not knowing of the drama on the other side of the wire, answered, "Let me tell it in my own way."

"You're calling long distance," Jed reminded Og, "get to the end. What did she say?"

"She said she'd tell him Saturday."

"She'll tell him Saturday," he told Maura.

"Saturday!" she said, disappointed, dropping her hands, feeling the frustration of another week of waiting.

"But . . ." Og said portentously.

"But?" Jed repeated and feeling his own frustrations, moved Maura's hands back.

"But she told Lillian she's going to tell him yes."

"She's actually going to marry him?" he cried, surprised he was surprised.

Maura's cry of triumph was long and loud enough for Og to hear it fifty miles away. "What's that?" he asked.

"Maura's pleased." Jed gasped as the girl, jubilant, ecstatic, lifted her body on top of his.

"She thinks he's the most wonderful man in the world," Og told him.

"No," he said to Maura, annoyed with himself for responding physically when mentally he was angry that Denise thought Barney, his creation, was the most wonderful—

"Yes," Og corrected Jed, then asked, "Should I call Barney?"

"No," Jed yelled. "He's not supposed to know!"

"Oh, Jed," Maura cried, positioning herself on top of him, encompassing him in her furious delight. "Do you realize what this means?"

Jed gasped into the phone, "Barney'd call her . . . it might slip out . . . that I was . . ."

"You sound peculiar, Jed." The doctor reasserted himself in Og. "You're not having a cardiac arrest or something, are you?"

"It worked!" Maura screamed, her hands on Jed's pectorals, her body rising, falling.

"I'm fine," Jed managed to tell the phone. "I'll call you back." He dropped the instrument.

"I'll sell my book," Maura told him, lifting his phone-free hand to her breast.

"Book?" he gulped.

Pumping, she said, "I showed it to a publisher." She continued in rhythm with her bouncing. "They want . . . the book . . . if they . . . get married!"

"Who?"

But something made her jump that question. "Igavethemtheoutlinelastweekandfivechapters," she said, grinding at him and at her words.

"Ohhh," Jed moaned, not sure whether he was responding to the information or the activity.

Riding ever faster, her words came in tiny gasps now. "And! They! Loved! It!"

"Wonderful! Won! Der! Ful!"

"Said! The! Writing! Was! As! Good! As! George! Plimpton!"

"Plimpton!"

"OHHHHHHHHHHHHHHH JED," she screamed. "We made it!"

Denise, having ruined the brownies but having decided there was no reason she shouldn't marry Barney, slept like a baby.

Lillian, having decided there might be a reason, was up all night. After all, she had advised, perhaps bullied, Denise into the decision.

When they faced each other Tuesday morning, bright eyes versus bleary over the double desks, Lillian had still not decided. Could she bear to disappoint her friend, who seemed at last to have recovered from the defection of her husband after twenty long months? Or conversely, could she allow her friend to marry a man who had agreed to marry her—heaven knows why—at the behest of this same fink husband?

They opened mail, discussed details of business, answered a phone call or two.

Suddenly, from nowhere, Denise asked, "What will I do with the boys when we go on our honeymoon?"

Unprepared, Lillian gasped.

"What's the matter?"

"I'm not sure I should tell you."

"Tell me what?"

Having proceeded that far, Lillian admitted, "I should tell you. I just don't know how."

"What?"

"Og," Lillian began, and it occurred to her all terrible things seemed to begin with Og.

"What about him?"

"I saw him when I left you yesterday. He wants me back."

"Oh," Denise said, about to make a sentimental comment.

"Oh don't be silly." Lillian shook her head. "We had an argument and then it slipped out."

"What?"

"Barney."

"What has Barney got to do with Og?"

"Nothing. Really. Well, I mean he cured his athlete's foot."

"Og knows Barney," Denise said slowly.

Lillian nodded. "Jed set him up."

"Barney?"

And then it all came out, the whole story, finding him, training him, re-creating him to serve for Denise. "And all," Lillian finished, "so Jed wouldn't have to pay you alimony and could afford to marry his child bride."

"Why would Og tell you?" Denise asked.

" 'Cause he's a fool," Lillian answered, and Denise could hardly argue that. "I don't believe it," she said.

"Why would Og make it up? Even assuming he had the imagination," Lillian asked.

"It's too absurd. Too wild. It couldn't be. I don't believe it." She was relieved that the phone rang then and she could return to real life. "New Freedom Real Estate. Miss Lavery speaking," she said into the instrument.

"Hello, Mrs. Lavery," a woman's voice said. "This is Rhonda Robotham."

"Oh. Have you decided to lower your price?" Denise asked.

"It's not about the house. I have something rather strange to tell you. . . ."

Chapter Eleven

Maura pressed the button under the box marked *Campbell* in the tiny entryway of the grey stone building near Central Park West. Almost immediately the door buzzed back and Jed opened it for her. He had not wanted to come but Maura had insisted. She knew that when you decided to get married, you introduced your fiancé to your family. She did not feel strong enough to drag out to Syosset and go through her mother, so it had to be her father first. "It's the third floor," she said to Jed.

Jed started up behind Maura, feeling more like a fool with every step. This is something you do when you're twenty-two, he told himself, not when you're . . . mature, he thought, avoiding actual numbers. And why? Nobody today asks a man's permission to marry his daughter. Most fathers are lucky to get a phone call or a note, actually should be relieved if their daughters bothered to get married at all. On the first landing he wondered if he had dressed correctly for father-in-law meeting. He had burrowed deep into the back of his closet and found an old shirt and tie that sort of matched his most sedate sports jacket.

He heard a door open above him, and as Maura reached the top of the flight, a man's voice called out, "Baby! Over here!" When he reached the top step, he saw Maura being embraced in the apartment doorway. She broke away and said, "Daddy, this is Jed."

The hair of his father-in-law-to-be was steely grey and rather thin and had been carefully arranged to cover his ears and an incipient bald spot and to dribble down his neck. He was barefoot, in jeans, and over his bare chest he wore a denim vest with rope toggles. Around his neck a link chain bore the weight of a large stained-glass amulet. He looked like a half-dressed, unfrocked priest. Jed felt overdressed.

"Jed, baby, this is going to be a beautiful experience." The man was advancing on him, hand outstretched. "I'm getting the vibes," he said and, grabbing Jed's hand, began to pump it.

For the first time in years, Jed said, "How do you do?" and wondered what about the man brought out this formality in him.

"Drag it in. Meet the lady," the host pressured them, and went in calling, "Sweet Stuff!" There were a lot of plants in the room and practically nothing to sit on.

A terrific figure, braless in T-shirt and shorts, came into the room, bringing with it the kind of face that was so plain you noticed it first. "Hi, Maur," she said with little enthusiasm.

" 'Lo, Jeannie."

"I'm cooking," Jeannie announced and backed into the kitchen. Jed felt a certain tension between the ladies.

"Well, sit down," Maura's father trumpeted and dropped with slightly arthritic abandon to the floor, pulling his feet together in a half-lotus position. Jed and Maura sat together on something that looked and felt like a wooden crate.

"Well, Jed"—their host was looking at Jed but playing

with his toes—"I wanna get it all up front. I wanna know where you're coming from."

"Worcester, Massachusettes," Jed answered and realized that was wrong from his host's expression.

"Maura says you're into market research, Jed."

"Yes." What the hell am I supposed to call him, Jed wondered. "What are you into?"

"Plumbing supplies."

There was a pause in the conversation and Maura's father turned to her. "Well, baby, you're finally gonna take the plunge, huh?"

"Yes," she nodded.

"Far out," he replied with attempted delight. "You're divorced too?" He turned back to his future son-in-law.

Jed nodded. "But my ex-wife's remarrying. That's why . . . I mean . . ." He was a little embarrassed. After all, he knew the guy knew he was shacking up with his daughter. "We'd've gotten married sooner, but . . ."

"The old alimony number. Been married four times. I'm singing it myself," the man on the floor sighed. "But you're getting it together now?" he asked. "Got it laid back? Life goals all hangin' in there?"

Is he asking about my financial condition, Jed wondered. Despite what he looks like, he's her father—and suddenly he was hurled back through the years to the day he met Denise's father and tried what had worked before. "I can support Maura if that's what you're worried about, Dad," he said.

The man turned away abruptly. "Hey, Sweet Stuff," he called, "how about a drink for the folks?"

"I could use a little help." Sweet Stuff's voice was a little sour.

"I'll go," Maura said, and her father watched till she left the room. Then he turned to Jed, and in a no-crap voice he said, "If you ever call me Dad again, I'll kill you."

Maura brought them each a glass of white wine and went back into the kitchen. The men sat staring at each other for a moment. Finally, Non-Dad, as Jed began to think of him, spoke again. "Have you met her mother?"

"No."

"If you're on anything, take a double before you go," he advised.

Maura returned with two more glasses of wine, followed by Jeannie, who carried a tray. She set it on the radiator cover, shoving aside an overgrown avocado pit. When she had filled their plates from a casserole and served them and passed some flat doughy things around in a bread basket, she sat in front of Maura and Jed on the floor beside her . . . her what? Jed thought. Consort?

Non-Dad raised his glass and offered a toast. "To Jed and Maura, may you kick back and get it all going with the flow." They all sipped.

"When are you getting married?" Jeannie asked.

"Couple weeks. There's a few details to straighten out," Maura answered.

"Marriage is a real ego-reinforcement. Cute," Jeannie said, and Jed noticed a cloud pass over Non-Dad's face.

Maura continued, "I want you both there, of course. I'm planning a big wedding."

Her father looked as though Maura had announced she planned to assassinate the mayor and changed the subject. "This is outa sight," he said, referring to the food.

"Yes," Jed answered, incapable of identifying it. "What is it?"

"It's this old Moroccan couscous recipe Jeannie adapted into a vegetarian number," Non-Dad said proudly.

"Don't you relate to bean sprouts?" Jeannie asked Jed.

"Whenever I meet them," he answered.

"He's more into steaks and like that," Maura admitted.

"Worst thing for you," her father said. "Macrobiotic vegetables. That's where it's at. That's how I keep my body"—and, making a little joke—"and that's how I keep Jeannie's." He laughed fondly and reached over and slipped his hand under the girl's T-shirt, running it up to fondle her breast, perhaps in apology for the lack of an ego-reinforcing wedding ceremony.

Maura's face pinkened and, noticing that, Jeannie leaned over and gave Non-Dad a wet kiss, achieving the desired ruby glow on Maura.

Jed thought he might toss his bean sprouts.

"I used to groove on steaks, lobsters," Non-Dad reminisced. "You remember, Maura? Your mother's stuffed fresh ham? Rotten! A cholesterol-covered hang-up. But when I met my Sweet Stuff"—he slid his hand down to her sugary thigh and rubbed it—"she set me straight. Got me behind diet."

"You practically lived on pizza in college," Maura reminded Jeannie.

"Infantilism. I bugged out of it," her former roommate said, and seemed annoyed.

Non-Dad seemed displeased, too. Maybe the mention of college, Jed thought. "You gotta go with your body," Non-Dad said. "Those junk foods are worse pollution than bus-fart." He rose, somewhat less than agilely, and took his plate and Jeannie's back to the tray.

"Any more couscous?" Jeannie asked her guests.

"It's great but no thanks. I'm up to here," Jed said.

She took their plates to the tray and Non-Dad grabbed her in an embrace, his hands falling naturally on her buttocks. "Ah, when I found this one, I got into health and feelings and the inside of me," he said. "Look at me!" He dropped the girl and pounded the tightly controlled flab over his belt buckle. "Would you believe I'm forty-two?"

"Never," Jed said, knowing he was forty-eight.

"Age is shit," Jeannie announced. "The only thing that counts is your karma," and because it obviously annoyed Maura she spread her luscious body around Non-Dad's in a "this-is-serious" kiss that ended with her hand slipping down his back and into his trousers.

They left as early as they decently could, found a cab, and rode back to the apartment and undressed in silence.

Maura turned out the light and crawled into the sofa-bed beside Jed, pressing herself against him, making her body a poultice to draw the infections of the dinner party from his. "It was awful, wasn't it?" she whispered.

"Well, that sort of scene can be sticky," he equivocated. "Your dad's a great guy," he said as sincerely as he could manage.

"Jeannie's a bitch."

"Yes."

"We won't have to see much of them," she promised and pulled his body over hers. He kissed her, brought his hand up to her breast, but saw her father's hand fondling the breast beneath the T-shirt and moved his hand to Maura's back, holding her closer to him. They kissed again, slowly, gently, tongues tangoing from mouth to mouth, but Jed could hear the other man's voice: "Would you believe I'm forty-two?" and broke away.

"I love you," Maura whispered, her lips grazing his face, his neck. When they had reached his collarbone and nothing had happened, she moved her hand down between them and caressed him gently . . . then more firmly . . . then with a certain frantic drive.

But Jed could not erase the picture of his future father-in-law, stained-glass medallion hanging from his overripe chest, his hands on the finely rounded fanny of his roommate, formerly his daughter's roommate. Jed clamped his jaw to keep from crying out, What's happening to me? as Maura worked him over feverishly. For the first time since I met Maura, for the first time since puberty, for God's sake, he thought, frantically . . . desperately . . .

"I can't get it up!" he screamed to Og, sitting on the doctor's examination table the next morning. "You've got to give me something!"

"Jesus, Jed, I'm a dermatologist."

"You're a human being! Aren't there shots? I mean, Christ, it never happened before. You believe me, it never happened before?" It was important that Og believe. It was only because Og was his friend that he could come to him, charge past the pimply patients in the waiting room, and demand to be seen. He could never have admitted what had happened to a stranger.

"I believe you! I believe you!" his friend assured him.

"And now! When we're getting married! What a helluva time! What is it, Og?" he cried, an orgasm of fear spurting from his eyes.

"It's probably just all these tensions. You're too young to—" A thought occurring, Og lowered his voice and asked, "You are only forty-two, aren't you? I mean, you told me the truth about that?"

"Oh, God, Og!" Jed howled, appalled his friend would think he had to lie about his age.

"It's nothing organic," Og assured him hastily. "You'll be fine when the pressures are removed, when everything's settled."

"Nothing will ever be settled! Maura will never marry a guy who can't get it up!"

"Please lower your voice. There are ladies in the waiting room."

"Then give me something," Jed pleaded.

"Jed, be sensible," Og snapped, remembering from medical school that it was imporant to be firm with hysterics. "It only happened once. You may be fine tonight." Jed looked down at himself, and for a moment Og thought he was about to try a manual experiment. "If not tonight, tomorrow. You've had all these things on your mind. They take a toll. Now, as soon as Denise is married . . ."

"What's she waiting for?"

"Saturday. She'll tell Barney Saturday and I'm sure you'll be okay."

"I can't wait till Saturday!"

"For God's sake, Jed, be a man!"

"I'm trying! I don't know if Maura can wait till Saturday!"

In a distracted flash, Og wondered if some people really needed it that badly, considered whether that was why Lillian . . . Veering away from the thought, he remembered his New Year's resolution.

"Og!" Jed demanded his attention.

"Shots are no good, Jed. You get to depend on them."

Jed moaned and Dr. Parmalee continued briskly, "You'll have to go now. I've got a patient waiting."

Jed rose from the examination table looking so mournful that Og said, "Did you happen to notice her? Young? Twenty-two?" The doctor's hands arced through the air, delineating the patient's abundant figure.

"She's got a face full of pimples," Jed said.

"She's much improved," Dr. Parmalee defended. Then Og leered. "Today I'm making sure they didn't move to her chest."

Jed, the picture of rejection, looked at his friend and spoke reproachfully. "You didn't even say take two aspirins and call me in the morning."

That night and the next Maura was energetic and adept in her attempts to remedy what medical science pooh-poohed. And what was worse, to Jed, understanding in her failure.

By Saturday his depression was such that bread lines of morbid thoughts waited to feed on his brain and horrible conclusions were nurtured in the shantytown of his heart and other organs.

Barney called from the lobby at five-thirty to say that he was double-parked and waiting to take Jed to Gaby's, where they had agreed they would wait for him to return from Westport and tell them The Great Decision.

As Jed went for his coat, Maura suddenly announced, "I'm going, too."

"No!" he said.

"Why not?" She settled herself firmly in front of the door. The week's events, or lack of them, had upset the girl, had made her search for reasons, and the only one she could come up with was Gaby. True, she could not imagine when Jed might have had the time to see her. Still, as her mother always said, "When they want to step out, they find a ladder."

"Because," Jed said.

"Because is a conjunction, not a reason."

"Stop editing me! The three of us have been a team,

and if there's going to be a Victory Celebration, it should just be the three of us!"

"You know what Denise is going to say. Why do you have to go at all? Just call up and tell them and have a glass of champagne over the phone."

"Suppose I told Barney Denise was going to say yes and she changed her mind? That poor guy would be shattered."

"But it's Saturday night!" Maura yelled.

"Well, people feel just as shattered Saturday night as Sunday," he yelled back.

"I don't want to be alone on Saturday night," she howled. "I'm alone all week. You're out playing tennis, bridge, dancing, God knows what, and I'm home reading romance fiction. I feel like an old-maid schoolteacher!"

"They wear cardigans," he yelled, and Maura crossed her arms over her naked breasts, protecting them.

"And how do you and Gaby plan to wile away the evening while Barney has dinner with Denise?" she asked, getting to the crux of the problem.

"We'll have dinner!" Then, finally getting it, he asked, as incredulously as possible. "You're not jealous of Gaby? She's a middle-aged lady with two kids and a live-in mother."

"Then why is she giving you dinner?"

"She likes to cook!"

"Let her make spaghetti for her children," she snarled.

Jed looked as maligned as he could manage. "Don't you trust me?" he asked with dignity.

"How can I trust a man who uses a washing machine to pick up broads in ice-cream parlors?" He had no answer for that. "Go!" she screamed. "Go have dinner with Gaby. But remember, there's a Howard Johnson on Eighth Street."

"You wouldn't!"

"I could use a good banana split," she said, making it sound more like personal service than food.

"You couldn't!"

"Oh no?" she asked and reminded him, "Barney is

double-parked!" She went into the bathroom, the slamming door putting a period to the conversation.

Denise had decided there were two ways to look at the problem and she had been looking at both of them all week and seeing no solution.

Now she was looking at herself in the mirror, checking the blusher, the eye shadow, the hair, knowing she looked as well as she ever had and not knowing what she was going to say.

There was A) for Audacity and Arranged marriages. How dare Jed, after taking eighteen years of her life, try to fob her off on some unwanted clunk he found at a singles club? The incredible gall of thinking he could reshape a man to what he thought were her specifications, like a builder redoing a house before he sold it, without asking the buyer if she wanted a sundeck? A sauna? A hip bath? The unmitigated conniving with her life so he would be solvent enough to marry. While she, herself, might not be happy the way things were, she at least had Jed over the barrel marked alimony and by standing pat could wreak a lifetime revenge.

Then there was B) for Barney. And Blame. And But how could she object to him agreeing to the plan when he didn't even know her? Except he did check her out. One of the most time-consuming puzzles of the week had been to reconcile well-dressed, sincere, sweet Barney with the neat figure and open smile as the alter ego or refinished version of the psychotic, moustached Mulligan who had frightened her so in the Cimini house.

And what about C) for Change and Cram and Cultivation of all the things Barney thought, or had been told, she wanted in a man. Which let's face it, was Charming. How many other women had had a man go through all that just for her?

She got to D) for Damn it! What am I supposed to Do? Forget them! Think about me! I think I love Barney . . . Jed will always be special . . . He was the first, but . . . I must not let him be the only. And he has certainly behaved badly. But I must not compare the two men. Jed is over, Barney is beginning. And I can make a life with him. If only there was some way that I could have what I want and not let Jed get what he wants.

Denise looked at the clock, saw that Barney would soon be there. She removed her robe, took the new dress from the bed, checked for overlooked price tickets, and stepped into it, wriggling it up over her hips. She squirmed for the zipper, was finally obliged to call Keith to help, except of course, he could never get the little hook at the top. There it is again, she thought. I need a man. She sent Keith away and looked in the mirror once again. I look sensational, she decided and suddenly thought E) Excelsior! I know how!

"Where do you think they are now?" Jed asked.

Gaby thought for a moment. "Well, we've just finished dinner. I suppose they've finished dinner."

And where do you think Maura is, Jed thought.

"Of course, you have to allow for travel time," Gaby added and, blowing out the candles, rose from the table. "Why don't we have some brandy?"

"Fine." He finished his wine and got up, too. "Do you think he'll come right back after dinner?"

Gaby moved close to him, pretending she was going to pick up his dishes. "I think," she said, "if a woman accepts a man's proposal, they'd probably want to be together for a while. You know, talk, plan."

Jed nodded. "Neck," he said.

Her blue eyes looked up into his. "We might have to wait all night," she whispered.

Oh my God, he thought, Denise wouldn't . . . Still . . . Gaby was a woman, she might be right. And if I waited all night, what the hell would Maura say? Gaby was still staring up at him. He nodded for an answer and reached over to pick up the plates.

"Don't bother," she said. "Go turn on some music. There's a lot of records in the cabinet. I'll get the brandy." She picked up a few of the plates and took them to the kitchen as long as she was going.

She was pleased with everything about the evening, except Jed. He was very moody, uncommunicative. Of course, he must be very tense about what was happening in Westport, she reasoned. But I'm sure Barney will come through. Why wouldn't Denise want him? He's attractive and if she's gone through what I have, she'll jump at the chance. Once Jed knows it's settled, he'll be all right. As for everything else . . . the dinner was perfect . . . the squabs just right, the wild-rice stuffing the best she'd ever made. And her chocolate soufflé was a foregone concluion. Even if Jed was nervous, it hadn't affected his appetite. He'd been very quiet, but what he had said was all about how terrific her food was. And the kids were with Len, that bastard, and Mother was playing a tournament with Aunt Harriet in the city and would stay over. Denise, she prayed silently, say yes, but take your time about it. She reached up into the cabinet for the brandy glasses.

Jed wandered into the living room, feeling the evening was anticlimactic. He knew what Denise was going to say, even if the others didn't. But still, as he'd told Maura, he had to go through this. Maura would get over being angry . . . as soon as Denise was settled. Og had guaranteed that would end his problem and everything would be fine with his girl once the sofa-bed was not just a place to sleep but the golden arena God intended it to be.

He moved to the record cabinet, his eyes roving over the albums of Sinatra, Streisand, Bennett. Suddenly coming to another shelf, he called out, "Hey! You've got musical-comedy albums!"

"I love 'em," she called back. "Put on any one you want."

"You got some really old ones. Some I haven't got. Or Denise hasn't got," he added regretfully. He pulled out an album of Mary Martin in *Lute Song*. "Do you think if Denise marries Barney, she'd give me back my records?"

"Why not?" Gaby asked, coming into the room with the brandy. She handed him one and pulled out another album. "Try this. It's a crazy one. Old Cole Porter cuts. There's some of Merman from *Panama Hattie*."

He put the albums on and sat beside Gaby on the sofa. Touching their glasses first, they sipped and listened to the old music. He realized how comfortable he was, that it was the first time in a long time he'd spent an evening in a room that looked like a family lived in it, with a woman who was fully dressed. That he was fully dressed. That he'd had the best dinner he could remember in a long time and the whole thing was . . . what was the word he wanted? Civilized, he decided. They were silent but it was not an uncomfortable silence, it was friendly and full of the shared interest of the music. When the two records were over, Gaby put on an album of *Pal Joey*, and one of a show he didn't know called *Tenderloin* that he thought was fantastic. By eleven they were on their third brandy.

As they touched glasses again, Gaby said, "Jed, no matter what happens tonight, I want you to know. I've enjoyed this. It's been a very . . . I don't know. It's been fun and in a way rewarding. We've done a lot for Barney."

"I couldn't have done it without you," he admitted, wondering what would happen to her when this was over. She deserved someone nice.

How the hell do I move him, she was thinking. She put down her glass and, trying to make it seem impulsive, leaned forward to kiss him, and the doorbell rang.

"This is it, Gaby," Jed said, tensely, feeling a sudden flurry of fear. He's back too early . . .

Damn you, Denise, Gaby thought. I told you take your time. "You go," she said.

He strode to the door, sure that everything was all right, that Barney in his excitement just couldn't wait to tell them, like a kid. That had to be it. He threw open the door and yelled, "Congratulations!" before he saw Barney's face.

"On what?" Barney asked.

Jed's hands turned to ice. "She turned you down?"

"No."

"Then what . . ."

"Can I have a glass of water?" Barney asked emotionally and walked into the living room. Gaby was already going to the kitchen to get it.

"What happened?" Jed demanded of his shaking, ashen protégé. Gaby returned with the water and Barney gulped it down. "Barney, please . . ." Jed said.

"Well, first . . . she said she loved me . . . but . . ."

"But what?" Gaby asked as both men seemed unable to speak.

Barney took a deep breath. "She said that nowadays there were so many options . . ."

"Goddamn it! She never talked like that before she went into real estate!" Jed exploded.

"Please," Gaby said to him.

"She said why didn't we just live together!" Barney blurted out, then handed the glass back to Gaby and went to sit, turned away from them, in a straight-backed chair in a corner of the room.

"Why? For God's sake why?" Jed howled.

"She said because it was just the same as being married and that way we'd get to keep the alimony."

Jed was next to him, pulling him up out of the chair, before Barney knew what had happened. "You'd shack up with her in front of my kids?" he yelled.

"No! I wouldn't do a thing like that," Barney protested.

"Denise suggested it," Gaby said gently.

"She doesn't think like that. I don't believe it!"

"It's true," Barney told him.

"Then there's something, someone, behind it. That's not Denise's style!"

"What did you say?" Gaby asked.

"I said I didn't think it was nice. My Mommy wouldn't have liked it."

Gaby noticed the trauma of the evening had caused some regression in their pupil's assurance.

"Then you left?" Jed asked.

"No. We discussed it for a while. I brought it up about

the boys," he assured Jed. "I said we can't do it in front of them."

"And what did she say?"

"She said, 'You're right. Let's do it away from them.' "

"Oh my God," Jed bellowed, and went back to the couch and knocked back what was left in his brandy glass.

"What did she mean?" Gaby tried to keep the report on a less emotional tack.

"She said she'd gone through one bad marriage—" Jed groaned and Barney said, "I'm sorry. And that in fairness to herself, before she married again, she would have to be absolutely sure, and she suggested . . . she suggested . . ."

"You go away somewhere together," Gaby finished for him since he didn't seem able. Barney nodded.

"You're not going?" Jed thundered.

"Why not?" Gaby asked sharply.

"Because . . . because you don't do things like that!" Jed phumphered.

"What's the difference between that and you living with a girl?" Gaby demanded.

"The difference is . . ." Jed started, and then could only think of one difference that he knew was a very weak argument.

"The different is she's your wife." Gaby was ahead of him.

"The mother of my children," he said, trying to make it sound better and failing.

Gaby turned to Barney. "What did you say?"

"I didn't know what to say. You can understand my shock," he said with a nervous look at Jed.

"Yeah," Jed barked.

"So I said I'd see if I could get away from the office. Was that right?"

"No," they both said and looked at each other.

Jed looked back to Barney. "You shoulda just said if you want me, you have to marry me!" Gaby laughed and Jed whirled on her. "Well, he should've."

Gaby moved toward Barney. "You're supposed to be in love with her," she said.

"I am," he mumbled.

"Well, what's the matter with you? If you love her and she wants that, why not give it to her? How could you not tell her yes right away? If a woman offers herself to a man and all he says is I'll have to ask the office, it's very demeaning." She flashed a look at Jed.

He stared back angrily because she was right.

"Well, I mean," Barney, who was not looking at them, said, "It isn't . . . you know . . . proper."

"Proper!" Gaby snorted. "Good Lord, people even go to bed on television now. In the afternoon!"

"If we were married it would be okay . . ."

"What would be okay?" Seeing the total ruin of her plan just when it was progressing so nicely, Gaby was losing her temper.

"Well, what if . . . that is, suppose it wasn't so great. At least at first," he put in hastily. "Then she couldn't back out that easily. I just don't know if I can pull it off with so much at stake."

"What is it?" Jed screamed, his own plans sliding away like Los Angeles in a heavy rain. "After all this, are you telling us you're impotent?"

"I don't know," Barney moaned.

"What do you mean you don't know? Can you make it with a woman or not?"

"I don't know!" Barney, goaded beyond endurance, cried out, "I never tried. I'm a virgin!"

Gaby and Jed collapsed into chairs, limp-bodied, like victims of a Mafia shootout. One of them whispered, "Jesus!"

For minutes there was no sound in the room except tiny gasps from Barney, who seemed to be trying to control tears.

At last, Gaby, feeling it was her apartment and up to her to say something, pulled herself together. "Well, we've taught him everything else."

"I did tennis. This one's on you," Jed shot across the room.

"I wasn't thinking of a demonstration. Perhaps just a fatherly talk," she said. "Haven't you done that for your sons?"

"Sure. Come on over and sit on my lap, Barney," Jed snarled.

Gaby stood up. "Your attitude is defeatist, self-pitying, and . . . and dumb!" she said. "After all the work we've put in, how can you give up now? There's more than Barney and Denise at stake. There's that girl!" And me, she thought, knowing the mention of the girl was a calculated risk, but the way things were going, she had to calculate. "Talk to him!" she ordered and went into her bedroom.

Jed picked up his glass and went into the kitchen to find the brandy. He poured a heavy shot and knocked it back, returning through the dining el into the living room. Barney was still in the straight chair, face to the wall, his smart new overcoat not even unbuttoned. "You want me to talk to you?" Jed asked.

"Talk to me."

"Just a second." Jed went back, refilled his glass, and returned, trying to remember exactly how he had put it to Scott. "Well, son," he said, sitting on the sofa, clutching the glass, "You know that men and women are different?"

"You think I'm an idiot?" Barney snapped.

"I think your condition is unusual, if not unlikely," Jed growled, "and goddamn inconvenient. I'm not sure where to start. Or if I should start," he added, getting up, disgusted.

"I'm sorry," Barney said humbly. "Maybe I should have told you before."

"Chee!" Jed exhaled and sat down again. "Do you know the mechanics? I mean, what fits where?" Barney nodded. "Well, then, what do you need to know?"

"How to get up to that point. I mean, I'm sure if I got that far, I'd be okay."

Jed nodded. "Well," he said, "you . . . you go out with a woman and . . . and you throw a little glitter on her

. . ." Barney looked up. "I don't mean that literally," Jed said. "I mean you . . . you know. Romance her . . . Put your arm around her. Good God! Haven't you kissed Denise?" Jesus Christ, what am I getting her into, he thought. I know we're divorced, but don't I have a moral obligation not to shove her into the sack with a sexual retardate?

"I kissed her," Barney said.

"You put your arm around her?"

"It made it more comfortable kissing," Barney explained.

"Did you . . ." Jed was unsure how to phrase his next question. Nervously he rose, pulling on his brandy, trying to remember how they put it in *The Ideal Marriage,* which he'd read in high school. "That is," he said, "did you fondle her?"

"How do you mean?" Barney asked.

"Did you feel her up?" Jed exploded. "Put your hand on her— No! I don't want to know!"

"I guess. Sort of."

"Well . . ." Jed said. "Well, that's it. Only you just go a little further." He was beginning to sweat now, wondering how to get through to a forty-one-year-old virgin mathematician. "Barney, fucking is necking carried to the third power."

"Shh! Maybe Gaby can hear."

"She knows!" he yelled and paced the length of the room to calm himself. "Do you have any questions?" Jed did not think he could take much more.

"Yes."

"What?"

"Undressing."

"Her or you?"

"Both of us."

"You start with your tie, then your shirt, and keep going till you hit your underpants. Denise knows how by herself."

"I'm very shy about my person."

"I remember!"

"Well, I mean, how do you get undressed in front of somebody? Of the opposite sex," he chose to specify.

"You can do it with your clothes on, Barney, but it isn't as much fun!" Jed shouted.

"All right," Barney said, trying to mollify him. "Let's say we're undressed. Now what?'

Jed pulled at the collar of his turtleneck shirt, which seemed to be balling up around his neck. "Now, you . . . you take her in your arms . . . you carry her to the bed . . ."

"Did I take the covers off before?"

"I don't know," Jed cried. "Maybe the maid did. You put her on the bed . . . you lie down beside her . . . you . . . you touch her . . . you kiss her . . ."

"Where?" the perfect student asked.

"Anywhere that looks interesting, for God's sake!"

"I mean is there anything special Denise likes? You know her. What did you do with her?"

"I'll be goddamned if I'll tell you that," Jed screamed. "For Chris' sake, I've got you naked on a bed with my wife. From there on in, you're on your own!" He slammed into the bedroom after Gaby. She was sitting tensely on the edge of her bed. "Mother of God," he said.

"I know it's very difficult," Gaby said, "but we've come so far. We can't go back to Square One."

"Square One is sitting in your living room!" Jed shouted. Noticing he still held the brandy glass, he finished the drink and set the glass on her bureau. "I think I'm going crazy. He's a man. He's forty-one years old. He's hung like a stallion."

"How do you know? '"

"Og told me." He crossed the room and stood before her. "Gaby, I can't teach a grown-up man sex. Nobody ever taught me. I just knew. Everyone I know, knew. Didn't you know?"

"I knew," she whispered. "I still know."

"It's insane. When is a guy ready? Fourteen? Fifteen? He's blown twenty-seven years of the greatest show on earth!" He reached down and, taking her arms, he pulled her to her feet, shaking her as he wanted to shake Barney. "There's nothing like holding a woman in your arms."

"For me it's a man," she reminded him, her breath coming in little gasps.

"Feeling your bodies together," Jed raved on, "her skin on yours, her legs wrapped around you . . . her mouth . . . her lips . . . her tongue . . . kissing her breast . . . or his breast," he said quickly, not wanting to sound sexist.

"Yes, yes," she breathed. "It's the only way to go."

"It's being with someone," he continued as though he had to prove it to himself or to her in order to reach the man in the next room. "Inside . . . outside . . . all wrapped together. It's fantastic. Isn't it fantastic, Gaby?"

"I'm on your side, Jed," she assured him. "I've missed it. Needed it."

He reached down and looked into her eyes, holding her face between his hands. "Then you will?" Silently, she nodded. He nodded too and they looked at each other for a long moment. "I'll go tell Barney," he said and started for the door.

"Why tell him?"

"I don't want it to come as a shock. He's sensitive."

"But why should he—" she said, moving to him. Then she stopped speaking, stopped moving.

Oh my God, he thought, understanding what she had misunderstood. And, remembering what she had said about a woman offering herself, he rushed back to her, took her in his arms and kissed her, wondering how to get himself out of what he'd gotten himself into. And as she kissed him back, her hands pressing him to her, her body grinding insistently into his, the yearning in her embrace and the long wait behind it forced him to consider the woman in his arms. Why not, he wondered. Wouldn't it be wasted on Barney? All this warmth and lovingness and passion and yes, charm and wit and . . . and civilization Barney would need a road map to find. And who knows what Maura is doing at Howard Johnson with their twenty-seven flavors right this minute? So, why not? And suddenly his memory zapped him with a reminder of why not. What if I couldn't, he thought, his stomach sinking to the affected area. No, it's only with Maura, he argued back. And how do you know? his conscience demanded. Suppose I tried and didn't make it? And main objectives! I want Maura! I've had Gaby. At least, I've had Denise and that was almost the same. I want Maura now. I want my youth!

He tried to pull away, whispering, "Barney will hear," but she refused to listen, pushing on against him. She was too sweet, too soft, had been hurt too much before to hurt again. Oh God, he thought, and all the wine and brandy. I can't think!

Slowly, gently, he pulled away, still holding her in his arms. "You're a wonderful girl, Gaby. I want to . . ."

And as he said it, he realized it was true. "But we shouldn't."

"We can send the student home and plan tomorrow's curriculum," she said.

"There's Maura," he answered, as kindly as he could.

"Are you so sure of her?"

I'm not, he realized, and if . . . for any reason, an obvious one popping up at once and being firmly pushed down, she should go . . . Gaby was not one to be dismissed.

"I need some time," Jed said.

She stared into his eyes, knowing she had gotten to him, knowing the truth about a girl of twenty-four was racing through his mind. All right, she decided, I lead into strength, Barney's the dummy, he'll throw some unimportant card. We'll see if Jed can play the ace. And whether Maura trumps.

"I've got time," Gaby said at last and walked to her dresser, picked up a comb and ran it through her hair.

"What'll we do with him?" Jed asked, nodding toward the living room.

Gaby dropped the comb. "What made you think I'd go to bed with Barney?"

"I didn't think. I haven't thought of anything," he said, hoping she'd understand. "I was so concentrated on Denise and him. I was . . . desperate. I don't know if I got through to him."

"Let's find out," Gaby suggested and went back into the living room.

Barney, still in his coat, was standing at the window, staring out over older, smaller apartment houses and one-family homes toward the river, none of which could be seen in the dark. He turned when he heard them.

"I've made up my mind," he said. They waited. "She wants to go to the Caribbean. Someplace warm. For a week. Together."

"Well?" Jed said.

"I'll go on one condition."

"What?"

"I want you both to come with me."

"No," Jed said as Gaby said, "Yes."

"If she sees me—" Jed began.

"I want to go!" Barney cried. "I want this to work out. I just need someone there to help if I get stuck!"

"What do you want me to do?" Jed yelled. "Hide under the bed?"

"No. But be there. Stay in your room so I can phone you. I can do it. I know I can do it! But," he pleaded, "I need help!"

"It's not so much to ask, Jed," Gaby said. "I understand. He's nervous."

"You go!"

"Both of you," Barney begged. "I need you both."

"I can't," Jed said.

"Well then, I guess it's over," Barney said tragically and turned to the window. Jed, frightened, took a step toward him, then realized it was the kind of window that opened sideways and Barney couldn't possibly squeeze through.

"You could just stay in your room," Gaby said sensibly. "Register under an assumed name if it makes you feel better. And I can carry messages. She doesn't know me. Jed, to give up when one more week would clinch it. We've come so far," and I want to go so much further, she thought. A week in the Caribbean could be my chance, too.

"But," he said, wavering, and they could smell his indecision.

"Please," Barney said, turning back.

"It would be nice to get away," Gaby pointed out. "The sun and swimming . . ."

"I'd be in my room," he reminded them but admitted he was thinking it over.

"Well, I'll take Denise out and let you know when it's safe," Barney pushed.

"I don't know if Maura would agree," Jed said reluctantly.

"Is she home?" Gaby asked. "Phone her."

Is she home, he wondered, but could not admit that she might not be, now, at midnight.

"Use the phone by my bed," Gaby said, but it sounded to Jed like, Are you so sure of her?

He went inside and dialed his number.

"Hello?" Maura's voice came through the instrument timidly as if afraid of midnight heavy breathers or people selling wear-ever light bulbs.

"It's me."

"Oh, Jed," she said, sounding relieved. "I'm so sorry for what I did."

"What did you do? With who?" he asked, suspicions clouding the reason for the call.

"What I said," she clarified. "To you. I should have known how nervous you are . . . with so much on your mind, Barney and your impotence and all. Jed, I could have cut out my tongue."

Why didn't you before you answered the phone, he thought, but said, "Are you alone?"

"Of course I'm alone. I'm reading *Tenderness Turned Terror*."

"You didn't go out?"

"No."

"Honest?"

"I read the book. Three hundred and twelve pages." And to prove it conclusively, she said, "It's about this Jewish Princess who is Tut-ankh-amen's mistress and they bury her alive with him and she puts a curse on the tomb but manages to get out and—"

"You don't have to tell me!"

"You know I couldn't make that up." Then, her first fears allayed, she remembered. "What happened to Barney?"

"Denise wants a trial honeymoon in the Caribbean."

"That's good," she said, and when he didn't answer, "Isn't it?"

"Yes and no. He won't go alone. He needs a security blanket and he wants me."

"Is Gaby going?" she asked, the old suspicions rising immediately over her guilt.

"No," he thought he'd better answer.

"You stay home. Send her."

"She can't go. She's got kids," he ad-libbed.

"Oh."

"Do you mind if I go?" he asked, and, sensing she was trying to decide, he amplified the emergency. "The man is a bundle of nerves. He refuses to budge without me. If I don't go with him, it'll wreck the whole plan."

"I don't understand why he needs you," she said.

" 'Cause he's a virgin," Jed whispered hoarsely.

There was dead silence from the other end of the phone. He's going with that woman, Maura knew instantly, it was patently obvious.

"Jed," she said quietly, "you've never lied to me before."

"I'm not lying."

"He's forty-one. You can't expect me to believe . . ."

"No I can't," he said, "but it happens to be true."

He couldn't have made it up, she decided. If you're going to lie, you don't say anything that incredible. "Jesus," she murmured. "Forty-one. A virgin. Doesn't it hurt?"

"You see? You see why I have to go?" Jed pressed.

Maura made a quick assessment. If Gaby was not really going, what fear of letting Jed go? Except other girls. But on the other hand, if Jed didn't go, neither would Barney, and if Denise wasn't settled, then Jed might never get settled no matter how many eggs and oysters he ate, and then what would happen to her? Jed was talking again, explaining, repeating, persuading; but she had no time to listen. The emotions of earlier in the evening, the argument, the guilts, the recriminations, her own desire to have things settled, even her book . . . what the hell? she thought, it won't work this way. "Jed," she said over his monologue, "Jed, go!"

"You don't mind?" he asked, interrupting his recital.

"No. For God's sake go. Get Barney laid so I can pick out my silver pattern!"

Chapter Twelve

"Pete, I know this is going to be difficult," Jed began as soon as he got his travel agent on the phone Monday morning. "I need four reservations for anywhere in the Caribbean next week."

"Jed . . ." Pete's tone was what-are-you-doing-to-me? "It's the height of the season."

"I'd like a big hotel, any island, maybe Puerto Rico." Any place I can get lost in the crowd, Jed thought.

"Puerto Rico's overbooked till Easter. I couldn't get you in the coffee shop of the Caribe-Hilton."

"Barbados?"

"I'll laugh later when I have time."

"Anywhere?" Jed lowered his requirements.

"Mmmm." There was a pause. "We heard about a guest house in Nassau. Five miles from the beach but it's gotta lotta charm and they serve breakfast. Only six rooms but I could check."

"Too small."

"How about March fourteenth?"

"Next week."

"Hold on." In the background Jed could hear a few yelled questions, then the phone clattered down on Pete's desk and a mumbled conversation. Then the phone was picked up again. "There's a swinging new beach club in Martinique. One of our guys checked it out. He says it's a fifty-acre mattress with palm trees. But the food is good and it's so new I could probably get you in there if I can get you on a plane."

"What's it called?"

"The Club Gomorrah."

Jed sighed. "It sounds perfect."

"Y'want four? You taking Miss Campbell again?"

"No."

"That over?" Pete asked. He'd been Jed's travel agent so long they were on friendly terms.

"Oh no. We're getting married when I get back," Jed assured him.

"When you get back . . ." Pete repeated slowly, then said, "Congratulations," with a doubtful overtone. "Okay, so it's you . . ."

"Yeah," Jed said, "but I don't want to use my name."

"Oh?" Pete said, as intelligently as he could manage. "Who are you going as? Fidel Castro?"

"Just put me down as . . ." Casting about for a name, Jed came back to, "Mulligan. John Mulligan."

"Uh huh. John Mulligan and who else?"

"Denise Lavery."

"Your wife?" the agent sounded startled.

"My ex-wife."

"Sure. And . . . ?"

"Gaby Marcotte and Barney Warburton."

"Okay. That's two doubles?"

It was Jed's turn to pause. He was still tempted. A week with Gaby was not something to give up lightly, and she wanted, obviously expected . . . However, it could only go that far, that week, and . . . No. It was unfair to the woman to do that. And unfair to Maura as well. Lightly regretting a basic morality that seemed incongruous in modern times, in his position and certainly in the Club Gomorrah, he said, "No. One double, two singles." Even so, he figured, if his moral position declined and his physical position rose, having them in singles left his options open.

"Divided how?" Pete said, his voice revealing a certain fascination in the order he was taking.

"Warburton and Mrs. Lavery are the double."

"Ahhh . . . sure."

"And about the plane tickets . . ."

"Please tell me about them," Pete said.

"I want to go as late as possible Friday, they want to go early Saturday."

"Sounds like a fun foursome," Pete said.

"I'd explain if I could."

"No, don't. I'd rather try to figure it out myself," the agent told him. "I'll call you back. And congratulations on your marriage," he added, and Jed thought he heard him laugh before the phone was quite cradled.

"Barney, I got the three of you on the nine A.M. flight for Martinique Saturday."

"What about you?"

"I can't be on the same plane as Denise. I'm going Friday afternoon."

"What kind of place?"

Jed took a deep breath. "It's new. They say it's terrific. "The Club Gomorrah."

"Gomorrah?"

"Listen, Barney," he said firmly, "it's the height of the season. There isn't another place from here to Caracas that'll take us."

"But I thought a small, family-type place—"

"This is it, Barney," Jed exploded. "Moonlight, palm trees, and an atmosphere drenched in sex. And you'll have both your coaches on the sidelines. You call Denise, I'll call Gaby." He hung up without giving Barney a chance to reply.

". . . and if anything happens on the plane, he'll give you a high sign and you'll go to the ladies' room and he'll go to the men's room and you'll stand there like you're waiting and you can tell him what to do."

"You've done a brilliant job, Jed. And how do I find you when I get there?"

"Just ask anyone for John Mulligan."

"Mulligan?"

"It worked before, Gaby, it'll work again. I'll see you Saturday night," he said and hung up.

I've waited this long, I can wait the rest of the week, Gaby thought. And with Mother here, I don't have to worry about a sitter. For once she felt grateful to her mother. Then she began to wonder how she could get her out of the apartment once she had firmly landed Jed.

His hands were sweating so he could barely hold the phone receiver as he dialed the number, but he didn't want to ask Miss Friedman to get it for him. The affair was, or at least she would think it was, sordid, and he didn't want to involve a good woman like that.

"New Freedom Real Estate. Miss Lavery."

"It's Barney."

"How are you?"

"It's all set for Saturday."

"Where?" Denise asked, her voice plummeting to where her stomach had been before it took off for lower regions.

"Martinique," he gasped out.

"How lovely," she managed to say. "Where?"

"The Club Gomorrah." His voice was an octave higher than usual.

Denise dropped the phone. Her hands had suddenly become quite slippery. When she got it back to her ear, he was saying, "Is that all right?"

"Fine!" she answered quickly.

Thinking she sounded shocked, Barney wondered if it wasn't wrong to take a woman like Denise, a woman of quality, to a place that sounded like a sunbathing orgy.

But it was her idea, he reminded himself, and gave her the time and place and flight number.

Denise considered whether, now that she had achieved her spiteful victory over Jed, she could go through with it, actually stay in a place like that. No, she told herself, face it, cohabit in a place like that, with a nice, sweet guy like Barney. Unmarried. Except, of course, he chose it. Maybe he wasn't so sweet and nice. Nonsense, he is! And she was a grown woman. With children. Who didn't have to know the name of the place, and even if they did, would not understand its connotation. (They teach them nothing in school, she thought, parenthetically.) And it was the ideal place. Obviously. In among all the adulterers, they would hardly stand out.

"Will I see you before Saturday?" she asked.

"No. I have a lot of work to catch up on because the office is letting me go," he said. The gym every night. Ten more pounds. I'll have to wear a bathing suit, he thought, and even, as he began to feel dizzy, not wear a bathing suit.

"I see," she said.

"But I'll call you," he assured her. "Goodbye, dear. I can't wait," he added because it seemed polite.

"Neither can I," she answered, because she thought she should, and hung up.

Oh my God, she thought, staring across the double desks to Lillian's empty chair. Can I do it? With a new man? At my age? Start all over again? Why not? she asked herself bravely and for the next little while fought against the reasons.

"Miss Campbell," she answered.

"It's all set," Jed's voice told her. "I leave Friday and they leave Saturday. The Club Gomorrah in Martinique."

"It's supposed to be fantastic," Maura said. "One of my writers was there. Said he didn't sleep the whole week but the bags under his eyes were very sunburned."

"Yeah," Jed said, slightly unenthusiastic. "It was all Pete could get me."

"Listen," Maura said, she had been busy that morning,

too. "They owe me some vacation time and I asked my boss if I could have next week—"

"No!" Jed said firmly.

"Why not?"

"I don't want to take you to a place like that."

"What's wrong with it?" and as Jed phumphered reasons, she answered her own question. Gaby. Gaby is what's wrong with it, I'm sure. "All right," she said when Jed paused for breath. "It would have been nice, but . . . I'll just wait for you at home."

"Yeah, it's better that way," he said and hung up.

Maura sat back at her desk, then leaned forward, shoved aside the galleys of *Cool Priestess, Hot Hun*, which she had been proofing, marking her place in the scene where Attila invaded the Temple of Athena. If I'm going to marry him, I have to know, she decided. Except, I can't let Jed know I'm checking on him. But, if he's hiding from Denise, it would be easy to hide from him. The others don't know me. They know my name. Okay, I could go under an assumed name. Jones, she considered. Brown? Attila? They all sounded fake. What was the name in my book? Mulligan. Fine. But it would cost about six, seven hundred. She thought a moment more, then swiveled her chair around with resolution and found the phone book in the bottom of the crowded bookcase behind her. Swinging back, she found the number, paused a moment thinking, I can do this. I've been on the other side so often, it should be easy. She dialed, asked for Mr. Trolander and gave his secretary her name.

"Hi," Will said, coming on immediately.

"I have wonderful news," she said.

"They're getting married?" he guessed.

"No. But they're going on a trial honeymoon at the Club Gomorrah. It's only a matter of time," she crowed.

"I hear Club Gomorrah's fantastic," he said, remembering the chest under the black sweater at Thanksgiving. Why not? he wondered. She didn't seem interested then but she did call after; it couldn't only have been the book.

How? Thinking rapidly, he came up with the answer. "But how are we going to cover it?"

Hooked, Maura thought. "Cover it?" she asked, innocently.

"We should know what goes on," he said. "And pictures. We have to have pictures. It could be a great chapter."

"I see what you mean," she said, telling herself just slide into it nice and easy. "But . . . well . . . I can't really afford . . ."

A feeling in his groin told him he had it made. And the legs, he reminded himself, and that wiggle when she walked into the restaurant at lunch. "What would it cost?" he asked.

"At least a thousand. Maybe twelve hundred."

Six hundred, not a penny more, he figured. But if it was an advance and not expenses, he could probably get away with it. "Look," he said, "if you're really sure, I think I can get you a contract on the book. An advance."

"Could you?" she asked, knowing he could probably write a contract for five thousand without having to ask anyone.

"I'm pretty sure I can get you a thousand."

"For expenses?" she caroled. "That's fabulous."

"An advance!" he was quick to correct her. It was his job, and who could be sure about the book? Or even the girl?

"Oh," she answered, and taking a breath, thinking of her trousseau while she was at it, "if it's an advance, I should get five thousand."

"Three," he said, deciding she was smart, too. That's a girl who's really worth the effort. Body and brains. If necessary, I'll go to four, he decided, the company owes me some fringe benefits.

Bingo, she thought, but asked, "No expenses?" not wanting to sound anxious.

"Not for a new author," he parried. "Three thou. Half now. Half on delivery."

"Well . . ." She drew it out, then said, "Okay."

Bingo, he thought. "We'll get this thing going right away. The contract," he added hastily, thinking she might have misinterpreted and heard the real meaning. "When will you go?"

"Saturday."

"Sensational. Get a camera. I'll call you when I've got the check," he said and hung up, feeling he had gotten a bargain. Maybe for the company, too. He buzzed his secretary and asked, "Has the company got a travel agent?"

"Yeah, sure," she answered.

"Will you call them and book me at the Club Gomorrah on Martinique for a week starting Saturday?"

"The Club Gomorrah? On the company?" She was shocked. Her previous boss had never tried for more than a couple of bottles of Scotch for the major agents at Christmas.

"Why not?" Will countered. "It's research."

"For what?" she asked.

"A book," he answered sharply.

"I'll bet," she said.

Jed opened his office door and looked out toward Felicity's desk. She was seated, not working, her elbows on the desk, a Kleenex at her nose, as though she'd blown it and forgotten to move her hand away. "Will you come in, Felicity?" he asked.

She turned, looked at him with sad eyes, and nodded. She dropped the Kleenex in the wastebasket, picked up her steno pad, and walked past him into the office. She settled silently on the oatmeal sofa and opened her book. She had been extremely quiet, passive, since her outburst two weeks before.

Jed closed the door. Felicity sniffed. "Is there anything wrong, Felicity?" he felt obliged to ask, not wanting an answer, hoping only for divine intervention, which came when the phone rang.

With a look of resignation, Felicity jumped up and answered it. "Mr. Lavery's wire." She listened a moment and said, "Please hold." She put her hand over the phone and said, "It's Mrs. Lavery."

Jed took the instrument, held it a moment, reminding himself he was not angry with Denise because he did not know she was flying off, hot-pantsed, to a tropical sex-circus with a man he had trained. "Hello," he said, carefully uninflected, and sat down, swiveling his chair around to concentrate by staring out of the window.

"Hello, Jed," Denise read from the paper on which she had typed her dialogue in preparation for the phone call. She knew he probably knew all about the trip but wanted to be sure she did not give away the fact she knew he knew. That way, she could needle without fear of reprisals. After all, he was a son of a bitch. "How are you?" she read on.

She sounded funny to him, almost stilted. "Fine. How are you?"

"I'm fine," she answered and made a checkmark on the paper, having correctly guessed his dialogue to this point. "I want to ask you a favor."

"Oh?"

"I'm going away on Saturday," Which you know, you bastard, but will pretend you don't.

"Vacation?" he asked, ready for it.

Her manuscript, which had been perfect so far, read, *Denise: (Lying) "Business"* and she thought she followed the stage direction perfectly, except of course, he knew she was lying and how could she fail?

"What kind of business?" Jed asked, amazed by the confidence with which his straightforward ex-wife had learned to lie. Probably at Real Estate School, he figured.

What kind? Denise asked herself, for she had written, *Jed: That's nice*. And he hadn't said it. "Personal," she ad-libbed and took a breath before reading her next line, but he cut in and asked "Where are you going?" which was also not in the script. "Lake Placid," she said because it was the first name that occured.

"On business?" he said, implying Lake Placid was the

sort of place people went not on business but to shack up, which of course, was exactly what she was doing.

"Why not?" she asked, so nervous that she dropped her script. "They have real estate up there."

"What was the favor?" he asked.

"Just a minute," she said and bent to retrieve the script, which had slid under the desk. When she had found her place, she picked up the phone again. "Could you come up and stay with the boys for a week?"

"No," he said, which she had not expected. Fink though he was, he loved his children.

"Why not?" Denise asked without referring to the paper, and thought, I counted on you. If it wasn't for you I wouldn't have to go away in the first place.

"I'll be out of town next week," Jed said.

"Where?" He wouldn't dare follow me.

"Flint, Michigan." Any place beside the Club Gomorrah, and who would lie about Flint, Michigan?

"Why?" Are you lying?

"Buick." They are the ones who aren't in Detroit, he tried to remember.

"Oh." He's either lying or he's desperate for money.

"I need the money," he said, luckily. "I pay a helluva lot of alimony." You don't want to give up the money, he thought, hire a sitter.

I was right all along, Denise thought. Get him in the wallet. That's where it hurts when you come down to the bottom line. "Well, never mind," she said, annoyed at a further complication. Angrily, she tore up her prepared script.

"I can't help it," he said.

"I'll get Lillian," she told him.

"Have a great time in Lake Placid," he said sarcastically.

"Enjoy Flint," she snarled and dropped the phone.

Jed swung around and dumped the phone back on the hook in a temper.

"You don't have Buick," Felicity said quietly from the oatmeal sofa. "You're getting married, aren't you?"

Oh my God, he thought. He'd forgotten she was in the room. "Nobody gets married in Flint," he snapped.

"Then wherever," she said. "And that means you got her married"—she nodded to the phone as if expecting it to throw her the bridal bouquet. She turned to him again, speaking forcefully, like an actress playing Greek tragedy. "You said you'd tell me!"

"There's nothing to tell yet. I am getting married but I don't know when. Mrs. Lavery may or may not be getting married. I hope I'll know by the end of next week. It all depends on . . ." He paused, realizing it all depended on whether Barney was a good lay, and Felicity was one person too many to depend on that. "I hope it will all be over very soon," he said.

"Yes," Felicity sighed. "It probably will all be over soon."

I don't need this, Jed told himself, but settled back in his chair to take it anyway. If he was going to be away for a week he would have to rely on Felicity. "Is something wrong with Perry?" he asked, trying to sound like a kindly but busy pastor who wanted to help but had a christening scheduled in ten minutes.

She nodded. "He's hardly ever home. He says he's working late, at the gym, seeing his children. Any excuse."

"No prospects for his wife?"

"None. Or so he says."

Having seen Rhonda, Jed was inclined to believe Perry but he didn't want to discourage Felicity. "Something will turn up."

"He says he loves me, but . . ." For a moment Jed was afraid she was going to cry like the other time, but her British upper lip only quivered and held. "It's frightf'lly easier at home. English men lie so well you can tell when they're doing it. But Americans are so goddamned straightforward!"

For a moment Jed wished he could tell her about straightforward Denise, lying in Connecticut like a blanket of snow, but then the phone rang again. Felicity picked it up and said, "Mr. Lavery's wire," efficiently. "It's Dr. Parmalee," she told her boss.

He took the phone and said, "I'll talk to you later," to Felicity, then waited till she had gone out, this time so discouraged she closed the door without being told. "Hello?" he said into the phone.

"I thought you'd call me Sunday, Buddy Boy."

"Why?"

"Well, I'm part of the team, too," Og justified. "I'm interested. When are they getting married?"

"I don't exactly know, Og. They're taking a honeymoon first."

"Denise??" Og was terribly shocked. "I don't believe it! Not Denise. I know people like Elizabeth Taylor do things like—"

"I don't believe it either. And she lied to me. Told me she was going to Lake Placid."

"—that, but Denise is a . . . a . . ." Og could hardly think, ". . . a pillar of the community . . ."

"Can you imagine? Denise lying to me? Because of that clunk that I trained . . . ?"

"Well, he's really quite good-looking now, you know, slimmed down, disinfected feet . . ."

"It's not the way she thinks at all . . . Somebody got to Denise . . . somebody advised her . . ."

"Well, it was probably Lillian—that woman will do anything. Do you know what she said to me . . . ?"

"Lillian? Why would she listen to Lillian? Denise is a grown woman with almost-grown sons . . ."

"She called me a blithering bore . . . said she'd rather marry Nixon than come back to me. Now, how would Lillian get to meet Nixon? And then, of course, there's Pat to consider, too . . ."

"Why would Lillian offer advice on a thing like this?"

"Oh you know Lillian. Tells everybody everything she knows. That woman is a busybody. I'm finally through with her, Buddy Boy. I mean, a man can stand just so much and . . ."

Jed's voice cut through icily. "What did Lillian know?" he asked.

There was a sudden silence at the other end of the line.

"What did Lillian know, Og?"

"Oh . . . well . . ." Og stammered. "I don't know what Lillian knows . . . pokes her nose in everywhere . . . That was really why I walked out on her, Jed . . ."

"You were the first to hear that Barney proposed." Jed sounded like a DA reaching his summation. "You told me that Denise was going to accept because Lillian told you. What did you tell her?"

"I can't talk all morning, Jed, I've got a patient waiting."

"You told her that I found Barney, sent him to her!"

"I didn't—"

"Then why did Denise change her mind, Og?"

Og knew when he was cornered. There was nothing to do but take the blame and put it on Lillian. "I didn't tell! Lillian wormed it out of me. But I made her promise to keep her mouth shut."

"You stupid bastard!" Jed shrieked. "You blew the whole thing!"

"Now, wait a minute, Buddy Boy." Og sounded hurt.

"If you hadn't opened your mouth, she'd've just married him. Now she's going to the Club Gomorrah just to get revenge on me!"

"Gomorrah!" Og had never heard of it but he was shocked. He could see it all, wild parties, dancing girls, that sort of thing.

"She may never marry him! Just go on living with him. Or somebody else. Once you get started on a thing like that, it just kinda rolls on its own."

"It was Lillian's fault. Get mad at *her*."

"Get off my phone!" Jed thundered. "Don't call me again. Don't call Denise. Don't even call Lillian!" And, realizing he had the choice, Jed hung up. He buzzed Felicity and said, "If Dr. Parmalee calls, I've gone to Flint, Michigan. Indefinitely."

Flint. Og stared out of the Penn Central's grimy window at the South Bronx, a burnt-out, boarded-up area that reflected his mood. He didn't go to Flint. He just won't talk to me.

By the time the train had reached Westport, Og had figured that Jed wouldn't let Barney go on his own, had either gone or would be going to the Club Gomorrah, too. Og slogged through the slush of the parking lot toward his car, pleased with his powers of deduction. And how dare he blame me! He got into his car and slammed the door, his mind moving to Lillian, the cause of all his trouble. Now. Before. Always. He pulled out into the mass of homebound commuter traffic, bumper to bumper, his nightly irritation increased out of all proportion this night.

And why should Jed be mad? He has Maura. And Denise has Barney. And Lillian has whatever it is she wants. The only one who doesn't have anything is me, he thought. Well, I'm still young and I'm darned if I'm going to wait around for Lillian to realize I'm waiting around. No more. No more Dr. Nice Guy. By the time he pulled into his driveway, he had decided he was going to swing. Find a girl. Two girls. More. And what better place than the Club Gomorrah? Besides, in the warm, tropical atmosphere, he'd be able to see Jed and convince him he had done nothing wrong. Even be of help if Barney had a recurrence of his foot problem.

He locked the garage and went into the house, called a hasty hello to the children before he closed the kitchen door and, not even waiting to put his roast in the oven, went directly to the phone and dialed Lillian. His anger and his determination increased as the phone went *buzz, buzz*. When she finally picked up and said, "Hello?" he yelled, "You told!"

"Who is this?" Lillian asked sweetly.

"You know goddamn well who it is!"

For a moment, hearing the language, Lillian thought perhaps she didn't know who it was, but Og's voice continued, "You told Denise when you promised you wouldn't!"

"I never promised anything," she said.

"You've finally done it!" he yelled. "You have destroyed forever a friendship of years standing."

"We were never friends. We were married."

"I meant Jed!"

Lillian thought that over for a moment. "I'm sorry about that," she said. "You deserve each other."

"I just wanted you to know," Og announced, "I am not taking you back. Not if you were the last woman on the face of the earth!"

"It's a deal," his ex-wife answered. "Anything else?"

"I was faithful to you, Lillian, before, during, and after our marriage. But no more. I could've been running around like everyone else. I see a hundred girls a week in my office, younger than you, prettier than you, better figures than you!"

"But worse skin," she threw in.

"I can fix that!" he howled. "I will. I'm not too old yet. Men are younger than women. I can still salvage something. If everyone else is running off having fun, I'm going, too. You can take the children for next week!"

"I'll pencil them in for January fifteenth," she said. "I've got Denise's children for a week starting Saturday."

Ah, he thought. That's when they're all going. "That's when I'm leaving, too. That's when you're taking them! You want our kids at Denise's or Denise's kids here?"

"That depends," Lillian said. "Do you have any of your pot roast in the freezer?"

"I'll make you some," he said graciously. "With the carrots and potatoes?" Then, remembering he was angry, "It's time you shouldered some of the burden. I'm leaving Saturday!" He slammed the phone down and, to make sure he wouldn't change his mind, went and told the children.

Lillian started at the phone trying to assess the unlikely rebellion, going over in her mind what had been said. "Everyone else is running off and having fun," was the key phrase when she remembered it. She dialed Denise.

"Packing?" she asked when her friend answered.

"It's only Tuesday," Denise answered vaguely.

"It's out-of-season clothes."

"I'm not sure I'm going," Denise admitted, and outlined her second, third, and fourth thoughts on the subjects of respectability, insecurity, and Keith had a sore throat. And Jed would be in Flint.

"Why would Jed be going to Flint?" Lillian asked, hoping to lead her friend rather than tell her.

"Buick," Denise answered automatically and immediately vaulted on to Lillian's thought plane. "Are you suggesting Jed plans to follow me on an assignation?"

"Assignation is a word that went out with Jane Austen," Lillian informed her. "You are going there to—"

"Never mind why! I have extension phones! And besides, you're wrong. Jed wouldn't dare follow me."

"It was something Og said. I'll bet you my half of the next three commissions."

"I don't have time to talk to you now, Lillian. I can't remember where I put away my bathing suits."

Even though he had said goodbye to Maura at the apartment in the morning, Jed decided to call her once more at her office before he left for the plane. She had been strangely quiet all week, annoyed, he supposed, since he wouldn't take her with him. He had been extra sweet to her, took her out last night for a farewell dinner and to the biggest musical show on Broadway, a revival of a hit of the fifties. He realized during the overture he had seen the original production when she was two and was depressed all evening. When they got home, he tried. God knows he tried. But still . . . and now he was leaving her for a whole week in a city crowded with karate instructors, photographers, and who knew how many other men who were ready, willing and, ninety-nine out of a hundred, able.

"I'm sorry about last night," he said miserably when she answered.

"It's all right. I understand," she said understandingly. "It'll be okay when you get back."

"I love you," he said.
"I love you."
"See you a week from tomorrow."
"Get some rest," she answered and hung up.
I wonder what she means by that, he thought.

Jed stood in the hot, steamy Martinique airport in a line of young, athletic-looking, Gomorrah-bound revelers. They had already been pushed through customs by a GF, which stood for Gomorrah Friend and actually meant a harried employee of the club, and were waiting before the desk of another GF who would give them room assignments before they boarded the bus. Most of the GG's, Gomorrah Guests, seemed under thirty though there was a small minority who seemed to have attained the ripeness of thirty-five. Actually, all the women looked ripe and the men looked ready for the harvest. If anyone calls me "Pop," Jed decided, I will go to my room, drop my bags, head for the nude beach and swim straight for the horizon till I meet a shark.

"Mulligan," he told the GF at the desk, and after a moment's terror remembered his first name was, "John. I reserved a single."

"No singles," the GF snapped back. "You're in Cabin 32B. Your roommate came in on the early flight."

"I don't want a roommate," Jed said.

"He won't bother you," the GF said. "You just work out a schedule. He uses the room at odd hours, you use it even hours. Like that."

"But I reserved a single."

"No singles, no refunds. You want 32B or a seat on the return plane?"

Going to the bus, Jed decided at least the problem of Gaby was resolved. He could just tell her he didn't know there were no singles, which was perfectly true, and that he was stuck with a roommate.

He removed his raincoat and flannel shirt and sat sweating in his cold-climate turtleneck as the bus moved off, past the airfield, through lush green fields and then past expensive modern-looking houses. Farther out, they passed villages of extreme poverty, rag-clothed natives who seemed to live in torn-down Coca Cola signs, who depressed him as much as his young companions. The Gomorrah Guests were already getting to know each other. He could hear some of the dialogue.

"My name's Marvin."

"Don't you remember? You spilled a J and B on me at Elaine's?"

"I hate skiing. It's too tough to make it in a cast."

And from just behind him, "How about a quickie to get in shape before we hit the beach and see who's here?"

By the time the bus pulled through the expensively shrubbed gates of the Club Gomorrah, Jed was convinced he was the only man on the bus without an erection.

They dis-embussed to the strains of "I Can't Give You Anything But Love, Baby," played by a steel-drum band, all gleaming teeth and mallets. Between the band and the new arrivals, about twenty men stood surveying the group. They were deeply tanned and wore beads and what looked like brightly colored diapers artfully draped to expose a maximum of pubic hair. Jed felt overdressed. He noticed that as certain of the girls who had layered down to T-shirts or tank tops during the bus ride got off, they got a nice round of applause from the onlookers.

One of the appreciative welcomers advanced on them and announced he was a GF and herded them all up the path to a roofed-over dining enclosure where what looked like the Head Gomorrah Friend, being somewhat older, say thirty-six, and wearing, as befitted his dignity, a T-shirt and shorts whose inseam must have been half an inch, welcomed them. He explained mealtimes, the beaches, one nude, one semi-nude, the beads, which he told them were pop beads used for buying drinks or anything in the gift shop. "Put all your valuables in the safe," he advised them, "except for you fellas, you can keep your family jewels." This sally brought a major laugh. "There are no keys to the cabins," the head GF continued, "they only lock from the inside, which keeps your roommate out if you're a privacy freak." He wished them all a happy week and said he'd be there for any questions.

Jed went up and asked if he could get a GF to take his luggage to the cabin.

"The GF's are Gomorrah Friends, not servants. You treat them the way you would anybody whose home you were visiting. So don't come complaining to me if you see two of them playing tennis when you want a court. Just wait your turn," the head GF snapped and walked over to a new arrival who had been unable to sit down during his talk due to the tightness of her slacks. Jed hefted his bag, went to the office and bought an opera-length chain of pop beads and deposited his valuables.

Someone pointed him toward 32B and Jed started down the network of small paths toward the beach, crunching pebbles beneath his heavy, New York winter boots, perspiring freely under the tropic sun, which was just edging its way down to the horizon. The place was green and luxuriously laid out, like most of the guests, he thought. Frangipani and bougainvillea seemed to be everywhere. At the swimming pool, he saw several topless sun-worshippers. As he passed, one rose, casually draping her towel around her top, and started down a path. A man stopped in front of her at an intersection. She paused, looking at the man, who leaned forward and whispered something. The girl silently looked him up and down, checked her watch, and nodded. He gestured and took the girl down the path at right angles to the one she had been on. Evidently the local mating dance, Jed decided and, setting down his suitcase, pulled off his turtleneck. Bare-chested and carrying sweater, shirt, and raincoat, he lifted the suitcase and started after the couple. He watched as they swung off the path and up to a long cabin with two doors, to his left. She was already removing her towel as her host opened the door.

Like the other cabin, 32B, when Jed found it, had two doors, one marked A and one marked B. It was at the top of a slight rise overlooking the sea. I'm glad it's a good view, he thought, it may be all I'll get to see. He set down the suitcase and, wondering if his roommate was busy, knocked.

"It's open," a man's voice called.

Jed went in. The room was furnished like a Spartan motel. Clean, uncarpeted floors, two beds, two dressers, two closets. A door at the back which had to be the bathroom was open and he called, "I'm your roommate."

"Your bed's on the left," the man called. "I just got outa the shower."

"Okay," Jed called back, and dumped his clothes and suitcase on the left bed. He turned to see the man coming out of the bathroom toweling his hair dry. "Hi," he said. "I'm John Mulligan."

His roommate pulled the towel from his head, looked at Jed, and said, "Like hell you are!"

Jed stared into the surprised and angry eyes of his future father-in-law.

Chapter Thirteen

A bubbling stew of sexual tension, moral anxiety, and old-fashioned fury that her friends referred to as Denise Lavery got out of the Connecticut limousine at Kennedy. A porter who always looked for emotionally disturbed women because they tipped better grabbed her bag and checked it through, and Denise walked gamely toward the flight gate as though a firing squad awaited her there instead of Barney. Lillian had moved in Friday night and had built up Denise's anger at Jed enough to overcome her basic qualms about the moral position she was putting herself in. "I know there's a new morality," she had screamed at her friend at two in the morning. "I know everybody does it. I know I packed the pills, but still . . . you didn't know my mother," she had ended pitifully. But Lillian had reminded her that Jed was waiting, Jed had to be shown, and then there was Barney, sweet and lovable and wanting to marry her.

"So how can he take me away like a fallen woman?" she had cried.

"That was your idea," Lillian reminded her.

"Then how can I marry Barney? He's a fallen man."

At four, Lillian had shoved her into bed, and had pulled her out again at six, got her through the final packing and into the car and down to the limousine. Now she was on her own.

She saw Barney standing in front of the check-in desk at the gate, nervously staring down the corridor. He is handsome . . . he is sweet . . . and if Jed is there I'm going to make this a warm welcome, she decided and began to run.

Barney had arrived early and waited impatiently for the two women to show, hoping Gaby would be first. She still hadn't turned up and there, running down the corridor, was Denise. You can handle this, he told himself; if it can't be "practice makes perfect," then think "beginner's luck."

Maura sat inside the lounge at the gate in the seat closest to the plane ramp, which gave her a commanding view of the waiting crowd and anyone getting on the plane. She was still cold from the few minutes she had spent in the open in her T-shirt and raincoat, selected to cope with the expected warmth of Martinique but encouraging pneumonia before she could get out of New York.

For the fifth time, she removed the camera, loaded and ready to go, from the top of her tote bag and stared at the picture of Barney that Stan Zabriski had taken in Jed's office. Of course she knew Barney had been redone, but there was no one around who even vaguely resembled the picture. She slipped it and the camera back into the tote bag and wondered if she had made a mistake about the flight or if there was another Club Gomorrah on another island. What if she was going to the wrong place, she wondered. She sat back, noticing an older woman, quite attractive, running to the man who had been standing in front of the check-in desk for some time. As she watched, the woman threw her arms around the man and they embraced, the woman's head peering around the man's neck looking at the people in the lounge, the man looking down the corridor over her shoulder as if he was waiting for someone other than the woman in his arms. Obviously married to other people, Maura decided, and scared their little fling may be discovered.

Denise's eyes roamed the crowd. He isn't here. Was Lillian wrong? If she was, then I don't have to play this big scene. She disengaged herself from Barney.

She knows I'm looking for Gaby. That's why she's pulling away. If she knows Gaby is coming, what do I say to her? For God's sake, Gaby, he implored silently, get here and tell me.

"Hello."

"Hello."

Somebody opened the door to the plane ramp and boarding was announced.

"Shall we get on?" Denise asked, and continued silently, or should we just go home and forget the whole thing? She could see that Barney was hesitating, too, obviously didn't want to go, didn't want to marry her, was just doing it for Jed. For what reason? Old college chum she didn't know about? Jed pulled him out of the ice when he was seven and saved his life and hadn't mentioned it to her? And now Barney felt the repayment was too large for the debt.

Should we get on, Barney wondered. Once we're on, it'll be harder to see Gaby. And suppose she doesn't come? Well, I'll still have to go. Oh God! But at least Jed is there. He wouldn't have told me he was going and not gone? Or would he? But what reason can I give for not getting on? I have to go to the men's room? No. That's too personal. "Yes," he said, unable to think of another answer.

He took Denise's arm and they walked through the lounge, past a girl shivering in a raincoat who stared at them. Why? Who was she? The girl gave no sign of recognizing them and they went through the door, down the sloping umbilicus, and into the plane.

Denise, flicking her gloves nervously, watched as the plane filled. It was easy to distinguish between the Gomorrah-bound passengers, young, swingy, sex-mad, some with scuba equipment, and just plain people, middle-aged, sedate, fine, upstanding community members who were going to Martinique only for the sun or to smuggle something. After a few minutes it occurred to her that Barney, in the aisle seat, had said nothing.

"Is something wrong?" she asked.

"What?"

"You're so quiet."

"I'm terribly nervous in planes," he said.

You want to go home, she thought. You regret this whole thing as much as I do. Could I just be open and frank and ask him, she wondered, the gloves flicking double time now.

"Why are you doing that with your gloves?" he asked.

"I'm nervous in planes, too," she answered.

Gaby, gasping, ran down the long corridor, following the young man who had grabbed her suitcase and told her if they ran they might make the plane. It was entirely her mother's fault she was late, except for the traffic tie-up on the bridge. Suddenly, just as Gaby was about to call the taxi, her mother had demanded a complete explanation of the trip and gotten it by threatening not to baby-sit. And while Gaby waited for the cab, her mother had filled in the time telling her she was crazy and why.

They reached the gate and sped through. A young girl in a raincoat stood just outside the entrance to the plane and, as though she had been waiting for Gaby, got on behind her. As Gaby made her way down the aisle, still gasping from the effort of running, her purse, swinging from her arm, hit a man in the head. He cried out (her travel iron was in it), and when she looked down to say "Excuse me," she recognized Barney. They both said "Oh," and she rushed blindly to a seat in front and forgot to fasten her seat belt.

Barney heaved a sigh of relief and Denise said, "What's the matter?"

"Nothing," he answered. "I always feel more relaxed when they close the door."

"Yes," Denise said. "Closing the door is always the worst part," and flicked her gloves.

Not having slept, Jed could not be said to have awakened at seven. He just got up, quietly slipped on some shorts and a T-shirt and tiptoed out of the cabin considering it a major triumph he had not awakened Non-Dad. On the way to breakfast he decided it had been the worst night of his life. Then he remembered the first night he had been unable to perform with Maura and the subsequent nights and revised his assessment to the worst two weeks of his life.

For openers, his instant reaction on seeing the man was that Maura had sent her father to spy on him. However, Non-Dad's furious accusation that Jed had come to Gomorrah to two-time his daughter, and in particular, his rage when he mentioned their coming marriage, made Jed decide that was not the case. In the interests of postmarital family relations, he had quietly and calmly explained the reason for his visit. Non-Dad refused to believe him and said even if his ridiculous cock-and bull story was true, he could not get behind having his future son-in-law as a roommate in Hump Heaven, and stormed out. Ten minutes later he returned to announce the place was booked solid and he could not change rooms and Jed goddamn well better go with the flow and keep out of his way. By now, it had occurred to Jed to wonder where Non-Dad's roommate Jeannie was, but he decided, the atmosphere being what it was, not to ask.

He sneaked off to dinner where the maître d' racked him up at the last half-occupied table, then skulked around the disco popping his beads for drinks till he felt it was safe to go back to the cabin. His roommate was not there, and Jed went to bed to organize his problems.

First, he would have to forestall an appearance by Gaby, which his future father-in-law would certainly report to Maura. He was still trying to figure that one out when the couple in 32A slammed in and launched a noisy performance, apparently against the wall beside his bed, which made concentrating difficult. Hardly had the lady's happy cries dimmed down when Non-Dad returned and Jed pretended to be asleep. He decided to move on to methods of avoiding Denise and implementing the end of Barney's virginity when 32A began their three o'clock show, which was, if possible, noisier than the early one. At four, Non-Dad began to snore and at five 32A presented a very early matinee.

Jed ate a magnificent breakfast but was still unable to think. He went back to the cabin, happy to find it empty, and put on his bathing suit, deciding to get as much sun as possible before the arrival of the morning plane put him under house arrest. He ate a hearty lunch, figuring it might be his last meal for the week, and returned to the cabin at about the time he assumed the bus would arrive. The indefatigable couple next door were in midperformance as he lay down upon his bed to begin his vigil. I've had everything else, he thought, when is He going to send down the boils.

As soon as they were through customs the more respectable citizens went their own ways, and Denise felt less mortified when they got their cabin assignment at the GF's desk in the airport. The GF, of course, did not turn a sun-bleached hair. Barney helped her get her things to the bus and she was not sure whether his face was red from registering or exertion, but once they were seated, he patted her hand and said, "It's going to be a great week, darling," only swallowing a little on the endearment. (He had had one hasty, in-front-of-the-lavatory, out-of-the-side-of-the-mouth consultation with Gaby on the plane, telling her he could think of nothing to say. She had replied, "Keep telling her you love her and call her darling.")

Once the square chaff of the plane passengers had been separated from the swingy wheat of the Gomorrah Guests, Maura hung back, still searching for Barney, and wound up near the end of the line at the assignment desk. "Jane Mulligan," she told the GF.

"Nineteen-A," he said, checking his list, and looked to the woman behind her.

"Gaby Marcotte," the woman said, stopping Maura dead halfway through removing her raincoat.

"Nineteen-A," the GF said. "You're in with Miss Mulligan."

"You mean Mr. Mulligan," Gaby said, heart fluttering at the excitement of realizing that Jed had made some commitment, that she was right to have come despite what her mother said.

"I mean Miss Mulligan," the Gomorrah Friend replied testily, annoyed at being questioned, and gestured to the girl, who was still standing there.

Maura finished taking off her coat, thinking the lying son of a bitch! Putting on what she hoped was a friendly smile, she stared at Gaby, who was not exactly Farrah Fawcett but on the other hand was a long way from the Wicked Witch of the West.

Gaby took a quick look at the girl's T-shirt, which was decorated with a vastly enlarged picture of a screw, the head up at the neckline, the point down in a crevice slightly shallower than Grand Canyon, and turned back to the GF. "I booked a single," she said.

"There are no singles, sweetheart."

"But I came for—" She intended to say "a rest," but the GF interrupted.

"I know what you came for. You'll just have to work it out with your roommate."

"Don't worry about a thing," Miss Mulligan interjected. "You'll be surprised at the way this'll all work out."

The GF was already trying to get the attention of the man behind Gaby whose attention was firmly screwed on Miss Mulligan's T-shirt. Well, she's trying to be nice, Gaby thought. Maybe she plans on giving me her rejects. And what can I do anyway? "Fine," she said, and walked to the bus with her new roommate. They sat together on the bus but kept silent, each pursuing her own thoughts.

Last on, they were first off, and when Maura descended she got a standing ovation from the welcomers. Smiling graciously, she led Gaby toward the dining enclosure for the orientation lecture. Maura was stopped three times on the path by men in varying stages of undress who whispered something Gaby could not hear. Maura's reponse to all was a charming laugh, a dismissing nod of the head and a return to the triumphal march. Nobody stopped Gaby. She began to think her mother was right, she should not have come. But right, as usual, for the wrong reasons.

It took a while for them to reach their cabin. Maura was stopped by men four times along the path but was smart enough to get the third to carry her baggage and the fourth to carry Gaby's. It then took a while to get the men out of the cabin, and they had just opened their bags to unpack when Barney burst in without knocking.

"What'll I *do* with her?" he asked urgently, without preamble.

"What happened to her?" Gaby asked, alarmed.

"Nothing. She's unpacking."

"This is my roommate, Miss Mulligan," Gaby said, collecting her thoughts. "Barney Warburton," she introduced.

The girl said, "My God!" and surprised that Miss Screw T-Shirt reacted that strongly to the man, Gaby took a closer look at Barney. He was still in his New York shirtsleeves but he really was quite attractive, looked at through the eyes of a stranger.

"Where's Jed?" Barney asked, ignoring the girl.

"I don't know," Gaby said. "Why don't you go play tennis?"

"Where will you be?"

"Well . . . I want to unpack. I want to see Jed. Then maybe I'll go for a swim."

"Which beach?" he demanded.

"The bathing-suit one."

"That's where I'll take her. Hurry," he said and started for the door.

"Just a second," Miss Mulligan said, pulling a camera from her tote bag.

"What?" Barney asked.

"I just wanted to get a picture," Maura said, taking his arm and leading him out of the cabin.

"Of me?" he asked, surprised.

"I just love to take pictures, pictures, pictures," Maura said, batting her lashes. "For my memory book," she added as she pushed him against the wall and backed up a few paces and snapped the shutter.

"But—" he said.

"One more. For a safety," she called, moving the film ahead. "Smile . . . tummy in." Barney did as he was told and the girl said, "Thanks. We'll get a bathing-suit shot later."

He looked back in the cabin and said to Gaby, "Please hurry. I'm so nervous." And sped off.

Gaby watched the girl reenter the cabin, drop the camera on the bed, and pull off her T-shirt. Hastily, she averted her eyes for the sake of her ego and went over and closed the door. God, she prayed, let there be better-looking men around. If that girl is throwing her T-shirt at Barney, Denise won't stand a chance. "What are you going to do?" she asked lightly, opening her bureau, checking the drawer for dust.

"Swim," Maura had decided, figuring there'd be no action till nightfall and the lucky circumstance of Gaby being her roommate would make it easy to check on the principals. Jed would be hiding in his room anyway and she might as well get the fringe benefit of the tropic sun while she decided what to do about Gaby. "The nude beach," she added.

Gaby spun around. "You better wear something to get there," she said.

"I know," Maura told her and put on her pop beads.

"I'll be back in a minute," Gaby said, deciding she better see Jed at once.

She had to go back to the office to get Jed's room number, then sped down the shell-lined paths following the signs. As she passed Cabin 24, a grey-haired man, his crotch wrapped in the ubiquitous brightly colored diaper all the men in Gomorrah seemed to wear, appeared before her in the path and blocked her way. She was actually rather relieved. The man leaned over, the stained-glass amulet he wore on a link chain around his neck swinging over his pudgy tummy, and whispered an indecent suggestion in her ear. All I had to do was get away from that girl, Gaby thought and, feeling the man had restored her ego, decided not to slap him. "Maybe later," she said, trying to be polite, and hurried around him down the path.

The door marked 32B opened a crack and Jed's eye peered out at her. Quickly, he pulled her in and slammed the door.

"Did anyone see you come in here?" he asked.

"Nobody knows me," she answered logically. "Oh Jed," she continued warmly, either in relief at seeing him again or excitement in seeing him clothed only in one of the diapers. "It's terrible!"

"What?" he asked, alarmed. "Didn't Denise come?"

"They're swimming," she dismissed them quickly. "I mean, I have a roommate."

"Me too." She was staring at his new swim suit. "It's called a niamu," he said. "Tahitian. I got it in the gift shop."

She pulled her eyes away, pushing them up past the deep chest and muscular arms, and made them look into the craggy, appealing face. "I didn't want a roommate," certainly not the one I've got, she thought. "I was hoping this week would be a . . . a revelation for us all."

She looked so genuinely upset that he put his hands comfortingly on her shoulders. As he said, with all the sincerity he could muster, "Don't worry. It will be," the door opened and Non-Dad burst in and said, "Aha!"

Gaby turned and saw the man in the stained-glass amulet, who looked surprised when he saw it was she. "How did you know my room number?" he asked.

"I didn't," she answered, confused.

He turned to Jed and said, "Aha!" again. Jed dropped his hands from Gaby's shoulders. "You lied to me," the man screamed. "That whole cockamamie story! You're here looking for what everybody else is looking for! And," he thundered with an imperious gesture toward Gaby, "I saw that one first!"

"I did not lie," Jed said, dignity welling from his niamu upward. "This is Mrs. Marcotte. The team's line coach." He turned to Gaby and said, "May I present Maura's father?"

Gaby turned pale. "Why is he your roommate?" she asked.

Jed shrugged. "Just lucky, I guess."

"I better get back to Barney," Gaby said, and raced for the door. She stumbled up the path in her city high heels wondering, is that man here to protect Maura's interests? It's impossible that they just happened to be roommates. But if he's here for his daughter, why did he make a pass at me? Is Jed lying to me? Leading me on? Except, she thought at the door of her own cabin, he didn't lead me on. I led myself. Oh my God, what am I doing here?

Miss Mulligan had sailed on, leaving a wake of clothing strewn around the room. What do I do? Gaby asked herself and, remembering Barney, decided not to unpack anything but a bathing suit and get to the beach.

She changed quickly, remembered the suntan lotion and a paperback book to serve as a spy cover, and raced out of the cabin. There were two city-clothed men carrying suitcases on the path. "Is this Cabin 19?" one called.

"Yes," she answered, and as they came closer was startled to hear the same man address her as "Mrs. Marcotte!"

Shielding her eyes to see, she recognized him. "Dr. Parmalee! What are you doing here?"

"Checking into 19B," he told her.

"But you can't! Denise will see you!"

"I thought of that," he answered with a do-you-think-I'm-a-child attitude? "But there is no earthly reason why I shouldn't just happen to be here. I decided I needed a little sun. If I should see Denise, I'll take care of it," he said reassuringly.

Rattled now beyond the bounds of politeness, Gaby hissed. "You idiot! You'll ruin everything!"

"Now see here, Buddy Girl"—Og sounded affronted—"I worked on this project, too, and I've been getting the short end of the stick. From Jed, from Lillian—"

"Who's Lillian?" Gaby demanded.

"My wife. No," Og corrected, "my ex-wife. For good. From now on, I'm going to be a good-time Charlie too. Besides, Jed wouldn't talk to me. I thought I'd just come down and straighten things out." His tone softened. "We've been best friends for twelve years, you know."

Gaby emitted an eerie sound of frustrated rage, learned from Liza on the *My Fair Lady* album, and started around Og down the path.

"Oh," he said, remembering his manners, "this is my roommate—"

Before he got to the man's name, Gaby snapped, "I've met enough people for one day," and, ignoring the other man, headed toward the beach.

Halfway there, she wondered if she should go back and tell Jed that Og was here. Then she decided, no, Maura's father will probably still be there and I don't want to see him. Should I tell Barney? was her next thought. No, again, it will only make him more nervous. She had reached the beach and, shading her eyes, scanned the sand strewn with baking humanity for the two bodies that had brought her to this unlikely place. After a moment, she saw them. Denise lay prone in the sun, Barney on a towel beside her, bouncing up every ten seconds to check the area for Gaby. On the third bounce he saw her and, looking nervously toward Denise to make sure her eyes were closed, waved frantically.

Sighing, Gaby picked her way toward them wondering, what am I doing here? Why is a woman my age, the mother of two, serving as midwife at the deflowering of a forty-one-year-old actuary?

Clad in the new cabana set with matching sandals he had just bought at Alexander's, Og strode purposefully toward the nude beach. The undeserved rudeness he had suffered at the hands of Mrs. Marcotte had firmed his resolve and rekindled his anger at Jed. Let him stew in his own juice, Og thought. I'm here to have fun, and let whoever I know from Westport who sees me, beware. He passed the swimming pool, noting several young ladies sunning themselves topless and thought, not good enough. From now on, for Ogden Parmalee, it's all or nothing.

The nude beach was the farthest stretch of sand in Club Gomorrah, the line of demarcation between nude and whatever they called the rest of it a small copse of palm trees. Og moved through them and cast an anxious eye over the scene. Heavily tanned bodies splashed in the surf. In the near distance a game of co-ed volleyball was in progress. Naked couples shared blankets beneath the tropic sun, some starkly laid out improving their already mahogany color; others, less careful of shadow marks, were variously entwined in each other. I have nothing to be embarrassed about, he told himself. I am a doctor. He ambled past the volleyball game, admiring the contestants' form, and on up almost to the end of the beach. An admirably proportioned young lady lay soaking in the sun, alone, her eyes protected by cotton pads.

Now how did one open a conversation, Og thought. Remember, you're a swinger. "Beautiful here, isn't it?" he said, pleased with the facility of his approach.

The young lady lifted one firm, round arm and pulled one pad away from one eye. The eye looked at him and the girl nodded her eyelid, replaced the cotton, and resumed her original position.

"Mind if I join you?" Og asked.

"You're getting your shadow on me," she said without moving.

Hastily he moved to her other side, pleased with how well it was going. Lowering his voice to what he presumed was a romantic pitch, he breathed, "Do you mind if I say you have magnificent skin?" Her hand came up again, removed the other pad, and that eye stared at him. "But you have to be careful about exposing yourself," he warned her.

"It's the nude beach," she said.

"I meant to the sun. I'm a doctor," he explained.

"It's the nude beach," she said again, the one exposed eye commenting on his cabana set.

An obvious invitation, Og thought. She's intrigued by my body. Taking a deep breath, he removed the top of the cabana set. The girl replaced the cotton pad and he took off his trunks, allowing himself to breathe out again while she was cotton-blinded. He sat down beside her, careful not to let his shadow fall across her body. He tried to remember any old Cary Grant movie for his next move. A young couple came from somewhere behind them, walking toward the sea.

"In the water?" the girl said, uncertainly, as they passed.

"I tried it last night," the boy answered. "It's the greatest."

"I'd hate to, you know . . . work up to the point and discover there was an undertow."

Og watched them plunge into the surf, swim past the breakers, and settle neck-deep in the ocean. The girl was still silent. Perhaps asleep? Obviously, she felt at home with him. But, I better say something, he thought. "You come here often?"

The girl removed both cotton pads, looked at him, and rolled over on her stomach, without speaking. Shy, Og thought. He stared over the glorious mound she made back to the end of the beach. A grey-haired man had left the volleyball game and was walking in their direction carrying a long strip of gaily colored cloth and what looked in the distance like a stained-glass Christmas tree ornament. Og wondered if it would be too blatant to say, "Busy for dinner?" and before he could decide was distracted by a woman's cry from the ocean. He turned and saw the young couple who had passed him moments before. They were on the crest of a wave. The young man seemed to be riding the girl to shore. These crazy kids and their surfing, Og thought. A man's voice beside him said, "I really groove on this view."

Og looked up to see the grey-haired man staring down at the sumptuous rise of the young lady's gluteus maximus. "You're getting your shadow on me," the object of his contemplation complained again and rolled over to look up at the source of sun blockage. Then she gasped, obviously stunned.

"You!" the man said.

"Daddy! What are you doing here?" the girl screeched and rose, hastily covering herself as best she could with a towel.

"Who is that man?" Daddy shouted angrily, pointing to Og with one hand, trying to cover himself with the other.

"I don't know. Some drip," the girl dismissed the question. "Is Jeannie with you?"

"I'm Dr. Ogden Parmalee," Og said rather formally, rising, wishing he had his card with him, but they were not listening.

The grey-haired father, seemingly further enraged by his daughter's question, was howling, "Didn't you know she left me?" as he desperately tried to wrap the gaily colored cloth through his legs and around his hips.

"Left you?"

"All your goddamn talk about marriage. She said if you could get married, I better goddamn well marry her or she was splitting!"

Og felt distinctly in the way, and reached down for the jacket of his cabana set.

"How the hell do you wrap these damn niamus?" the father asked the sea breeze.

"I don't wear them," Og answered. "You really shouldn't expose the pubic regions in the tropic sun." The man looked at him, fury steaming from his eyes, "They're sensitive," Og explained.

"Get the hell outa here," the man yelled and, turning back to his daughter: "A church wedding she wanted!"

"But why did you come here?" the girl cried over her towel.

"I couldn't stay in the apartment alone. The plants kept dying!"

At least the loss of his young mistress had restored her father's vocabulary, Maura thought, and was distracted by a man's voice saying, "So there you are." All three whirled in the direction of the sound.

"Oh," Maura gasped. "What are you doing here?"

"Protecting my investment," he smiled.

"Who is THAT one?" the father cried apoplectically. "And what's his investment?"

"He's my roommate," Og said, slightly befuddled.

"I don't even know who you are," the father bellowed.

"This is Will Trolander. Will, my daddy." Maura introduced the two naked men, admiring, despite everything, her editor's trim, young body and wondering what she could do to keep its arrival unknown to Jed and still keep friendly enough to get her book published. Except, Jed lied to me, she suddenly remembered, stealing a further, furtive look at Will's editorial equipment.

"You ruined my life!" her father cried, ignoring Will's outstretched hand. "All your talk about a big wedding with the other one and you're still screwing around!"

"I'm not. I'd no idea Will would be here. There's nothing between us except business!" Feeling now she ought to look more like an author, she reached for the tea-bag-size bottom of her bikini and, in attempting to put it on behind the towel, lost her balance and dropped both.

"Cover yourself!" Her father spun his body between her and the two men and his niamu slipped back into a strip of cloth. "Anybody got a safety pin?" he asked, trying to rewrap himself. Og held out the bottom of his cabana set to the man, always sympathetic to a father in distress, but the man's furious self-pity had again overtaken his modesty and he turned back to the girl. "And you don't think that son of a bitch is going to marry you, do you?"

Shut up, Maura thought, slipping into the bikini bottom, you're dropping my options in every direction.

"Well, he's here!" her father announced, as she hadn't

spoken. "Here. In make-out paradise. Did you know that, Miss Big Wedding Reception?"

"I know Jed's here," Maura answered, by now stung to anger at her big-mouthed father. "How do you know?"

"He's my goddamn roommate!" In total fury, the man threw the slippery niamu to the sand and grabbed for Og's shorts.

Jed, Og thought. If Jed is her fiancé, then any fool can tell this is Maura, and grabbed his shorts back. "What's your cabin number?" he asked.

"Thirty-two-B. Who the hell are you?"

Og decided it would be foolish to answer, and while he hesitated, his roommate, seeing the girl had settled the top of her bikini and looked calmer, asked, "How's the book going?"

"Almost at the climax," she answered.

Og said, "Excuse me," and ran off clutching his shorts, knowing he must warn Jed that Maura was here.

"I can explain everything," Maura said to anyone who wanted to listen and Og, at some distance, heard the father yelling, "He told me some cock-and-bull story, but he had a woman in the room this morning . . ."

Even if Jed is angry, Og thought, the importance of telling him Maura was here would more than suffice to bring them together. But should he tell Jed about the young man who said he had an investment in Maura? And he seemed such a clean-cut boy, taking a shower the moment we checked in, Og remembered. He turned to look back at the group. They were coming in his direction, Maura and her father still yelling at each other as the young man tried to help the older one wrap the niamu. Young people have no respect these days, Og thought, and rushed into the palm trees, where he could have privacy to put on his shorts. He realized when he reached the rocky path that he'd forgotten his matching sandals, but decided not to go back and face Maura again. Maybe she'll forget me, he thought. If she tells Jed I made a pass at her . . . but that was too awful to contemplate and he ran on to Cabin 32B.

"Arrrragggggh!" Jed screamed like one demented when he opened the door and saw Og. "Get away from me. Go home. What have I done to deserve this?"

"But—" Og began, and found himself facing the slammed door. "Okay, Buddy Boy," he said with injured dignity, "if that's the way you feel . . ." and Jed heard his retreating footsteps crunching on the gravel. He locked the door and, feeling that he might go mad, lifted his head and bellowed, "Arrrragggggh!" once more, then hurled himself on his bed.

Through the wall, practically in his ear, a woman's voice asked, "What was that?" and he heard a low mumbled answer. "But I never heard anything like that," the woman's voice continued. "What are they doing? Maybe they know something we don't know. Maybe we should ask them over?" There was another low-toned comment, then a crash of bed springs and a high-pitched giggle from the woman.

"Goddamn it! I can't stand this anymore!" Jed said aloud to himself and, knowing it was cabin fever, knowing no matter what, he had to get out, pushed himself from the bed and hurtled to the door. He opened it to find the enraged figure of his roommate, fist upraised to knock.

"Get back in there!" Non-Dad snarled, and shoved him back with a quick punch in the stomach.

"I've got to get out!"

"You're always in this cabin except when I want you here," Non-Dad stormed back. "How the hell do you expect me to get laid?"

"Take it now. For as long as you want."

But Non-Dad was beyond listening. "Do you know who came in on the plane?"

Jed was startled. "Yes. But you don't even know Og."

"Og? What's Og?"

"Never mind," Jed said and, as they both registered a high-pitched female keen from the next room, started for the door again. Non-Dad pushed him back.

"Maura is here," Non-Dad trumpeted.

"Maura? Oh my God!" He rushed at his father-in-law-to-be, intending to grab him by the lapels except there weren't any. "Did you tell her about Gaby?" he demanded, his hands flapping around with no place to grab. For a moment, Non-Dad seemed not to know how to handle the question and, pressing his advantage, Jed grabbed him by the pop beads. They popped and he felt foolish. "Does Denise know?" he demanded as sternly as he could in the circumstances.

"Denise? Gaby? Og?" Non-Dad repeated the names apoplectically. "What the hell have you got here? A harem? No wonder you're in the room all day!"

"I've got to see her," Jed yelled and started for the door.

"You come back here and explain this," his future father-in-law rasped, grabbing Jed from behind, his forearm crushing Jed's Adam's apple.

"Let go . . ." he yelled, and they grappled ineffectually for a moment.

"Can we have a little quiet in there?" a man's voice called through the wall.

"Screw you!" Non-Dad yelled back, and while his attention was diverted, Jed broke from his grasp and pulled open the door. Directly in front of him, a little distance away on the path from the beach, he saw Denise and Barney. Some thirty yards behind them Gaby was ostentatiously reading a paperback as she walked along. He slammed the door shut and faced the wild-bull roommate. "That's better," Non-Dad gasped.

"Button your niamu. Have you no sense of decency?" Jed asked coolly.

Pulling at the cotton band hopelessly, the man said regally, "Maybe I haven't been much of a father to that girl up to now, but so help me God, I'll stop her from marrying a middle-aged cocksman like you if it's the last thing I do."

"You can't. She loves me!"

"Then why did a young guy—if he's twenty-six it's a lot," he interpolated, rubbing it in sadistically, "follow her all the way from New York here?"

"Rod?" Jed asked turning pale beneath yesterday's suntan.

"Rod? Who's Rod?" Non-Dad asked, turning red on top of today's. "This one's called Will."

"Will? Who's Will?"

Barney, shivering in his bathing suit in the warm, sunlit cabin, looked at the array of cosmetics and curlers and brushes and combs on top of Denise's bureau and listened to the sound of water from the bathroom where she was taking her shower. Mommy never needed that many things, he thought. I thought Denise was more a . . . a natural beauty.

What happens now? he wondered. He had managed earlier to put on his bathing suit in the room while she put hers on in the bathroom, but now? She was inside, showering, probably completely undressed. Would they go to dinner first? Or should he make advances before dinner? Or might she make the advances herself, considering they were living in sin? Only for seven sun-filled days and six romantic nights, but still . . . he added hastily when the phrase upset him. It wasn't that he didn't want to . . . He searched for a euphemism even in the privacy of his own mind and found . . . do it with Denise. He wanted to. Had wanted to for weeks. For years, even before he met her. But . . . He knew he was starting late, knew she was accustomed to a slick, assured man like Jed . . . What if he bungled? No, on the whole, it would be better after dinner. So what do I do now? he asked himself. Can I get dressed before she comes out? The water was still going. Quickly he assembled a clean pair of shorts, a sports shirt, and slacks on the bed and pulled off his damp bathing suit. Towel! he thought. They're all in the bathroom. He ran to his bureau and got two handkerchiefs, using them to dry himself as best he could. The water stopped and he dropped both hankies on the floor and pulled on the shorts, the slacks, and was just buttoning the shirt when she came out.

She wore panties and a bra and her skin was glowing

from the sun, the water, the towel, whatever. She looked sensational and his hands were like blocks of ice. "Don't you want a shower?" she asked.

"Later," he answered, husky-voiced. "It's bad right after the sun. If you have a burn it brings it out." He thought he remembered having heard that. She shrugged and walked closer to him, put her hands on his shoulders. Now? he screamed silently. I'm not ready yet.

"Are you glad we came away together, Barney?" she asked.

"Yes," he strangled out.

"So am I," she said and snuggled into him.

He put his hands lightly on her back. "Hold me," she whispered.

"My hands are so cold."

"I don't care," she answered and kissed him.

She felt warm and pliable and altogether nice, and down below he felt a stirring, a hardening. Afraid that she might feel it too, he jumped back.

"What is it?" she asked.

"I'm very hungry," he replied.

"You're right," she said, trying to keep her voice light. "Later, there'll be more time. We mustn't rush it the first time. Not after waiting so long."

"No," he gasped out.

Denise stared at him, thinking, well, that little-boy naïvete is one of the things I love about him, but enough is enough. She dressed quickly and determined to eat lightly and fast.

Gaby had rushed through her shower, done the best she could with her hair, slapped on the make-up, one of the false lashes was already slipping, and dressed and was watching through the window before Miss Mulligan got back from the beach with a nice-looking young redheaded man who went into 19B. Miss Mulligan looked at Gaby strangely when she saw her staring through the window, and all she could think of to say was. "I'm watching the sunset," although they faced east. Miss Mulligan went into the shower and Gaby returned to her vigil. In a moment of inspired improvisation just before they left the beach, Barney had managed to ask her cabin number and say he'd walk Denise past her cabin on the way to dinner so she could follow and be at the same table. His distress by late afternoon was so evident she had hastily agreed.

Just as Miss Mulligan came out of the shower, starkers, of course, Gaby observed the happy couple to the left of the window frame. "I'll just run along to dinner," she said.

"Wait a sec. I'll go with you."

"Well . . ." Gaby cast a hasty glance out of the window. They were walking rather quickly. "You're not dressed," she told her roommate. Instead of answering, Miss Mulligan pulled on some shorts and a T-shirt, shook out her long, dark hair and, walking to the door, opened it.

What's even worse, Gaby thought as they started down the path, she looks better than I do.

"Who's Jed?" Will asked, slipping into his loafers and running a comb through his red hair.

"Jed who?" Og countered carefully, tying his shoelaces.

"I don't know. Maura mentioned him. On the beach."

Og considered trying, "Who's Maura?" and thought that was too much. "Oh, that girl," he said, as if recalling her vaguely. "I only met her today. I thought you knew her," he added, feeling like that rumpled television detective.

"Slightly," Will said and dropped his comb on the bureau.

"Odd," Og said, underlining it heavily, "she's in the next cabin."

"Convenient." Will looked at him and smiled. "How do you like her roommate?" he asked.

"I've known her for some time," Og answered without answering.

"Let's fix it so you get to know her better," the redheaded boy said conspiratorially.

Shocking, Og thought, loose-moraled, and then remembered he too, was a swinger. "Not a bad idea," he said, trying to sound mature and lascivious but still a pillar of the AMA. They heard the door on the other side of the cabin swing shut.

"Let's go," Will said.

"Where?"

"They just left for dinner. Let's follow them and get the same table."

Nice young man, Og thought, following his roommate out. Ingenious. Except, Maura's Jed's girl. He shouldn't be ingenious about her.

The Gomorrah Friend maître d' was stationed at the entrance to the roofed-over dining terrace slotting arriving diners in the next empty chair at the tables for eight beginning at the far end of the room. It was regimentation, but it worked. By the time the last chair in the last table was filled, the first chair at the first table was empty, and he enjoyed shoving the guests around like so many backgammon pieces. Barney and Denise were among the first arrivals and the maître d' walked them through the banks of snowy-white tablecloths, fresh flowers centered on each, to Table Two, where a young couple had just settled and were pouring themselves wine from waiting carafes.

Quickly, Denise scanned the only other occupied table looking for Jed. Sure she would see him at dinner, but not yet sure how she would act, she positioned herself in a chair that commanded a view of the entire room. "We're Denise and Barney," she told the young couple, still too uptight to go into last names. "Eddie and Karen," the boy answered in kind, and a woman roughly Denise's age came up to the table with a young girl who looked like a Vic Tanney commercial.

Barney leaped to his feet and held out his hand to the older woman. "Barney Warburton," he said, "and this is Mrs. Lavery." Denise could have killed him.

"How do you do?" the woman said elaborately. "I'm

Gaby Marcotte," and Denise could have sworn she saw her wink at Barney as she sat down.

"Jane Mulligan," the centerfold announced and sat beside her.

"I'm Karen and he's Eddie," the young woman announced truculently, making it sound like "He's mine."

"Well, well, well, where are you folks from?" Barney asked Mrs. Marcotte, establishing the fact he didn't know.

Denise thought the woman looked as though she didn't like the question, but answered, "Riverdale," and Miss Mulligan laughed. Denise looked to see why and, catching her eye, the girl serioused up and said, "What do we do about food?"

"When the table's full, the waiter comes," Eddie told her with a personable smile.

"I'd like some more wine," Karen announced loudly.

When Og saw Denise at the table they were being led to, he stopped short, causing Will to crash into him. "Sorry," Og mumbled and decided daringly, so what? I have a perfect right to be here, and, assuming a look he hoped was startled, cried, "Denise! What a surprise to see you!"

"Yes," she agreed, wondering if Jed had sent Og in his place. But wouldn't Lillian have known? And who was the man behind Og? Meanwhile Barney had leaped to his feet again and was introducing himself to Og rather hastily, and the girl in the distended T-shirt was staring at the skin doctor. Denise began to feel there were forces at work she did not understand, but decided if Og were here for Jed, she had better start the performance she had planned for her ex.

"Og's my neighbor in Westport, darling," she said to Barney and pulled him down.

Barney said, "What a coincidence," heartily, and Denise noticed he was sweating. A GF waiter brought a huge tureen of soup, looked around the table, and set it in front of Barney. "You be mother," he said, handed him a ladle, and left, walking past Og, who had bent toward the T-shirt and was saying, "What happened this afternoon was all a mistake."

What happened? Denise wondered, but the girl was paying no attention to Og. Instead she was making what looked like signals at the redheaded man with him. The young man spoke to Jane Mulligan. "Hello Maura," he said. The Marcotte woman, who was sipping some wine, suddenly choked on it and spun toward the girl beside her.

"Careful," the girl said, smiling, and took the glass from Mrs. Marcotte, who was red in the face and coughing. Barney, next to her, began to pound Mrs. Marcotte on the back. Og said, "Hands to the sky," to her and sat down. Mrs. Marcotte gave Barney a warning glance, and he left off pounding. The red-haired man sat down. Mrs. Marcotte stared at the girl in the T-shirt.

"I thought you said your name was Jane," Karen said.

Maura/Jane wondered how to field it. Obviously Gaby and Barney and Og knew who Maura was. Did Denise? And did it matter to Will if she was Jane? "Maura is my pen name," she said.

Eddie leaned across the red-haired boy and Og to say, "Oh? You're a writer?"

Shoving him back, the redhead said firmly, "I'm publishing her book."

Karen leaned across Eddie to the publisher. Exuding charm, she asked, "What's it about?"

"It's called, *How to Marry Off Your Wife,*" Will told her. "It shows how a divorced guy gets out from under alimony by finding a guy for his wife, fixing him up, and then getting them together."

Denise became aware of a blinding light around the table that revealed everything, starting with the true identity of the girl in the T-shirt. It was as though she could see everything that was happening in every direction although she sat perfectly still, and with a corner of her mind she tried to remember if her will was in order and wondered if Lillian was the one to break the news of her death to the children. Barney had crumpled, head in hands, to the table, narrowly missing the soup. Og, after a hasty, too-late restraining gesture to the young publisher, put his napkin over his face, and even the Marcotte woman looked upset, though she was the one puzzle-piece Denise could not fit in.

Karen, oblivious to everything but the two young men, smiled past her escort to the new prospect and said, "I'll bet it'll be a sensation."

"It is already," the authoress murmured.

For what seemed like an eternity, under his napkin, Og heard nothing. Then, knowing it was unwise, as compulsive as Pandora, he lowered his linen veil slowly and looked around. It was as though the other seven were frozen.

"What happened?" the little blonde girl on his right asked. There was something familiar about her. "I saw you surfing at the beach today," Og said suddenly. "Exciting. I really enjoyed watching."

The girl turned beet-red and her escort rose, balling his fist threateningly, moving behind Will to stand over Og. "Is that a crack?" he asked ominously.

The waiter returned and said cheerfully, "Finished with your soup? I'll take your orders."

Suddenly, as if magically released from a spell, the Marcotte woman burst into tears, jumped up, and stumbled from the table. Maura, Jed's girl, it was now obvious to Denise, dropped her napkin and started after her.

"Maura!" Will called, jumping up and accidentally grinding his chair into Eddie's foot.

"Big-mouth!" Maura called over her shoulder. "I think you blew the finish of the book!" and hurried after Gaby, sure she was on her way to Jed and determined to prevent it.

"What the hell's the matter with you people?" the enraged Eddie cried, and threw a punch at Will, who was already chasing after Maura. He hit Og, who was just rising. Blood spurted from his lip.

"Oh my God! Get a doctor!" Karen cried.

"I am a doctor," Og said, and fled after Will.

"And what would you like for dessert?" the waiter asked.

Karen threw down her napkin and, eyes flashing, yelled at Eddie, "You coward! Hitting a man twice your age!"

He followed her out of the room saying, "He made a crack about us surfing."

"Just coffee," Denise told the waiter, who bowed and left. Barney looked at her. "I knew," she said quietly. "About everything except the book." He just stared at her, unable to speak. "I don't really care. You're a good man, Barney." And there in the dining room, she kissed him. "Let's go back to the room," she whispered.

It was too much for him, knowing all those people knew why they were here and what they could be doing in the room; knowing Denise knew all about the training, the day he went to look her over disguised as Mulligan, all of it. She is very understanding, he thought, I could be happy with her. Everything'll be fine, but first, "I think I need a drink," he said.

Denise nodded, and as the waiter served the coffee they got up and went to the bar.

One drink was not enough, and after the third, Barney decided he should show Denise how well he did the hustle. "I learned for you," he told her, "all for you." They went on to the disco. Through the night, his vivacity, his daring on the dance floor increased in direct ratio to his nerves. It was almost midnight by the time he had popped all his beads and Denise persuaded him to return to the cabin. Along the way, they passed Cabin 19 and Barney had the impression the cabin was brilliantly lit, both doors were open, and there was a great deal of going back and forth and angry shouting between the rooms.

Jed sat on the bed in his dark cabin and counted twelve twangs of the bedspring behind the wall. It must be midnight, he thought, and I'm starving. And nobody has come to tell me what's happening. Well, I know what's happening to Barney. Rising, he paced the small area. He's in his cabin with Denise, going through his graduation exercises. All right, that's what I wanted, that's what I got. He was annoyed that the thought annoyed him. But Maura? Where is she? And who the hell is Will and where is he? He had a sinking feeling he knew where they both were, because Maura had to be angry with him. Otherwise, why would she follow him here? And Og! Og is a walking catastrophe and he's bound to introduce Maura to Gaby . . . except he doesn't know Maura. But he'll find her, he's that kinda guy. And anyway, I introduced her father to Gaby and he hates me. How dare he hate me? He's the cause of all my problems. Or is Og? And where the hell is Gaby? She could at least come and tell me what's happening. Or bring me a sandwich.

Chapter Fourteen

First Maura was aware of being hungry, then aware she was awake. Of course, I never got any dinner last night, she thought. Turning cautiously on one arm, she looked across the cabin. Gaby was faced to the wall, but her regular breathing told Maura she was still asleep. Good, she thought, and rose as quietly as possible, found a T-shirt and shorts, decided not to brush her teeth, to take no chance on waking the woman.

Maura knew she was physically more attractive than Gaby, but she could still recognize the threat the woman was. She was more mature, which was different than being older, more nearly like Jed's first wife, Maura realized, now that she'd seen Denise. She was the kind of woman he was used to and therein lay the danger. And there were all the lies Jed had told her about Gaby, suggesting he was not unaware of her as a woman. If I want to keep Jed, I have to keep an eye on Gaby. Her stomach growled noisily and she tiptoed to the door, carefully unlocking it, and left, not even closing it fully for fear the click of the latch would wake her roommate. I want her to sleep till I get back, she thought. All I need is coffee, then I can figure my next move.

As soon as she left the cabin, Gaby got up, thankful that as the mother of small children she had gained expertise in feigning sleep. She did not want to have to talk to Maura. Having seen the enemy in battle dress, or out of it, as it were, and discovered last night at that awful dinner that she was the enemy, Gaby accepted defeat. Maura had all the weapons. Youth, beauty, and tank turrets that were unassailable. As for the noble experiment, now that Denise knew all, there wasn't a prayer of its success. Which at least left Maura unmarried as well. The only decision left was whether to go home today or stay out the week and salvage a suntan from the wreckage. She went to brush her teeth and decided to stay but not to enjoy herself.

Crouched behind the palm tree, Barney saw Maura go off in the direction of the dining room. He had wakened early and left Denise asleep, hoping to return with newer, fresher instructions before she woke. He preferred to discuss the latest developments with Gaby. He waited cautiously till Maura was lost to view behind some cabins and then went up the path, rapping softly on the door, not wanting to wake Og in the other side of the cabin.

The door, unlatched, fell open at his touch and he went in, snapping it shut behind him. The room was empty. Was it possible that Gaby had left even earlier? He paused, uncertain, and Gaby came out of the bathroom and, seeing him, gasped. He held a finger to his lips and gestured with his head toward the wall. She nodded and stood silent, waiting for him to speak. She wore a foamy kind of nightgown, ruffled straps sliding down into a scoop neck, the ruffle crossing above her bosom. It occured to him that he had seen more women in nightgowns in the last eight hours than ever before in his entire life. He liked it.

Finally Gaby whispered, "What happened? Did she throw you out?"

"Oh no. She was very understanding."

"About the whole thing?"

"Well, not about the book."

"Well, that's Maura's fault," Gaby dismissed that part and sat on her bed. "How did it go last night?"

A look of absolute agony welled up in his puppydog eyes and he crumpled to the foot of Maura's bed. "It was awful," he moaned. Gaby's hands flew to her mouth and she stared, unable to think of how to phrase the one question in her mind.

"We got back to the cabin at midnight," he went on, "and while she was changing, I put on those silk pajamas, you know?" She nodded. She knew about the silk pajamas. "And she came out in this kind of see-through white thing . . . there were feathers on the bottom and she smelled so good . . . She came right up to me . . . so close . . . she unbuttoned my top button and she kissed my chest . . ." He stopped, apparently unable to go on.

"And what did you do?" Gaby prompted.

"I threw up."

"My God!"

"Some of it got on her feathers," he confessed.

"My God," Gaby said again, as he seemed to want some reaction. He nodded. "Didn't you want to . . . ?" She let it dangle.

"I wanted to. But I don't know . . . the excitement . . . and then that terrible scene in the dining room. And then I drank an awful lot. And all that dancing. I was sick all night," he whimpered.

"My God," she said again, feeling unoriginal.

"She was very nice about it," Barney assured her. "Held my head and everything. Till I fell asleep. It must've been five o'clock before I stopped heaving."

"Well . . ." Gaby hardly knew what to say. "You'll have to make it up to her."

He rose in his agony and almost bayed, "How??? Why did I drink? I know I can't take it. Why can't I just go to bed with her? Everybody here is going to bed with total strangers. Do I love her? Is something the matter with me? Why didn't she marry me in the first place? Then everything would have been all right!"

Somehow, it was a final straw for Gaby. She rose and crossed the room to Barney and slapped him.

"Why did you do that?" he asked, amazed.

"For her! How dare you do this to Denise? She's a lovely woman with feelings, emotions, desires. Only a cad goes around turning on women and then short-circuiting the whole affair!"

"I'm not good enough for her," he mumbled.

Gaby slapped him again. "Yes, you are," she said firmly. "You've got everything you're supposed to have, haven't you?"

"Yes," he whispered, folding his hands in front of him.

"Stop that!" Gaby ordered. "Take off your shirt!"

"Why?"

"I want you to look at yourself. Take it off!" Obediently, he unbuttoned his new sport shirt and when he had removed it, Gaby yelled, "For God's sake, Barney, you don't need underwear in this climate." Truly angry now, she pulled the cotton T-shirt from his trousers and over his head. "Look at yourself!" she commanded and shoved him toward the mirror over her dresser. "You've got terrific shoulders," she said from behind him and slapped them both. Walking around him, she felt the newly acquired muscle in his arm. "You're strong. You've got a nice chest . . ." Her hand trailed along his pectorals, went back for a second feel. "And you're not fat anymore," she finished, giving him a solid punch in the stomach for emphasis. "Look at it!"

He nodded dumbly, staring into the mirror.

"Take off your pants," she said.

"Please!"

"Oh, forget it," she said. "You've seen one, you've seen 'em all. All right." She moved between him and the mirror, staring up at him. "Now you go back there, and you take her in your arms"—she pulled his arms around her—"and you kiss her. Long and hard." Her hand shot up to the back of his head and shoved it down, pressing his lips to hers. Suddenly, she yanked at his hair. When he cried, "Ouch!" she slipped her tongue inside his mouth.

"Mmmm," he said, but he was not objecting

She grabbed his arm and pulled it around till she had his hand in hers and slipped it inside the top of her nightgown. "That's a woman's breast," she snarled. "Hers, mine, they're basically the same." She made a mental reservation about Maura's, but pressed on. "Nice? You like it?" she said sharply, professorially.

"Wonderful," he gasped.

"And you react when you touch it?" she asked and, without waiting for an answer, ground her pelvis into his. "Yes, you react," she said, and this time he kissed her, open-mouthed and longingly. Just as fast as he was at bridge, Gaby thought with some satisfaction. She wriggled in his embrace, lowering her other shoulder strap, then let her gown fall to the floor. She broke the kiss and whispered, "Now, Barney."

"You?"

"Yes!"

"But . . ." he said, "if we do it now, will I be able to do it with her later?"

The frustrations and insecurities of the night moved her from anger to fury and, using the tone she used to her children, she yelled, "Barney! Eat what's on your plate!" and shoved him over to the bed. He kissed her again and she struggled with the fastening of his trousers. When at last she got them open and he shucked them off and she saw him, she whispered, "My God, what a waste!"

"It's all right?" he asked.

"It's just fine," she said. "Mother knows," and pulled him down onto the bed with her. For a moment they stared into each other's eyes like frightened fawns.

"Be gentle," they said together.

"Is there a doctor in the house?" Denise asked the GF in the office, then decided the question had come out more melodramatic than she intended.

"Why?" the girl asked. "Don't you feel well?"

"I'm fine. My . . ." She hesitated, never having had to describe what Barney was before. ". . . friend was ill last night and when I woke up he was gone and I thought maybe he'd gone to the doctor."

The sad look in the girl's eyes told Denise the GF thought her friend had gone somewhere other than to a doctor. You're not *my* Gomorrah Friend, she thought. "We have a doctor in town we send people to," the girl said. "but no one asked today."

"Thank you," Denise said and marched out of the office. Where? she wondered. Where would he go? The logical answer was Jed. For more coaching. Except if Jed was his sex coach, he had failed miserably. But he wouldn't have coached him in that! Or would he? And if he did, what happened? Except Barney was sick. But why? Oh my God, Denise thought, seeing a long list of questions ahead of her. The answers lie with Jed. (And so does Maura, she thought, parenthetically.) But is Jed really here? No one had actually admitted it. She turned and went back into the office. "Pardon me, Gomorrah Friend," she said, "but is there a Mr. Lavery registered?"

The girl flipped through a large flat, file. "There's a Denise Lavery in 51A."

"I know that. I want Jed Lavery." The girl looked up and shrugged. Denise started for the door again, then turned in a moment of blind inspiration. "How about Mr. Mulligan?" she asked, and with a flash of annoyance the girl went back to the file. "Not Miss Mulligan, Mr. Mulligan."

"First name?" the girl asked.

"I'll take whatever you've got," Denise answered, sure she had hit on it.

"John. 32B."

It was a loud rap and Jed woke instantly, jumping up to sit on the side of the bed, all his senses alive and functioning. He was hungry and cold. There was another knock and he looked across the room. Non-Dad was gone but his bed had been slept in. Could it be him? Jed wondered, then decided I don't care who it is. Maybe they brought food. "It's not locked," he called.

Denise threw open the door and said, "Barney—" and was startled to see that Jed was alone.

He jumped off the bed. "Denise!" he said.

"Don't pretend to be surprised," she said. "I know the whole rotten story. Everything. Except where Barney is now."

Jed's stomach growled. "Maybe he's eating breakfast."

Denise nodded. "I didn't think of that," she said and started out.

"Denise . . ." Jed said, and she turned back to him, one hand on the edge of the door. He looked at her a moment, and then away, down at the floor, his toes. He wiggled them and then, as if satisfied his motor functions were operative, he said, "I'm sorry."

"What is that *ridiculous* garment you're wearing?"

"It's called a niamu. They sell 'em here."

"You're too old for something like that," she said, nastily, untruthfully. His body was hard and muscular and every bit as good as it was twenty years ago when she first saw all of it.

Trying to find a way to get into the apology he felt she deserved, he asked, "Have you seen Maura?"

"More of her than I cared to," Denise admitted, thinking, all right, I can understand. Maybe I did let myself go a little. Maybe, facing it, I never looked that good in the first place. But I was taking care of children, taking care of him . . . loving him.

He looked up at her. "She's a wonderful girl," he said.

She looked down, not wanting to talk about it. "How does it work?" she asked.

"What?"

"The niamu."

"Oh. You just kind of wind it around and tuck it in." He indicated the tucked-in end. For a moment they were silent. "A lot of guys just walk off," he said, "forget about the alimony. Go to Mexico or something. I couldn't do that."

"It just seemed so premeditated," she said bitterly. "Making me into Mrs. Average Consumer and designing a man around me. What if he'd been six-foot-four? Would you have shortened his legs to fit in my bed?"

"I'm so happy," he said miserably, "that I wanted you to be happy, too. I realized the ways I disappointed you when we were married. I didn't want to make the same mistakes again. It was as though I had another chance to fulfill you through Barney. That's why I went and took the dancing lessons and the bridge lessons with him. I'm afraid I flopped on tennis."

And elsewhere, she thought, but said, "You took dancing?" and laughed as sardonically as she could manage.

"Just to encourage Barney. I did everything I could to give you the perfect marriage."

"With Barney," she completed his thought.

"Was that so wrong?"

Yes, goddamn it, she thought, the enormity of his deceit hitting her again. It was wrong. I invested my life in you. I loved you and you thought it would be perfectly all right to transfer your account and give my dividends to the T-shirt kid. Barney is a good man, she thought, but she knew, had realized last night that it would be years before it could possibly be right between them, if ever; that Jed had cast a shadow over Barney and her from which the man might never recover. Barney would always think of himself as an inadequate replacement of the man she loved. But Barney is better than nothing, she thought, and I will take him and work to make it right. But I deserve one thing.

"No, it wasn't wrong, Jed," she said. "I remember the first Mr. Mulligan. You did a fantastic job. In every way but one. You didn't teach him what to do in bed, did you?"

"Well . . ." He shuffled his feet. "I mean . . . you've got to draw a line somewhere. I . . . I remember what we had, Denise, and I couldn't . . . I mean I couldn't spoil that by sharing it with him." And then he verbalized his greatest guilt. "I'm sorry. He must've been awful."

"You misunderstood me, Jed," she said as sweetly as she could, and kicking the door shut, went and stood before him. "He was utterly fantastic."

"What?"

"I mean," she continued, as though she didn't want to hurt him but was determined to be truthful, "you were a wonderful lover, Jed, but he knows things you've never even dreamed of."

"Barney?"

"When that man took me in his arms last night, you could never believe what he did to me." I may never be able to get it out of the feathers, she thought, but carried on, delighted by Jed's stricken look. "I reached heights and depths I've only read about before. Over and over and over," she said, adopting the most ecstatic expression she could manage.

"Well, I know he's got a big one—"

He does? Denise thought. Well, that's encouraging.

"—but it's not the size," Jed said desperately. "It's what you do—"

"He does it all," Denise virtually sang and, in fake-remembered ecstasy, twirled around the little room. "It went so deep, Jed, it stirred me in a way—"

He grabbed her arm in mid-twirl. "You mean he's better than I am?"

"Not better, darling," Denise said with pseudo-tact. "Just . . . different."

"Like what? What did he do?"

"Well," she said, smiling slightly, "you couldn't share us with him, Jed, and I don't feel I can share us with you. Not . . . specifics."

"Look, I just want a plain, simple reading. For the record. I mean, for crying out loud, he was my pupil!"

"And he dances well," she assured him.

Jed grabbed her shoulders, forcing her to face him. "I know what I can do with you. My God, we did it often enough. Remember that first night in the Holiday Inn?"

"The Ramada," she corrected.

"That old landlady in Truro? Remember that?"

"Of course," she said, "and it was very sweet . . ." implying it was all a different league.

He slid his arms around her, roughly drawing her close. "And I could do it again," he said huskily, and remembering his problem, wondered if he could.

"Jed, Jed," she said as coolly as she could, but it was becoming difficult, "that's all over now . . ." He kissed her. "You have that lovely girl, so young and yet so experienced-looking—" He covered her mouth again, pulling her body tightly into his until she felt their ribs might interlock like bumpers. "And I have my wonderful Barney," she managed to say as soon as he released her.

"Shit!" he cried and kissed her again, his tongue tangoing in her mouth till he had unbuttoned her blouse, then he lowered his face to kiss her breast. Her hands flew to his head, riffling through his hair, pressing him closer. His whole body tingled, trembled, and he felt himself rising, expanding, knowing at last the problem, if it was one, did not include Denise. He rose and pulled her blouse away, threw it somewhere. She stared at his familiar body as he backed off a step to look at her.

"But I'm engaged to someone else," she cried as he pulled the tucked-in end of his niamu. "Oh isn't that cute!" she gasped. "It just unwinds," and they trampled on the fallen niamu in their haste to reach each other.

Maura distinctly remembered having left the door unlatched and now it seemed to be locked. She pushed against it, hard, and rattled the knob.

Barney arrested his piston movement in mid-revolution, his body suddenly hunched like a cat discovered on the buffet table.

"Keep going, please keep going," Gaby whispered urgently. The second round had started much sooner than she would have expected, but she supposed he'd squirreled away a lot of energy in forty-one years, and could only be grateful it was she who'd found the supply shed.

"But . . ." he whispered.

"I don't care," she said fiercely, twisting and jerking her body in the way some people kicked a motor to get it started. The motor turned over, purred, and chugged away, to her relief. It was amazing how quickly he caught on, had remembered the second time all the things she'd shown him the first. He didn't know the little tricks, the extras, Len, that bastard, kept on file, but she knew them and she'd get to them all as soon as possible.

Maura knocked softly.

Gaby dug her nails into Barney's back, hoping to distract him.

Maura knocked loudly.

"Go 'way!" Gaby managed to shout while keeping the rhythm going.

"It's Maura," she called but Gaby's lips were occupied with Barney, keeping his accelerator pressed to the floor.

"Let me in!" Maura yelled and pounded on the door.

In the other half of the cabin, Will woke up.

"I love your body," Gaby whispered. "Don't even lose the last ten pounds."

"Is Jed in there?" Maura screamed, knowing he must be.

"Noooooo," Gaby cried, pleased that Barney was ignoring the disturbance now.

Will hurried to the window, moved the shade a trifle, and saw Maura smashing her fist against the door.

"I don't believe you," she shrieked and waited for an answer.

Will dropped the shade, ran to the dresser, got some shorts and pulled them on.

Maura launched a barrage of blows against the door.

Og woke up. "Morning," he said. "What's the weather like?"

"Hot," Will said and pulled on a shirt.

"He isn't . . ." Maura heard Gaby cry, and after a pause, "here." And after another beat, "Go 'way."

Will rushed back to the window.

"I'll look for him," Maura was yelling, "and if I can't find him, I'll come back and kill you!"

Will moved to the door and opened it a crack.

"Where are you going?" Og asked.

"Out," Will said, peeking carefully around the door.

"Do you understand?" Maura yelled.

"YES! YES! YES!" Gaby cried, but Maura was not at all sure it was an answer to her question. She turned on her heel and, remembering her father was in 32B, sped off down the path.

Og rose, suddenly galvanized. "Was that Maura?" he asked, remembering he had never told Jed she was here. "Who did she say she was going to kill?" He ran toward the bathroom. "Wait for me. Won't take me a minute to shave," he said.

Will left the cabin, closing the door behind him, hugging the side of the building, not sure yet that he wanted Maura to see him.

Gaby and Barney lay gasping in each other's arms. "I suppose we'll have to get married now," he said.

"Have to?" she asked.

"Well . . . I mean . . . it's only honorable. I've . . ." He hesitated. ". . . known you."

I could just say yes, Gaby thought, except it didn't seem fair to play on his naïvete. She remembered how she had explained it to her ten-year-old son when he was eight. "You should only know," it was not the verb she'd used with Steven but she didn't want to bother to translate, "someone you really love." Barney nodded. "Without love, it doesn't mean anything." That had been hard to get across to Steven, but Barney seemed to buy it. "And you marry someone not because it's honorable, but because you love them."

Barney rolled away from her, got off the bed, stood looking down at her. Oh God, she thought, did I goof?

Haltingly, he spoke. "It's easier to be with you than her. I . . . I feel at home." Gaby nodded. "Do you . . . do you want me to speak to your mother?"

"About what?"

Barney sank to his knees beside the bed. "Will you marry me?"

Gaby leaned across the bed and took his face in her hands and kissed him. "Yes," she whispered, leaning her face against his.

"And this . . ." He indicated their situation. "This is all right?"

"All right? It's sensational!" she said.

He pushed her back upon the bed and lowered his body on hers, as ready as a Boy Scout with two sticks to light her fire. And as his hands, third time experienced, ran up and down her body and he covered her with kisses, almost weeping with joy, she whispered, "Oh Barney . . . and you play such good bridge, too!"

Running down the path, Maura could see a man and woman standing before the door of what she thought was Cabin 32B. She slowed to a walk, catching her breath, wanting to see the lay of the land in the original sense.

Fearing she might stop, Will moved behind a palm tree thirty yards behind her.

As Maura moved closer she saw the man raise his fist and pound upon the door. He was yelling something she could not hear, but suddenly the grey hair came into focus and she recognized her father. But who was the woman?

Will sped from the palm tree to a closer rock as Maura began to run again.

"Let me in! Goddamn, it's my turn!" Maura could hear her father now, and then the woman saying, "We could go to my place."

"No!" her father thundered. "The bastard hasn't been out of that cabin since he got here!"

They clung together tightly inside the drum of a cabin, on which his roommate beat a frantic solo.

"This is where I should've stayed all along, isn't it?" Jed whispered. Denise, tears streaming down her face, nodded. "Can you forgive me?" he asked. "Can you understand what happened to me? The way I felt? It wasn't you . . . I was never unhappy with you." Denise kissed him, and from outside they heard the woman's voice again.

"What's the difference? Your place or mine?"

"It's a matter of principle," the roommate yelled. Then, slightly lower but they could still hear him. "Besides, I think he's humping my daughter."

"No, he isn't."

Jed sat bolt upright, and Denise understood this new woman's voice was Maura's.

Her father and the woman turned to her. "Then who the hell's he got in there?" her father asked.

"He's *your* roommate," Maura answered.

"I thought he was yours," her father said.

"You came here with your daughter?" the woman asked, sounding justifiably puzzled.

Maura looked at her. She was in her mid-thirties. Not a bad figure but certainly no Jeannie. Maura moved around them and pounded on the door. "Jed! It's Maura! Let me in!"

Will scuttled to the corner of the cabin, not wanting to be seen, not wanting to miss the dialogue.

"No," Maura's father told his new friend. "We just happened to meet here."

"If you're thirty-six, how old is she?" the woman asked suspiciously.

"Seventeen," he answered hastily. The woman reached into the beach bag she carried and withdrew a gold lamé eyeglass case. As she pulled her glasses from it, Maura's father, realizing he had to move fast, joined his daughter at the door. "Open!" he yelled, "or we'll break it down!"

"What about Maura?" Denise asked.

"She was wonderful," Jed admitted. "But she wasn't you. She could almost have been our daughter."

"Not mine," Denise snapped.

"I'd like to be a little fat and flabby," Jed said. "I'd like to have a home. I'd like to grow old in the accepted way. I'd like to do it with you."

"Are you sure you've got it all out of your system?" Denise asked. "I couldn't go through it—ask the boys to go through it—again."

"I'm sure," he said and, leaning back, he kissed her.

"Who's in there, Jed?" Maura screamed, beating on the door again, her father landing a counter-rhythm of heavier blows. The woman had her glasses on but their backs were to her.

"Shut up out there!" a man's voice yelled from 32A. "We're trying to sleep!"

"What are you people? Gypsies?" the woman in the cabin added.

"Shut up!" Maura's father redirected his rage at them. "You two are the noisiest lay in the Islands!"

"Donald! They listened!" The woman's voice sounded shocked.

The man stuck his head out of the window and yelled, "You perverted, big-eared son of a bitch!"

"Come out here and say that," Maura's father howled at him, apoplectic.

"Kill him, Donald!" the woman's voice screeched.

"You bet your ass," he said and withdrew from the window.

"We'll have to face them," Jed said, helping Denise up.

"I know," she answered, getting her blouse.

He picked his limp and dusty niamu from the floor and, winding it, said, "And Barney. If he was really better than I, will you . . . will you be sorry?"

It was a difficult question for Denise to answer, especially while dressing and with the yelling going on outside and the furious threats coming from the A side of the cabin. "We've both made mistakes, Jed," she said. "Of course, yours was longer than mine. But we'll forget about it." And, laying it out so that the memory would haunt him till his dying day, "It's sweet with you. With him . . . we were like raging, driven, mindless animals. You must forget everything I've told you about Barney."

The woman in the glasses tapped Maura's father's back

insistently and he turned to her. "I don't believe your daughter's seventeen," she said.

Angry, frustrated, and determined, Maura's father grabbed the woman in a rough embrace. "We mature early in my family," he said. As though he was about to kiss her, he removed her glasses, rubbed his body against hers and whispered huskily, "That's why they call us the Royal Family of the Mattress."

As Jed and Denise opened the door, he heard Og's voice calling his name from the distance.

"Maura's here, Jed! Maura's here!" Og bellowed, gasping and breathless as he ran down the path.

Maura looked at Denise. "Oh," she said, "I didn't expect you."

"I guess not," Denise said and saw the young, red-headed publisher coming from around the corner of the cabin. "You'll learn. Life's full of surprises."

"Can we have the room now?" Non-Dad asked with icy sarcasm, his right hand kneading his friend's behind in a groping attempt to hold her interest.

"It's all yours," Jed said and moved Denise through the doorway.

"He's really much too old for you," Will whispered into Maura's ear.

"We had something lovely," she said, not even wondering how Will got there.

The man called Donald burst from 32A and charged up to Maura's father. "All right, you big-mouthed bastard, here I am." He wore a brief pair of shorts and was obviously into body-building.

"Not now!" Maura's father said, with as much authority as he could muster, and shoved the woman into the cabin.

Og stumbled up to the crowd. "I tried to tell you last night, Jed, but you wouldn't let me."

"He listened, Donald," the woman in 32A called from the window. "To all our beautiful moments!"

"Now!" Donald yelled, enraged, and grabbing Maura's father by his amulet, pulled him back, set him up, and delivered a roundhouse punch to his jaw. Non-Dad's hands flew up as he crashed back against the door frame and sank to the ground.

"My glasses!" the woman in the doorway screamed, seeing them fly into the air. "You're not supposed to hit a man who's carrying glasses!" she cried, and rushed from the room looking blindly around at the ground. A few GF's and GG's stopped on the path and watched, accepting the event as an after-breakfast floor show.

"You were looking for a father," Will said.

"I've got a father."

"That's what I mean." Will looked at the grey-haired, red-faced man, muttering curses as he pulled himself up. Donald, bouncing on the balls of his feet, fists clenched, waited for him to rise.

A voice in the distance called, "Denise!" and, turning, she saw Barney and the Marcotte woman running toward them. "Who is that woman?" she asked Jed.

Using the cabin wall as a springboard, Maura's father launched himself, plunging below Donald's fists, butting the man's solid midsection with his head. With an "Oooof," sound Donald thudded to the ground, Maura's father on top of him.

"Kill! Kill!" the woman screamed from the window of 32A.

"I've got to tell you something, Denise," Barney said, puffing a little.

"I'm very sorry, Barney . . ." Denise began.

"Are these yours?" Og offered the glasses, which he'd stepped on accidentally, to their owner.

"Oh, they're cracked," she moaned.

"I'm Dr. Parmalee," Og told her.

"Doctor?" she said, sounding interested. She slipped her glasses on but they were too damaged for her to see much.

"I'll never forget you," Jed told Maura in apology.

"I know," she said. "You never forgot her either."

". . . so I'm going to marry Gaby . . ."

". . . and after all, he is the father of my children . . ."

Neither Barney nor Denise were listening, but somehow they understood.

"Wanna go swim?" Will asked.

"I don't have my suit," Maura answered.

Will shrugged. "We'll go to the nude beach."

She looked at him a moment." No," she said. "I'll go back to the cabin for my suit. We don't need that scene anymore."

"You were terrific, Barney," Jed said, stepping over Donald and Non-Dad, who was clinging insecurely to the big man's biceps, trying to kick him in the groin as they rolled on the ground. "You really tried. I'm proud of you." And though it was difficult, feeling that Barney deserved it, Jed added, "You grew up. Denise told me how fantastic you were last night."

"But—" Barney began, and only Denise noticed the Marcotte woman kicked him. "But she loves you," Barney finished.

"Come play bridge with us sometime," Denise invited.

"We'd love to," Gaby accepted.

They were quite some distance up the path when Maura looked back. Two of the more conscientious GF's had separated Donald and her father. The woman from 32A was washing Donald's face and the GF's were trying to control her father as he struggled to go after his woman. She and Og, his hand on her waist, were walking purposefully down the path. As Maura looked, the woman pushed Og's hand down to a more comfortable position on her behind. Jed and Denise, Barney and Gaby were deep in friendly conversation. None of them seemed to notice she and Will had gone. It was the end of a wonderful experiment.

"Oh my God!" she gasped and turned to Will. "The book. They ruined my book. And the advance and all . . ."

"Keep the advance," he said. "Turn it into fiction."

Maura considered that for a moment. "Mmmm," she said. "I could call it *All Passion, Pooped.*"